THE TRUTH ABOUT YOU AND ME

EMMA COOPER

Boldwood

First published in Great Britain in 2025 by Boldwood Books Ltd.

Copyright © Emma Cooper, 2025

Cover Design by Lizzie Gardiner

Cover Images: Adobe Stock

A CIP catalogue record for this book is available from the British Library.

Paperback ISBN 978-1-83656-948-0

Large Print ISBN 978-1-83656-947-3

Hardback ISBN 978-1-83656-946-6

Trade Paperback ISBN 978-1-80656-065-3

Ebook ISBN 978-1-83656-949-7

Kindle ISBN 978-1-83656-950-3

Audio CD ISBN 978-1-83656-941-1

MP3 CD ISBN 978-1-83656-942-8

Digital audio download ISBN 978-1-83656-943-5

This book is printed on certified sustainable paper. Boldwood Books is dedicated to putting sustainability at the heart of our business. For more information please visit https://www.boldwoodbooks.com/about-us/sustainability/

Boldwood Books Ltd, 23 Bowerdean Street, London, SW6 3TN

www.boldwoodbooks.com

For Nicki,
Who's been beside me through every kind of plot twist, every blooper,
on and off-screen. Thank you for your loyalty, your unwavering
friendship, and for always laughing at the same bits I do, even when no
one else in the cinema does... This one's for you.

1

FRIDAY 6TH SEPTEMBER

Maggie

When I was a child, I wanted to be an astronaut. I yearned for space. For the quiet; my skin covered in layers of thick white fabric, hands in those puffy white gloves that held the American flag on the moon; my face protected by a smooth glass dome. I wanted to be an astronaut *so* badly that I'd once got my head stuck in a glass bowl. A foster father – I forget his name now – had to cut my pigtails away so he could shimmy the bowl over my ears. I'd screamed and screamed as his hands yanked and pulled.

OK, so I might have been a *tiny* bit optimistic on the whole astronaut thing, but I found the next best thing.

I'm a cleaner.

I know that it might seem like one small step down from my childish dreams and one giant leap into minimum wage but I *love* it. I like imagining the smile on a person's face when they come home after a stressful day to a clean house. I picture their reflection smiling in the stainless steel of their kettle as they notice the way the polished floorboards catch the light of the setting sun. I think that, in my own way, I have an impact on their happiness; I make their lives a little brighter, a little easier.

I get to be part of their life, while still keeping the distance I need.

They say love your job and you'll never work a day in your life, and that is how I try to live, but sometimes, shit just has a way of happening. Which is why I'm about to say the following words:

'I quit.'

I pull off my lanyard, careful not to get it tangled in my chaotic curls, and throw it onto one of the many mattresses housed in the showroom for *Pillow Paradise!*

'What?' Doug, purple with indignation, stares at my face. It makes a refreshing change – he's usually staring at my boobs. I knew what was going through his mind as he reached over while I bent down to empty the waste-paper basket but he *needed a paperclip*. What a load of shite. I have to quit before I do something I regret, despite really, *really* needing this job. Or maybe I wouldn't regret strapping him to the Massage Master? It might shake some sense into him.

'You can't just quit! It's Mattress Madness tomorrow!'

'Actually' – I pull on my cerise fake fur – 'I can.' I zip up my backpack with my cleaning products in, wrap Henry Hoover's nozzle around my neck, and make for the glass doors. Henry is a British icon: London-red-bus body, cartoon-happy eyes peering up above his hose-for-a-nose, permanent smile beneath. I've had Henry for ten years now, the only reliable man to ever be part of my life.

Doug rages as I sweep past the Snooze Ease Double and the Snuggle Rest Divan.

'Feel free to make a formal complaint. My email is Maggie dot Wright at yahoo dot com. I'll be sure to get back to you promptly. Actually I may as well save you the bother.' I pause, adjust the hose around my neck and wiggle my fingers like they're hovering over a keyboard. 'Dear Doug.' I clear my throat. 'Thank you for your email, but given that you're an egotistical dickhead who has "accidentally"' – I finger-quote then continue with my imaginary keyboard tapping – 'brushed yourself against me, I'm afraid your contract has now been terminated and a complaint has been made to Pillow Paradise Limited. Will that do? Or would you like me to recite the specific areas of misconduct you've breached?'

He narrows his eyes and folds his arms. 'Nobody will believe you. I'm a husband and father and you're just—'

'The cleaner. Yes, yes I am. Good luck with Mattress Madness by the way. It might be a bit quieter than you were expecting though, as I've popped a post about you on the Facebook page.' I make my way past the mattress of my dreams with a touch of regret. There goes my ten per cent discount... so long FirmHaven. I grab the door and swing it open, the sounds of the Friday morning rush leaking in as he begins furiously unlocking his phone screen. 'Oh and Doug?' I fix him with a stare. 'I would think again about planning to let the store cupboard door accidentally slam behind you and another employee.'

His overgroomed eyebrows meet his slicked-back hairline. 'What? I—'

I let the door swing closed behind me rather than respond.

* * *

'Almost there!' I lie back on my bed, suck in my breath, and force the button of my jeans into place.

'Come on, Mags, I haven't got all day!' Tess's voice from my phone has me vaulting from my mattress.

I drop a hip. 'So? What do you think?' I twirl. 'Bargain, right?'
She leans forward, Velcro rollers almost hitting her phone screen.

'Nope.'

'What do you mean nope? These are vintage 501s and' – I
bend over and flick the tab on the back pocket – 'Judd Nelson
wears these in *The Breakfast Club*.' I turn around and run my
hand over the thighs.

'Mate, life isn't a John Hughes movie. It's not the eighties and
Shermer, Illinois, doesn't even exist.' She leans closer to the
screen. 'I can practically see what you've had for lunch, not so
much a camel toe as a whole bleeding foot.' I deflate, the button
pops and fires its way across the room. Tess snorts, mouthful of
coffee almost spirting out of her nude-glossed lips.

'OK, OK... I'll stick them on Vinted.'

I begin yanking the jeans off and reach for my denim skirt.

'Nice knickers by the way, very rrrrawgh!' My head shakes at
her enthusiastic imitation of a lion. This isn't the first time she's
seen me in my undies. I'm Tess's adoptive sister, and we spent
most of our childhood in a shared bedroom with a small set of
bunkbeds. Even at the age of thirty, this is the only real friendship I've ever had. 'Where's your gig?'

'Comedy Corner, in Nottingham. It's usually a good crowd.
So, tell me more. I hope you told him to stick his job right up his
double divan?'

'Words to that effect.'

'Good for you.'

'Yeah, but' – I pull my red jumper over my head – 'I've now
got to hustle to find another cleaning job. That five mornings a
week slot is what has been paying my rent for the last three
months.'

'Have you set up a webpage yet?'

I hesitate. 'Not yet... I'll scour the ads and apply for something.'

'Mags!' She lets out an exasperated sigh. 'I keep telling you to—'

'Put myself out there more. I know, I know. But most people like to meet me first and it's usually in a public place and you know how hard—'

Her voice softens. 'I know, but you've got to stop living your life as though you're the side character and everyone else has the lead roles. Make up an excuse. Tell them, I don't know, that you're a germaphobe or something.'

'A germaphobe who is a cleaner?' I snort. 'I'm sure that will go down well.'

'But if you start your *own* business, you could set the terms. Have a Zoom call first or something?'

'I do set the terms; I choose which jobs to apply for—'

'But if you set up your own company, rather than working for other people, people would come to you with the jobs not the other way. Speaking of which, did I tell you Wes *Goode* asked if he could have free VIP tickets?'

'*Wes*?'

That name is a blast from the past. He used to call her Ten Tonne Tessy and once wrapped her a pack of lard up for her birthday, *for your arse* he'd said. Dick.

She'd laughed it off. She always made fun of herself to stop being bullied, and now, she's taken that and made it into a career choice.

'What did you say?'

'I didn't say anything, just replied pretending I was my own PA and attached the link to the ticket site. Oh and included him in one of my set pieces.'

'*Nice.*' I glance up at my watch. 'Crap! Gotta go. I'm cleaning Riz's in half an hour. Love you millions.'

'Love you billions.'

2

MAGGIE

I pull out my phone, selecting my 'songs to clean to' playlist. 'Wake Me Up Before You Go-Go' by Wham! blasts through my one working ear pod. An hour ago, Riz's kitchen bin was full, the surfaces splattered with coffee grinds and dirty teaspoons and now? Lemony fresh, shining tiles, gleaming toaster. My sense of pride peacocks inside my chest, fluffing up like my feather duster as I close the kitchen door and make my way into the lounge, while trying not to question how I'm going to pay my rent next month without the five days a week at *Pillow Paradise!*

Mrs Hancock, Riz to her friends, has wall-to-wall photos of every stage of her adventurous life. I pull out my microfibre cloth and go about dusting them. The pictures range from her in her twenties, a firm athletic body atop an elephant in Kenya; in an army green flak jacket as a photographer and war correspondent, cigarette between red lips; in her thirties holding an award, silver dress; her wedding day, garter showing as she sits on the back of a transport lorry. I take my time with each frame, with each piece of glass, making sure every stage of Riz's life remains unblemished. I imagine myself in those scenarios. Riz's chin is always slightly lifted, as though she's challenging the world to take its best shot, whereas I keep my head down, avoiding the world as best I can. I'm also short rather than tall, my mouth is fuller, my nose isn't as strong, and I have dark green eyes instead of light blue.

The only travelling I've got under my belt is a few wet weeks in Wales, which my foster mum, Hellie, had saved all year round to pay for. God, how I would love to travel to those kinds of places. I'll be lucky if I can make it to China City down the road for a chicken chow mein, given I only have twenty-five pounds and fifty-three pence to last me until next Monday. And now, after Doug and his search for paperclips, I'm going to have to find another gig. Maybe Tess is right and I should set up my own company rather than working for other people.

On the plus side – I straighten a frame – I might not have enough to splash out on a takeaway, but I have a roof over my head that's mine, a bedroom that I'm not sharing, and a job I love, when I'm not avoiding the likes of Doug and his roaming hands.

I look to the window where September hail is hailing on the Georgian panes. It's a good job I've already set the timer on my heating so I can have a long bath before my last job of the day. I say job, but cleaning the local cinema and getting free entrance and snacks every Friday night is hardly what I would call work.

The playlist has flicked on to 'White Wedding' by Billy Idol and I sing along as I dust the rest of the surfaces. My finger catches on a piece of paper poking out of the top drawer of Riz's dresser, and I reach over to put it away. My heart sinks as I read the words at the top of the letter: *Dear Mrs Hancock, we are thrilled to confirm your placement at Heritage Retirement Home.* Riz has been looking frailer lately, and I know she doesn't have any living relatives. I close the drawer quickly as Riz shuffles into the room, the steel-framed walker making her progress slow. Even at eighty-four, her white hair is still thick, but it's flat on one side; she must have been napping in her office. I unplug Henry and pull out my ear pod.

'Do you want me to turn up the heating a bit?' I rub my hands together. I'm cold... even in the summer, always feeling the need to have a jumper or coat on hand. I nod towards the window, landing my foot on Henry, the lead tidying away with a whoosh.

'That would be wonderful, thank you, Mags.' She pushes up her sleeves and begins manoeuvring herself. I step towards her high-backed chair, give the cushions a quick plump and stand back, not touching her. She grips the side of the walker, bracing herself as she releases the bar and reaches out towards the arm of the chair. I take a small step in her direction, but keep myself far enough away so we're not touching. Riz flinches, a flash of pain crossing her features before being replaced with a look of frustration. Her eyes meet mine, defeat softening her gaze. 'Would you be so kind as to give me a hand, Mags?'

I look at her in panic. *Of course* I want to help her. It should be a simple request; I should already be moving towards her, hands at the ready, but touching someone is not easy. It never has been. My eyes search the room for the pair of bright yellow Marigold gloves, but realise I've left them in the kitchen.

I back away, but I already know my fight is lost. The tension in her body is making her shake, and if I hesitate any longer, she will be on the floor.

My feet move towards her: mouth dry, heart jack-knifing against my ribs. My hands stretch outwards, one at her bare elbow, the other at the bottom of her back.

Nausea tightens at the base of my throat as I try to speak, to continue my life on the outside as I've taught myself to do since I was a child.

'Almost there.' I hold on to her elbow and shift the cushion as she lowers herself down.

I'm on the verge of passing out. I take a steadying breath, and manage to land her into the chair, letting her go as quickly as I can without ceremony or fanfare, while inside, my body reacts to the release with breakneck relief.

My hand reaches to the back of my neck. It feels as though my pulse is about to explode through my veins. Riz shifts and leans her head against the chair, eyes tearful as she looks to the ceiling rose. I know how much it's going to hurt her to tell me that I no longer have a job. I can help with that at least. I ignore the pulse throbbing at the top of my spine and crouch down in front of her. In normal circumstances, I would take her hand in mine, and run my thumb across her paper-thin skin. But I'm not normal. 'Can I get you a glass of water?'

She shakes her head, closes her eyes briefly then straightens, resilience and tough-upper-lip expression as she meets my eyes. 'Mags, I'm afraid I'm going to have to let you g—' she begins, earnest.

'Riz,' I jump in. She leans forward, sapphire-blue eyes widening as she takes in my expression. 'I'm... well you see... I'm so sorry, Riz, but I'm not going to be able to clean for you any more. I'm going to be studying' – I pick a plausible subject – 'script-writing. But the thing is... the hours will probably conflict with my time here.'

Her eyes search mine, tears pricking behind them as she smiles. 'How marvellous for you, Maggie! I honestly couldn't be happier for you.' She beams. 'I once dated an English professor – did I mention that? Two decades my senior... mind you, he taught me more than English that summer and I dare say I taught him one or two tricks myself.' She winks and we laugh. 'How about you open that cabinet and pour us both a glass of rum to celebrate new beginnings?'

* * *

The hail has turned back to rain, and my thick more-brown-than-blonde curls are now rat-tailing above my shoulders. I drag Henry along the path, his face smiling, regardless of the strain on his ligaments. 'Come on, Henry,' I encourage, giving his hose-nose a tug over cracked paving slabs. I've parked in the lay-by and walked the ten minutes needed to get to Riz's rather than park in the pay and display outside her place.

Harrowsby Bay has been my home for the last twenty-three years. And honestly? I couldn't imagine living anywhere else. We have our fair share of sandy beaches, plenty of high street shops, rolling hills and top-notch restaurants – or so I've heard. The buildings that line the bay are a mismatch of the old and new, shops and houses that rub alongside each other despite their differences. It's like they echo the personalities of the small population who call this home. We're not far from Brighton, on the South Coast, and up until the last decade, our little slice of paradise had remained pretty much under the radar. But best-kept secrets never stay kept for long. And lately there have been more and more visitors and property owners joining us. I don't mind, not really. But the more people that come, the more people I avoid.

I approach the lay-by outside Harrow's Hawkers where my red Fiat Punto is parked beneath a flickering street lamp, rain sliding down the rusty bonnet into the giant pothole puddle next to it. My lilac boots are starting to leak, but it was either these or my white house pumps that I wear when I'm cleaning, and they'd be ruined by now.

My next job isn't for another few hours and my plan is to get home, take a long hot bath, and change my clothes before my Friday night date at the cinema. I know *technically* it's still work, but as soon as I've hoovered up the popcorn, cleaned the loos and polished the lobby, Friday night belongs to me. The last session on a Friday night is usually a quiet one, so I give it a good clean beforehand, then it just needs a swift once over before I leave, which leaves me with two glorious hours in front of the big screen with as much popcorn as I can eat, and a large Diet Coke.

I lean Henry's hose next to the car and fumble with the keys, as the rain pelts at my skin and falls into my eyes. My fingers are still cold regardless of the thick wool of my green gloves. For once in my life, I would love to have a car with central locking that works and heated seats and – crap! No, no, no, no, no! Scrambling to my knees, I crouch down next to my car. I take off my gloves and shove them into my pocket, a hole already forming in my fishnets. I scan beneath the car in the dull light, searching for my keys, tapping my fingers around, but sit back up with nothing to show for my efforts. I pull my phone out of my pocket, slide my damp fingers three times across the surface until it opens the torch. I get on all fours, tilting the light across the pavement until it lands on the six slots of the drain. My keys lost beneath them.

Perfect.

It'll take me too long to walk home then back into town. The thought of getting on a bus makes me feel sick. The last time I was on public transport, in close proximity to so many people, I found myself wedged in the 'wheelchair only' space of the bus.

But maybe I can get on the bus this time. It might be quiet; I reckon most people are at home, staying in from the hideous weather. I dig my hands around in my pocket and find I have just over three pounds, as well as a packet of Tic Tacs. That's enough to get me and Henry a bus ticket. I shake two mints into my palm, pop them into my mouth, put my gloves back on, and employ a determined stride.

'Not long now,' I reassure Henry as much as myself, pulling him along the stretch of path towards the bus stop, the rain still unleashing itself on us.

Pausing for a second to catch my breath, I wipe the mascara from beneath my eyes again before dragging poor Henry onwards. Waterproof mascara, my backside. There is a heavy rumble behind me and a blast of dirty puddle water hits my right side as the bus hurries past.

Perfect. Just perfect.

I carry on walking. The few shops that edge around town are closed. Some date back to Tudor times, others built in the seventies and eighties, each window dark, reflecting me and Henry as we walk. I pass a boutique, eyeing the clothing inside that even if I saved all of my wages and didn't buy one packet of Super Noodles, I still wouldn't be able to afford. I continue on, taking my usual shortcut through Fleetwood Road. It's a narrow cobbled side street; blink and you'd miss the entrance. It's the perfect shortcut to avoid the busier parts of town. Just a few small rows of neat bungalows. Hellie used to clean number six. Tess and I would climb the tree in the backyard. I glance at the blue door with fond memories, following the quiet street until I cut back out onto the main road.

To my right is the beachfront, the waves loud as they crash against the shore. I drag Henry past the bakery, and the 'Grab a Gift' shop on my left.

We sidestep the smokers outside the White Lion, my head dipped against the smell of stale beer and the sounds of a sports match playing in the background. I continue past Smithfield Road, and the '*Best-Pork-Pie-in-the-County*' shop.

Ahead, a group of women grip umbrellas and chatter amicably, one holding the door into a bookshop open with one hand, shaking rain and closing the umbrella down with another. I trail slowly behind them; my stomach rumbles almost as loudly as Henry's wheels.

I'm hit with a waft of fresh coffee as the door closes. I step cautiously closer. On the inside of the door facing me is a poster advertising a book club, a grainy black-and-white picture of the book of the month: '*Great Expectations! Join us for coffee, cake and bookish chat. All welcome. Entrance £3.*' I peer in through the blurred windows, rain distorting the view. My stomach rumbles again as I eye the warmth inside, and the group of people taking their coats off. Their hugs and smiles are being passed around like a biscuit tin. The chairs are arranged in a semicircle, and there is space around them. My hand reaches for the coins in my pocket, warm and comforting like the inside of the shop. I wish I could be one of them. They wave and embrace, their conversation flowing easily. A head turns. A woman in a polka-dot dress and straight black fringe catches me looking in and begins to smile.

But I already know how this ends.

With a slow exhale, I give the bookshop one more wistful look, and pull Henry behind me. There is a chippy down the road with a three-star hygiene rating, which is bound to be empty. I'll go there instead. I should have enough to get a bag of three-star chips and if I'm lucky, they'll take a while to reheat.

3

JACK

Ever since I was a young boy, I used to find comfort in the order of letters and words; in the alphabet; in the breaths between commas and semicolons; between paragraphs and chapters. My father is a writer, my mother is the chief editor at a publishing house, so words have always been part of the tapestry of my life. There was always comfort to be found in the middle, beginning and endings of books. At least, that's what I thought a year ago, before everything I loved was ripped away, gouged out from deep in the cortex of my brain.

I'm an imposter now, an outsider forced beneath the skin of my own body. I'm a walking contradiction: a reader who can't read, a bookshop owner who no longer loves books.

I reach for the bathroom cupboard and pop a diazepam into my palm. I know it's diazepam because I've coloured the label yellow. I squint at the symbols:

♎ ♓ ♋ ⌘ ♍ □ ♋ ◯

I throw the pill to the back of my tongue, lean down, drink directly from the tap then splash my face with water. My hands grip the edge of the sink as I close my eyes, waiting to feel the effects of the diazepam ease their way into my nervous system, waiting for magic fingers to untangle the knots of fear that have me hiding in my own bathroom wearing an expensive suit that I bought a year ago, which I never made it down the aisle in.

Even after so much time has passed, I can't grasp my new normality; it's intangible: a wisp of reality that is too faint to hold. I still hear the same phrases that screeched inside my head when I was told I have alexia. *The stroke damaged your left visual cortex;* the words sounded like they were being shot at me, bullets of information: *your right visual cortex can process visual information, but it can't send the information you need to decipher the words.* Each pitying explanation delivered in a pitch that set my teeth on edge.

I had hope back then; they were wrong. *They.* The neurologists, the doctors, the therapists, my family, my colleagues. Hope still sometimes lingers when I occasionally see the consultants, when they tell me the ways I can flex the muscles of my brain to help me read again.

The irony of it all is that I can still write, but can't read a damn thing I've written; it feels like I'm on an acid trip every time I try. I had no idea that my life as I knew it was about to end on a Friday night.

I loved my life back then. I loved waking up in the morning and only having to commute down the stairs into my bookshop. I loved the weight of a box of deliveries, fresh covers and new voices ready to be slotted into their rightful place: thrillers in one section, romance in another, children's books at the back, cookery books behind the counter holding glass domes of freshly baked muffins. I loved the huff and puff of the coffee machine, the peel of the bell above the door, the smile when a regular customer came to pick up the new release of their favourite author. I loved my fiancée. I loved my job.

But that was then. Before I had a stroke two days before my thirty-second birthday.

A Friday was the last day I found comfort in the order of words.

All I remember is leaving the pub, a blurred image of a man, then a crack at the back of my head. The same kind of crack and physical pain that pulses every time I try to read.

The doctors have said this is *normal*, that the trauma has caused my memories to become impenetrable, but not *knowing* what happened that night, not understanding *why* this happened to me, makes me feel like even more of a failure. Deep inside my gut, I know that if I could remember *what* happened, it could help me read again. Or maybe I'm clutching at straws.

The fact that I was steaming drunk didn't make a solid case for the police that anyone else had caused my accident. There was nothing to say that I hadn't just fallen over.

The bell above the shop door downstairs compacts the air in my chest. It's book club time. Downstairs there will be fifteen to twenty eager readers *exploding* with thoughts about their pick of the month. Paperbacks will be excavated from bags, notebooks will be smoothed down; Nell will be hurrying around taking drink orders in her usual Wednesday Addams' style of dress, while the volume of conversation rises to *cataclysmic* heights.

I used to love Friday nights. Before, they meant books and the comfort of being around people who were like me. Now they confirm that I don't belong in that world any more. I *dread* Friday nights.

I take a few deep breaths, unlock my fingers from the edges of the sink, and head back into the lounge, sinking into the edge of the sofa. A bubble of laughter climbs the stairs and leaks into the room. I try to swallow the block of air in my chest. The life I wanted, and my ambitions, all compacted behind it.

Nell raps on the door. 'Jack? Taxi's almost here!'

I pull myself up, smooth my hair down, and open the door. 'Wow,' she says, smiling. 'Just look at what something other than joggers and workout gear can do for a man.'

'Very funny.' I run my finger around my collar; it feels like it's shrinking with each passing second. 'I feel like a priest.'

'No priest I've ever met looks like they're about to walk the red carpet at the BAFTAs.'

'Not true – Andrew Scott.'

'Andrew Scott isn't a real priest.'

'Remind me again why I'm going to the awards when you're the one who has run the shop all year?'

'Because, it's *your* shop, with *your* name above it.'

Nell stands on tiptoes and adjusts my bow tie. 'You know, if I were into the whole *man* thing, I reckon I'd be climbing you like a tree dressed like that.' Nell has absolutely zero filter but has worked here since she left school, came at a moment's notice after I was hospitalised, worked long hours without asking, and has held my business together for the last year. 'Keep still,' she instructs, blowing her razor-sharp black fringe out of her eyes while her fingers continue fluttering beneath my chin.

She drops back onto the flats of her Doc Martens, strokes down my arms and gives a little nod. 'You'll do. Time to go.'

The diazepam hasn't kicked in yet, and fear slams through my back into my chest like I've been bucked from a horse. I take a step back.

'I don't know if I can do this.'

Nell lifts her chin. 'Yes, you can. You smile *that* smile and you talk *the* talk and you keep your head held high when you win the best indie bookshop of the year.'

There is the thrum of a heated discussion climbing the stairs. '*Great Expectations*,' Nell says in explanation. 'Mrs Keller thinks Pip is a whining little—'

I interrupt her before she can finish her sentence. 'Well, respectfully, I disagree. Pip's not only the...' I'm trying to find the word that's out of reach pro... pro... but the word doesn't come; the pill is kicking in. 'He's the lead character and the narrator. It's his words that shape the whole narrative. He's caring, passionate and he might not make the best choices, but he learns from them and... what?'

She pinches my chin and grins at me.

'Listen to me, Jack. You're going to walk onto that stage and own the room. You'll probably get laid too looking like that. How long has it been? Six months?' I open my mouth and close it. 'A year? Jesus, Jack, you'll tear a wrist ligament. Will you promise me something?'

'No.' I fiddle with the collar again.

'Fine, you don't have to promise me but if you see someone you're attracted to, will you at least *try*?' I let out a breath, tired of Nell constantly telling me to *get back out there*. 'You deserve to be happy, Jack; being on your own doesn't suit you. It never will.'

'You're on your own.'

'But I love my own space, Jack. You've always been part of a group – your family, your friends – your whole life you have been part of *something*. It's time to stop hiding yourself away from folk.'

As I say, Nell has zero filter. 'Now come on, get a move on. If I get one more taxi notification vibrating in my pocket, I'll be needing a post-coital cigarette.' She grins and hurries down the stairs. I wait a beat. The pill begins to work its magic, and the man I have become awkwardly steps outside of my body, leaving the ghost of the person I was, inside the suit. I can do this. I can pretend to be the man I was, for the next four hours at least.

This award won't fix me. Or repay the money Vicky took back when she left. It's not going to unsign the loan papers either. But it will be good for business, and I desperately need that right now.

I grab my coat from the back of the door, and close it behind me.

The rain is hammering down as I head into the station. Platform four, I repeat over and over. As long as there have been no major changes to the layout of the station, I know where I'm going. I look up instinctively to the screen to check my train is on time.

I take a deep breath and head for platform four, just as the word 'protagonist' arrives in my thoughts.

4

MAGGIE

'Just a few more minutes,' I encourage Henry as I reattach his nose-hose for the third time as we turn into one of the many back streets forking away from the main promenade. 'We're almost there.' I tug him along the last leg towards 'Flicks'. Pausing for a second to catch my breath, I look up at the small two-storey shopfront. It's set back from the road, two grey-tinted windows either side of the silver door. Above the door, the billboard promises one of my favourite love stories: *Some Kind of Wonderful*. Vanity lights surround the small billboard, and they glow onto the pavement. It's like the puddles are trying to steal a small taste of Hollywood. I'm out of breath, but happy: we made it.

I lift Henry up the steps and open the small black box to the left of the door, pull off my gloves and tap the code into the keypad. The wind lifts again, then there is a small noise like a fizz. I grimace then punch in the number again and the door clicks open. I slide my gloves back on, and climb the stairs, pushing open the doors to the main foyer.

Five years ago, this small space used to be a sweet shop. Now the walls are a deep red velvet with gold-embossed panels. There is an eclectic mix of film posters from *Gone with the Wind* to *Moulin Rouge*. Slap bang in the centre of the square space is a booth that could be sitting in the middle of a casino. It's gold, hexagonal, and the top rises and dips like the peak of a crown. Romy sits behind the three glass windows, feet up, giant headphones over her pink space buns. She licks her finger and turns the page of her magazine before clocking me and Henry. She pulls off her headphones and exits the booth at the back.

'Holy Mary, what happened to you?!' She goes to touch my arms but stops her movements instinctively. Romy had assumed I have OCD on the first day we met. I can see why.

I had been desperate to make a good first impression, while at the same time avoiding accidentally brushing her skin. It made for a *pretty* awkward interview and we ended up performing this kind of dance as she waited for me to walk into her office, while I took a step back making space for her to do the same. When we finally got into the room, the two chairs set for interviewing were mere centimetres away, and so I ended up moving the chair three times before sitting down, and desperate to impress, I continued to describe my enthusiastic love of cleaning by pulling out a tissue and wiping down the edges of the chair and door handle. Retrospectively, I can see that my actions were, maybe, a little too enthusiastic. It was no wonder that I did a Gwyneth-level acceptance speech when she called offering me the job.

On my first day, she mentioned a friend who had OCD. It was only by chance that I looked up and realised she was saying this to me with understanding and sympathy.

I wish I could tell Romy the truth. The only person who knows is Tess, but other than her, my attempted friendships, or relationships as a whole, crash and burn. But it doesn't stop the edges of the lie sharpening itself against my conscience.

'I dropped my car keys down the drain,' I answer.

'You poor thing!'

'I'm fine, honest. I've got a spare set in my cleaning cupboard.'

Romy is in her early fifties and after divorcing her husband of thirty years, she bought this place, renovated the bottom floor into a small cinema and is embarking on her own sexual revolution: she is currently dating herself. Every Friday, she goes on a date: a table for one in a good restaurant, a bottle of decent wine, a new book and a set of double A's for her vibrator. So, Friday nights, I clean, watch the last showing, and lock up afterwards; she goes on her date and gives me free entry anytime I want. It's win, win. She's also going through something of a fashion renaissance and currently looks like a cross between Tina Turner and Cyndi Lauper circa 1985.

'I'll dry off in no time and Henry is looking forward to watching the best kissing scene from any movie. Ever.'

'Agreed. Here—'

She returns to the booth and digs out a black lace shirt. 'Pop this on until your clothes are dry.' She throws it over to me.

'Thanks, you're a lifesaver.'

'It'll be a quiet night with the weather like this,' she adds as a gust of wind sends a gravel-like splatter against the glass. 'The next showing starts in an hour and a half. Colin is already in the projection room, but can you give him a nudge? Hypothetically,' she adds. 'Yesterday he was asleep in his Pot Noodle – not that it'll matter. I've only had a handful of customers today. The Odeon has a two for one deal so...' She trails off, nonplussed. This is a passion project for her. Despite her rather eclectic fashion sense and devil-may-care attitude, she had been a successful injury solicitor.

Heading through the foyer, I open my cleaning cupboard, take off my coat, shimmy out of my top and replace it, the black lace visibly showing my purple bra. My navy cleaning apron covers the lace, and I swap my green gloves for a straight-from-the-packet pair of Marigolds, holster my disinfectant and polish, then finish the look by hooking three black bin liners over my belt before following the gold glittered arrows that point downstairs to the cinema.

The room is dark until I flick on the overheads, the light bathing the forty flip-down seats. The walls are deep red with gold edging around the panels, and heavy deep red curtains cover the screen. It can be a bit much at first glance, but after a while, it stops feeling like you're inside a gilded vagina.

I set to work, picking up discarded popcorn bags, empty cups and a rogue bag of dried mango – who in their right mind takes dried mango to the cinema? I shrug and add it to the bag.

An hour passes quickly and I finish polishing the taps, add fresh loo rolls, and squirt toilet duck around the rims. There. All done. I throw my plastic yellow gloves into the recycling bin, open my bag, untangle my hair, run some tinted Vaseline over my lips and add a small layer to my eyelids – a tip from Marilyn Monroe's make-up artist. I add lemon and ginger essential oils to my wrist and neck and rub my lips together. Hardly Monroe but at least I don't look like I've been pushed into a swimming pool fully clothed. I slide my fingers into my new baby-pink flip-top mittens, fix the button in place, and head to the back of the building, giving the projection room door a tap. Colin is sitting behind a small desk, dozing; the square glass window to the auditorium above. 'It's almost eight,' I say, ignoring the stale smell.

'Righto.'

He swings on his chair, runs his finger down the small leaning tower of hard drives in white boxes, tracking his finger along the names until he finds *Some Kind of Wonderful* amongst the other films for the month, all John Hughes classics. Last week it was *Sixteen Candles*. He opens the box, takes out the drive and slots it into the player. It looks like a black stereo that could be straight from a film set in the nineties.

'Pass me the trailers would you, love?' I hesitate, before picking up the thumb drive with this week's date on, quickly placing it on the desk next to him, which he slots into the USB port above the main driver slots.

The film begins to upload, the file flicking up on the computer monitor desktop. He opens an email with the authorisation code and jots it down on a piece of paper with several other codes.

'It's going to be a quiet one so... no worries if you're a bit late.' I smile at Colin but he's already clicking on the screen, checking on the download progress.

'No worries, it'll be done in about twenty.'

Back in the foyer, Romy is throwing on her leather jacket.

I take off my apron – my jumper on the back of the door is still wet through – but my fake fur is dry, having been hung over the radiator. I slip my arms through, the gloves less conspicuous now.

'I'll hang on for another fifteen then get going,' Romy adds. 'Colin can take over here once the film's rolling.'

'Okey dokes.' I push my arms through the jacket. 'I... I don't suppose you need me for any more days, do you? I've got more slots available, so if you need any extra hours... I'm free.' Like *really* free. Losing *Pillow Paradise! and* Riz means I'll now have more free time than I'd like.

'Oh, Mags, I would but—'

'I can offer you a discount?' I'm one step away from pushing my mittens together in prayer.

'You know I would in a heartbeat, but I'm tied into the cleaning contract with CleanPro... Claire has three kids, and has been with me since the beginning. She would work Fridays too if she could get a sitter.'

'Oh, no worries.' I wave away her apologies and put on a smile.

'But if she needs to cut her hours, you'll be the first person I call, OK?'

'That would be great. Now scoot! You've a date to get to.'

'See you next week?'

'Yep. I'll be here.'

'Don't forget to help yourself to snacks!'

The door swings behind her, as I try to calculate if I will have enough after my final week's pay to top up the electric meter. My reduced hours will mean budget beans on toast and cheap Super Noodles for the week. I make my way over to the snacks, undo the pearl button of my gloves so the tips of my fingers are free, grab a bag of popcorn, and pour myself a large Diet Coke from the dispenser. Henry smiles over at me.

'Come on then,' I say to him, arm-pitting my popcorn and picking him up with my Coke-free hand. 'You can keep me company and be there in case I spill the popcorn.'

I slurp my Diet Coke, dipping my hand into my bag of sweet and salted. Henry is planted on the seat next to me; the rush and creak of the red curtains pulling back fills the room. Not for the first time I question if I'm losing my mind, having a portable hoover as my Friday night date. I'm thirty minutes into the film when the door opens, Colin sauntering down towards the front row. 'Mags, I'm going to head off – you all right to close up?'

'Yep,' I whisper back even though there's only us here. There is a kind of reverence to the inside of a cinema. It's as though the rest of the world is on hold: no emails, no phone messages, no red light blinking on the electric meter. Just me and the life unfolding on screen.

'Great. The doors will lock behind me. You've got the code?'

'Mmmhmmm.' I nod, smiling at him even though I'm desperate to land my eyes back on the screen. He's a sweetheart and I don't mind him knocking off early tonight. He has a wife, two teenagers and a pet iguana called Horatio. 'And you know how to turn off the console?' he fusses.

'Yep.' I give him a thumbs up. He casts his eyes across the empty seats.

'Just you tonight then?'

'Yep. Just me.'

5

JACK

I climb out of the taxi and stare up at the hotel. Large symbols naming it Salisbury House loom above me. At least, that was what the taxi driver has assured me. I climb the steps between the two stone pillars; they are lit up in blue lights with a banner wound around them. At a guess, I'd say they announce the DeWinter book awards.

Inside the large foyer is a hive of activity. Editors, literary agents, press, bloggers and authors all holding glasses of fizz and talking loudly. A tall woman wearing a black dress approaches me as I begin to take off my coat.

'Hi!' she greets me energetically. 'Nominee or guest?'

I hesitate, the diazepam taking the edge off her words. 'Nominee,' I reply, eyes scouting the room, looking for familiar faces to avoid.

'Congratulations! If you would like to follow me?' I nod my assent, dip my head, and follow her into a larger reception room. The noise is louder here. I recognise some attendees; others are new and unfamiliar. 'Lanyards are over there,' she continues, arm swooping towards a large table with lanyards set out in neat rows. 'And do help yourself to a complimentary drink.' She smiles through deep red lips.

'Thank you, I'll...' I nod towards the bar.

'Enjoy the evening and good luck!'

'Thank you,' I reply a second too late; she's already striding past me and back out into the entrance hall. I grab a glass of champagne and take two large sips. My uncomfortable, polished shoes lead me towards the table where I'm met with about forty white squares edged with deep blue, all with matching blue lanyards. But I may as well be looking at hieroglyphics. My heart is pounding in my ears as I redundantly search for something that resembles a 'J'.

The room shrinks, the sounds loud and yet distant: a shriek of laughter behind me, an announcement from a microphone in the next room, a confusing concoction of musical instruments resembling jazz. I scour the white squares for a few seconds more, but the symbols aren't stationary. Heat rushes to my face; my throat tightens. I knock back the rest of the drink before I turn and walk back out of the building and into a recently vacated taxi.

'Train station, please.'

I rest my head against the back of the seat and close my eyes, the symbols and white rectangles dancing behind my eyelids. My phone vibrates: Mum's face.

'Jack? Where are you? Edna said she saw you leave?' I look out of the window at the rain blurring the view of the street lamps as the taxi weaves across town.

'I'm not well. Migraine.'

'Jack?' she challenges softly. 'I know it's difficult, but—'

'Can you give my apologies? And if I win, accept the award?'

'Sweetheart, you—'

'Can you do that?' She pauses. 'Mum?'

'Yes.' She sighs. 'Yes, I can do that but this is the last time, Jack. You need to move forward.' I close my eyes and pinch the bridge of my nose.

'I'm trying.'

'You can't keep hiding from your responsib—'

'Sorry, Mum... signal's sketchy. I'll speak to you later.'

I glance at my watch, the hands telling me it's almost nine. I'm back outside the station. Two train journeys, and nothing to show for my efforts except a blister on the back of my heel. The rain is unrelenting. I can't go back to the shop yet; I can't face the interrogation and so I begin to walk. I have no destination other than 'not home'. Familiar streets, with unfamiliar signposts, follow my progress. My hands are inside my pockets, the gold-edged invitation scratching against the inside of my palm. I stop next to a bin and discard it. A light flashes in my periphery; my eyes are pulled towards the flickering bulbs surrounding a billboard. I'm momentarily disorientated. I don't recognise the street I've found myself on, and the signposts are as confusing to me as the words on the invitation. I can't remember the last time I went to the movies – two years ago? Maybe three?

I don't consciously make a decision to walk up the steps, or open the door, or follow the pull towards the ticket office, and yet here I am. It's richly furnished in reds and golds and at odds with the humble building. My eyes are drawn to the sounds from the film echoing through into the room, but it's empty. I step towards the ticket booth.

'Hello?' I ask, but there is no response.

I take out a twenty, place it in the small tray beneath the glass ticket sales booth, and follow the sounds of the film. The way is signposted by golden arrows, and my feet step carefully down into the secrets of the building.

Music plays from behind a red door, something from another era, eighties maybe? I put my hand on the door at the foot of the stairs and push.

6

MAGGIE

Here we go. It doesn't matter how many times I've seen this movie, this scene gets me. Every. Time. Eric Stoltz, aka Keith, in his dark blue mechanics overalls, under a car. Watts, short blonde hair – the ultimate 'tomboy' and hopelessly stuck in the friend zone – is convincing him that maybe he should consider practising kissing on her before he makes a move on the popular chick. I chew on another piece of popcorn, the warm and fuzzies expand inside my chest as she asks him what he intends on doing with his hands. I let out a loud sigh as their lips meet, as her hands run through his hair, her biker boots hitching around his waist.

I'm swooning up at the screen as the kiss deepens and increasing music volume intensifies the moment. God I wish I could lose myself in a kiss like that, to be swept off my feet by that kind of need and want. I wish I could have that kind of—

The room sinks into darkness, Watts and Keith disappearing from view.

Panic catches in my throat as my eyes adjust to the absence of light. I'm alone. In the dark. I let out a long steadying breath, reminding myself that it's the same room as it was a minute ago while Watts and Keith were getting it on; all that's missing is light. That's all. Just a simple power cut. It'll be the storm. I take another breath in, counting to five, then exhaling to ten. I stand and begin to make my way past the empty seats to the end aisle, walking slowly towards the door, the bare tips of my fingers tracing the edges of the seats.

There is a split second where the air changes, when I know I'm not alone.

'Hello?' The voice is deep, questioning, and breaks into the silence. 'Is there someone in here?' My breath is coming in sharp bursts and I reactively undo the buttons on my mittens, covering my fingertips. 'Do you know what's happened to the lights?' the voice continues. I'm deliberating answering when the lights flicker back on. The screen behind me resets to sky blue.

I take in the man stood still in the aisle. He's tall, broad and looks like he's stepped out of a 1950s film, like he's one scene change away from leaning against a wall in the shadows and lighting a cigarette: dark hair parted on the side, clean-shaven, tux, buttons open at the neck, tie loose around the collar. Jesus. Maybe I wished for the perfect man and this is a *Sixteen Candles* scenario. I've made a wish and it's come true. I shake sense back into my brain. I'm alone in this building with a stranger, no matter how knee-trembling, stomach-swoopingly gorgeous he is.

'Don't come any closer,' I warn, inwardly wincing at my sharp tone. My defences are instinctively up, but he looks like he's completely confused and worried by the situation, which is to be expected. I have practically accused him of being on the verge of attacking me without a valid reason.

He puts up his hands as though I'm about to fire a gun at him and takes another slow step down the aisle, hands still raised. He's not far from me now. I can smell his aftershave: clean,

expensive, like the scented candles from the new Marks and
Sparks shop in town that Riz bought me for my birthday. He
takes in my anxious state and softens his voice. 'I'm not...' He
lowers his hand and places it against his chest. 'Jack.'

'You're not Jack?'

'No, I mean, yes. I am Jack, but I'm not a weirdo.' He takes a
deep breath, exasperated with himself, or me, or the situation. I
can't quite tell. He places a hand on his chest and says, 'Jack,' in a
'Me Tarzan, you Jane' motion. He stops still, raising his hands
again. 'I promise you I'm not here to harm you, I' – he runs one of
his hands through his hair – 'I've had a crappy night and I just
wanted to catch a movie. There are no ulterior motives here, OK?'

Neither of us breaks eye contact. I can hear each breath in my
lungs inhaling and exhaling. 'Is the storm still storming?' I ask,
not knowing how to respond.

He nods with a small smile. 'I like that. Storm still storming.'
He takes a moment to appreciate my turn of phrase before
continuing. 'I'm guessing that's what caused the electric to go off?'
He raises his eyebrows.

'I think so.' I shrug. Or wishes do come true and I've *Aladdined*
you into this room.

Jack breaks eye contact first, his focus landing on my recently
vacated seat, Henry still staring at the screen. 'Unusual companion.' His eyes flick back to mine, mouth cracking into a lopsided
smile. It's unnervingly self-conscious, as though he's afraid of
unleashing it.

'I'm the cleaner,' I say, pride in my voice.

'You know, James Joyce used to take his notebook everywhere
with him. A true artist is never far away from their tools.'

'You should see my feather duster – I'm a magician with that
in my hands.' *What?* I sound like I'm offering him a good go-over
with my tickling stick. He doesn't respond other than a slight

twitch of his mouth: top lip Cupid's bow, bottom bee-stung. We both hesitate, a small ripple of nervous laughter comes from within my chest. He lowers his hands slowly. 'Well. Seeing as the movie isn't playing, I'll be on my way.' He tucks his hand in his pocket. 'It was good, not quite meeting you...'

'Maggie. Wright. Not that you need to know, but...' I chew the inside of my cheek.

'Maggie.' He smiles and oh God, the way he says my name... it sounds like it's wrapped in velvet. I stand still, then remember that my purple bra is visible from beneath Romy's black lace top. I pull my coat closer, cross my arms and nod towards the door. 'I'll see you out?' He goes ahead and I follow a few steps behind, trying not to sniff the Jack-scented air behind him like Scooby-Doo.

'So why was your night crappy?' I ask as we round the top of the stairs into the foyer. I walk next to him, aware of maintaining some distance, while at the same time trying to make the gap look natural.

'I... it's just that I didn't feel like being around people, you know?' He looks across at me, a fleeting glance that hits me in all the right and wrong parts of my body.

'I do.' He must register the sincerity in my voice. 'People are the worst,' I add and find myself smiling at him. Neither of us move as we arrive at the door. The air feels still. 'Well, if you ever want to escape people again, in my experience, the cinema is the best place to avoid people. Nobody speaks once the film starts.' He raises his eyebrows, but nods as he sees the logic behind my suggestion.

Jack turns his head towards the door. 'I'd better...' He reaches for the handle then stops, turning to me. 'Before I go, and we undoubtedly go our separate ways—' His eyes drop to the keys in his hand, a small charm in the shape of a book that he flicks open and shut with his thumb. There is a small mole, the size of an eyeliner pencil dot beneath his right eye. Slowly, they drag back upwards, deep brown stare meeting mine as he clicks the small silver book shut. 'I wondered if you'd like to grab a drink?' His dark eyes meet mine. I lick my bottom lip, pulling it between my teeth.

My body tightens, my mouth opening a touch; all the words I imagine I could say in this scenario are filling my mouth, trying to get out.

'Thank you,' I reply. *Thank you?* But I don't know what else I can say. There isn't a world where I can have a relationship with this man. He'd run a mile – no doubt without breaking a sweat or pulling a hamstring – if he knew the truth about me. And after the *disaster* of my last attempt at a relationship, I know this can't go anywhere. My mouth tries to open again but I clamp it shut, our eyes drawn to the sound of a fresh wave of rain hitting the glass outside. 'I... I'm sorry. I mean, I *would* like to but... it's... I'm complicated.'

'Understood.' He gives me a nod, lands a hand on the door and pulls. The door remains locked. He frowns and looks back at me.

'Oh! Sorry, automatic locks. They should have been on when you arrived, actually. Give me a sec.' I stride across to the keypad trying to compose a different reply, where I say yes I'd like to go for a drink with him. Instead I quickly move the conversation away. 'So you like John Hughes films?' I ask, opening the black box beside the door and glancing over. Under the brighter lights, he looks more Mediterranean than I'd first noticed, Italian, or Greek maybe? He frowns, possibly due to the breakneck speed I've changed the conversation, but there isn't a hint of recognition. '*Some Kind of Wonderful*?' I nod to the poster on the wall. He follows my line of sight and shakes his head. '*The Breakfast Club*?

Pretty in Pink?' Nothing. '*She's having a Baby*? *Ferris Bueller's Day Off*?' A glimmer of recognition.

'I thought that was Matthew Broderick?'

I shake my head. 'It is but it's written and directed by John Hughes. I'm a massive fan. He always strikes the right balance between humour and heart. And I know most of his films are for teens, but he always champions the underdogs, and makes all that awkwardness feel *normal* somehow. The soundtracks are always *so* good too.'

I punch in the number and frown. There is no reassuring click from the doors. Weird. I peel back my mitten and try again.

'Right. And I guess *Some Kind of Wonderful* is a Ted Hughes—'

'John.' I smile, stepping towards the door, giving it a yank. 'I must have hit the wrong number.' I head back to the keypad. 'It's my favourite of his actually,' I add, punching the code in again.

'And is it?' He pauses, drawing in his eyebrows. 'Wonderful?'

'Oh, it's dreamy.' I walk back to the door, Jack stepping away to allow me space as if he senses the distance I need. 'It's about two friends' – I yank the handle – 'she's a drummer, he's a mechanic,' I explain over my shoulder, 'and she's, like, totally in love with him.' I pull on the doors again but they don't budge. 'But he's in love with this popular girl and there's this scene where she lets him practise kissing on her and it's—' I sidestep, landing my hands on my hips, puzzled.

'Dreamy?' he prompts. There is a hint of a smirk in the corner of his mouth, but his gaze is sincere, like he's genuinely interested in what I have to say.

'Yeah.' I clear my throat. 'Dreamy. Let me try the code again. They should be opening.'

The lights flicker, and both of us look up towards the ceiling. I try the number a third time, but the door is locked. 'It must be the electrics. Not to worry.' I smile. 'There's a fire door downstairs; you can go out that way.' I give him a reassuring smile, but something in the air between us shifts, like it's alive. He tilts his head, eyes serious.

'I wasn't worried.'

If this were a movie, maybe he would step closer and tuck a lock of my hair behind my ear. I wouldn't feel the need to secure the pearl button on my gloves; instead, I might move closer to him, the camera picking up the way I'm looking at his mouth, the intensity of his gaze as he leans in, his lips finding mine.

But this isn't a film.

Because this leading lady can never have the kind of love you see in movies.

Not when she would hear exactly what he's thinking the moment they touch.

7

JACK

Shit.

I shouldn't have said anything. I've let Nell get into my head and now there is this monumentally awkward situation where the two of us are stuck in the same place, her knowing I've asked her out, and both of us knowing that she has shot me down. And if someone asks you out for a drink, and they don't come back with a positive response, then the writing on the wall is pretty clear, isn't it, even for me. What the hell was I thinking?

Despite Nell's insistence that I should move on, I know I'm not ready. A year ago, I was ready to stand in front of my family and friends and commit to spending the rest of my life with Vicky. I still wake up expecting her to be next to me, or hear her in the shower; I swear I can still sometimes smell her perfume. And now here I am asking a stranger out on a date.

But there is something different about Maggie – a familiarity.

I've read about this feeling, that certainty of *knowing* someone with one look. But reading about this feeling and experiencing it are two very different things. I'm trying to explain this to myself as she approaches the fire escape to the right of the screen.

My sister, Charlotte, wrote her dissertation on the love at first sight phenomenon; if I recall correctly, she had described it as our brains creating a perfect storm. We see someone, something ignites, and our brains flood with chemicals that cause an addiction: a need to be closer to that person. Ironic. In the short space of time I've spent with Maggie Wright, I have come to understand that she is fiercely protective of her personal space. I get it. I'm a stranger to her, even if she feels nothing like a stranger to me.

Maggie meets my eyes, her pink gloves on the fire escape door, which has refused to open more than a few centimetres. There is another jolt, deep in the pit of my stomach. She has eyes the colour of moss and hair that hasn't quite made up its mind whether it's curly, straight, blonde, brown, long or short. She makes a small grunting noise and pushes the bar again, but it doesn't open any further. She looks at me over her shoulder: bright pink fur coat, purple boots, and feline eyes.

'There must be something parked in front of it,' she explains. Even the tone of her voice is appealing to me. Or maybe I've had another stroke and this attraction is nothing more than a new symptom.

'Maybe if we both push?' I suggest, walking slowly towards her. I'm careful with my steps, keeping a good distance, especially given my recent confession. If we can't push the door open any further, we might well be trapped in here for the night. Although, if I'm honest, there are worse fates to be had.

'It's no use.' She crouches down, selects the torch app, and looks through the small gap, her voice dampened. 'There's something blocking it.'

She stands back up and yanks the door closed.

'So' – I lean against the front row of seats – 'what now?'

'Well, *I'm not Jack*' – she grins at me, walking in front of the blue screen, dimples forming in both cheeks – 'we could try calling for help, but—'

I wiggle my phone at her. 'No signal.'

'No signal and the Wi-Fi is down. Must be the storm.' She scoops up her hair then lets it fall back on her shoulders. 'There's a landline in the projection booth though. I'll go and try calling Romy or Colin from there.'

* * *

'Sorry about the smell,' she warns, scrunching up her nose as she leads me along the corridor above the auditorium. 'Colin's diet consists of Pot Noodles and pork scratchings, but he's a sweetie. He'll come and let us out, or Romy will. Fear not.' She grins as we come to the end of the corridor, a door with two words on it in gold glitter:

I don't bother trying to take the time to sound out the letters like my speech and language therapist encourages me to do. Sounding out letters in the same way as my five-year-old niece is not something that raises my mood. I used to read Shakespeare. Now I can barely read the word 'sit'. I managed the 's' sound after following the letter six times with my fingers first. Reading is beyond exhausting.

At first I was determined to find my way back: to books, to me; I've never quit a thing in my life, but after Vicky left and after months of endless failures, it all seemed... pointless. I'd rather focus my energy on something else. Besides, I consider, as I watch Maggie switching on the light and looking at the small room; stories can be found in places other than books. 'Here we are!'

Maggie's excitement at the inside of the small room is infectious and I find myself feeling lighter than I have in months despite the embarrassment of my earlier confession.

'This is where the magic comes from.'

On the walls are more film posters.

'So how long have you worked here?' I ask, leaning in at the original *Jaws* poster: red letters, the shark's mouth pointing upwards beneath blue water, a woman swimming across the surface.

Maggie steps over the boxes on the floor towards a desk at the back of the room.

'Three years. I came here for a late-night showing of *Before Sunset*. There was an advert for a cleaner and the rest is fairy-tale, popcorn and lemon-scented history. Are you a fan?' she asks. I realise I'm squinting and drop the muscles in my forehead, focusing instead on her as she begins lifting magazines and coffee cups on the desk.

'Of *Jaws*?'

She nods.

'I don't know. I've never seen it.'

'You're joking?' She stops searching briefly and laughs, shaking her head. 'Everyone has seen *Jaws*.'

Our eyes meet and I try to ignore the electric charge currently climbing up my spine. 'I've read it though,' I rush on, looking back at the picture.

'I didn't know it was a book. I don't think a book could ever beat the film version.'

I laugh quietly. 'That's the first time I've ever heard anyone say that.' I run my finger down a stack of boxes piled on top of each other. 'What are these?'

She frowns. 'They're the films... *The Breakfast Club*, *Pretty in Pink*...'

'Ah, Mr Hughes?'

'Yep.'

'The films are played from here?'

'Yeah. You load the film into the DVP, type in the passcode on the PC and away we go. Ha! Success!' she announces, revealing a phone from beneath a pile of discarded McDonald's napkins. She lifts the cradle to her ear and taps the button on the base. 'Nothing.' She lands her hands on her hips before tugging the phone line with her finger and following it around the edges of the room, finally crouching down in the far-right-hand corner, holding up the end of the line, which is three wires without an adapter.

'Guess calling for help is out then?'

She drops it, blows her hair from her eyes and stands. 'Yep.'

'Windows?'

'All top-opening.'

We're quiet for a moment before I speak. 'It's not the worst place in the world to be trapped though.'

'No. No it isn't.' She pulls her earlobe.

'And I came to see a movie, which, I'm told, is dreamy.'

'You were told correctly.' I don't let my eyes drop to her lower lip, which she tugs with her incisor.

'And, it would be a shame if I didn't find out if the mechanic chooses the drummer or the mean girl.'

'It would. A real shame.' Maggie's on the verge of a smile, but it's guarded. She wraps her arms around herself. 'If we're going to do this, I need to explain something, Jack. You seem like a good guy and' – a small smile – 'everything, but I'm not... available. And it's not that I don't think you're hot, because you definitely *are*.'

'Good to know.'

'But when I say I can't be around people? It's not like I don't like people or anything, on the whole people are pretty great but I can't be physically close to them. I have this... thing. It's hard to explain but the upshot is—'

'You don't have to explain,' I interrupt.

'No, it's fine, I want to, and if we're going to be together all night then you need to understand.' She lets out a long breath, eyes on the ceiling. 'I can't touch anyone.' She meets my eyes and holds up her hands, still inside a pair of gloves. 'It's a... a germ thing. I'm not saying you look like the kind of guy who is, you know, germy or anything; you actually smell really, *really* good. It's nothing personal; it's just the way I'm built.'

I meet her eyes directly. 'Understood. And I apologise... I didn't mean to make you uncomfortable earlier.'

'You didn't.' Maggie tucks her hair behind her ear, but it takes seconds before it falls back along the curve of her cheek. She looks to the floor, then back at me through her eyelashes. I continue. 'Maggie? Tonight, I'm supposed to be somewhere I didn't want to be, surrounded by people I didn't want to talk to. I do, however, very much like talking to you. And seeing as we have no choice, how about we grab some popcorn and watch a movie. I can keep my distance. We can be alone. But, together.'

Alone but together. Did I actually say that? I'm about to try and retract the whole sentence but her face softens.

'Alone, together?' She pulls at her bottom lip again. My eyes drop to her mouth then correct themselves.

'Yeah. Well, you, me, and Ted Hughes.'

'John Hughes,' she corrects gently.

'We can have your vacuum between us if it'd help?'

'Henry.'

'No.' I place my hand on my heart but I'm smiling. 'Jack.'

'I meant... Henry's my hoover.'

'I know,' I say softly, tucking my hands into my pocket. 'And you have my word, Maggie.' I meet her eyes, keeping my focus steady and sincere. 'I'll respect your space. I know you have nothing to base this on, but you *can* trust me.' I wait for her to process my words.

'You can't even share my popcorn,' she says, pulling at the tips of her gloves.

'I don't share my food, either. Seeing people share their food gives me the ick.'

'The ick?'

'Yep. I needed counselling after watching *Lady and the Tramp* when I was six.' I shudder. 'I can't even eat spaghetti.'

She laughs then narrows her eyes, mock serious. 'Are you a noisy eater?'

'No. Are you a loud slurper?' I lean against the wall and cross one foot over the other.

'No. Wrapper crinkler?'

'Only during loud action scenes.'

'Phone checker?'

'Nope.' I wait as she looks around the room, hand tapping against her thigh then laughs to herself, shaking her head.

'What's funny?' I ask.

'I was wondering, why?'

'Why?'

She puts on an American accent. 'Why in all the cinemas, in all the towns, in all the world, you walked into mine.'

'Guess, I'm just lucky.'

And for the first time in almost a year, I feel it.

8

MAGGIE

Jack is shrugging off his jacket while on screen Mary Stewart Masterson, our heroine, holds her drumsticks in red leather biker gloves and pounds on the drums as the eighties intro music starts. I sneak a glance at him as he folds his jacket, placing it on the seat beside him. He's wearing cufflinks. Actual cufflinks. I've never seen anyone wear cufflinks in my life. They catch the reflection from the screen as he settles back into his seat.

My encounters with the opposite sex have been few and far between. It's hard to build a relationship with someone when you have a running commentary to their thoughts as they kiss you.

Jared Hill behind the bike sheds at school:

How long do I have to kiss her before I go for her tits?

Not long, as it turned out.

Joseph Simm in the common room:

She tastes like cheese and onion crisps.

Rude considering he tasted like cigarettes and garlic.

Pip Finnegan, while snogging me at the school disco to 'My Heart Will Go On':

> **This will get Clara's attention.**
> **Is she looking?**
> **Yes! I'll grab her ass... What's her name again?**

It did get Clara's attention, and ruined *Titanic* for me forever.

And then there was Luke.

I met Luke in the supermarket. Not exactly Richard Curtis levels of meet-cute, but when his bag broke, and tins of tomatoes and sweetcorn careered along the aisles, I helped pick them up. He was kind, funny, liked to cook, and he was patient. With me. But that was all before I found out, just six months later, that he thought it was perfectly fine to shag someone else behind my back. That was one of those moments when I was both resentful of yet thankful for my gift.

The first time I heard thoughts, I didn't realise that what I was experiencing was different. I knew my parents had died, that they had gone out in a car and that it took my parents to heaven, but I think I was too young to grasp the concept of death. When I revisit my first memory, when I try to unpick it, I remember a deep sense of confusion. There is the image of a small house with a cherry tree in the garden. But no matter how many times I try to imagine opening the door, and stepping inside to where my early memories are hidden, I get no further. There are no images of the family I was once part of. Nothing but a locked door with ivy growing around the porch.

My first real memory is of Grandma sitting on a pale blue sofa.

The sun was streaming in through the windows. It was a

warm day, I had a red polka-dot dress on, and my hair was in pigtails. There was an ice-cream truck outside playing 'Greensleeves'. It was a happy day and Grandma was smiling when I asked if I could have an ice-cream. I don't remember the journey from the sitting room to the pavement, but I remember her hand taking hold of mine. She was smiling, her eyes were kind, but then I heard her:

> What am I going to do with her?
> She doesn't belong here with me.
> I'm too old.
> Too frail.

But she was smiling, she bought me an extra flake and strawberry sauce. It was a sunny day and children were laughing, and I was happy because I had an ice-cream.

'Aren't I staying with you, Grandma?' I'd asked.

'Of course you are! I will always be here for you. Now how about I take you to the park?'

It was the first time I realised that what people say and what they think are two very different things.

Grandma put me into the care system by the time I was five and a half.

The last time I saw her, she had held my shoulders and told me to never tell people that I can hear them thinking. It was the first time the words in her mouth matched the words shouting in her head:

> They won't understand.
> You'll never fit in.

So dating, to me, is something that happens mostly in a world created and compacted within the four corners of a movie screen, all high-definition, professionally chosen outfits, make-up dusted along cheekbones. The dates that play out behind that secret, pixelated screen are filled with witty one-liners or awkward silences, where the characters say *exactly* what they mean. And when the hero doesn't go off shagging people behind the heroine's back.

And I know this isn't technically a date, and that we have Henry grinning up at the screen between us, but it's pretty close. I shift my focus back to the blonde pixie-cutted drummer. From the corner of my eye, I see him opening his bag of popcorn, salted not sweet. I take a long pull through my straw, eyes now focused on a young Eric Stoltz walking along the train tracks, daring the train to get closer to him before he steps safely away. I side-eye Jack.

'You're smiling,' I find myself saying, eyes back on the screen.

'I am.' He throws a piece of popcorn into his mouth. 'I like the metaphor.'

'Metaphor?'

Jack nods to the screen. 'Yeah, wrong side of the tracks?' He glances in my direction. 'Low income, thinks he's setting his sights too high?' I nod. 'Classic. Classic character archetype. A' – he frowns in frustration for a second before composing himself and continuing – 'a main character, who sees himself as extremely average, but is better-looking and more talented than he thinks. He wants more from life, right?' To prove his point, on the screen Eric aka Keith is looking at his oil-stained hands while his crush, Amanda Jones, is getting it on with the rich popular guy in the background. There is something in the way he is looking at the screen, an excitement that – God this is going to sound *soooo* naff – lights him up from the inside.

'But also, sexy,' I add. He coughs on his intake of lemonade.

'You think he's sexy?' Jack gestures to the screen with his paper cup, straw sticking out.

'Eric Stoltz?' I fold my arms and lean back. 'Yep. I should say that he's not *actually* a teenager. He was in his twenties when they filmed this.'

'Huh.' He seems to assess the man on the screen.

'What about you?' I bring the straw to my lips.

'Me?'

'No, Henry.' I roll my eyes. 'Yes you, I'm-not-Jack. Who tickles your fancy, the popular girl or the drummer?'

He laughs, deep and slow. 'Tickles my fancy?' He raises an eyebrow.

'Yeah, which leading lady floats your boat?'

'My boat?' That slow smile again.

'Watts or Amanda Jones?'

'Amanda Jones. Isn't that a Rolling Stones song?'

'Yes, and stop avoiding the question.'

'Amanda is the mum from *Back to the Future*?'

'You still haven't answered the question. Blonde, brunette, or are you a redhead kind of guy?'

He frowns, as though he's thought of something, but then he smirks. 'I don't know yet. I need to see if I like their personalities.'

'Smooth,' I say shaking my head. 'Very smooth.'

We're both smiling as we return our attention to the screen. Conversation passes easily between us as the film continues, our voices raised above the eighties nostalgia.

'Is it weird to be nostalgic for a time you weren't even born in?' I ask, taking in the lack of phones and social media as the family eat around the table. He looks across Henry at me.

'I don't think so... There's something...'

'Innocent?'

'Yes, but it's more than that, isn't it? It's like being nostalgic for a life that can never be yours. I guess there is a sense of safety around wanting something you know you can't fail at. We're never going to be teenagers in the eighties.'

There is a vulnerability around his words. What could this ridiculously attractive, intelligent and funny man have failed at?

I recall what he said earlier: *Tonight, I'm supposed to be somewhere I didn't want to be, surrounded by people I didn't want to talk to. I do, however, very much like talking to you.*

'I get that,' he says, attention back on the scene playing out where Keith is rebelling about his father's pressure for him to go to college.

School is hard enough, but by the time I was seven, I had already been to more schools than I could count. My uniforms were often second-hand, and I would be told that I looked nice and smart, while hearing the opposite.

I would try to fit in with friendship groups and they would smile and laugh at something I had said, while thinking that I was weird.

My first school disco was when I was six. One of the older girls in the group home let me use her make-up and lent me a dress. It was bright blue, but two sizes too big, so I had used the belt I wore to keep my school trousers from falling down. I tried to disguise it by wrapping tinfoil around the leather. Looking back, I'm sure I must have looked a right sight, but I had perfume and make-up on, red shiny lips, silver belt, and I'd pinned two heart-shaped badges on my shoes to try and hide that they were my school ones.

'You look amazing!'

Oh bless her, poor thing.

'Where did you get those shoes? They're super cute!'

Oh. My. God.

Does she really think we can't tell they're her tatty school ones?

'You smell so nice!'

She smells like Mum's disinfectant.

But then a year later, Hellie took me in, and the next school disco I went to, I had a whole new outfit on. It was a white dress with daisies on and my feet were slipped into sunshine-yellow sandals. Not a scrap of tinfoil to be seen. Tess and I had danced the Macarena and Cha-Cha Slide together.

Jack slurps the last of his drink, with a grimace, apologising.

'Your parents put you under pressure?' I ask.

He shakes his head.

'No. I put myself under that pressure.'

'Why?'

'I guess, I didn't want to let them down. My brother and sister were head girl, head boy, captain of the football team, and I, well, I wasn't.'

'Did they care? Your parents?'

He laughs and shakes his head. 'No. Not really.'

'So why put that pressure on yourself?'

'I didn't want to fail.' There is that word again, 'fail'. 'How about you?' he asks, smoothing over the unspoken conversation.

'*Zero* expectations. Oh, here's my favourite scene.' I shift my legs so that the hole in my fishnets, is facing away from Jack. I'm suddenly very aware of Jack's presence as the music builds up and they begin kissing. I keep my eyes fixed on the screen and try to ignore the thoughts rushing through my mind of what it would feel like for him to kiss me like that, to have that kind of connection.

I hazard a brief look at Jack, but his face is unreadable as he focuses on the screen. 'Just nipping to the loo,' I explain, gathering myself and leaving the room. 'I'll check the doors too.'

'Want me to come with you?' he asks then chews the corner of his mouth, 'to check the door, not to the loo.'

'I'm good,' I reply and hurry from the room.

In front of the mirror, I take in my appearance. Cheeks flushed, eyes bright. I wash my hands, give my underarms a quick sniff. Passable. I rearrange my boobs. The elastic in my bra gave up a long time ago, but it was either a new bra or a replacement dust bag for Henry.

'What are you doing, Mags?' I shake my head recalling his words: *There is a sense of safety around wanting something you know you can't fail at.*

I can already feel myself stepping towards the threshold of tomorrow. I imagine it will feel something like homesickness.

I check the doors. They don't budge.

I smile.

9

JACK

The credits are still rolling, indecipherable symbols flashing and fading; the film crew lost to me while Maggie and I discuss the ending. Is it the best movie I've ever seen? No. But is it the most I've enjoyed watching a film? Unequivocally, yes.

'So... what now?' Maggie asks.

'I guess we should check the fire door?' My suggestion is immediately followed by an unfamiliar urge to cross my fingers like my nieces when they ask me for one more piggyback around the garden. My body is behaving oddly, like it belongs to a different man than the one who walked into this cinema a few hours ago. Maggie's green eyes flash towards the door; I'm hoping she feels the same reticence as I do for this night together to come to a close. This strange, mystical realm filled with shoulder-padded angsty teens and drum-machined music that smells like popcorn, citrus, and ginger biscuits.

'We should,' Maggie replies. 'There could be a zombie apocalypse happening out there and they're outside right now waiting to eat our brains,' she says, green eyes widening. I resist the thought that they will find mine lacking.

'Damn it, I forgot my' – my voice drops off while I try to find the word... *mash, mash* – 'axe.' I recover quickly, tapping my trousers down. 'Of all the days to choose style over concealed weapons.'

I make my way towards the fire door, Maggie at my side.

'Shall we both push. Again?' she suggests, flipping back her mittens so her fingertips are free.

We both clamp our hands on the bar.

'Ready?' I ask. 'On three?'

She nods and we both begin pushing but it doesn't budge.

'Maybe if we put our backs into it?' she asks turning around. I follow suit. It's such a strange thing, to be feeling such happiness in this moment. My thoughts are loud in my head, the past year banging and clattering against the inside of my skull. How much I've lost, how this is the first time that I can feel that dark, suffocating cloud of depression lifting. How much I miss my old life, the old me, and how, right now, this is the most alive I've felt for a long time. Maggie's feet slip as she pushes back; instinctively, I reach out to steady her. My hand holding hers, fingertips cold against my skin. She doesn't pull away immediately but the colour and humour drains from her face and she steps back and I realise what I've done.

'I...'

'It's nothing.' She waves her hand dismissively but secures the gloves back in place. 'Let me have a look.' I step aside, cursing myself for not thinking when I reached out to help her. It must be so difficult to live a life where even the simple touch of a hand can force her to distance herself. A fleeting thought of how that would work for us, if we *were* to have a relationship after tonight. I push it away quickly. It's way too soon to be even thinking that, and yet... No. Shut that down right now.

She opens the door a fraction, cold wet air blasting her face through the small crack. 'Bad news, I'm afraid,' she says into the dark cold street. She looks over my shoulder.

'Zombies?' My hand dramatically clutches my windpipe. My appalling attempt to lighten the mood.

'Worse.' Her words are faux sincere.

'Aliens?' I shudder. 'I hate aliens.'

'Me too. Green. Slimy. Big googly eyes.' She widens her eyes and I laugh. Thank God. I haven't blown it. She peers back through the crack. 'It looks like a truck is blocking it. I doubt it's going anywhere soon,' she concludes, meeting my eyes and closing the door back in place.

'Oh. Well, that's a relief.'

'It's a bit of an anticlimax, actually. I was hoping you were going to go all Rick Grimes from *The Walking Dead*.'

I grimace. 'Not seen it, sorry.'

'Really? I love a good zombie flick. Oh well... at least our brains are safe then.'

I pause.

Machete.

The word finally comes to mind.

'Fancy grabbing that coffee, now?' she suggests, flushing, her words rushing on. 'I'm no great cook but I have learnt to tame the coffee machine.'

But then my phone comes to life with a barrage of notifications.

We've got signal.

'We might be saved!' Maggie is beaming as she stands and takes her own phone out of her pocket.

'Great!' I say overly eager and stand too.

She hesitates, seeing my actions.

'You stay here. I'll be back in a jiffy,' she adds.

'Oh, yeah. Sure.' I sit back down as she hurries from the room.

Shit. Shit, shit, shit.

OK, let's think this through. This doesn't have to be the end. I can come back. See her again. For the last few hours, I've seen a glimpse of a version of myself who might be able to navigate the mess that is now my life. And we might not be able to have a relationship in the *normal* sense but I do want to see her again. The screen turns blue, the lights lifting back to full.

I click on Mum's picture, hitting play: 'Hi, darling! Congratulations! You won! I'm so proud of you, sweetheart. Call me back.'

Dad's face next: 'Jacko!! Well done, lad – knew you could do it. Give your mother a ring, will you? She's celebrating for the two of you and if you don't call soon you'll get nothing but repeats.' I snort at that. Mum is well known for repetition once she's had a few glasses of fizz. There are voice messages from my siblings, too, both thrilled for me, at my success. It's too late to call, but I'll leave a message, Mum's phone will be on do not disturb. I hold the mic down on WhatsApp: 'Hey, Mum, that's great news. I'm so pleased and Nell will be too.' My leg bounces. 'Sorry for ducking out but at least you got to have my share of the bottle, eh?' I pause, looking around the room. 'Funny thing, I actually ended up going to the cinema and I...' I've met someone? Feel like myself for the first time since the night everything was taken from me? 'I've had a good night. Been introduced to John Hughes. Not the real one, obviously, but, anyway, thanks for picking up the award. I bet your acceptance speech was class. Hope you've had a fun night and that you've drunk some water. Night, Mum.' I release the button.

A smile pulls at the corner of my mouth; Nell *will* be thrilled. It should have been her picking up the award. It's been Nell who has introduced more author events, Nell who has kept the shop flourishing. If I hadn't had the stroke, right now I'd probably still be celebrating, staying in a good hotel with thick white sheets. Vicky lying next to me, wedding bands on our fingers.

I take in my surroundings, Henry's smile, the plastic purple cup with a faint lipstick mark around the paper straw, a screwed-up napkin, and the trace of Maggie's lemon scent. The image of white sheets and wedding bands fades. I click on Nell's face, playing her message: 'Hey, heart-stopper, congratulations! Hope you get lucky. I've left you a box of ribbed, extra-large' – Maggie comes back into the room with a bright smile, her phone being passed between her hands. I fumble with my phone, urgently swiping at Nell's message – 'and a bottle of strawberry-flavoured lube next to the till... I'm *kidding*. It's cherry-flavoured.' Nell continues despite my furious thumb swiping. 'I've locked up so have fun, oh and Jack? If you think there's a chance you will get lucky? Maybe knock one out first, eh? Girls have high expectations and looking like you do—' I finally close the message. Maggie lifts her eyebrows. 'Sorry. That's Nell. She's, um, a joker,' I add.

'Cherry lube?'

'She's joking.'

She raises her hands. 'Hey, each to their own. No judgements here.' She smirks like she's enjoying watching me squirm. 'So, Jack.' She sits side-saddle on the armrest. 'I've typed out a message to Romy, telling her we're locked in. She lives two streets away and can be here in ten.' Disappointment pulls at me, like my spine is made of steel and the floor is magnetic.

'Great.' I can hear how false that sounds. There is a spark of something behind Maggie's eyes: mischief, excitement, a glimmer of something unexpected.

'But, you see. The thing is... I, well, I don't get to do this' – she gestures around the room then at me – 'very often.' She tucks her thick curls behind her right ear. They stay there for a second before falling back over the curve of her cheek. 'I mean I do this' – she gestures to Henry and the screen and then herself – 'but I'm normally alone. And so... I guess what I'm trying to say is I would really like to not press send.' She holds her phone up to me. 'But if you need to go, I—'

'Don't press send.' My voice is quiet. 'Don't press send,' I repeat, more certain this time.

10

MAGGIE

I know more than I should about the man beside me.

After a brief intermission where I battled with Colin's password system, I've managed to get *The Breakfast Club* running. We've also managed to find an unopened bottle of tequila in lost property and added some to our slushies.

Jack is broken. His thoughts as he touched me were so loud, so clear. I know he's had his heart shattered; I know he's lost something of himself. That he wants answers to a question I couldn't quite place. It was as though there was a gap behind his thoughts. It's hard to explain exactly. For the most part, I just hear people's thoughts. But when they are stressed or upset, it's well... it's more than thoughts burrowing their way into my head. I can feel their emotions, like they're so strongly attached to their thoughts, they're unable to separate them. Sometimes, I even get flashes of memories, images, as if they're being projected into my mind. I suppose it's like when you smell a specific perfume or hear a piece of music that is so tightly linked to a memory, it's hard to differentiate one from the other. Thoughts... memories, emotions are so extraordinarily tethered to the other parts of the brain, it's understandable that elements of these would also pass on to me.

That's how I know that right now, here, with me, he feels happier and lighter than he has for a long time. And that gives me a glimmer of hope that *maybe* I can help him find his way back to the man he was. Hearing thoughts has held me back from a normal life for so long, but fate has brought us together for a reason; I could help him fill in those gaps in his mind, help him find those answers.

Our students on screen – Emilio Estevez, Judd Nelson and Molly Ringwald – are navigating their way through social differences while sitting in the library, all of them having different reasons for being in detention.

Right now, I'm happily tipsy and talking to Jack comes easily, despite my knowledge of the things he's hiding. Our conversation has ranged from socks and Crocs – a yes from me, an absolute no from him; best boxsets ever – me, *Buffy the Vampire Slayer*, him *The Sopranos*; chess or draughts? I would go draughts every time. I tell him about Romy and her dates; he tells me about Nell and his family. He had dogs growing up, but had his heart broken when his last golden retriever, Bumper, died.

'Did you always want to be a cleaner?' I'm struck by how genuine he sounds. My occupation is usually met with pity or judgement as though I must have failed at everything else, but the way he asks could be the same as, 'So, did you always want to be a brain surgeon?'

'Actually, I wanted to be an astronaut.'

'Really?' he asks, his tone impressed not mocking.

'I always loved the idea of being in space, of having my whole body protected in a space suit, millions of miles from the earth.' My voice has taken on a wistful tone. 'But... I realised I wasn't any good at maths or physics...'

'And then there is the issue of aliens.'

'Right.' I smile. 'Aliens are the worst.' We look back to the screen. Our teenagers are telling each other their deepest secrets.

'So what's your day job? Wait, let me guess.' I tap my fingers on my bottom lip. 'You've never seen *Jaws* but you've read the book, you mentioned James Joyce, you like avoiding people—'

'Not all people,' he says. The way he looks at me sends goosebumps along my skin.

'Got it. You're a writer.'

'No, but you're getting close.'

'Journalist?'

He shakes his head and pulls away from the straw. 'Too intrusive.'

'Hmmm...' What else do I know about Jack? 'What's your surname?'

'Chadwick.'

'Chadwick? Why does that ring a bell?' I frown. 'Are you anything to do with the bookshop in town?'

'I own it. Well done – full marks.' He smiles but there is a brief tightening around his mouth, the light behind his eyes muted for a split second.

'You're not going to believe this, but I almost went into your shop tonight.' His eyebrows rise as he chews. 'But I couldn't.'

'Why?'

I hesitate. 'Germs,' I reply holding up my gloves.

I wait for him to frown, to react to my gloved jazz hands, but he doesn't even look at them. I take another sip of my drink.

'Maybe' – Jack tilts his head – 'we were destined to meet tonight, one way or another?'

I swallow. 'Maybe.'

'I'm glad we did.'

'Me too.'

'Do you think he feels left out?' Jack faux-whispers out of the side of his mouth, eyes directed at Henry. I reply using the same corner-of-mouth diction.

'He doesn't have emotions. He's a vacuum cleaner.'

Jack laughs slowly; it pools in my stomach like warm toffee. Of course, that could also be the tequila.

'Can I ask you a question?' I begin, emboldened by the alcohol zinging its way around my body.

'Shoot,' he says twisting around in his seat, elbow leaning on the armrest.

'Where were you supposed to be tonight?' He takes a moment, eyes darkening, deep in thought, thumb tapping against the armrest. 'Sorry, I shouldn't have asked. You don't need to explain...'

'No, it's fine.' He gives me a small smile. 'My shop was nominated for an award.'

'Congratulations!'

'Thank you.' Jack's leg is bouncing a little as he takes another sip.

'Or commiserations?' I probe. Jack focuses on the slushie logo on the outside of the clear plastic. The cup tips to the right then left. Slowly, he drags his eyes from the cup.

I don't need to touch him. I don't need to read his thoughts to experience the sense of pain behind those brown eyes as they meet mine, because it's there, shouting through the taut air between us. 'I'm sorry, I... I didn't mean to pry. Your business is your own.' I fumble for the right words. That's the thing when you live with a vacuum cleaner for company: rusty social skills that need buffing.

'No, it's fine.' He gives me a gentle smile, shifting in his seat and pulling at his earlobe, a healed ear-piercing hole above his thumb. 'I had a—'

But his words are swallowed by the lights coming on in all their full end-of-credits brightness. Jack and I shield our eyes.

And Romy walks into the room.

* * *

Outside, the storm has lost its enthusiasm, a light drizzle coating the fur on my coat.

'I'm...' Jack and I both say.

'You first,' I add.

'I'm glad I chose to come here, Maggie.'

'I'm glad too.'

Tactfully, Romy begins to walk away.

'I'd like to see you again,' Jack says. But this time, when he says it, this isn't the man I didn't know, who asked me out moments after meeting me. This is the man who has become part of the tangled labyrinth of my life. Who knows and has seen that I'm different.

The person he knows, this woman who has flirted and acted out her part in a life that she can never have, isn't real. But that invisible thread that somehow makes me feel connected to him tugs and the words fall out of my mouth.

'I'd like that too.'

'So... next Friday?' he asks, his head leaning to the right. 'You, me, Henry...?' He meets my eyes with that intense gaze that I have come to recognise, eyes searching mine as though looking for answers.

'Oh, I think Henry can sit the next one out. He's already seen *Notting Hill*.'

Jack lets out a soft laugh that runs up my body from the soles of my purple boots to my scalp.

Romy gives a not very discreet cough. We both glance in her direction, awkward smiles passing between us.

'Goodnight, I'm-not-Jack.'

'Night.'

He hesitates like there is more he wants to say, but then begins walking away. Panic expands inside my ribcage, that feeling of homesickness already beginning to rise. I step forward, in case – despite his offer to see me again – he realises that it would be a mistake for this to go further; that this special relationship born through soft lighting and magic reveals its true self, and he sees me with all my flaws, in the cold light of day. 'Jack?' He stops, half turning in my direction. 'Hold on...'

My hands are already fishing in my bag for a pen and paper. I pull back my gloves and scribble down my details. He walks back towards me, my breath hitching, his dark eyes so intense that it feels like he could read my mind if he wanted to. 'Here's my number. In case you ever need a friend or, or someone to fight aliens with.' I reach out. His face falls, eyes drawn to my scribbles with a frown. 'Forget it, I...' I rush on, retracting the paper but his hand dashes out, his fingertips brushing gently against mine as he looks down.

There is a crack of sound as Jack's thoughts and emotions crash into mine. Then there is a snap, like an electrical current and I know I'm about to see as well as hear his thoughts. There is a rip, a resistance, and symbols and words collide and disappear; there is a pain at the back of my head and then the noise stops, like a void has swallowed his memories. Before I have time to prepare myself, an image forms. A man.

A face I recognise.

Realisation hits me hard. My breath is hot and dry at the back of my throat.

It's my fault.

I'm the reason Jack's life fell apart.

He takes the paper, smiles at me all enigmatic and relaxed, despite everything I've experienced through his mind.

'See you soon, Maggie Wright.'

And with that, he tucks the paper in his pocket and walks across the road.

11

FRIDAY 13TH SEPTEMBER

Maggie

'Not the yellow. No offense, mate, but yellow isn't your colour; it makes you look jaundiced. Try the turquoise.' Tess throws over a jumper. Once I'd told her about Jack and our second 'date' she had insisted on getting the train down.

I gesture to my walls. 'I like yellow. It's a *happy* colour.'

I pull the jumper on and sit down on my bed. Tess pulls her blonde hair up into a topknot, pushes her glasses up her nose and joins me, sitting cross-legged.

For the past week I have tried and failed to find another cleaning job. My bank account is dangerously low, but I have another interview tomorrow for a night shift in a department store one town over. I'll have to walk as I don't have enough to fill up my petrol tank. And all the time, as I scoured online for cleaning jobs in my area, I've tried to process what I heard and saw from Jack. I could be wrong; the face I saw might not be the same as the one Jack had pictured, but my gut tells me it is.

'You look gorgeous, Mags.'

I let out a long breath.

'How do I even begin to tell him—'

'Like I keep saying, you don't need to tell him anything yet. It's not like you've not been wrong before.'

'Not very often.'

She crosses her arms and challenges me. 'You once thought I was pregnant because you knew I was worried and saw a flash of a positive pregnancy test.'

I laugh at the memory. I hadn't paid attention to the fact she was watching *Grey's Anatomy* when I passed her a cup of tea. 'I worried for a week before I asked you.'

'Pillock.'

'I was twelve! I didn't know quite how my thing worked back then. But this... it was so vivid, Tess. It was *him*. I'm sure of it.'

She reaches over for the book on my wonky bedside table and frowns. It's *The Invisible Life of Addie LaRue*; Jack recommended it to me. I'd gotten it from the library – the first time I've set foot in one for years. I'd suggested he watch *The English Patient* and dared him to tell me the film isn't better than the book.

Tess puts the book back down next to the green wine bottle I'd filled with fairy lights.

'Look. You said it yourself: he felt happier than he had for a long time just spending time with you.'

'I know but maybe I should cancel? It's Friday the thirteenth. Is that not screaming out loud that I should cancel? I mean, it's not like it can go anywhere, even before I realised that I might have wrecked the guy's life.'

'You didn't wreck his life and why can't it go anywhere?'

I give her a look that says, *you know exactly why*.

'Look, he knows you're a bit...' She scrunches up her nose.

'Weird?'

'I was going to say hesitant, but weird works too.' She throws a lemon-shaped cushion at me. 'You've told him the truth about not being able to touch anyone and he still wants to see you, so why not take the shot?'

'I haven't though, have I? Told him the truth, and you know as well as I do that if I ever did, he would run a mile.'

'You don't know that. Hellie didn't. I didn't.'

'You're different; we'd lived together for years and Hellie knew I was telling the truth after I showed her.' Hellie was the first person who had ever believed me, believed in me. She knew the truth about me and loved me anyway.

I miss her so much it burns.

She died in her bed, sound asleep. A heart attack they said, as we waited for the paramedics to carry her away.

She was the first person who, despite understanding my reality, made me believe that maybe, just maybe, I could have a life where I am loved, where I am wanted, where I belong.

'So get to know him first. Let *him* tell you what happened before you blow the first chance at a relationship with a guy you *really* like.'

I reach for my jewellery box and push on a couple of plain rings that won't snag on my gloves, my mind whirring.

'Or at least make sure that you've got your facts straight. You don't want to go and mess this up if it's another pregnancy-test scenario.'

'Maybe I could help him? It felt like, I don't know, like there were gaps. In his thoughts.'

'That's the spirit!' She claps her hands. 'This curse or gift or *whatever* you want to call it has held you at arm's length for most of your life. Here's your chance to use it to your advantage.'

'I'll have to tell him. About me. About what I can do.'

'*Eventually*, yes. But not yet, eh? Get to know each other a bit

more and besides, you might go out tonight and realise he's a bit
of a dickhead.'

I think of Jack, his smile, his sincerity.

'He's not a dickhead.'

She shrugs. 'You need to find the right time to tell him who
you are. Nobody fesses up everything on the second date.'

'So how many dates until I do? Fess up?'

She squints while she thinks. 'Five.'

'Five? Why five?'

'The first few are when you're on your best behaviour, fourth
is when the cracks start to show, the fifth? That's when you'll
know if he's worth risking everything for.'

'He won't understand. They never do. He'll think I'm crazy.
Every time I try to be honest, it blows up in my face.'

Her voice softens. 'Mags, don't push him away before he's got
to know you. *Then* give him the chance to decide for himself.'

'So five dates?'

'Five dates, then you can spill the beans as much as you want
and at least then you'll know if he's worth it.' She leans over, picks
up my make-up mirror and turns it to face me. 'Just look at yourself, Mags, *really* look.' I take in my reflection. My skin is clear;
the acne I'd battled with throughout my teens has gone. My eyes
are bright; the dark shadows from lack of sleep have lifted. My
make-up is natural – even my hair is behaving itself thanks to the
curl serum Tess had brought with her. 'You're not a wallflower,
Mags, you're the bleeding centrepiece.'

OK. Date number two.

* * *

I walk up the steps towards Flicks, carrying my secret in my
pocket like a closed book. If Jack is willing to hear my full story,

then maybe I can help him find answers. And maybe there could be a chance of something more.

But when I take my seat after cleaning the theatre, and the lights dim, and the curtains pull back, the seat beside me remains empty.

Jack isn't here.

12

JACK

I'm running late.

I got pulled into the book club discussion about Kazuo Ishiguro's *Remains of the Day*, then I took over from Nell when one of our customers requested a refund because they didn't like the paperback he bought last week after reading the whole book. I mean, who does that? It's like asking for a refund of a tin of paint that you've decorated your lounge walls with only to discover that it wasn't your thing after all. Nell can hold her own when it comes to complaints, but this guy was relentless and not listening to a thing she was saying. He'd calmed when I approached, a look of 'at last, someone who will understand me'. Arsehole. And now here I am, on my way to Flicks, jogging in jeans and a new pair of brown boots that could as easily be used by the SAS to increase my tolerance for pain. Not exactly the cool, calm and collected entrance I wanted.

The trailers have already started as I take in our empty seats, my stomach tumbling towards my uncomfortable boots. I can't see Maggie. No Henry either.

I scour the room.

A trailer of the next big superhero film is playing. My eyes bounce across the rest of the faces lit up in flashes of light while the sounds of superheroes landing their knees into concrete vibrates around the room. There is a row of four women in the middle, all chatting through the *not-on-my-watch* dialogue. Towards the back is a couple in their forties, the man on his phone, the woman demolishing her chocolate as she glances angrily at her partner. Behind our seat are a pair of women in their late forties. Easy body language, and the way they are interrupting each other tells the story of a long friendship, both women accepting of each other's habits, both talking animatedly, hands moving rapidly, laughter punctuating their conversation. Next to them a man is standing up and taking off his jacket – but I can't see Maggie.

Shit.

That twat will never buy another book from my shop. I give the room another once-over. Still no sign of those heavy curls. The screen darkens, my eyes drawn to the symbols telling the viewers the age certificate.

Then I see her. She's not in our seats, but further along the row in front of the man, who, now jacketless, has just sat down.

'Excuse me?' I say. 'Is anyone sitting here?' She raises her eyebrows, cat's eyes sparking. I look up, taken aback once more by that unsettling feeling that came over me the first time I'd seen her, that sense of knowing her.

'I was expecting someone, but it looks like he's ditched me.'

'My lucky night then.'

She shifts to the right, a cloud of her scent reaching out to me as I sit. She's wearing a turquoise jumper, off the shoulder, a pink corduroy skirt resting above her knee-high navy-blue boots, a pair of soft grey gloves, the same type that she wore last week where the mitten part can be pulled back revealing fingerless gloves. Her hair looks softer than it did last week, curls bouncing as she shifts to the left. 'So this guy who stood you up,' I whisper. 'What's he like?'

'Clever. Bookish. Nice' – I tilt my head waiting for the end of her sentence – 'teeth.' She flashes me a grin.

I let out a snort. 'I bet he had braces as a kid. Had a lisp for most of his early teens.'

'Maybe. I'd say it was worth it though. The guy has a great smile.'

'Well' – I put a hand to my heart – 'I'm sorry you're stuck with me.'

'You'll do.'

The film has started and our conversation stalls for a few moments as Hugh Grant narrates, explaining that he lives in Notting Hill.

'Hi,' she says, eyes on the screen.

'Sorry I was late. I'm normally annoyingly punctual.'

'How can you be annoyingly punctual? Being on time can't annoy someone, surely?'

I think of Vicky's face when I would be pacing the floor, checking my watch as she finished an email that was urgent, or hunted for a necklace that the outfit wouldn't be complete without. 'Depends if that person is laid-back about punctuality.'

She meets my eyes. Hers look a little different, and I recognise the impact of an eyelash curler. Growing up with a sister and having a niece who likes to practise on you leave their mark. I wonder if Maggie opens her mouth when she uses it.

'I get that.' She sucks a chocolate, pocketing it in her cheek. 'It kind of implies that their time is more important than everyone else's.'

Without knowing it, she's just summed up Vicky. My stroke and recuperation was quite the inconvenience, as it turned out.

I'm being unfair, really. It turns out that it was the '*in health*' part of our impending vows that she was committed to, the '*in sickness*' part... not so much. And I guess, she was always going to break me, stroke or no stroke. I didn't realise she was going to ruin me financially too.

'I'd have understood, you know. If you'd had second thoughts.' Maggie's voice brings me back. It's tender, cautious. Hugh Grant's monologue about where he lives continues in the background as he strides along the streets of Notting Hill. The flirtatious atmosphere has dimmed, something like insecurity dipping her eyes before they meet mine.

'Are you kidding? I've been looking forward to this film all week.'

'Lies,' she says shaking her head, curls skating along the pale skin of her shoulder.

'I never lie. Well not never. I once told my fiancée she looked nice when she had her eyelashes done...' I enact spider legs with my fingers in front of my eyes. 'But that was a kindness.'

'Fiancée?' she questions gently.

'Ex. Ex-fiancée,' I clarify.

'Sorry.'

'It's fine. Well, you know' – I scratch along my jawline – 'not fine. Nobody wants to be dumped a month before their wedding, do they? Pretty tragic, isn't it?' I'm being flippant, but the look she gives me, the sadness cuts through my chest. It's been months since I've mentioned Vicky to anyone, and yet here I am.

'Wow. So when you say fiancée, you really mean fiancée. Like not let's get engaged, post it on Insta then never actually plan the wedding. You were one top hat and tails away from the aisle?'

'One tux away... actually.' Her eyes widen as she registers my meaning. I shrug. 'I didn't see the point in buying a new suit last week.'

'Can I ask what happened?' She shakes her head as if the action will rub out her question.

I think of the days and weeks after the stroke. Vicky was at my bedside, there to help me through for the first few weeks but then... she became more distant. There were excuses not to come over, to not attend the hospital appointments. Then: 'You're not the same man I fell in love with,' she'd said. And I wasn't. I'm not. That man doesn't exist any more. Kudos to Vicky. She realised it before I did.

'It's fine. We didn't fit any more. I changed and...' I shrug. 'She didn't. That's about it.' That and the fact that she took the money she'd invested in the new shop with her. I push that thought aside.

'I'm sorry. That it didn't work out.' Maggie looks genuinely upset. More upset than Vicky did when she told me it was over.

'Thank you, but it was for the best.'

There is a pause and for a moment, I think she's going to reach out and touch me but instead, her hands fold in her lap and she puts on a brave smile, shifts in her seat, and angles further away to the left.

'I loved the book by the way. Addie LaRue? So beautiful and relatable.' She frowns as she lifts her gloves and gives me a knowing look. Something changes in her demeanour, a kind of eagerness to hear what I have to say but something else.

I change the subject. 'I watched—'

'*The English Patient*?'

'Yes.'

'And...?'

Her eyes spark with a challenge but then I nod. 'You were right.'

'Hah! Told you.'

We get a 'shush' from the friends behind, and grimace at each other, sinking down into our seats. The film is good but I'm finding it hard to concentrate with her next to me. Ten minutes in and we've had our second meet-cute: Julia Roberts has met Hugh in his bookshop and then they've bumped into each other on the street, orange juice spilt all over her top.

'Classic,' Maggie says quietly, grinning up at the screen as she pops another chocolate into her mouth.

'Who knew finding love was so easy?' I whisper, leaning towards her a little but still keeping a respectful distance. Maggie turns her head. Her eyes widen a touch and I realise the implications of that sentence. I rush on. 'If I'd known I just needed to be clumsy with my orange juice, school would have been a whole lot easier.'

'Huh,' she replies, gently nodding, then she whispers, 'It would have made my life easier, too.'

'Good job we didn't go to the same school and have this superior knowledge back then. It would have been orange juice chaos.' What the frick am I actually talking about? *Orange juice chaos?*

'Shush!' one of the friends from behind reiterates. Maggie shakes her head at me and points to the screen, a finger on her lips. I glance back at her, but her lips are clamped, holding in a laugh.

As Hugh looks for his glasses and takes Julia Roberts to the cinema in a pair of snorkelling goggles, Maggie shifts in her seat, pulls out her phone and frowns at the screen.

I risk the wrath of the friends behind.

'Everything OK?'

'Sorry... I need to take this.'

She unfolds herself from her seat, apologises to the women behind and makes a hasty exit.

13

MAGGIE

I frown at the screen as I head into the foyer; Riz's name under the two missed call notifications. Why is she calling me at this time of night? I wave my phone at Colin in the booth and make my way outside. The wind hits me, and I pull my arm around myself against the salty air, returning her call.

'Riz?' I raise my voice over the wind, my hair tangling across my face.

'Mags? I'm so sorry to be calling at this hour, but, well... the thing is, I seem to have gotten myself into a spot of bother and the truth of the matter is, I had no one else that I could call.'

'Are you OK?' I think of the thoughts I'd heard flash through her mind the last time I was there when I'd had to help her into her chair.

Almost there. Getting old is such a shit.

The pain in her hip, the retirement home, the feeling of closure that had ricocheted through her words as she thought about boxing up her things, locking the door of her house for the final time.

> I know how she depends on this job.
> She's such a bright spark.
> I see myself in her.
> If only life had thrown her a few more favourable rolls of the dice.
> This will probably be my last true act of independence.
> And it's going to break my heart.

'Well, there's the rub. I seem to have gotten myself in a bit of a fix, and I wondered, if it's not too big an inconvenience, if you could possibly pop over? You still have your key?' There is a gasp on the other end of the phone, as though she's shifted her position and is in pain.

Riz's key is on my keychain in my jacket pocket, which is still folded under my seat next to Jack. 'Yep. Do you need an ambulance? I can...'

'No. No. I don't need all that fuss, but I would be grateful for a little help.'

'Just hold tight. I'm on my way.'

The wind almost pulls the doors straight from my hands but I close it behind me, and make my way back to Jack.

'Problem?' Jack scans my face as I look over to him. There is concern and kindness in his eyes.

'It's Riz,' I begin in a rush, gathering my jacket. 'I'm her cleaner. I think she's had a fall. I'm sorry, I need to go.'

'I'll come with you.'

'No, no... you stay. Watch the end of the film.'

But he's already standing.

* * *

I slip my key into the door, Jack behind me. The lights are off in the hallway. I flick them on.

'Riz?'

'Upstairs, Maggie dear.' Music is playing from somewhere upstairs: 'Moon River'. I recognise it from *Breakfast at Tiffany's*.

I take the stairs two at a time, Jack following. A rectangle of soft warm light spills from her bedroom door onto the mauve carpet.

'I'll wait here,' Jack says, staying in the hallway as I push open the door gently. Riz is sitting in the middle of the room, her walker on its side, boxes surrounding her, photo albums stacked up, jewellery and clothing in wayward piles. She's dressed in an aquamarine sequined dress, long beads around her neck, bright red satin shoes on her feet with three-inch heels. A bottle of champagne is sitting in an ice bucket on her chest of drawers; her red lipstick is smudged around the corner of her mouth.

'Riz.' I rush to her side, crouching down.

'Darling, I'm so sorry. You must think me a silly old fool to get myself into such a bother at this hour.'

'Not at all.'

She glances around the room wistfully. 'I thought I'd have a last hurrah before this all gets packed up and sent away to charity shops but' – she casts a glance around the room then gestures to her ankle with a lift of her chin – 'it seems my dancing days are over.'

'Never say never, eh?' I smile gently. 'Can you move your foot?' She tries to shift but winces, tears filling her blue eyes.

'Blast.'

'Riz, I have a friend with me: Jack. Do you mind if he comes in?'

'Oh, my dear. You were on a date.'

'No. Well, not exactly.'

'Darling girl, if your face lights up at the mere mention of his name then yes. I'm quite certain you were on a date.' She leans forward a touch as I shift back as subtly as I can. 'Is he handsome?'

'Jack?' I call. Riz shifts her neck to see him over my shoulder. Jack steps into the room, all six foot something of him filling the doorway.

'Well, well.' She takes him in, raises her eyebrows at me in appreciation.

'Hi,' he says. He doesn't look around the room, just smiles at Riz as if he's meeting her over lunch in a restaurant, not sequined and lipstick-smeared. 'I'm Jack.'

'Of course you are. Come on in, Jack. I'm afraid it's been a while since a handsome man has been in my bedroom and it appears that you find me in quite the state of disarray.'

'I think it's sprained,' I say, looking up. Jack smiles at Riz, but I can see his mind is working. He walks to the ice bucket, takes hold of a discarded cloth and wraps the ice inside. He goes to pass it to me but must see the resistance registering on my face. Instead, he pauses and crouches on the other side of her.

'May I?' he asks, gesturing to her ankle.

'Be my guest.' She flinches as he applies the ice.

'Sorry,' he replies.

'What for? You didn't waltz yourself onto the floor.'

'I'm more of a tango dancer.' He smiles, catches my eye with a grin, shifting the ice pack so it can lean against her without him applying pressure.

'I can imagine.' She raises a furiously plucked eyebrow at me suggestively. She shifts. 'Maggie, be a darling and pass me my cigarettes, will you?' I scan the room, my eyes landing on a packet with a diamanté-encased lighter sitting on top. I place them next to her. Riz quickly finds one and clamps it between her teeth. Not missing a beat, Jack ignites the lighter, the flame flickering as Riz inhales deeply, blowing out a long plume of purple-grey haze.

'So, Jack, tell me about yourself.'

'Oh, there's not much to tell.' I hold on to my knowledge, surveying the room. He sits down on the floor next to her, back against the wall, legs crossed over at the ankles, head tilted towards Riz. 'I'd much rather hear about you. Maggie tells me you're a photographer?'

I love how he says it in present tense. It strikes me that I've not seen Jack interact with anyone other than a brief conversation with Romy. It's strange seeing this confidence in him, this easy charm and charisma. Gone is the vulnerability that he revealed to me last week. Riz laughs; Jack compliments her easily. *This* is the man who was engaged. The man with ambition and drive who wins awards and owns a successful business. There isn't a hint of the pain and the void behind those eyes. I begin picking up items of clothing as the two talk. Jack remains seated on the floor beside her, his focus on Riz as she tells him she once worked for a French magazine that I've never heard of but which Jack is familiar with.

'There's a whole box of them...' She frowns looking at the chaos around her. I take in the boxes. The house is filled with the evidence of a life well lived. I see the leaflet about the retirement home, and recognise the determination in her. She's planning on doing all of this herself.

'Are you moving house, Riz?' I ask tentatively. She takes a long pull on her cigarette, then nods, eyes on me then Jack.

'My final adventure. A retirement home they call it, but it's where I'm going to be putting myself out to pasture. I've lived a full life, known the love of a good man. And it's time. I'm fed up of being stuck in here on my own. I have no family and all of my friends have kicked the bucket or lost their marbles.' She inhales again and waves around the room on an exhalation. 'Most of this can go.'

Jack glances up at me. An unspoken conversation: she can't pack all this away by herself. 'I need company, you see.' She turns her attention back to Jack. 'Laughter!' Her focus is back on me. 'And not before long, I dare say, a bedpan. And I shall be taking myself under my own steam. This way, it's my choice. I'm not going to be put in some godforsaken institution without decent care. The place I've chosen is perfect. Music on a Saturday night and well... there's bingo, which I can't abide... all those silly phrases set my dentures on edge, but the daily menu is good, made by a proper chef and I get to take my own things for my room.' Her eyes roam the discarded items, the photos still on the walls. 'It's how I want to spend my final days, just as I have lived. My choices guided by my own decisions.'

She finishes her cigarette, twists it out into a small saucer. Jack lifts the ice from her ankle. 'Well, you're made of stern stuff, Riz,' he says. 'The swelling has gone down a little already.' Jack looks up at me; I'm clutching a vinyl record against my chest. 'But we can take you to the doctors' tomorrow to get it checked out?' I don't miss the *we*. The invitation. The question in his eyes.

I want to say yes, of course we can take her to the doctors', but I can't. There will be too many people and it's too much of an intrusion to have access to so many private thoughts. He must see my hesitation, and an understanding softens his expression. I need to tell him the truth; this is going too far. I mean, a second date at Flicks was OK – it's not that huge a commitment – but now I've let him into my life outside of the cinema and... and I'm not sure if he *can* be part of it. Or that I can be part of his, not until I've explained.

'How about I swing by tomorrow morning,' he continues, 'and take you to get checked out?'

I should say: no, it's fine. You're a busy man. I'll take my elderly friend to a busy doctors' surgery, no problem. But I know what it will be like, even if I'm able to avoid touching people with their own worries and fears. I could call her a taxi but then who would help her down the steps? I know she has no children, no husband...

'I'm sure you two have much more interesting things to be getting on with than taking care of the likes of me. I'll grab a cab and I...' She looks around the room at the debris of her life. There is a switch, something not quite defeated, but there is a drop in her shoulders, like the weight of the task at hand is suddenly pressing down on her slight frame.

'It's my day off,' Jack continues.

'Mine too. I can give you a hand, sorting out your things if you'd like?' I suggest tentatively. 'You'll probably need to rest your ankle,' I add for good measure.

She looks between the two of us, then around the room.

'Very well.' She smooths down the sparkles of her dress. 'If you insist. Thank you. But I will pay you, Maggie dear.' I try not to show how much this will mean to me. 'I've never taken advantage of people's good intentions and I don't intend on doing that now. Now, Maggie... you're sure it won't interrupt your studies?' It takes me a moment to catch on. The fake course I'd told her about.

'It won't. I... it doesn't start until the new year so I have plenty of spare time.'

'Well then. I always believe things happen for a reason, so it was a good job I got tipsy and fell on my derriere. Thank you both.'

Jack helps Riz up, and we wait outside the bathroom while she changes.

'Studies?' he asks, leaning against the wall, hands in his pockets.

'It's' – I lower my voice – 'she felt bad about me no longer cleaning for her. I told a little white lie to make it easier for her.'

Riz shuffles out, holding tightly to her frame. We get her settled, say our goodbyes, and make our way to the front door, an unspoken conversation passed through glances towards each other.

'Sorry you didn't get to see the end of the film,' I say, shrugging on my jacket.

'I'll catch it next time.' He smiles, softly.

'Thanks again. You've done more than enough.'

Jack nods before opening the door and stepping outside. He stops, turns, and makes his way back towards me. My heart is pounding again. 'Forgot my coat,' he says. I have to talk myself down from being so ridiculous. What did I think was going to happen? That he was – what? Going to ask me out again? Come back and snog my face off next to the door jamb?

'I'll get it.'

I rush upstairs, grab his coat, something heavy inside knocking against my thigh. I say goodbye to Riz again.

My mind is so filled with him, with what I should say, that I don't notice that my gloves are peeled back, my fingertips bare. He steps towards me, hand outstretched for his jacket.

And we touch.

Again.

14

MAGGIE

What am I *doing*? This is too soon.
I'm not ready.

I snatch my hand back.

'Sorry,' he immediately responds as I tuck my hand in my pocket.

'It's OK.' He looks appalled by his actions.

'I—'

'Really, Jack.' I smile despite reeling from his thoughts. 'It's fine. It was my fault; I wasn't paying attention.'

I clutch the inside of my pocket, like I'm trying to hold on to something that is already lost. 'I'm fine,' I reassure him again, but he's standing still, his eyes locked on my pocket.

I turn away, trying to push away the grainy image that was at the back of his thoughts. The road outside the White Lion pub. Just down the road from where *I was* that night. I close the front door behind us, the security light spotlighting us on the pavement, my heart knocking against my ribcage as I pull the mittens

back over. His thoughts replay over in my mind: *This is too soon.*
I'm not ready.

'I'll swing by tomorrow and—' Jack begins.

'That's... it's really kind of you but... look.' I drag my hands
through my hair. 'I... I think it might be better if...' The muscles
in my forehead tighten and I force myself to concentrate on my
breathing instead. 'I, if we... do you remember when I said that
I'm complicated?'

'I do, but—'

I bite down the pain before I continue. 'I... this... you and
me... I'm not available, not how you would need me to be if this is
going where I think this *might* be.'

He puts his hands in his pockets and looks to the right of the
street.

I soften my voice. 'And I don't think *you're* ready either.'

There's a stillness around us, the air heavy with all the things
we're not saying. He gives a small nod, a fraction of a movement.

'So where do we go from here?' he says quietly.

I want to touch him again, to hear what he's thinking. Is he
relieved? But I can't do that. Not with him. 'I would like us to be
friends?'

His head leans, just a fraction. 'Friends?'

I nod, glancing at my boots. 'But...' I meet his eyes. 'The kind
of friends who don't spill orange juice on each other.' I give him a
small smile; I want to look away. I don't.

He lets out a long breath, eyes searching mine. A car passes, a
dog barks twice, life carrying on around us as though I've not
said goodbye to the one real chance I've ever felt at a normal life.

'OK. Friends,' he says, and I try to ignore the pain that is tightening my chest.

'But we could still see each other, on Fridays?' I ask hopefully.
'I always think that Friday is the best day of the week, isn't it?

There is something that is even more special than the weekend –
it's the conclusion but there is still the promise of what could
come next. If you'd rather not though, I'd understand.'

'No, I mean yes, I'd like that.'

'*You've Got Mail* is on next week. It's about a bookshop owner
so should be right up your street.'

He runs his knuckles along his jaw and nods. 'Oh' – he
reaches into his inside pocket and pulls out a book – 'I thought
you might like this?'

He hesitates, glancing down at the book and my gloves, like
he's unsure how to pass it to me. I reach out, taking the book from
his hands. '*The Time Traveller's Wife*?'

'Yeah.' He takes a step back. 'I think you'll like it. It's one of
the book club's favourites.'

'Thanks, this looks great. I love a bit of time travel.'

There is an awkwardness to our exchange now. It's as though
we're less like friends and more like strangers. 'I'll start it tonight
and let you know. As we're swapping favourites, check out *Pride
and Prejudice*, the Keira Knightley one.'

He raises his eyebrows. 'There is no way that it's better than
the—'

'Book. I know, I know...' I roll my eyes. 'But the music is
gorgeous and there is the best hand acting ever.'

'Hand acting?'

'You'll see.'

'Will do.'

'We can compare notes?'

He nods, but his eyes are already scanning the road. There is
a chill in the air, the winter fast approaching, leaves already
dying and falling to the kerb.

'Goodnight, Jack.'

'See you soon, Maggie.'

I watch him walk along the road until the evening swallows the outline of his figure.

Only then do I let the air back out of my lungs.

* * *

Tess is curled up on the sofa, asleep, when I get back home. *Bridget Jones* is playing quietly in the background.

She looks out of place in my sitting room in her pale beige pyjamas and carefully highlighted blonde hair.

My small sitting room is a riot of colour. The walls emerald green, the sofa a dark orange, warm colours contrasting with the perpetually cold temperature inside the room. Above the sofa are postcards of places I will never travel to in the summer, not on my wages, and not without gloves and a coat.

I've always wanted to fill my home with things to look at, to enjoy. But now, it feels like they're all symbols of a life I can never have.

'Hey,' she says, yawning. Her face falls as she takes in the time and my expression. I slump down next to her, taking off my gloves and throwing them across the room.

'Want to talk about it?' she asks.

'Not really. I...' Jack's thoughts come back into my mind, and the image of the path outside the pub: *What am I doing? This is too soon. I'm not ready.*

'He's not ready. And he knows we can't be anything... and I think I saw him thinking about the road outside the White Lion.'

'That doesn't mean anything, Mags. He might have fancied a pint.'

'I know but I was only across the street when I—'

'Just take a breath. Tell me what happened.'

'Riz had a fall so we went to hers, and I wasn't careful enough when I passed him his coat.' I rush on. 'And then I saw him thinking about the pub and I heard that he wasn't ready and I... I hate lying to him, you know? And not just about the whole germ thing. I know he's not OK, and I think it was because of me that his life turned to shit, but I can't tell him that without explaining that I'm, well, me—'

She sits up. 'Take a breath, Mags. You don't know any of this for certain.'

'I know I'm lying to him.'

She pulls the cuffs of her pyjamas over her hands. 'You're not lying to him, you're just not telling him everything *yet*. And has he told you the truth? Why his life is shit?'

'Well... no.'

She holds out her hands like she's balancing plates in a 'there you go' motion. 'See? He's got his own secrets too. You both need time.'

'I told him we can only be friends.'

Her shoulders drop a little. 'Being friends is a good place to start, I reckon.'

'Maybe.' I chew my thumbnail.

'Although I was hoping you would have at least got to first base tonight.'

I give her a weak smile. 'What and hear how I use too much tongue like I did with Luke?'

'Luke was a tit, and you said yourself that he thought he was doing everything right when in fact he, as you so delicately put it, would knead your baps like Paul Hollywood on speed.'

'True.'

I lean my head back on the sofa and tilt my head towards her. 'Jack's given me another book to read.'

She frowns. I catch a glimmer of the protectiveness she used to show when the girls at school would tease me. 'What, like homework?'

'No... he's not like that... It's something we do. I suggest a film; he recommends a book.'

'Well that's a start, isn't it? He must want to see you again?' She props her cheek on her hand. I've always admired Tess's natural beauty. She could be on a skincare advert.

'Yeah, we're meeting again next Friday.'

'You really like him, don't you?'

I nod, my eyes hot, tears already pricking.

'I should end it.'

'It's early days yet. We've all got shit that we don't spill on the first few weeks of a relationship. Hot chocolate?' she asks.

'I'm out.' I sniff and shake my head.

'Oh ye of little faith. Brought supplies, didn't I?'

She lands a quick kiss on my head as she gets up, so fleeting all I hear is:

I'm here.

15

JACK

The shop is almost empty, the last of the book club – already with their coats on – are still talking, laughing, exchanging recommendations. Despite Maggie's words, the old sense of pride rekindles in my chest at the community Chadwick's has created. But I soon deflate.

Because in the corner of the room, sitting on the leather armchair, is my father.

Who I've been avoiding.

Shit.

He unfolds himself, makes his way towards me.

I raise a hand in acknowledgement and stride behind the counter. 'How long has he been here?' I ask Nell out of the corner of my mouth as she stacks the cups behind the counter.

'About an hour,' she replies. I avoid my father's steps and instead focus on the book cover: a yellow cover with a pair of eyes staring out. She continues talking to me under her breath. 'I told him you were on a date.'

'It wasn't a date—' She raises her eyebrows, her sharp fringe lifting with the movement.

'We're just friends.'

Friends. Is that all we are? I push the thought aside. Maggie is right. Things were moving too fast and—

'Riiiight. And that's why you've changed your outfit three times today?'

Dad makes his way over. 'Business is booming!' He pauses, smiling at the customer. 'Great read,' Dad continues. He has what is often described as 'kind' eyes. And it's true. He does. He's a kind man, a good father. A talented writer. But he also *kindly* refuses to accept that I am no longer the man I was.

'Can we go somewhere and talk?'

There is laughter coming from the group beside the door and I look over. Anything not to face the conversation that I know is coming.

'I can't.' I straighten the already neatly stacked pile of book-marks. 'I'm needed here. Nell's shift is over and I need to lock up.'

'Oh I'm fine here,' Nell says. 'They'll be nattering for another half an hour yet.' She smiles oh so sweetly at me. Traitor.

'But—'

'Of course. I wouldn't want to put your Nell out.'

I let out a sigh and dig my hands into my pockets. 'She's not *my* Nell.'

'Apologies. Five minutes, son. That's all I'm asking.'

'Fine.'

He follows me up the stairs, chattering about the book that he'd signed for a fan while I was at Riz's. 'I can barely remember writing the ending to that one, you know. It was when...'

I've heard this story a million times. How it was when me and my siblings all had chicken pox and he'd had hardly any sleep for days. *The subconscious—*

'The subconscious at work.'

I click on the lights. At least the flat is tidier than the last time he gate-crashed my time.

'Coffee?' I ask heading into the kitchen.

'No thanks. Already had one downstairs. She's quite something, your Nell.' I shake my head; he just doesn't listen. He walks over to the bookshelf, fingers the pages facing the room. Charlotte, my little sister, had commented on this, layering over the real conversation that needed to be had with a smirk that did nothing to hide the horror as she looked at my flat. '*Getting your Insta on?*' she'd asked. '*I like it, very minimalist. Very Marie Kondo.*' I look to my shelves, each of my books facing the wrong way so that only the buff-coloured paper edges show. Dad runs his fingers along the pages, with a tight expression. 'Very good with the customers.'

'I know. That's why she manages the shop.' I can hear the snap in my voice, the irritation. I walk over to the window, focus on the lights outlining the bay in the distance.

'Jack, pluck the thistles off your skin for a moment. I'm not here to attack you.' I turn to face him as he looks to my reading chair; you can barely see it for the laundry hanging over it. He sits on the sofa instead.

'No? Then what are you here for?' I fold my arms.

'You know why I've come to see you. The new shop is still only half renovated, Jack.'

'I know. I'm working on it.'

'Are you? Because from what I can see there has been no progress in the last four months. You've told the landlord that it would be open by the end of the year. You know the holding fee only reduces the rent until then.'

'I've made my decision. I don't know how many times I need to say it. I'm not capable of opening and running a new shop.' I let out a long breath. 'I'm going to sublet the space.'

'Right. And your dreams for a chain of Chadwick's bookshops?'

'That was something I dreamed of before... I've tried to tell you this.'

'How do you know if you don't even try?'

I shake my head, turn back to the sea, imagining the waves crashing against the shoreline.

'I know things have been... difficult for you.'

I turn around again. 'No, you don't. You don't know.' My voice is low but brittle, like it's flaking away.

'You're right. How about you tell me?' His voice is annoyingly calm. He was the same when we were growing up, would always de-escalate our sibling quarrels in the same calm and controlled manner. He never shouts, never loses his cool. It's infuriating.

I look over to the bookshelves, to the drawer with the letter from the bank inside, then back to him. His eyes are soft behind his glasses, filled with love and concern, determination and curiosity.

There is no point trying to explain. My answer will still be the same. 'I can't do it, Dad.'

'Now, you see, this is where we disagree.'

Growing up, there was never a limitation in my parents' eyes of what we could or couldn't do. Go out and get shitfaced if you want. Call us when you need picking up. Want to take a year out of uni? Sure, fill your boots. Go back to uni when you're ready. Marry a girl who is completely wrong for you? It's your call. But we'll be here if you change your mind. We can cancel the wedding at any time. They always believed in letting us find our own path, our own limitations, our own triumphs – which is why this intervention from him is so hard to take.

'You have never given up on anything in your life, Jack. It's not in you. Chadwick's was your dream, and we have done everything we can to support you. But enough is enough. I'm not going to stand by and watch you throw it all away because of one setback.'

Maggie's words echo through my thoughts: *I don't think you're ready either...*

'A setback?' I raise my voice. 'A fucking *setback*?'

I walk over to the bookshelf and pull out a book – I recognise the cover as *The Water on Horseback*. The spine is cracked, the pages well worn. I've read this book at least five times. I take a breath and open the pages, clearing my throat dramatically. 'Page one.' I stare at the symbols dancing around the page then stride towards him pointing to the text, flexing open the pages.

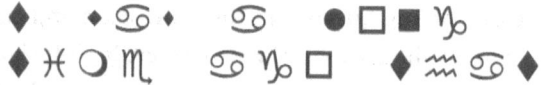

I stare at the symbols, the pain at the back of my skull already pounding, the feeling of failure sitting squat-like in my stomach. 'Do you know what it says?' I ask him. 'DO YOU?' Dad doesn't flinch, doesn't break eye contact. 'No, because you can't see the fucking words on the page from there. That's how hard it is.' I drop the book onto the coffee table. A dirty wine glass tips. The sound of the glass cracking in two rings out, like an exclamation mark.

'Have you finished?' Dad asks calmly.

'Yes. We're done.'

'I hate to break it to you, son. But we're not. I have never inter-fered with your life, because I knew you would learn from your own mistakes, but it's been *months* and you still haven't learnt a thing.'

'I told you that I couldn't do it after the stroke. After Vicky walked...'

'And yet you still took out the loan to cover her share. Why would you do that if you didn't think you could do it?'

'I didn't know then how hard it would be, Dad. I thought I could *fix* it, fix *me*, but I was wrong.'

'Maybe you're right. But we have one job as parents and that is to teach our children to live a happy and fulfilling life, and to find happiness.' I roll my eyes at his attempt at an inspirational speech.

I'm breathing heavily as I slump down onto the sofa.

'You have to understand... that dream died the moment my head cracked open.' I take a minute. 'A new shop needs a *good* manager, Dad. Someone who can at least read.'

He shakes his head. 'You can't keep burying your head in the sand. It's time for you to take control of your responsibilities. Here's what I propose. I've found a specialist. An intensive course that—'

'Dad, I—' I let out an exasperated sigh. 'No.' I'm breathing quickly. My ears are filled with a rushing sound. Dad stands and clamps his hands on my shoulders, guides me back to the sofa.

'Just hear me out. Dr Levin has helped hundreds of people with reading difficulties gain back some of their abilities. It won't "fix" you, for want of a better word, but it may mean you will regain some of the missing cognitive function.'

His words are slamming into me like a train crash, each one concertinaing into the other. 'He's had incredible results. He can help you.'

'He can't.'

'So what then? Subletting the place is your answer?'

'If that's what it takes.'

'You're going to throw away your dreams and replace it with... I don't know, a palm reader or one of those woo-woo tenants with crystals and incense sticks?'

I let his words land, the implications of the financial burden I've put on myself. The lower rent from the holding loan will run out soon and once it goes up to full price? I could lose everything. This shop, my flat, Nell's job would be gone. Something like shame encroaches into the room.

But I know it won't work. I've already tried.

'Just... promise me you'll think about it?'

I look at the hope in his eyes and find myself nodding, even though I know that I'm already too broken, and no one, not even this Dr Levin, can help.

Dad's face breaks into a grin and I hate that I'm letting him hope. He claps his hands together, all optimism and sunshine.

'Now then. Tell me all about the new lady in your life.'

16

Maggie

'Riz?' I poke my head around the lounge door. 'I'm off now. Seren will be here in half an hour to help you change, OK?'

She grins at me over her glasses. 'Say hello to Jack for me.'

'How did you—'

'Oh, give me a little credit, darling. Your face is flushed and you've been like a cat on hot coals all afternoon.'

'It's not like that... We're just friends.'

'Mmmhmmm.'

The last week has flown by. Jack kept me updated on their trip to the doctors', how Riz told him about some of her past and that he enjoyed her company. He pushed for social services to arrange some care, and she's now got a nurse who comes to check on her twice a day.

Even more good news is that I got the night-shift job too, and started straight away. It's three nights a week, Monday to Wednesday; I don't get as much as I did at *Pillow Paradise!* But it'll help make ends meet... when I get paid next week, at least. It's hard sleeping in the day, but there is also something so freeing and magical about being in a department store in the middle of the night. I take my time exploring the different sections: sportswear, camping, and the tech department. I've managed to work the state-of-the-art stereos so can blast my music while I clean. I get to browse the designer clothes, try the sample perfumes, while not having to avoid intruding on people's thoughts. It's like I'm in the film *Mannequin*, even if I'm no Kim Cattrall, and Andrew McCarthy is nowhere to be found. Coming home as the sun rises has its bonuses too. No people, no searching for the easiest way to navigate my way past.

Most afternoons, I've been here. Riz's bedroom is mostly packed up, and I've piled the boxes up along the hallway.

'Does this look OK?' I ask stepping into the room. I'm wearing a jade green skirt, knee-high brown boots, and a burgundy cashmere jumper Riz had insisted I take. Luckily my apron will protect it from any rogue blasts of toilet duck.

'You look gorgeous. Pass me that box, would you?' I walk to the sideboard, lifting up a small blue velvet box and placing it next to her. She flicks it open and turns to me. 'Now, how about these?'

I lean forward. Inside are a pair of earrings. Gold ovals, green gemstone inside. 'I... I couldn't...'

'Poppycock. You can and you will.'

'Thank you, Riz. They're beautiful.' She nods. I take the box and head to the mirror above the fireplace, sliding them into my ears. I turn to her, wiggling the tips of my fingers beside my ears.

'Perfect. Now off you go. Have fun, darling, won't you?'

I want to kiss her on the cheek. But instead I kiss my fingers and blow towards her.

* * *

Jack is early for our third date. Although, I guess it's not a date any more, but still, Tess's countdown to the truth beats through my racing pulse. Jack is already in his seat by the time I've finished cleaning the loos. I pause my steps as I head towards him. The lights are still on, the trailers yet to start. I take a moment to capture him: broad shoulders beneath a navy sweater, thick dark hair, the way he tilts his head when he looks at his phone. Inside my gloves, my hands are more clammy than usual. I need to broach the subject of what has happened in his life that has caused him so much pain. I want to help him find answers, and if I can't, I'm going to have to try to explain how I know that his life is more complicated than he's showing. I hesitate. Maybe I should turn around and walk back out, send him a message and say I've got the flu? But I take a breath, straighten. We're friends. *Friends*. And friends help each other through dark times. But my throat still tightens as I step towards our seats.

Like he can sense me, his head turns. He gets up, the movement too fast, too awkward. 'Hi!'

'Hi!' Our voices are too loud. Jack tries to overcompensate by tapping his watch. An overly eager laugh escapes my mouth.

'Well, well... on time, I see?' I smile.

'Yep. Annoyingly punctual as promised.'

We stand awkwardly before Jack sits down, checking the space between us. A slushie already sitting in the cup holder. 'I took the liberty of buying them... no tequila, I'm afraid.'

'Thanks.' I shrug off my fur and fold it beneath my seat. 'You smell nice.' Crap. I shouldn't have said that. But it's true – he smells fresh but with that hint of clove. 'Sorry, was that a bit weird?'

'No.' He scratches the back of his neck. 'Friends can compliment each other. I think. I'm a bit out of practice. And so do you, by the way. Nice earrings.'

'Thanks. Riz insisted.'

He shifts, his leg is bouncing and he's fiddling with his straw. 'So' – he clears his throat – 'how's the packing going? Sorry I haven't been about much... I've had a few' – he pulls at his earlobe – 'things on.'

'No worries.' I smile even though I've tried to push down the disappointment in the distance growing between us.

'So how's things?'

'Good!' I tell him about the new job and how fun spending time with Riz has been. Going through her things has been like watching a soap opera unfold, stories about her travels, her wedding day, her life as a photographer.

'It's going well. She has so many stories. Did you know she worked on a cactus farm in Peru and that she had lunch with Salvador Dalí? And she's so full of wisdom.'

'Rizdom?' Jack suggests and I laugh.

'Yeah, Rizdom.'

We're trying to talk as though things haven't changed, even though they have. Jack is a little more guarded, my laugh a little too enthusiastic.

Behind us, the cinema starts to fill.

'I can believe it,' he says. 'I think she was the inspiration for one of my favourite books: *The Water on Horseback*?'

I look over, curious. 'Really?'

'I talked to her about it when we were waiting at the doctors'. She made me laugh, told me it was full of purple prose.'

I half-smile, frowning. 'Purple prose?'

'Too much flowery writing, but I *love* that book. Must've read it five times, maybe more. Anyway, before that she was telling me about her and Art being in Thailand and that he was there too, studying temples and it suddenly clicked: *The Water on Horseback* is set there, and the main character, Adam, gets obsessed with temples and' – Jack is talking quickly, like he's trying to repair the barrier between us with more words – 'there is this absolute powerhouse of a woman, Clarissa, who happened to be a... guess.'

'Photographer?' I venture.

'Right? She said Chris Renford, the author, never liked Art that much. Apparently he used to call Chris out on his bullshit all the time.'

'Did you ask her if it was her?' I take a sip of my drink.

'Couldn't help myself. Clarissa is one of my favourite characters of all time. Tall, red lips, feisty as hell.'

'And?' I question.

'She shrugged. Said, "Who knows?"'

I shake my head. 'Oh she knows all right. Every time I pick up an ornament, or scarf, or book, or record, she has this incredible story to tell. Her life with her husband Art sounds incredible. Real, proper, true love, you know?'

The lights dip and the trailers begin.

'So, what is this one about, again?' Jack asks, opening his popcorn.

I adjust my skirt. 'A bookshop. Two actually.'

He hesitates, the popcorn halfway to his mouth. 'Right.'

There is a late arrival: a tall man and his shorter girlfriend have chosen to sit on our row. I'm about to comment on Meg Ryan's bookshop being similar to Jack's but the woman's leg bumps into my bare knees, as does the guy's, and the joy drains from my face.

17

MAGGIE

I shouldn't have agreed to meet her here.
Harry is so nice.
What if my wife finds out or goes into labour?

The couple scrape by, sides of legs and dangling hands grating past my knees: the rush of excitement and hope from the woman. The truth about his circumstances. I stand, anger pulsing through me. There *are* times where this curse comes in handy. The absolute *snake.*

'Harry?!' I exclaim. The guy spins around, confusion on his face. 'I thought that was you! How *are* you?' He frowns, looks around, panic etched around his eyes. 'And how's your lovely wife, not long now; she's due any day, isn't she?'

'*Wife?*' the woman asks, her hurt expression swiftly turning to anger. '*Wife?*' she repeats and storms off. Harry looks at me with confusion then glares as he chases after her.

'You OK?' Jack asks gently as I sit down.

I nod, but I'm shaking.

'What a tool,' Jack adds and I laugh despite my mouth being

dry, the aftershock of the couple's thoughts throbbing sharply in my right temple.

We watch the rest of the film, but I'm distracted, my headache blooming.

I want to tell him the truth.

But I don't want to lose him.

* * *

Outside the air is cool, the night sky clear. I dig my hands into the pockets of my skirt as we walk out of Flicks.

'So what did you think?' I ask, pulling on my gloves and zipping up my coat against the sea air. 'It's not my favourite Nora Ephron but...'

'It was good.' Jack walks beside me as we descend the steps onto the road.

'But?' I ask, smirking up at him.

'But...' He pulls up the collar of his coat. 'I mean, he was a bit of a twat, wasn't he? Keeping his identity a secret?'

'Oh I don't know. He had his reasons, didn't he?'

'Maybe. I still think he should have been straight with her.'

I hesitate on the path. His words ringing in my ears.

'Jack, I—'

'Do you want to go somewhere else?' He cocks an eyebrow. 'Let's go get something to eat? Something that isn't ninety per cent air.'

This is my chance, my chance to tell him.

'I know a place...' he continues. 'It'll be just the two of us. Sorry, that sounded a bit murdery didn't it?'

I shake my head. 'It's fine. I guess if you were going to murder me, you would have done it while we were locked in the cinema.'

'Fancy a drive?'

* * *

The car is quiet. I've never been in an electric one before, and the sound is low and calming. He reaches over and flicks on the radio, selecting a local music station with long confident hands, hands that could be the undoing of me in more ways than one. He turns the volume down low.

'So that guy, huh?' he asks. 'How do you know him?'

'Oh... I used to clean for them.' The lie swells on my tongue.

'I hope he gets what's coming to him.'

'Me too.'

I watch the headlights lead the way away from my home town, the sea to the right a constant companion as we talk more about the film. I tell him about Tess and her comedy and he laughs as I land one of her jokes.

When he pulls up outside a quiet row of shops, I blink, surprised. We're in Bayside. I've been here before during off-season – charity shop hauls, mostly.

Jack parks outside a row of shops. One looks empty; next to it is a kebab shop. 'Wait here, I'm going to get us dinner. Any allergies?'

'Besides people?' I joke. 'No. I'm pretty easy to please. And you don't have to do that. I can pay,' I say, heart pounding, knowing my bank balance is only skimming into the black.

'My treat. I suggested it and you haven't lived until you've tried one of these.' He smiles and leaves the car. I lean back in the comfortable leather seats. I bet these babies heat up. I lean towards the window, watching Jack as he laughs and jokes with the man behind the counter. Christ, he's gorgeous. I groan. I can practically already feel the way my heart is going to rip open when I tell him the truth and he bolts. My eyes graze over the shop next door. It's a shame it's empty. It has an old-world charm about it, the kind that speaks of a building once loved. The front window is rounded, the glass splintered into small rectangular panes, with dark forest-green paintwork flaking away in places. The step that leads up to the door is uneven; the glass pane in its centre boarded up.

Jack exits the shop, a plastic bag in hand, but rather than join me inside the car, he walks past and hesitates outside the empty shop, beckoning me. I join him on the kerb as he pulls out a set of keys. I recognise the pendant on the keychain, the small silver book that he flicks open and shut when he's thinking.

'You have the keys?' I ask, brows furrowing. He looks over at me as he turns the key, gives a small nod as the door opens, and then he steps inside and flicks on a light switch. The low-lit lamps on the walls catch the dust motes in a warm glow.

The deceptively wide room is scattered with boxes – some with brown tape hanging forlornly – others unopened. There is an overturned bookcase in the centre of the room, and slabs of wood and a workbench stacked in the back. It smells like sawdust and aches with potential.

'Wow...' I look around the room, my gloves touching a box. I can make out the spine of a book through the small opening. 'This is yours?' I ask.

'It's... yeah. Kind of.'

He fiddles with the key fob again and walks further inside, setting the bag down on a stack of unopened boxes.

'What do you mean?'

He turns and leans against the wall, hands in his pockets.

'I took out the lease before...' He scratches the back of his neck. 'It was going to be the second Chadwick's. Another bookshop by the sea, a new one based around building a community, but this time I was going to add a bar, figured it would be good for business, and sales might go up after a few pints?' He huffs a laugh, but it doesn't land.

My eyes roam around the room taking in the boxes, the books suffocating under large polythene sheets.

'What happened?' I question gently. 'You said "before": before what?'

I brace myself. Whatever he's about to tell me will be hard for him; I'd felt first-hand the pain and loss and confusion it has caused him.

He pauses, opens his mouth like he's about to answer, then avoids the question, grabs the bag and rummages for the polystyrene boxes. 'Lamb kofta and mint sauce for you. Trust me, it's the best.'

I take it with a thanks, still watching him. 'Jack?'

He stops, eyes focused on taking out another takeaway box.

'Why did you bring me here?'

'Because I wanted to tell you a bit more about me. About who I am.' He takes a beat, then sits on the windowsill, flipping open the box in his hands.

'I... I had a stroke. Last October.'

I don't know what I was expecting him to say, but having a stroke wasn't it. I look for the signs we've all been warned about – slurred speech, loss of movement in one side – but there is none of that, then again, some of the most debilitating illnesses are invisible to outsiders. That explains the gap in his thoughts, the void I'd felt. 'I'm sorry.' I inwardly wince at the words. They're so loose, so lacking in texture. *October.* It's the right month. My mouth dries.

He gives a small smile – an 'it is what it is' expression that doesn't match the hurt behind his eyes. 'That must have been terrifying.' I want to say something more, *do* something more. If I was normal, I would take his hand. I still could. I want to. My hand tingles with the possibility.

'I can't read.' His words are delivered bluntly, but each one is sharply edged. I register shock on his face, as though the words have been hidden backstage and have crept up on him: *boo*. I stay silent, giving him space to pilot the conversation. 'It's called alexia?' He waits, questioning if I know the term. 'I hadn't heard of it before. I can see words but my brain can't process them. It's like they're hidden, no... not hidden...' He looks upwards at the ceiling, at the cobwebs hanging like eighties Christmas decorations. He drags his eyes back to me. 'They're there, but they're not in a language I can understand. That's why I ended up at Flicks that night. I tried to go to the awards, but it was filled with people from my old life: writers, publishers, agents.' He looks back at me. 'I couldn't stay. I felt like a fraud. Like I was in the same room as those people but outside of them. Does that make sense?'

'It does.' The real reason why I can relate to being an outsider thuds against my ribcage. He looks out the window; a woman walking her dog passes by. 'Do you ever feel like you're watching your life from the outside? Like, you know you're in it, but it's almost like it's happening to someone else?' He shakes his head. 'Ignore me – that made no sense whatsoever.'

'It does actually.' The moment I stood outside his shop, the night I met him, shimmers in my mind.

His face kind of lifts at that. 'It was like that at the awards. Like I was living someone else's life.' His eyes cast around the room slowly. 'I used to be able to run the shop myself. I would read three, four books a week... now, trying to read a street sign is like reading Shakespeare, harder in fact.'

'So...' I gesture to the room.

'I was going to expand. We' – he glances back at me – 'Vicky and I...' I try to ignore the jolt inside at the mention of Vicky and the hurt behind his eyes. 'We were going to expand, hence this place.'

'What happened?'

'I wasn't the person I was before the stroke. Vicky was – still is, I suppose – ambitious. We both were, had our future all mapped out. But then' – he runs a hand through his dark hair – 'when it was clear that I… that I'd changed, she ended it, took her share of the money and I was left with a shop I couldn't run and another waiting to be opened. I think it highlighted that there were already problems in our relationship. She tried at first, to stay, to help…' He hesitates. 'I thought I could still do it at first, thought I could fix it, fix me, the alexia, so I took out a loan to cover the rest. But now, now I avoid books, and the place where I have always felt like I belonged, feels like a prison.' He looks back around the room, almost as if he can see this shop as he intended, filled with light and conversation, books filling the shelves, soft music and laughter coming from the bar. He resets, his whole body shifting as though embarrassed that he's spoken out loud by mistake.

I take off my gloves and set them beside me.

Jack glances down, eyebrows hitched then meets my eyes.

'How about' – I smile at the memory of the first time we met – 'we be alone, but together?'

His eyes flash with recognition; I dip my head, offering him a small, encouraging smile.

'That's a terrible line, you know,' he replies, but the light is back behind his eyes.

'Really? I think it's pretty great.' I lift my kebab and take a small bite. It's delicious. Jack takes a bite of his own as I swallow.

'Good?' he asks, covering his mouth before placing his back inside the container.

I nod. 'Yes, you weren't kidding.'

He reaches into the bag. 'Water or...' He squints at the label; his whole body tenses. How did I miss how hard reading is for him? I replay our time together and realise that it's not only me who is good at hiding the truth about themselves from the rest of the world. The liquid is pink. He looks up, body relaxing a touch. 'I'm guessing pink lemonade? I pointed to it in the shop, looked like something you might like? It was the brightest colour.'

He looks at the label again then passes it to me.

'Thanks.' I smile and he gives me one in return, but it's like the confidence has been knocked out of him. He takes another bite, the air thick with lost dreams and secrets.

'How did it happen?' I ask tentatively.

'I honestly don't remember.'

I take another small mouthful.

'Anything?'

'I'd been to the pub, had a few. Bumped into some guy and then... nothing until I woke up in the hospital.'

I swallow hard, the pitta bread too thick in my throat.

'What did he look like?'

Jack frowns, looks off into the distance. 'Pretty average really: medium height, medium build, blond hair.' My heartbeat quickens. 'He was pretty pissed about something... But that's all I can remember. Well that and the pain at the back of my skull.'

'So he hit you?'

'Honestly? I have no idea. Maybe I tripped over. I'd had a fair few beers and a shot... one for the road from my mate. All I remember is saying goodbye and then his face, the feeling of being pushed, and a pain that sounds like a crack. That's part of the problem with my reading. When I try, it's like the trauma of that night stops me. I get a searing pain, right' – he turns his head and points to the base of his skull – 'here.'

'Is there ever a chance it could get better?' I suggest tentatively. 'Like, with support or therapy, maybe?'

He hesitates, opens a bottle of water and takes a long pull, taking his time screwing the lid back on.

'I've tried... I had a speech and language therapist but the words, they... won't come. It's exhausting, trying to read. And painful. But my father has found a specialist – Dr Levin, he's had good results. Apparently.'

'That's great... isn't it?' He places the bottle on the windowsill, turns the label to face him, a finger skating across the 'w'.

'I guess I'm afraid.'

'To try?'

'To hope.'

We sit quietly, his eyes focused on the inside of the shop, mine focused on him.

'Maybe I can help?' He draws his eyes back to me. 'If we talk about it some more, we might be able to get your memories back and then maybe you won't feel that pain, maybe it won't be so hard to try to read?'

He shakes his head. 'I've tried. That's all I remember.'

I lean in a touch. 'Humour me?' I encourage. 'What was he wearing?'

Jack takes a bite and chews thoughtfully.

'Black. All black.'

'Like a leather jacket?'

'Yeah. Maybe.'

I try to keep my composure. I try not to let my body react.

'There is one thing... I think he might have had a scar on his eyebrow.' He shakes his head as though trying to discount his own memories.

'Here?' I point to where the 'scar' was while knowing he shaved it in on purpose.

'Yeah? How did you know that?'

My thoughts go back to that night. We'd gone for a walk after Luke had cooked me dinner. I had been thinking how kind he was being. He'd bought me flowers and had been so attentive that night and I'd figured it was the right time to tell him.

When we began to take the next step in our relationship, and things were more physical, I had tried to block out his thoughts in lots of different ways: reciting the alphabet backwards, singing in my head, anything to avoid hearing him. Over the years, Tess and I had suggested many weird and wonderful methods to control it, but little snippets always managed to leak through. And then I'd kissed him, and the first thing I'd heard – as I tried to focus on naming as many fruits as I could – was the name Becca, and the way she was more 'into' him. I'd pulled away fiercely.

'You're sleeping with someone else?!'

'No!'

'Don't lie to me, Luke! I know you are!'

'Well what did you expect? You hardly let me touch you and when we do, it's like your mind is on a million different things. You make me feel like a waste of space.'

He'd shouted then, thrown in my face all the things that were wrong with me, how being with me was so hard, so weird and that I should learn a few things about how to make a man feel wanted.

Then I said the words that would wreck Jack's life: 'Don't take the fact that you've been caught out on me. *Take it out on someone else.* I'm done.'

I was right. I didn't get the image mixed up. It was my fault.

18

JACK

'Jack...' Maggie exhales long and hard. 'I think... I think I might know who it was.'

Do I want to know more? Do I want to know who he is, the man who took so much from me? Yes. Yes I do.

'How? How do you know who it was?' Maggie looks up at me. There's hesitation there, more words to be said.

'I... you see, I think that I was there, Jack – the night you had your stroke. And I' – she rubs the space between her eyebrows – 'I think it was my fault. Well not my fault exactly but—'

The room is too hot, the air too close, too full.

'How can it be your fault?' My words come out scratchy.

'Luke? The guy who you think shoved you? He had a scar on his eyebrow, was wearing black that night, and he has blond hair. He was my boyfriend and I'd, well, I found out' – she looks away then back to me – 'that he was sleeping with someone else. Behind my back. I said something. But at the time I was so hurt, so angry that I wasn't... I wasn't at my best. Anyway, we were on the beach wall and we had this blazing row... and—' She rubs the side of her face with both hands. 'I told him to take it out on someone else. And... it seems... that someone else was... you.' Tears have filled her eyes. 'I'm so sorry, Jack. I shouldn't have said it.'

There is an image, then. It's fleeting, but it comes with a throb and I touch the back of my head to ease the pain. When I came out of the pub, I'd heard raised voices from across the street. I can remember shadows around him as he shouted, the etch of another figure in front of him, the sea at their backs, the moon a half-crescent hanging low in the sky. But then I'd looked at my phone. Vicky said that I'd messaged her but I couldn't remember sending it, and when I tried to check my phone in the days after... I was too embarrassed to ask what I'd said. But now I remember holding the phone in my hand.

'He was pretty riled up,' Maggie says, scanning my face. 'I think that's why he might have shoved you.' I look down at the label on the bottle of my water; the pain at the back of my head starts to ease.

I sit still, fleeting images that were so hard to picture starting to form. The way the wind was blowing against the right side of my face, how I squinted at my phone screen as I typed out a message to Vicky. How the last shot of Sambuca hit me as I started to walk.

'You were there?'

'No, I mean, I didn't see you fall or anything. I walked one way; he walked the other. I was angry, upset...'

I nod while something feels like it's worming its way into my brain.

'I'm so sorry, Jack. If I hadn't said the things I did, he would never have stormed off.'

Images are sharpening, pushing against each other like pieces of a jigsaw trying to fit in the spaces they don't belong: *watch where you're going...* My voice? Or was it his?

I look up. Her cheeks are flushed, her eyes verging on tears. I blink, back in the room now.

'I know sorry isn't a big enough word, but I really am. I'm sorry that this happened to you and that I started the whole chain of events.'

I sit. Stunned. Unable to find the right words or thoughts to process what she's saying.

'Jack?'

'I...'

'I wish I could take it back.' She clasps her hands together.

'You don't need to be sorry.' I look up at her. 'This isn't your fault.'

19

FRIDAY 27TH SEPTEMBER

Jack

Over the past week, I've replayed our conversation over and over. My memory is becoming... not clear as such, but... it's like when I've read a thriller, been blindsided by the twist, and realised that the answers were staring me in the face the whole time. It's as though my brain is starting to work again, to connect in ways that it hasn't over the past year. And maybe, if I keep piecing things together, I can do this... Launch this shop. Run it, even.

I don't blame Maggie. Not even a little bit. She wasn't the one who got pissed. And she wasn't the one who knocked into me. I can see she feels responsible though, and I hate that.

My eyes scan the stack of unopened letters in my hand, and that glimmer of possibility, that I could make a success of the new shop evaporates, like the words on the envelopes.

I try to pinpoint the exact time I realised that I would never read again, as I riffle through the pile of letters.

When I first woke up in the hospital, I had put it down to the pain meds, the headache that made even the small crack through the hospital blinds feel like someone was piercing my retina with a red-hot needle. When they explained the real reason, I thought that there must be a mistake. I had grown up surrounded by literature, by books and stories; of course I would read again. The other option was too hard to contemplate.

My memories of that time come in pieces, tiny splinters. Vicky visiting me and unpacking a bag with pyjamas, energy drinks, grapes and a book. She wasn't being unkind, or insensitive. I always had a book with me, or a Kindle... She had joked that there was no point buying me jewellery; books were always my accessory.

She had kissed me, arranged my hair to cover the bandage. *'You'll be OK. Nobody loves books more than you. You'll find a way.'*

And honestly? I believed her. After she'd gone, despite the pounding headache, I had reached for the hardback. It felt heavier in my hands than usual, and the picture on the cover swam before my eyes. Words that should have been familiar sneered back at me. I couldn't read the chapter heading, couldn't decode anything on the page. It was as if it needed a cipher. Nausea came over me like a wave, the kind of seasickness that takes over your body and leaves you gripping the sides of the hospital bed like a life raft. I'd reached for the bedpan and thrown up.

I remember the police coming, asking me questions, but I couldn't remember anything back then other than leaving the pub and a vague impression of Luke's face, but I couldn't confirm that he'd attacked me. All I knew was that he was there. I told them I was drunk, my blood alcohol level confirming this. There were no unknown substances in my test results, no other injuries, and my wallet was still in my pocket. I was told to call them if I remembered anything else but it was assumed that the injury was caused by some drunken misdemeanour.

The weeks that followed are a tightly knit line of failures, and frustration, but I do remember reaching for a microwave meal and spending ten minutes trying to read the instructions. I'd cried with it in my hands. The doors shut. The curtains drawn. Alone.

That was the moment when I knew.

Knew that my life would never be the same as it once was.

The door is stuck and Maggie comes into the shop with an 'Oof.' Her hair is wild, cheeks flushed, Henry Hoover trailing behind her.

Only Maggie could make walking through the door with a vacuum cleaner look charming. We had agreed to make a start on clearing the shop, so that if I decided to sublet the lease, the place would look more like a shop and less like a half-finished project. A bit like me, I guess.

'Hey!' She blows her hair out of her eyes. 'I came prepared!' She lands her hands on her hips and looks around. The sunlight is tracking a path through the grimy windows, lighting her up as though she has her own spotlight. Maggie always has this typhoon of energy swirling around her. I shouldn't find it appealing, I should be running away from the chaos, but instead, I find my body calming, the ache of anxiety in my chest releasing. I know this is too soon for anything more than friendship; I'm still healing in more ways than one, and she said 'just friends' and I agreed. What else could I do? This is all I'm capable of right now. I'll just try to ignore the way the room expands and brightens when she's in it.

Maggie is determined to speak with Luke, to see if she can find out more about what happened. So far though, he's ignoring her messages. I'm trying not to get swept up in the hope that finding more answers about that night might help me on the road to recovery. She's convinced that he's not the violent type... The vague memories I do have and that my stroke was caused by a blow to the head seem to contradict that. Even so, I trust her judgement.

'You wouldn't believe the morning I've had.' She shrugs off her backpack and her pink fur coat and dumps them on the floor, a cloud of dust flying up. 'First I went to see a new potential employer, Ola, who is a *hugger*.'

I dramatically wince for her benefit.

'Right? I had to take three steps back and fell on the sofa. I'd like to tell you I styled it out, but I looked more like I was gate-crashing a photo shoot for Furniture Land. Needless to say, I didn't get the gig.' She bends over and starts taking out cleaning products, holds them to her chest, and looks around with a frown before making her way towards me, landing them on the over-turned bookshelf. 'Then, my car wouldn't start *again*, which made me late for the next interview and the job had already gone. Anyway I'm here now!' She pauses, clasps her hands.

The sight of her hands without the protection of her gloves hits me. She's putting her trust in me as her friend. I need to do the same. And this is good. I need a friend right now. And that's what friends do. Help each other out, tell each other about their day, tell funny anecdotes. Does that also turn every Friday into something I look forward to all week? I push the thought aside.

'Where do you want me?' Her eyes widen at what she's said, embarrassment hot on her cheeks. 'I meant...'

She has no idea how much light she brings into my day, how she makes me feel like I'm not failing at my own life. But what gets me is she doesn't even know she's doing it. She doesn't realise how much my world has already started to open up because she's in it.

'Coffee?' I ask holding out a cup towards her.

'You, Jack Chadwick, are a bloody lifesaver.' She reaches out and takes the cup. I don't miss the concentration in her eyes as she takes it from me.

'Any response to your messages?'

'Nada. He will though; I've found one of his precious vinyls in the back of my wardrobe.'

'Are you sure it's safe to see him?'

'Luke? Yeah. Honestly, Jack, he's not a tough guy. That's why what you remember doesn't add up. Despite what I said' – she looks away, pink blossoming on her cheeks – 'to him. I've been thinking...' she begins.

'And?'

'And there must have been CCTV?'

I shake my head. 'The police checked. Nothing was picked up.'

'Maybe we can get some more information, see if it jogs your memory? Have you asked your pals?'

'*Pals?*' I laugh.

'Yeah, buddies, mates...'

'Not really... We've kind of lost touch.'

I think of Steve and his unanswered messages. The sound of him knocking my door and me reaching for the painkillers by the side of the bed that would take me away to oblivion. Steve is on the sales team from one of my favourite publishing houses. I should have got in touch before now, but my pride, and I guess my imposter syndrome, have kept me away from my old life. My parents said the police spoke to him, but as far as I know, nothing he said shed any light on what happened.

'I could ask Steve? He was out with me that night...'

'Well there we go!' She grins. 'Let's ask him if he saw anything, even a little clue might help?'

'Maybe.'

'Good. That's settled then. We'll go and ask him. I can be your partner in crime or, you know, the Daphne to your Freddie. Or Velma. I always thought she was the coolest one.'

She pops the lid off her coffee and blows over the top, eyes drawn to the window. 'Shall we start there?' She gestures to the grime covering the glass with her cup.

I take a deep breath. 'It's as good a place as any.'

*　*　*

The windows are clean, and while the plaster is still hanging off the walls, and the shelves remain in the plastic covering, and the boxes filled with the first stock I ordered remain hidden inside, the neglect and expectation of the room feels less suffocating.

Maggie is reaching up to the corners of the room with her feather duster, singing to 'Private Dancer' by Tina Turner. The local radio station has been playing non-stop classics for the last two hours and Maggie has sung along to almost every song. I follow her movements, watch the way she balances on the steps of the ladder, hands working. I realise I'm smiling and wonder – not for the first time since I've met her – how being around her seems so... easy, and question if my life could be as simple as this. She stops singing, sneezing five times consecutively. The ladder wobbling. I step forwards and hold it still, looking up.

'You OK?'

'Wha—' She sneezes again, a tiny little 'ssnnnyyup' sound.

I steady the ladder as she climbs down. My eyes linger on the small part of her lower back between her jeans and the edge of her navy T-shirt as she descends, her skin smooth and porcelain. Get a grip, you arsehole. She's put her trust in you. We can't be more than friends, right now. Even after today, I don't think I can fix this. It will fail. *I* will fail.

'You sneeze like a kitten,' I say.

'Like a wh—? Ssnnnyyup!'

I laugh and shake my head as she climbs off the ladder, stepping back, her eyes searching the room, landing on the gloves. Her bright yellow Marigolds, sitting untouched on the counter next to the remains of our lunch from next door. I don't know why it catches my attention now, but it does. And I realise her hand brushed mine as she climbed down the ladder. The air between us changes ever so slightly.

'You OK?'

'Yeah, it's the dust...'

She heads towards the other side of the shop, humming now, not belting out 'Private Dancer' the way she was minutes ago. My stomach tightens. Her hands reach for the gloves, but she puts them back down, looking around the room, as though she can see its potential. 'I, um, I hope you don't mind, but... I checked out Dr Levin.'

Her words quickly hammer me back down to earth. If this was anyone else, I would be angry. But right now, do I mind? Strangely... no. Maggie didn't know me before, and unlike with my family, or with Vicky, she doesn't want to fix me, she wants to help. Those are two very different things.

'You did?' I pull at a thread at the edge of my cuff.

'Yep.' The softness in her voice pulls my attention back to her. 'He's... well, I get the impression that his methods are a bit out of the box, but—' I want things to go back to how they were a few moments ago, where everything felt easy.

I deflect quickly, 'What, like he's going to hypnotise me and make me think I'm a squid trapped in a fish tank in a restaurant?'

She snorts, the tension in her face falling away. 'I don't know, I mean, maybe? It could be fun to watch. I can see how much this means to you, Jack, and I can help, or maybe this doctor could?'

She looks away, before meeting my eyes. 'Sorry, I'm overstepping; forget I said anything.'

The question Riz had asked as we'd sat in the waiting room at the out-of-hours doctors' surgery comes into my mind unbidden. I'd found it so easy to open up to her about the stroke before I'd mentioned it to Maggie.

'Is there anything that can be done? I'm a bit out of touch these days, but you always hear of these groundbreaking treatments...'

'No. Not really.'

'And what is the "not really" treatment?'

'I will never be... for want of a better word "fixed" but I can retrain my brain a little. Sounding out the words, copying the letters and repeating the sound. Sand trays and all that...'

'Nonsense?'

'It's... not for me.'

'Why? Why isn't it for you? You're a young man. I learnt how to speak some Mandarin using that wonderful app and I'm eighty-four. What's stopping you?'

'Reading isn't part of my life any more. I've come to accept it.'

'Forgive me, at my age I have little time for beating around the bush, but that is utter poppycock. You're too proud to try.'

I look back to Maggie, at her hopeful expression. 'You're not overstepping.' There is a catch in my voice, and I clear my throat. 'Thank you.'

'For suggesting you see a therapist who could turn you into a giant squid?'

'No.' I scratch the back of my head. 'For this. For, you know, helping.'

'Help is my middle name; actually it's Gertrude but we don't talk about that.'

I laugh, the sound lightening Maggie's expression, and filling the corners of the empty shop.

'Gertrude?'

'Mmmhmmm.' She winces playfully. Her cheeks are flushed. Maybe it's from the warmth of the sun streaming through the clear windows, but part of me wonders – or hopes? – that it might also be because of me.

'Promise you won't tell anyone.'

'I shall take it to the grave.'

Her phone pings and she swipes the screen, eyes scanning the message easily. She looks up, eyes bright.

'He's replied. He wants to see me in half an hour.' She glances up at the recently hung clock and smiles. 'Look, it's happy time!'

I frown. 'It needs new batteries. That's not the right time. It's half four.'

She dismisses my comment with a wave of her hand. 'Doesn't matter, it still says ten past ten, like a smiley face...' she explains. 'Maybe it's a good omen?'

I love these things about her, the way she finds joy in the smallest things.

'And if it was twenty past eight?'

'Bad. Baaad juju.' She pitches her head towards the door. 'I don't suppose you have your fancy car here, do you?'

20

MAGGIE

I scan the small park. The playground that is usually full of excitable kids in the summer months is empty. Apart from a few determined joggers, it's quiet, the clouds heavy and promising rain. I spot Luke sitting at a picnic table next to the old bandstand. Drinking what I'm guessing is his usual takeaway oat-milk latte. It's been almost a year since I've seen him and in that time he's decided to grow a beard. An unkempt beard. I still feel the sting of rejection, of anger, even more so since discovering what happened to Jack. But, I suppose I appreciate him agreeing to meet me in a place where he knows I can keep my distance from people. I never did get the chance to tell him that I could read his thoughts. I'd tried a few times, but in my gut, maybe I knew he would never understand. But that was before he kissed me and I heard him thinking about the previous night spent in Becca's bed.

'That's him,' I say to Jack, nodding to his table. 'Ring any bells?'

Jack slows his steps and looks over. 'Not really, it might not be him. He didn't have a beard.'

'Oh the beard is new. You OK? I can do this on my own and tell you what he said?'

He digs his hands into his pockets. 'Thanks, but I want to hear what he has to say. Look him in the eyes. See if I can remember anything else.'

I'm still hoping that Luke isn't the one who caused Jack's stroke. Or that my words spoken in anger started the chain of events.

'Hi, Luke,' I say. He looks up, bits of coffee froth on his moustache.

'Mags.' I can't pretend that I don't feel a little buzz as he looks up at Jack. I know that we're only friends, but still, it feels good to be next to him. Albeit with some distance.

'Good to see you,' I begin, even though it's not. He was the first person I slept with, had a relationship with, which made his infidelity hit even harder. I sit down, shifting to the edge of the bench. 'This is Jack.'

Jack, to his credit, puts out his hand, which Luke limply shakes, eyes widening a touch.

Jack takes a seat, far enough away that we're not touching.

'How've you been?' I ask.

'Not bad. Yourself?'

'Good.'

'So my vinyl?' he asks, looking to the bag on my shoulder.

'I'll get to that in a bit. I actually wanted to meet for another reason.'

'Oh?' He takes another sip of his drink.

His blond hair is longer too. I used to love the way his hair was always doing its own thing, like it was waging its own rebellion. It looks scruffy in comparison to Jack's.

'I wondered if you might help us with something? It's about the night we broke up?'

He frowns. 'What about it?' He adjusts the zipper on his leather jacket.

'Well Jack thinks you might have met before.' I look to Jack who gives me a small nod that lets me know this is the person he saw that night.

Luke gives Jack a thorough up and down. 'No. I don't think so.'

Jack begins, 'We bumped into each other, outside the White Lion pub?'

Luke wipes his milk froth away with the back of his hand and scans Jack's face. 'I don't think... wait. You're the guy who knocked into me.'

Jack tilts his head, questioning. 'I bumped into *you*?'

'Yeah, too focused on your phone to watch where you were going. You need to unplug, man.'

'Wait, so you didn't push him?' I ask.

'Push him? No!' He shakes his head and takes another sip.

Jack's hand is tapping his thigh. 'Luke? Is it OK that I call you Luke?'

'Well, that is my name; don't wear it out.' He grins as if that's the most original comeback ever spoken.

'Right. Well, you see the thing is, Luke,' Jack continues, leaning forward on the table, 'I had an accident that night. A head injury. I'm just looking for answers, that's all. We're not here to accuse you of anything. I'm trying to piece a few things together.'

'Can you tell us exactly what happened?' I ask Luke.

'I'll try but there's not much to tell. After we'd, you know "gone our separate ways"' – he air-quotes; I'd forgotten that he did that – 'I was on my way home and this guy...' He gestures with his cup.

'Jack,' I correct.

'Yeah, you, well as I said, you were on your phone, bumped into me, said sorry and that was it.'

'You didn't say anything?' Jack asks.

'Yeah, well I did tell you to watch it, or something like that. I might have yelled a bit actually. I was a bit emotional for' – he looks pointedly at me – 'obvious reasons, but that was it.'

'Nothing else?'

'No, man. I swear down.' Ugh. *Swear down*? My memories of my time together with Luke are filled with moments where he'd make me laugh, when he would cook delicious meals and was patient. Endearing even. And he liked me too, despite keeping my distance as much as I could. He didn't push me for more. I'd tried to make it work. God how I'd tried. To prevent his musings and critiques, but his words always had a way of getting through. That's why I made the decision to keep my distance after that night. From people as a whole. Until Jack, I had started to accept my lot in life. I can't have the kind of easy relationships I see around me every day, on the screen, in love songs. But right now, if I'm going to help Jack, I need to know Luke's telling the truth.

I clasp my hands together and rest them on the table next to Luke's so that my pinkie is close enough to touch his skin. He doesn't notice. I take a quick glance at Jack, but he's focusing on Luke's face. 'It's important, Luke. Do you remember anything else? Anything at all?' I prompt.

He shakes his head and continues to look at Jack.

'No.'

'Can you try again? Try really hard to remember that night.'

I didn't do anything.
Is he her boyfriend?
Slick bastard.
He should have watched where he was going.

'Did you see him fall?' I ask.

> No.
> I walked back to Becca's.
> What did Mags expect?
> It's not like I was getting much from her.

I move my hand a fraction. Pushing down the sense of hurt and betrayal that within minutes of breaking up with me, he went to her house.

'No. I carried on walking. Look, I'm sorry this happened to you, mate, but it wasn't anything that I did.'

'You're sure?'

'Certain. There were a couple of smokers outside... They could confirm it, maybe they're local?'

I look to Jack, but he's already getting up.

'Thanks for your time,' Jack says, standing now. 'It was good meeting you. And I apologise. For bumping into you.'

'You too, and I hope you find out what happened.'

'Thanks.' Jack waits for me to unfold myself from the bench.

'How's Becca by the way?' I ask.

'Becca?' I can see him trying to piece together how I know her name. 'Wouldn't know. Um, my album?'

'Oh that! Sorry,' I say, grimacing. 'Turns out *Sergeant Pepper* didn't quite make the cool placemat that I thought it would.' He takes it from me with a look of horror, hands already scrambling to pull the disc out.

Jack and I head back to the car. The rain starting to spit. 'Did you really use it as a placemat?'

'Nah, but it was worth it to see the look on his face.'

Jack's deep laugh fills me with warmth.

'Did it help you remember anything?' I ask, as he double clicks to unlock the car.

'A bit.' Jack opens the door for me, like it's second nature. It's old-fashioned but he doesn't make a show of it. 'I remember him telling me to watch it, so that's new. And he's right, I remember stumbling into him. It wasn't the other way around.'

I climb into the car. Jack joins me. 'He's telling the truth. Just so you know.'

'You're sure?'

'Mmmhmmm.'

I click the seatbelt buckle into place.

'So what's next?' I ask him as he turns on the ignition and begins pulling out.

'I guess I need to find out what happened after. Maybe ask at the pub and see if any locals saw anything?'

'And see Dr Levin,' I probe. He side-eyes me.

'And *maybe* see Dr Levin.'

The wipers begin sectioning the view in rhythmic beats. The mist on the windows – which would take me several rounds with my sponge to eradicate – disappears almost instantly.

'I do have one question?' he asks, turning at the junction.

'Hmmm?'

'What the hell did you see in that guy?' He glances my way, eyebrows raised.

I laugh. 'Oh he wasn't that bad. He was funny and he was kind... most of the time. And patient. With me and...' I waggle my fingers.

'I think he's the world's biggest idiot.'

'Oh, he's very clever actually, a wiz at game shows.'

'No I meant—' He turns to look at me. 'Because he had you and thought someone else was better.'

Oh *holy hell*.

'Thank you,' I say and look away so he doesn't see the way heat is rushing to my face.

We're quiet for a while as I gather my composure. Outside the rain is coming down harder, umbrellas raised and mad dashes are being made by pedestrians.

'I was thinking...' Jack stops at a zebra crossing, a woman with a pushchair rushing past.

'About the accident?' I ask.

'No, I was thinking I'd like to repay you, for your help at the shop and well' – he pulls at his earlobe – 'everything else... I've made more progress in the short time I've known you than over the past year. Are you free next Friday afternoon? Before your shift at Flicks?'

'I'm not actually working next week. The projector is being cleaned so it's shut...'

'Great! I've got an idea.'

I frown. 'What kind of idea?'

'That would ruin the surprise. I guess you're going to have to trust me.'

I tuck my hair behind my ear. 'I don't know, Jack. Can I trust you?' I challenge.

The tone has shifted, something more peering out between the cracks of humour.

'You can.'

21

FRIDAY 4TH OCTOBER

Maggie

'So what did he say... exactly?' Tess leans forwards towards the screen. I prop my phone up next to the kettle as I pour the rest of an almost-empty box of cornflakes into a bowl. Despite Riz paying me to help her pack, and the night shifts, I've had to pay double my rent as I'd begged my landlord to give me a few weeks' grace while I waited for payday.

I hesitate. She means about the surprise that Jack had planned for today, but I can't help thinking of the moment when I climbed down the stepladder, before we went to meet Luke. The slight graze of my hand on his as I sneezed.

We can't be more than friends. It will fail. I will fail.

It turns out that Tess's prediction of cracks starting to show on the fourth date was right.

I need to help Jack find his way, to find the answers he needs before I tell him. I know we can be nothing more than friends, despite the way my heart feels like its folding in on itself every time I take in the small idiosyncrasies that make Jack *Jack*. The way the right side of his mouth arches higher when he teases me. The way his eyes glint as if he's challenging me. How he runs his hands through his hair, like he's trying to repair his mind beneath it. How he says my name, like it's something only he knows.

'Mags? Hello? You look like you're away with the fairies.'

'Sorry.' I swallow down the images. 'Just that it was a surprise. To say thank you, for helping him. It's no big deal.' I shovel a mouthful of cornflakes in.

'And that was it?'

'Yep.' I take another big spoonful. 'He's being, you know... kind.'

'Hmmm.'

'Hmmm?' I say, milk dribbling down my chin. I wipe it away with the last of my kitchen roll.

'This screams romantic date vibes.'

'It's not like that – I've told you. I don't think it can be like that. He's picking me up at Riz's in' – I glance at my smartwatch, a TikTok Shop spesh – 'an hour, shit. I'd better get going in a min.'

'How is she doing?'

'She's good. She's such a character and the more I work my way through her things, the more amazed I am at the life she's had. She had this photo, right, old-school, black and white in a fancy hotel and the woman on the sofa was Jackie O.'

'You're kidding?' Tess leans back in her chair and begins twisting her blonde hair into an artfully arranged messy bun.

'Nope. She said she was on the photo shoot for a *Life* magazine interview... post JFK dying. Honestly, the woman is a legend.'

I think of the way Riz told me the story, how that photo was the one that changed the trajectory of her career, but the glamour, the places she went to, all of it, she tells it like it's the backdrop to her life with her husband Art. I can only imagine how hard it must have been for her when he died, to have that part of her taken.

'I'd like to meet her, sometime. I'll come over in a few weeks? Just got to finish this circuit.'

'How did last night go?'

She sighs, and leans away from the camera and flicks her eyelashes with mascara. 'Not great. I'm thinking of knocking the whole thing on the head to be honest.' My heart sinks. Tess has always wanted to be a comedian.

'But I thought things were going well?'

'If you call' – she dips the wand into the tube and continues applying her mascara – 'getting booed off the stage "the dream", then yeah. I am living it. Maybe I'm not cut out for this amount of rejection, you know? There's only so many times you can keep repeating the same thing and expect a different outcome. I think it's time I stopped trying to chase "the dream" and became a bit more practical. I'm almost thirty-two and... it's time for a change, I think.'

I let her words sink in. 'Shall we have a brainstorm later? Pros and cons?'

This is something we used to do a lot when we were younger.

'That sounds great, but I'll be out till late and besides, you never know where tonight is going to lead you.' She frowns at me. 'I know you're both skirting around the friend-zone thing Mags, but how do you really feel?'

I pause. I don't even know how to begin to navigate this question, but I try regardless. 'Happy because I have him in my life, terrified that I'm going to lose him, guilty for lying to him – take your pick.'

'Just remember that you are perfectly you, and if he can't handle that, then he doesn't deserve you.'

'Let's talk more tomorrow. We need to sort out your career first.'

* * *

'What do you mean I can't look!' I turn to Jack.

'It'll ruin the surprise.' He shifts the gear stick and passes me a ridiculous bright-purple eye mask with closed eyelids embroidered onto the material. He also passes me a pair of brown leather gloves. 'You did say you trusted me...' He raises an eyebrow.

'I did.' I hesitate. 'I do.' I shake my head and pull on the gloves first then with a faux-exasperated sigh, put on the eye mask. My senses are heightened. The fear of not seeing where my hands are should be more terrifying. I've always been afraid of the dark. I can't even sleep without nature programmes playing and the warm dulcet tones of David Attenborough in the background. I guess that comes with the territory of always needing to see where I am, or rather where other people are. Instead though, with Jack beside me, with the windows down and the smell of cut grass and warm sun on the leather of the seats beneath me, I feel... safe. Still, my heart is crashing inside my chest like one of those battery-operated monkeys clashing symbols between its hands. 'But if you take a photo of me in this, that is it. Friendship over.'

I smile as Jack's deep laughter rumbles through me.

His phone rings through the speakers. 'It's Steve,' he says.

'Your friend from the pub?'

'Yep.'

'Good to hear from you, mate!' his voice booms into the car.

'You too, and sorry I've been a bit AWOL.'

'Ah no worries. You've had a lot on. How've you been?'

'Good. Good. You?'

'Dad life mainly!' He laughs. 'Thanks for the fruit basket by the way. Very cool.'

'You're welcome. How is he?'

'Lungs like a foghorn!' He laughs again. They chit-chat about the baby until Jack's tone changes.

'Steve, I'm trying to piece together a bit more about my accident, and I wondered if you remember anything?'

He lets out a long breath. In the background there is the muffled cry of a baby.

'I'd love to be of some help, but there's nothing much to tell. I stayed for another and left. You were nowhere to be seen.'

'You didn't see an ambulance?' I question.

'Oh hi, Vick—'

'Steve, this is my friend – Maggie. She's trying to help me find out a bit more about that night.'

I'm glad I'm blindfolded so I don't have to see Jack's face as he corrects his friend.

'No, mate, you must have been long gone by then.'

'What time did you leave?' Jack asks.

'Just after eleven? They'd called last orders.'

'How drunk was I when I left? I keep thinking that I might have passed out or fell or something?'

The crying in the background increases and he must have covered the mouthpiece as he speaks to someone in the background. 'Sorry about that – Milo is teething. Well, we'd both had a skinful. You were drunk, mate, but not that drunk. Listen. I've gotta go, but let's catch up soon, eh?'

'Yeah. Thanks, man.'

He ends the call.

'Does that help?' I turn my face to him, even though I can't see a thing.

'The times don't add up. The police said it was eleven when the ambulance arrived. He should have seen it. Anyway,' he says breezily. 'Sit tight, we're almost there.'

According to the forecast ten minutes ago, it's going to be warm for October, which is perfect according to Jack, and I'm glad I wore the lighter long-sleeved blue blouse rather than the jumper I had originally chosen. Jack turns up the radio, Taylor Swift shaking it off. I laugh at Jack singing along.

'You're a Swifty?'

'God, no, my niece is.'

The indicator tocks, the car turns, the road becoming more unsteady. I reach out my glove to the dashboard, to steady myself. Outside, I can hear the crunch of gravel and something like a lawnmower in the distance, but louder. The car turns, the motion sensors beeping until Jack kills the engine. My fingers move to remove the sleep mask.

'No, not yet,' he says. His voice is gentle but there is also a hint of excitement to it. 'I'll come round and help you out. Sit tight.'

His door closes with a soft thunk before I hear his steps rounding the car and my own door is opened. I'm hit by the smell of grass and hedgerows and something else, something like tarmac after rain.

'Do you feel comfortable taking my hand?' he asks. Ah, now I understand the gloves. I hesitate for a split second, not because I don't want to, but because I do. I stretch my fingers towards him, his warm hand holding on to mine. I know that with the thickness of the gloves, his thoughts will be mostly hidden from me, but it still feels so intimate, electric even. My heartbeat ratchets up as his grip tightens a touch. He steers me out of the car.

I try to hum *shake it off*, but still hear whispers of his thoughts.

Don't rush.

Mind the pothole.
Careful.

'Can I take this off now?'

'Just a bit further,' he says. His tone suggests he's smiling as I try to balance and navigate the uneven ground. I concentrate on the strength of his hands, smelling the Jackness of him. I start reciting the periodic table, but still, I hear him.

This might be a mistake.
She's nervous.

He stops us, my feet now on flat ground.

'OK.' He releases me. 'Turn to your right.'

I follow his instructions.

'Ready?' he asks, his voice laced with excitement, with an undercurrent of nerves.

'As I'll ever be, I guess.'

'You can take off the mask now.' I pull the velvet from my eyes, blinking in the sunshine. Jack is smiling, his deep brown eyes taking in my face as our surroundings come into view, my mouth opening wide. Ahead of me is a small building; to the right, there is a large grey hangar and nestled in the large expanse of grass, is a small runway. I blink away the sun, covering my eyes as they land on a small blue aeroplane, a propeller at the front, and two flames painted on either side. Set further back are three other planes of similar size. I turn to Jack, his head leaning to the left as he watches my expression. He ducks slightly, eyebrow raised. 'Surprise?'

'I... I don't understand...' Out of the building a man is walking towards us. He's mid-to-late forties, salt-and-pepper George Clooney hair, and he's holding a clipboard.

Jack tucks his hands in his back pockets. 'You said you wanted to be an astronaut, and well, I couldn't quite stretch to that, so I thought this might come like a close second?'

My chest constricts, with excitement, but also with a terrifying wonder that he would do this. That he listened to me talking about my ridiculous musings as a child and is handing me a gift that is so much more than any grand gesture I've seen in the films I love so much. Heat pricks the backs of my eyes, and Jack looks at me in a way that is both self-conscious and proud.

'You're taking me on a plane?' I swallow down the excitement and nerves.

'Yep and don't worry, I've explained about the germ thing and—'

My eyes are drawn to the pilot then back to Jack; the urge to throw my arms around his neck is so strong that I move forward. The air between us is taut with what-ifs. His eyes search mine, before dipping to my mouth. He steps closer, the air lifting his hair; I see my own longing reflected back at me.

His head leans fractionally closer. The need to kiss him is like nothing I've ever experienced before.

'Jack! Good to see you, my man!' The moment is broken and I step back. Jack's eyes scan my face before he turns to him. They shake hands as I try to decipher what just happened. What was I *thinking*?

'I take it this is your Maggie?'

'It is.' Jack clears his throat, rephrasing. 'Err, Maggie... Maggie Wright.'

'I'm Greg. Good to meet you.' He gives me a nod, no hand-shaking for me. I wonder how the booking conversation went between them. 'Looking forward to the flight?'

'I... yes, I am.' I look to the plane, to Greg and then to Jack. His eyes are lit up, and he's smiling again, the awkward moment lost in the air that smells of tarmac and petrol.

'Ever flown before?' Greg asks, his blue eyes crinkling at the edges, his whole body relaxed.

'Me. No!' I glance back to Jack.

Greg smiles. 'Well, it's a great day for it. I'll go through a few safety points then we're cleared for take-off in' – he checks his watch – 'twenty minutes.'

Greg goes through the safety checks before we make our way towards the aircraft. 'You'll be wearing seatbelts and headsets so listen carefully to me during the flight. So the big question is' – he turns to me – 'would you like to take the back with our man Jack here, or would you like to fly?'

'Sorry?' I frown.

Jack leans forwards. 'Greg is a great teacher. Don't worry, you'll be in good hands.'

'I...'

Greg smiles. 'There's no pressure, Maggie. The choice is yours: in the back as a sightseer or... you can take control of Penelope here?' He taps the nose of the plane. 'Once we're up.'

'No pressure.' Jack meets my eyes. 'It's up to you.'

I look from Jack to Greg then to the plane, *Penelope*.

'So, Maggie, what'll it be? Wanna learn to fly?'

'Yes.' I take a deep breath, my head nodding. 'Yes, I... thank you.' I spin round to Jack and he nods encouragement, a smile in his eyes before he reaches up and lifts himself into the back of the plane.

Greg leads me to the front, opens the door, and I pull myself into the co-pilot seat. I swallow down the dryness in my throat as I look at all the dials and levers in front of me. Greg climbs in, first turning around and passing a headset to Jack who is sitting behind the pilot, then he hands me my own before securing his. I fasten the seatbelt, again staring at all the dials in front of me.

'Ah don't worry, it looks more complicated than it is. I'll take care of everything and once we're up, you can take the lead... Sound good?'

'Yep.' My whole body is shaking as my eyes look out to the stretch of tarmac ahead. The engine starts and the whole machine begins to rumble, as it slowly moves towards the runway.

'Good morning, control,' Greg's voice comes through the headset, as relaxed as if he's ordering a chow mein from China City, not about to launch us into the sky. 'This is G-ADCF, Cessna 172, requesting clearance for take-off. Three on board and ready for departure. Over.'

I look over my shoulder at Jack, who is leaning back, as relaxed as if we were about to watch *Top Gun* with Henry between us. He mouths: *you good?* I nod, turning my head back, facing the runway.

'Roger, G-ADCF, cleared for take-off.' I look at Greg in awe as he smiles at the response. It's like he's waiting at a roundabout rather than on a runway.

Greg points to the lever and explains it's the throttle and pushes it forwards. 'All right there, Maggie?' Greg says over the sound of the engine increasing as we begin along the runway. My body feels like it's being pushed back into my seat as we bump along the tarmac.

'All good!' I reply. He pulls back on the steering and the nose lifts. I lean forwards as the plane banks to the left. The ground sinks beneath us, trees and fields rushing past. I hold my breath tight in my lungs as the aircraft lifts higher until it levels out. Beneath us, the fields look like a patchwork of greens and yellows, light bouncing off the sea in the distance.

Roads and cars look like kids' toys, the coastline curving around the sea to the west. It's everything I dreamed it would be.

'Holy shit, is that Harrowsby?' I ask after a short time.

'Yep,' Jack's voice comes through. He leans forward, his arm stretched, finger pointing. 'There's the high street.'

I look down and think of the times I have walked those streets. We head towards the sea, the plane evening out.

'So, Maggie, you want to take the reins?' I look over, startled, but I can already feel the need to put my hands on the steering, or yoke, as Greg calls it. I look over my shoulder at Jack who grins and nods. 'Go for it,' he says through the headset then leans back, and crosses his leg over his thigh.

My hand is shaking as I tentatively reach out. It's strong and powerful beneath the leather of my gloves. I take hold, the vibrations of the plane now more emphasised beneath my fingers. It's powerful, exhilarating and terrifying, yet I also feel a deep sense of calm, of feeling grounded, which is ironic given how far the ground is beneath me. Greg explains how to apply gentle pressure; the plane reacts to every little movement but right now I'm in complete control.

'That's it, nice and steady.'

'I'm bloody flying, Jack!' I say, cheeks already hurting from smiling so much. I hear his familiar laugh.

'You are. Tom Cruise eat your heart out.'

Greg leans back, head turning briefly. 'Don't look away!' I shriek, panic tensing my whole body. 'Ah you're doing great. I might have a little nap.' His eyes crinkle at the sides, but stay on the dashboard.

Greg points out the key landmarks, the church and the cliffs, and then we settle into comfortable silence as I – *me!* – fly us over the bay.

'How's your dad, Jack? Loved his last book. Stayed up till the early hours to finish it.'

I'm concentrating on the yoke beneath my fingers, but the conversation surprises me. Jack's dad's a writer?

'He's good, thanks.' Jack's voice is flippant.

'You read any of his stuff, Maggie?'

'I...'

'Maggie is more of a film buff,' Jack intervenes.

'Really? What's your favourite?'

'Um, I like anything really, but particularly romance films. I love a good horror too though. I'd recommend some but I'm finding it hard to reply and concentrate on not killing us all.' My hand shakes and I feel the slight movement of the plane, all of it under my control.

Greg lets out a small laugh. 'You're doing great. Let's turn right now, gentle movements. You'll feel us bank slightly. That's it, keep her steady. Perfect! You're a natural! Completely in control.'

His words snag on my thoughts. There is a pull inside, an anchoring, and I grip the stick more firmly. I can't remember the last time I felt like I was in the driving seat of my own life. My eyes find Jack's briefly as I pass the controls back to Greg. And just like that, I'm a passenger again.

I look at Jack's side profile against the backdrop of the sky, his high cheekbones, dark hair and the Mediterranean glow of his skin. There are a few white clouds scudding the horizon behind him. I take a mental snapshot – of Jack, of this moment – before it all crashes to the ground.

We almost kissed.

I want more than friendship with Jack.

Tess was right. Date number five. It's time. I need to tell him the truth.

Or I need to end it.

22

JACK

The look on Maggie's face as she flew the plane will stay with me for a long time. On the drive home, we talk about the flight, about Greg, about everything other than *that* moment. I park the car outside my shop and turn off the engine.

'Hungry?' I ask as the silence in the car pushes down on us.

'I'm always hungry.' She smiles but it's guarded.

'Pizza?' I ask.

'I, actually... I think I might turn in early tonight. It's been' – she looks up at me, green eyes almost jade in the setting sunlight – 'a pretty big day.'

I've been trying to deny how I feel when she looks at me like that, like she sees the truth beneath the façade.

'But a good day?'

'Definitely.' She smiles. 'Definitely a good day.'

She opens the door and climbs out.

The physical distance feels symbolic. She's about a metre away but it feels further somehow. The open door is between us, like a pause at the end of a chapter that I can't read.

I've waited too long, or moved too soon. But in that moment, as she stepped towards me, I was so sure she felt the same. That she wanted to kiss me as much as I wanted to kiss her.

'I guess we should talk?' I suggest. 'About earlier—'

'Listen, Jack.' She turns to me. 'I'm not sure I can do... this.'

And here it is. This is why I've been holding back, ignoring the attraction I've been feeling for her since the minute the lights went on and I saw her standing in front of a cinema screen. I don't want to lose this, *her*.

'This?'

'You and me. It...' Her voice is scratchy, pained. 'It's not going to work. We can't have...' She meets my eyes. 'There are things you need to know and, and... I can't even touch you and—'

I was so certain. So convinced that I wasn't ready... and now I might have blown it. For the first time in months, I've felt like me. But she's scared too.

'Maggie?'

I hate that there are tears in her eyes.

'I like you. A lot,' I begin.

A smile twists in the corner of her mouth. 'I know. I like you a lot too. But—'

'Can I ask you a question?'

She exhales long and hard.

'If this was a scene in a film, what would you want to happen?'

'This isn't a film, Jack.'

'Humour me. Let's say we have this couple, they are friends but *I think* there might be something more there, but there are the usual – OK, not *usual* – barriers standing in their way. What would you want to happen next?'

'I...' She looks away, and then back to me. But there is a moment's hesitation, a hint of possibility. 'If this was a film? I'd want them to overcome those barriers, I guess.'

'Even if it might be hard? Even if they're scared to let themselves get close?'

She nods. 'But this isn't a film...'

'Or a book. But they always find a way, don't they? Our heroes? Even if it might get a bit complicated along the way.'

'This isn't a fairy tale. We don't get to have a happy ever after. Fairy tales aren't real.'

'Who says?'

She throws her hands up. 'Everyone!'

'Most stories are based on the truth. And OK, the Grimm brothers were pretty Grimm, and Goldilocks was a selfish little know-it-all, but stories at their core are all about the journey. We're at the beginning of ours. Please don't tear up the script. Not yet.' I close the car door, step a little closer, hope clutched tightly in my chest. I incline my head towards the shop. 'It's book club night...' My voice trails off as I look towards the window, a display of new books matching the stickers in the window, then back to Maggie. 'Can you wait here?'

'I...'

I take off my jacket and hand it to her. 'Keep this; you'll need it.'

'What? Jack, I...'

'One more scene?'

She gives me the briefest of nods. 'One more scene.'

* * *

I push open the door and rush through, taking the steps to my flat two at a time. Thoughts bouncing around inside my mind like a ping-pong ball.

I gather everything I need, shoving it into my overnight bag. I hurry down the stairs and back into the shop, where I'd left Nell with a look of surprise and her questions about why I'm back so early and what I'm doing. I take the two hot chocolates I'd asked her to make and pour them into a flask. The buzz of discussion is heated; the book of the month has clearly divided the readers. Nell springs up from where she was perched on the edge of a chair as I hurry across the room.

'Jack!' She tails me. 'What's going on?' I stumble over my words as I explain about the events of the day, grabbing a handful of sugar sachets. 'She's *outside*?' she asks aghast, then practically skips towards the window. She cranes her neck, a beaming smile across her face. I follow her line of sight. Maggie is sitting across the road on a bench, looking along the street. Nell chuckles. 'You've given her your jacket? That is so *cute*!'

'It's not cute.' I dip my head under the counter, looking for my spare battery pack. 'It's turned cold outside. I'm being practical.'

'Readers!' Nell turns, gathering the attention of the book club. 'Jack's on a date!' I fire a furious look at Nell. 'And he's given her his jacket!'

'Jesus Christ,' I mutter under my breath as the book club members rush to the window, all trying to see Maggie.

The comments from the book clubbers fire quickly. 'Oh, she's pretty! Invite her in. What's her name?' Nell deftly answers and allows me to ignore the questions as I shoulder my bag, grab the flask and push my way through the throng, Nell following me to the door.

'What are you doing?' I ask.

'You don't think I'm going to miss meeting her, do you?'

'Well. Yes. I've told you,' I say pulling her aside. 'She has a phobia.'

'Right, right. Germs.'

'I mean it, Nell. You. Can. Not. Touch. Her.' The excitement behind Nell's eyes dims.

'Understood,' she replies. Her mouth opens as if she wants to say something more. I open the door, but Nell follows me, the book club clutching around the doorway.

'Go back inside,' I say.

'Not in a million years.' Her eyes are challenging. 'I'll keep my distance,' she says voice lifting in innocence. 'I don't hug *everyone* I meet.'

'You do though.'

'I'll be on my best behaviour. No touching. I swear to Captain Birdseye.' She salutes.

God help me.

23

MAGGIE

What am *I* doing? I take a seat on the bench opposite the shop.

The bell rings above the door and I'm hit deep in my solar plexus at how beautiful he is, such a cliché. He's looking along the street. The open door frames him in a lozenge of warm light, wind ruffling his hair. A smile stretches across his face as I turn my head.

Oh, who am I kidding? I was never going to walk away from him. I'll tell him I can hear thoughts at the end of the night. Who knows? Maybe he won't think I'm insane and leg it as far as he can from me.

The moment is broken as a woman steps by his side. Nell, I gather. I stand and cross the road. Jack moves slightly in front of her as though he's ready to tackle her to the ground if he has to.

'You must be Nell?' I ask.

'And you are the woman who has made this miserable pillock slightly more bearable.'

I pause before replying. 'Miserable?' I question, a touch defensively.

'I should clarify that he's only miserable around me. I'm sure around you he is a positively bouncing beam of rainbowy unicorn farts.'

I laugh. I like her.

'Great,' Jack interrupts. 'So now you've both met, Nell, you can go back inside and—'

A group of people are now on the kerb. Various ages, genders, all relaxed yet excited at the spectacle that is me.

Jack gestures to the group chatting under their breath. 'Maggie, this is the Friday night book club gang, and they were going *back inside*.'

They chatter in one stream of noise like a gaggle of geese flying overhead.

Nell is appraising me. I look away, focusing instead on rolling up the cuff of Jack's jacket. 'It's good to meet you, Maggie,' Nell says.

'You too,' I reply brightly.

'Right, you lot, back inside.' Nell ushers the group towards the doorway, fairy lights framing the glass windows. 'I think Jack can take it from here.' She gives Jack a wink. 'Take care of our boy?' Nell adds over her shoulder. Her smile is relaxed but there is something pointed in her words.

'Nell...' Jack gives her a warning.

'Of course,' I say, looking away from her gaze.

'Sorry about that.' Jack looks over his shoulder as if he expects the book clubbers to be watching on.

'Nell is protective of you.' I look up at him. 'Have you two ever...?'

'Me and Nell?' He laughs slowly. 'No. Me and Nell as a couple?' He lets out a long plume of air. 'We'd kill each other. Also, I don't have boobs. This way,' he says leading us further along the road, heading towards the park from the main entrance.

'First you give me your jacket to shield me from the cold, then you suggest a moonlight walk.' I look up at him. If I was normal, I would nudge him with my shoulder. 'The romantic hero looks good on you, Jack Chadwick.'

'I'm no Hugh Grant.'

'No, you're not. You're more of a—' I turn my head to him, stopping my steps. I step back assessing him. 'Theo James.' His eyebrows rise quizzically. 'It's the whole Greek descendant vibe, I think, dark hair, dark eyes, high cheekbones... and you're, well...'

'What?'

'A bit posh.'

He laughs and shakes his head.

'Actually it's Italian. My great-grandad on my mum's side was from Sicily.'

We continue walking. 'Do you still have family over there?'

'Some, but I haven't been over since...' He gives me a look that reads 'my stroke'.

'So where are we going?' I lighten the conversation.

'Linton Park, if that's OK?'

'Sure.'

We continue walking. 'The book club people seem like a fun bunch.'

'They can be.' He hesitates. 'I've mostly avoided them for the past year.'

Both of our heads turn to the sound of steps behind us, an owner being walked by their dog, the lead straining against his gloved hands. I step onto the empty road, letting them pass. The flustered man gives out a *'sorry!'* as he narrowly avoids bumping into my shoulder. I hop back up onto the kerb.

'Did you always want to own a bookshop?' I ask.

'Honestly? I used to want to be a writer. Apart from reading in stairwells, it was all I did in my spare time when I was a teenager. I was a bit of a nerd. Never quite fit in with the popular crowd.'

'I find that hard to believe. I bet there was a bevy of hormonal teenagers slapping on watermelon lip gloss and straightening their hair before class.'

'Well if socially awkward, gangly boys with bottle-top glasses, braces and a lisp are your stereotypical teen crush.'

'Bottle-top glasses?'

'Yeah. I was always losing mine and after the third pair of thinned lenses Mum decided to put her foot down. And I couldn't afford to replace them. As soon as I was old enough I had laser surgery.'

'Oh, she's a tough-love mum?'

'More of a learn the value of money because she comes from a working-class background kind of mum. We grew up with a pretty privileged upbringing. Dad comes from what Mum calls "old money". Our family home, Chadders, is... it's kind of a big house. Not that grand or anything but it's been in our family for over a century. Both my parents were keen to correct our heritage by making us pay our own way with pocket money we earned through chores. And if we asked to borrow money, we had to pay interest. But they also gave us complete autonomy, let us learn from our mistakes and supported us if things went wrong.'

'They sound great.'

'They are. They'd like you,' he adds. 'Sorry, that sounded like I'm already inviting you to meet the parents.'

'They sound great,' I repeat, redundantly, avoiding the fact that when I tell him about me, the last thing he will want is to introduce me to his parents.

'So, what happened to the Jack Chadwick novel?'

He nods towards the right and we cross the road as he points towards the entrance to Linton Park. 'My dad is Tom Ridgeway.'

I frown.

'*Midnight Runaway*?' he adds, knowing I would have seen the film.

'No way?!'

'Yep.'

I let out a low whistle. 'So have you, like, met Henry Cavill?'

He adjusts the shoulder of his backpack, ducking as we head under the stone archway leading into the park. 'Once. He's nice. Normal. Huge.'

'Wow.' I shake my head. 'We lead very different lives. How come your dad's not Tom Chadwick?'

'Pen name. In case it all went horribly wrong.'

'So why did you stop writing? There's space for more than one family member to be a writer?'

'I, well, I wasn't good enough. As a kid I thought it was the coolest job in the world. Dad would wear pyjamas until lunchtime. He didn't have to "go to work". But as I got older, I could see the reality of being a writer, the deadlines, the stress when Dad struggled with the next book; I knew it wasn't for me. Recommending books is easier.'

I scan the pathway beneath the Victorian-style street lamps towards the main courtyard of the park. The path is low-lit, swaths of fir trees lining the ribbon of pathway. The moon is high as we approach the small courtyard, casting a pale blue glow over the large and imposing circular fountain. In the centre is a sculpture of a woman, her body braced for battle, hair blown back from her face by a wind long gone. In the summer, the fountain can be heard gushing from where we are, but tonight, the warrior remains silent.

'We're here,' he says.

'You've brought me to see a fountain that's not fountaining?' He smiles and drops the bag off his shoulder.

'We missed the end of *Notting Hill*.' He climbs over the ridge of the fountain, automatically turning and offering me a hand. I give my head a little shake; he looks like he wants to kick himself. I climb over the ridge and drop down into the basin. He takes out his laptop, opens it and props it up next to the base of the horse, the ta-dum of the Netflix logo playing into the cold night air. I laugh, my cheeks warming. He lays out two yoga mats, with a wide enough space between them to keep us from accidentally touching and unfolds two blankets.

'Wow. I...' I swallow hard and clutch the tops of my arms. 'Thank you, Jack.'

'I thought I'd better make scene two special.'

'Well, you've nailed it.' I sit down as he pours hot chocolate into two takeaway cups, placing them on the ground before leaning over the laptop and selecting *Notting Hill*.

'What, no whipped cream and marshmallows?' I tease.

'One step ahead.' He pulls out a bag of marshmallows and a battery-operated church candle, placing it further around the bowl of the fountain.

'No fairy lights hidden in there? Dry ice machine?'

'Sorry to disappoint.'

'I doubt you ever do.' My eyes meet his. There is a buzz of connection between us: that spark that was there earlier and is so often shown in romance films.

For my whole life I've come to accept that I will never be as happy as the couples on the screen, as the people I see from outside a restaurant window, holding hands across a table. But while the film plays and we talk through it, while I laugh and tease him, and while I tell him about Hellie; my pet goldfish,

Bruce; and he explains about the time his siblings pretended he was invisible for two whole weeks, I realise that this is possibly the happiest day of my life.

But then the film ends and I realise it's time.

I turn to him.

'Jack? There is something I need to tell you.'

24

MAGGIE

Jack is cricking his neck from side to side. The feeling of inevitable nostalgia for this night, this time with him unburdened by the truth, shrinks the air around me. The clear night presses down, the light from the moon heavy, the cold crisp air filling with dank, dark moisture. I'm about to destroy this day. The perfectly imperfect Friday night.

I turn to him tentatively, tucking my legs up. I wrap my arms around my knees, and take a deep breath as I turn to him. He's leaning back, head resting on the back of the ridge of concrete, eyes on the stars above.

'Hmmm? Look!' He points, mouth cracking open. But I don't look. There could be a thousand shooting stars, the northern lights could be strutting around in all their flamboyant colours and glory thrown across the sky like a feather boa and neither would be as spectacular as watching Jack's face unfolding, relaxed yet excited at the same time. I let my eyes rove along the curve of his jawline, the Roman nose, the Cupid's bow of his upper lip. I want to count every bristle of stubble along his skin, measure the exact width and length of the mole beneath his eye. The wind lifts and drops his hair, the moisture unlocking the hint of repressed childhood curls. 'Never mind,' he says, the excitement falling from his face. 'False alarm. It's a satellite.'

The words I need to say cluster together, heavy in my throat. He turns to me, takes in my expression.

'What's wrong?' he asks.

'I—' I pull my knees in tighter. 'I need to tell you something.' He sits up, shoulders pulled back, the concern in his eyes out of step with the wariness in his body language. It's natural that he should be on his guard. 'This is going to sound—' I close my eyes briefly, trying to think of how to release the words that I'm so terrified of unshackling. But Jack deserves the truth. 'I've been lying to you, Jack.'

The laughter lines around his eyes fade, the skin between his eyebrows tightening.

'Bruce isn't a goldfish but a Danish prince?' he asks hopefully. I can see he's scared, that he's trying to direct the conversation towards humour despite the crack in my voice.

'No. He's definitely a goldfish.'

'So...?'

'Before I tell you, can I ask that you listen to everything I have to say before you run?'

'I'm not going to run.' The words sound truthful, but he doesn't know yet.

'You might.' I lift my head, pressing my lips together to stop the wrong words falling out in the wrong order. 'I'm not afraid of germs. That... that isn't why I can't be around people.' Jack shifts backwards. Defensiveness flashes in his eyes, swiftly followed by confusion. 'I can hear thoughts.' I rush on. 'When I touch someone. I can hear their thoughts. *See* them sometimes too.'

'What?' The word slams up a wall between us. He's breathing

heavily, arms folding then unfolding. The air around us is frozen, like I've hit pause.

'Look, I know how this sounds, I know that what I'm telling you sounds like something out of a Marvel film, but I *promise* you, Jack... I *promise you*, it's the truth, it's the way I was made. And I'm sorry I lied to you, but I know how it normally goes when I try to explain the unexplainable.' I lean towards him slightly. 'And that's why we can't have a relationship, not that you'll want to see me again after I've told you this *ridiculous* truth.' I wait a beat, desperate for him to say something.

He doesn't.

I climb out of our nest of blankets, standing, ready to walk away from him. From us.

'Wait.' I turn slowly, Jack is standing stationary, but it feels like his whole body is vibrating. 'Is this a party trick?' he says, hope and fear lacing his words as he looks up. 'You ask me to think of a number and then give me some maths problems?'

I shake my head. 'It's not a trick.' I look back up at that heavy sky, the sparks of starlight blurring. I blink, a solitary tear rolling down my cheek. 'I don't know why, I don't know how. It's always happened to me.' He gets up, stands beside me, my eyes searching his face, begging him to understand what I'm saying.

'You think you can hear thoughts?'

'I don't think I can. I *can*.'

Jack shakes his head, looks away.

I rush on. 'I've tried so many times to stop it, to think of other things, to meditate. I told the doctor that I had too many thoughts buzzing around my head, and she prescribed anxiety medication that made me barely able to function, but all it did was numb my ability to process, to unstick their emotions and memories from my own. It was harder to escape the thoughts and—' He puts up a hand – a stop-talking motion. I clamp my mouth shut.

'So you're not afraid of germs?'

'No. Just people. People are the worst,' I add but he doesn't smile.

I look to the lamplit path that led us here; the dense trees on either side of the park leaning away from each other, embarrassed to watch our relationship self-combust. I don't speak, not wanting to say anything more that could bulldoze the crumbling space between us. During all of my time with Jack, the distance separating us has only been physical. Not any more.

He walks slowly around the circular rim of the fountain. I analyse his movements, the way his shoulders have tightened and lifted, the tension corrugating the muscles along his jaw. He does two full circles of the fountain, finally stopping to look up at the woman on the horse. He turns then, leaning back, hooking one leg behind the other, and fixing me with a stare I can't read. 'Let's say what you're saying is real—'

And there it is. This is always how it goes. I don't know why I hoped this would go any other way.

'It *is* real.' He looks away. 'I'm not a charlatan, Jack. Why would I lie? Why would I tell you this if it wasn't true? Surely you must know how I feel about you?'

'Maybe you're trying to figure out the world's most original way of dumping someone?'

'That isn't what this is. I didn't want to lie to you.'

'But you did.'

I nod, swallowing hard.

'I did. Can you imagine how this would have gone if I'd told you when you found yourself locked in a cinema with me?'

'You've had plenty of opportunity to try to explain *that*...' The way he says *that* is enough to tell me that he doesn't believe me. And I get it. Who would? 'Before I—' He looks away then back at me. 'Before I let myself get close to you.'

'I know. That's why I'm telling you now, before this goes any further. Do you have any idea how much I want to kiss you?' His dark eyes skirt over my mouth before they sear into my own. I swallow the desperation in my throat. 'How all I've been able to think about over the past week is that I needed to tell you the truth while at the same time wanting one more night with you?' He looks away, eyes off in the distance, his stance fixed, defensive, unbending. 'I can never have a normal relationship, Jack. You'd never be able to have secrets, privacy,' I say softly. 'I can never have the happily ever after that I yearn for, or that you deserve.' His eyes are fixed on the ground. A flock of leaves gather around our feet before a gust of wind makes them take flight. 'Say something.'

'I don't know what to say.' His voice is exasperated. 'You tell me you can hear people's thoughts, Maggie. Do you know how—'

'Insane?'

Jack looks towards the way we came, to the road that leads him back home then comes back to me. He lowers his voice, but it wavers. 'You tell me you can *hear* thoughts? That you want to kiss me, but you can't. You tell me you can't have a relationship when for the past few weeks all I could think about was you. What do you want me to say, Maggie?'

'Tell me to leave, tell me this was a mistake, tell me you wish you'd never decided to go to Flicks that night. Something!'

'I. Can't.' The words slice out of him. Jack is a man who lives his life through knowledge, through the need to be in control of his own destiny. His stroke stole that from him and now I've taken the only piece of stability that has grown from our relationship and broken it. He clutches at the thick hair at the nape of his neck, eyes back on the road home. He doesn't need to say anything. I don't need to touch him to know he wants to leave, to go back to the warmth and safety of his shop, to Nell, to the people he surrounds himself with; a place I can't be part of.

The colour has drained from his face and he steps back. The truth is too much. I take off his jacket and fold it up then place it beside him. 'I want you to know that I've never hated what I am... more than when I'm with you.' He nods, eyes fixed back on his boots. 'I will always be glad you walked into my cinema.'

For a small moment, it looks like he's about to say something, but those words are locked away under the weight of my truth.

He looks away.

Doesn't respond.

And I know this is the end.

'Goodbye, Jack.'

I turn my back on him. Hot tears are already falling from my eyes as I pick up the pace, but they can't wash away the truth, and I can't outrun the loss of the only relationship I've ever wanted.

25

FRIDAY 25TH OCTOBER

Jack

It's Friday. I know where she will be tonight, just as I have for the past three weeks.

Outside the train window, the edges of Guildford come into view; the sun sinking behind the crooked buildings; the cathedral bruising the sky. The train is busy and each time a person bumps into me, each time there's a nudge against my shoulder, I think of her.

I've replayed that conversation over and over. Questioned if she's *just* really good at reading people. But she believes she can hear thoughts, *see* thoughts. It's ludicrous. I must be mad to be even considering this.

I rub my forehead, a migraine already on the way.

Then again, I can write but not read... how many times have I had to explain that? They're the thoughts that have been turning around in my mind for the past three weeks, like a scratch on a broken record.

What if it's something more though and she really *can* hear what others are thinking? If I told Nell what she'd said, she'd laugh and tell me to get as far away from her as possible and yet... Yet, I can't stop my mind questioning. It wakes me up in the night. It haunted me as I tried to draft the email advert to sublet the shop that I still haven't sent.

I've even tried to recall any time that Maggie *could* have read my thoughts in the days that followed. What would she have heard? That I feel like a failure? Did she know about my stroke before I told her? Is that how she knew Luke was telling the truth?

That's the toughest thing to take. Because since I've met her, I haven't felt the need to hide anything. And if I'm being honest, part of me *wants* it to be true, to have one person see the darkest parts of me, the parts that scared Vicky away, that I try to hide away even from myself, and want a relationship with me anyway. That's what she said. She wanted to kiss me, she wanted me to know how she felt. If she heard what I was thinking, would she still want to do that? I shake my head. This is ridiculous. People can't *read minds*.

* * *

Dr Levin's office is not far from the uni campus, and I'm going to have to try and navigate my way through a town I don't know, with road signs I can't read. I wait until I hear my stop and disembark. I've been counting the times I've been accidentally touched since I left home. I've made it out onto the street and I've already hit sixteen. Sixteen people who Maggie says she would be able to 'hear'.

I squint against the sun. I have no idea whether to walk left or right, or whether I've used the right exit from the station. I open up my voice note with the instructions, cross the road outside the Black Swan Inn – easy to spot by the colours. I stop still. The sound of the town is playing its own chaotic symphony: traffic parping horns, a couple arguing, and a man asking me for a fiver so he's warm for the night. I give it and ask him directions.

I make a few wrong turns, getting more and more frustrated as my feet hit the pavement. The ground is cobbled, and the air feels compacted around me. There is something about this place that feels like it expects something of you, a greater knowledge of the world, which only amplifies as I make my way around the outskirts of the campus. I unwind my scarf, shove my gloves into my pockets.

I looked at pictures of his office before I left, but I still have to ask three more people until I find a small row of houses at the end of a cul-de-sac. According to Google Maps playing in my ear, I have arrived at my destination.

I take a breath, looking up at the plaque on the front of the Victorian building.

☐ ♏ ❖ ♓ ■

There is a woman around Mum's age outside the house next door. I squint at the words, stepping forwards. In my mind, I know that there will be a space between the two smudges of shape if this says Dr Levin but still my finger hovers over the buzzer. I scratch my neck, squeeze my eyes shut and reopen them to see if I get any more clarity. Since finding out more about Luke, that he wasn't the one to cause the stroke, the pain has eased a little.

'Forgotten your glasses?' the woman asks, joining me: short blonde bob, bright red lipstick.

'I... yes.' I give an exaggerated eye roll. 'I'm looking for Dr Levin?'

'You're in the right place.' She looks back to the building, her face softening, and gives my arm a gentle squeeze.

I knock on the door, the sounds of a dog barking coming from behind.

Dr Levin is short, hairy and has thick glasses. He reminds me of a mole.

'Hi, I'm Jack Chadwick. We have an appointment – sorry, I'm a bit late...'

'Not to worry. Come on through.'

His office has high ceilings, yellow walls, battered leather sofas and arched windows that do little to block out the sounds outside.

'So, Jack.' The chair he's sitting in seems to almost swallow him. 'What brings you to my door?'

'Well, I had a stroke and—'

'Yes, yes. I know all about that, but why are you here?' He peers at me over his glasses. *Because if I didn't come, I could financially ruin myself and end up losing my home and cost Nell her job. And it gives me something else to focus on.*

'I... I want to read again.'

'Are you sure?'

What a question. Of course I do. I frown. 'Yes.'

'Because I've looked at your history and you've only made it to seven of your speech and language appointments in the past six months and I don't have time to start the trial with a patient who isn't fully committed.'

I shift in my seat. 'Things have changed. Before, I didn't remember much about the night it happened and any time I tried to read I would feel this pain at the back of my skull.'

'Psychosomatic pain.'

'Sorry?'

'That's what it's called. When you experience that type of pain that is connected to trauma.'

'Right. But since then...' I push away the image of Maggie, of the way she tried to help me find the answers. 'Since I've started to piece together a few things, the pain isn't as... excruciating. So now I am. Committed.'

He taps his note pad with a pen. And waits. And waits. And waits.

'Reading is part of me it's...'

'No. It's not. Not any more.'

'What am I doing here then?' I ask, frustrated. 'Isn't that your job? To teach me? Shouldn't we be reading right now?' I'm being unnecessarily rude, but losing Maggie, not sleeping and the pressure of the new shop is taking its toll.

'You can't read.'

'I know!' I throw my hands up.

'Good. Now we can start.'

Wait, what?

He leans forward with a green plate in his hands. 'Choccy biccy?'

Christ. This is going to be worse than I thought.

Over the next hour I'm forced to try to read for his baseline assessment. He told me not to think too hard, to be honest. And honestly? I can hardly recognise any of the words on the page he gives me. I'm sitting at the desk in the corner of the room, the sun too warm on the back of my neck. Dr Levin is sitting opposite. The setup is the same as my parents' desk at home. He barely blinks; eyes scrutinising my every move, every attempt.

'Lllllllll—' I stop take a breath and look back at the paper. 'Lll-llll... aaaaaa.'

'Move on.' He uses an extended pointer stick and taps the paper.

I don't know what I was expecting to happen, but as I made my way here, I'd be lying if I didn't feel a small seed of hope trying to grow. All the last hour has taught me is that I. Can't. Read. And that Levin seems to have little patience with my pathetic attempts. I let out a breath, waiting for him to tell me I'm a lost cause. Instead, he produces another sheet of hieroglyphics.

This test is different. Four or five sets of 'words'.

'Can you tell me which of these are real words and which are fake?'

'I can't read.'

'I know. Now tell me which is real and which is fake.' He taps the paper again and I want to take the stick and shove it right up his— 'Today, Jack. Not next week.'

I let out a long breath, staring back at the paper. 'This one is fake?'

'No, that one says "king". Try again. Next box.'

When I look at the next box, something clicks. I can't read it, but my body seems to shift internally, like I'm readjusting my balance when I'm standing on a bus and it brakes.

'This one is fake.'

'Good. Next one.'

I do as he says. I can somehow differentiate some of the fake words and even more bewilderingly, on the next sheet, I can spot words that are in Italian as opposed to English.

I finish the list. My head is pounding but I feel... I feel. Pleased? 'How do I know that?'

'It's a common aspect of alexia. You can still recognise syntax patterns.'

'Huh.'

'That's it for now. It's lunchtime and if I don't get to the deli all the pumpernickel bagels will be gone. I'll see you Monday.'

'Monday?'

'As I explained to your father, this is an intensive course, Jack; I see you three days a week for six weeks.'

'Oh. OK.' I fold the paper.

'Same time?'

'Um. Yeah. I'll be here.' I pull on my coat and head towards the door.

'Before I go...' I should push the thoughts aside, keep Maggie and her confession locked away with the rest of my old life. I'm behaving like a kid still trying to believe in Santa Claus even when the evidence is stacked up against the truth. Even so, *if* what Maggie is saying is real, or some part of it is, I've just destroyed a relationship with the one person who gets me without having to pretend I'm someone I'm not. The words come out anyway.

'Before I go, I have this... friend and she thinks she can hear thoughts.'

'A *friend*?' His eyebrows rise sardonically. He takes off his glasses and cleans them with the corner of his navy jumper.

I catch on. 'A *real* friend. *I* don't think I can hear people's thoughts.'

'Right.' He puts his glasses back on.

'Is there, I mean...' I look to the picture on the wall of a much younger Dr Levin holding a pint to the camera. 'Are there any studies about it? Or any theories?'

'It's not my area, I'm afraid.'

I'm being ridiculous. What did I think he was going to say? Give me the answers to explain it all? I can't ignore the way that it hurts to let that small glimmer of hope fall away though. I'm clutching at the smallest of straws and I can't deny the way I wish

I had some glimmer of tangible evidence that I could hang on to. If there is even a small chance that what she is saying is true, then I wouldn't feel like I'm losing my mind for wanting to believe her.

I nod. 'Well, thanks anyway.'

'But there will be some papers on it somewhere. Have a dig around. You'll find something I'm sure. Us academics can't help ourselves researching one thing or another.'

I don't ask how I'm supposed to do that when I can't read.

'And Jack?'

'Hmmm?' I wrap my scarf around my neck.

'You did good.'

26

MAGGIE

I rip the brown tape off the cardboard box and lean back on my knees.

Heritage Retirement Home is nothing like I was expecting. I suppose, what came to mind was one of the more institutional homes that I was placed in, but this is like a five-star hotel. The large building is Georgian, set amongst acres of lush green land, tall oaks around the perimeter. From Riz's room, you can see the sea and the whole place smells like furniture polish, and not the cheap stuff either.

I look around her room, or maybe suite is a better word? It's large, two big windows behind a neat round table, a small kitchen area, and to the right is her bedroom. Her bed is large and the only hint to this being anything other than a hotel is in the hospital-style bed, the call buttons to the side, and the handrails in the bathroom.

The removal firm had brought her things, and now Riz looks perfectly at home, sitting in her favourite chair, a large black A4 portfolio on her knees.

'Of course, I turned him down,' Riz continues.

'John Lennon?' I blow my hair out of my eyes. 'You turned down John Lennon?'

'I absolutely did. Even if I wasn't already married, he wasn't at all my type. Here, look.'

She tilts the folder open. I get up and peer over the back of the chair and there smiling up at the camera is the man himself. He's young, early twenties I'd guess. He's wearing a black tie and a white shirt. He has a spark of mischief and is clearly flirting with whoever is behind the camera. She turns the page and there he is again, laughing at a woman with thick black hair beneath a jockey cap, mini skirt, three-quarter-length leather jacket, her camera held in her hands. 'Art took that one.' She sighs and shakes her head. 'He never could get to grips with proportions, far too much of the brick wall to the left. It was navy blue that jacket. It should be in one of those boxes I left for you; it'll suit you.'

'You are stunning, Riz. No wonder he had eyes for you.'

'I think he liked the chase more, to be honest. It must have been refreshing to meet a girl in her twenties who wasn't falling at his feet. Tragic what happened to him.'

I shake my head. The more I learn of her life, the less believable it all is. But each time I think she may be exaggerating, she produces some kind of evidence.

I wipe down the dust from my purple tights. 'Fancy a cuppa before I go?'

'That would be wonderful.'

'So, how's our Jack?' she asks with a tone that is more than a gentle enquiry.

I fill the kettle as my stomach knots.

'I don't know. I haven't seen him.' I flick the switch and grip onto the counter.

'And why is that?' she asks.

I turn and lean back, dragging my eyes up to her.

'It's complicated.'

'Pssssh. That word should be banned. Complicated just means there are lots of elements that need to be unpicked, so unpick them.'

I close my eyes briefly, remembering the way he'd looked at me, like I was one step away from being sectioned.

'I'm not good for him, Riz.'

I replay the way his whole body had tensed when the truth landed. The look of betrayal and hurt that followed. I should have stopped seeing him after that first night. In the past, my ability has hurt me more than those around me. This time though, it cuts deeper. I deceived him at a time in his life where he needed stability. The way he looked at me, after everything we've shared... and I know that I'm asking a lot of him to believe me, but part of me... I hoped he'd be different, that he would at least try to understand.

'Not *good* for him? Maggie, I've seen the two of you together; you're more than good for him.'

'We don't work. As a couple. It's better this way. I will only cause him pain.' I place the cup down next to her.

'Of course you'll cause him pain. That's what love is: pain and joy and everything in between.'

'You and your Rizdoms.' I shake my head. 'I'll see you tomorrow?'

'That would be lovely, but don't you have better things to be doing than visiting me?'

'I *like* visiting you. Now, behave yourself and don't get into any mischief.'

* * *

I push aside my thoughts about Jack. I'm about to tap the visitors' pass to open the doors when my attention is drawn towards an elderly man, smartly dressed in a suit and waistcoat. He reminds me of an older Pierce Brosnan. He hesitates, turns and begins walking up along the corridor then turns again, a look of confusion there.

'Hiya,' I say, smiling.

'Hello!' he says brightly. 'I... I...' He looks up and down the corridor again then back to me. 'I was going somewhere and...'

My heart breaks a little for this proud-looking man, who is clearly lost. I scan the corridor, but can't see any staff. 'Shall we go and find your room?' I suggest. He brightens as I step towards him. 'I don't know about you, but I always get lost in this place, so many doors!'

'Quite right. That would be... thank you, young lady. This way!' he instructs. I walk beside him.

'I'm Maggie.'

'Derek Hill.' He grins up at me. 'Pleased to meet you.' He puts out his hand; it's unavoidable. I can't try to explain to him that I can't touch him and I don't want to cause any more distress. I let my hand fall into his and recite the digits of pi. His thoughts are quiet, distant, his mind whirling as he looks to the long hall with doors on either side.

Which one. Which one.

'So, Derek,' I say, linking my arm through his. The action feels alien to me, but I don't recoil because his thoughts are quiet, his emotions dampened. I stop reciting digits and let myself relax. 'Tell me about your room. Did you get a sea view or can you see the hills...?'

I hear his thoughts as he tries to recollect: deep green walls, a painting of a ship, dark furniture. There are trees outside the window, no sea in the background, which must mean he's on the other side of the building.

'Oh, now there's a question.' He smiles up at me, giving me a wink. 'Are you asking if you'd like to see my room, young lady?'

'Derek, are you flirting with me?' I smile.

'I never pass on a pretty face. You've got to be in it to win it, as I always say.'

There is a flicker of a thought. It's hard to describe, but it's like he's remembering to act a part. We continue slowly along the corridor. I glance into the rooms as we pass, seeking out green walls and dark furniture. Rounding a corner to the right, we continue. I hear his thoughts before he says them, like it's a well-rehearsed script and he's reading out the lines. But it's quieter than I'm used to; there is less background noise in his mind.

'So what's a pretty girl like you doing in a place like this?' he asks, a twinkle in his pale eyes.

'Quite the charmer, aren't you?'

I scan more rooms, listen to his thoughts, but there is a mist there, something dampening his memories.

I spot his room, as a sense of relief floods through him.

Silly old fool. Here it is.

He taps the side of his head. 'Ah here we are. Might you fancy a drink?'

'Let's get you inside and I can make you one?'

'Perfect. I take my tea with honey and lemon if you don't mind.'

'Not at all.' I let him go as he makes his way into the room. It's clean, fresh but there is something sad about it too, like it's not him, somehow.

He folds himself into a large green armchair and picks up a discarded newspaper. I turn and look for a kitchen area but there isn't any tea and the fridge is empty. I frown. *Is* this his room? I scan the photos on the wall and lean in. There he is, much younger, standing on what looks like a yacht; beside him is a man with red hair and ruddy complexion. I step around the room. There are more photos of the two of them, getting older but smiling from various destinations.

'Derek! There you are!' A pretty nurse in a uniform more suited to hotel staff than a carer comes in. She has thick black hair in a neat bun and walks in with a palpable look of relief on her small face. Ravina her name tag reads. She looks to me with gratitude. 'Thank you,' she breathes.

'No problem. I brought him to his room, no harm done.' She chews her bottom lip and tries to convey something that I can't quite get the meaning of as she moves towards him. 'I turn around for one minute.' She shakes her head. 'Derek, love. It's time for your dinner.'

'I'll have it in my room,' he says from behind his newspaper. Her shoulders drop and she gives me an almost sympathetic look.

'How about we go downstairs and...'

'No thank you. Here is fine.' He drops the newspaper and confusion descends across his features again.

'Derek, your room is downstairs. This is your... *friend's* room.'

I'm pulled back to the photos of the two men and sadness fills me. The act. The script.

'Well, where is he?'

She crouches down and takes his hand in hers. 'William has

stepped out for a moment. Let's get you some food. It's lamb chops – your favourite.'

Derek gets up and folds the newspaper. 'Would you like to dine with me?' he asks, putting out an arm, that twinkle back.

'I can't today, Derek, but another time?' I smile.

He taps me on the hand. 'Very well. Don't be a stranger now, will you?' He winks. 'I never forget a pretty face.'

'Come on, you old rascal,' she says, as he walks towards the door. Another nurse with dreadlocks and kind eyes approaches them and takes Derek by the arm.

'His partner, William, died last week,' Ravina says sadly as we watch them leave. 'He's forgotten. This was Will's room and... he's regressed. When they first came to us, they were a right pair! Always holding hands, laughing and getting into all kinds of mischief but the dementia started to take its toll. Broke William's heart when Derek started to pull away from him in public, started flirting with all the women. Put himself firmly back in the closet, William said. It was so sad to watch.' She straightens. 'Thank you, for finding him. He's a clever bugger when he's lucid, watches when people go through the safety doors and tags along as brazen as you like.'

'What happened to William?'

'Heart attack. He died peacefully though. That's all we can hope for in this job.'

'Does he have many visitors?'

'No. Not any more.'

'If it's OK, I'd like to look in on him? I have a friend here, and it would be no bother.'

'That would be lovely...?'

'Maggie.'

'Maggie. Good to meet you.'

We follow the large staircase down to the reception area.

Sounds from the communal area leak towards me: a TV, a cough, laughter, something like ping-pong being played from further along. I pick up the pen and sign myself out. My thoughts return to Jack. Is he already trying to forget me, the time we spent together? I push the thought away.

I might not be able to have Jack in my life, but maybe my curse doesn't have to be something I hide from, not all the time.

27

FRIDAY 1ST NOVEMBER

Jack

The rain powering down distorts the road signs flashing by. I flick on the windscreen wiper. If only clearing my questions about Maggie was this easy. I've relied on the Google Maps narration to get me to Guildford. I know the roads well now and I trust myself enough to navigate my way to Dr Levin's.

I follow the instruction to join the motorway, checking over my shoulder as I join at speed.

I've spoken to my parents and they've confirmed that it was eleven when the ambulance came. And that I was not found outside the pub but two streets along. Completely the wrong direction to where I should have been heading. As I have for the past week, I try to force my brain to remember more details. But there is just Luke's face.

The next episode of the podcast I've been listening to is waiting like the guilty secret it is. But instead, I put on the radio.

Today will be my fourth session with Levin and every time I think I know what to expect, he comes out with something new.

Last time it was listening to Darth Vader's imperial march as I stepped on a huge letter J laid out on the floor in bubble wrap, popping the air pockets beneath my feet. For 'Ch' it's Bob Dylan's 'Times They Are a-Changin'' And honestly? Even though his methods are... unique, I'm glad of them, and I'd be lying if I was to say that I'm not starting to be able to spot my name on a list, even if I feel like a walking cosplay fan on his way to Woodstock when I read it.

And coming here fills my spare time with something other than thoughts of Maggie and what happened that night. Maybe my drunk ass fell over and that was that. All this time, I've been trying to blame someone else, when in fact, it's probably my own fault, that and a shot of Sambuca.

I'd walked towards Flicks last week, desperate to see her, to talk to her. Every day I think of something I want to share. Hear her laugh as I acted out the bubble-wrap death march; see her smile.

My finger taps on the steering wheel are becoming relentless. I've resisted for about half an hour before I click on the podcast.

Thanks for joining us, listeners. Last time we ventured into the realm of premonition, but this week we're going one step further: Are we hearing people's thoughts without knowing it?

Sounds crazy. And sadly I haven't suddenly found the ability to read minds like a superhero, but current studies are saying that the idea of hearing someone's innermost thoughts is not just something for science fiction lovers, it might actually be possible.

I turn up the volume a fraction.

Let's dig deeper into the facts, firstly with a very real piece of the brain called 'mirror neurons' the part of the brain that allows us to feel, or mirror, the responses of others at the same time as they do. Researchers have found that not only is 'mirroring' a reality, but that it's more dominant in empathetic people. When they observe someone experiencing a deep moment of emotion, or are experiencing pain, these neurons spring to life as if they are experiencing it too.

I think of Maggie, the way she cares for Riz… the way she can almost sense when I need space and when I need to talk…

These clever little neurons are why we cringe when someone slams their fingers in a door, or why we feel so awkward that we blush when we watch someone in an embarrassing situation. Empathetic people in particular, often simulate the experience, kind of like eavesdropping on someone else's lives.

I know, I know, you're waiting to get to the nitty-gritty; so what if those lines become more tangible and it's not only second-hand emotions those neurons are capable of? Here's the kicker, folks – scientists now believe that these neurons might be able to actually simulate internal ideas or even modes of thought.

Stay tuned after this short advertisement.

I sigh in frustration and slip down a gear.

I know I should turn it off, but over the last week, I've found more and more 'evidence' of this 'hearing thoughts' thing. Have I shared this with Nell or my family? No. If I could see myself from the outside looking in, I'd be questioning who the hell this person is, who listens to podcasts about seeing the future and reading minds. But if there is even a tiny little thread of truth in what Maggie said, then I'm going to listen.

I exit at the next junction, and wait at the traffic lights.

Welcome back! Glad you're still with me. To recap, we're looking at how mirror neurons might be capable of more than simulating emotions when we take into account other somewhat unexplainable functions of the brain.

Here's another real condition: synaesthesia. This is where the senses cross over with incredible results. Some people taste sounds, others see emotions as colours, or feel days of the weeks as specific shapes.

Huh. I think back to my last session. I could *hear* the letter J, hear the sounds of the Star Wars music.

These types of synaesthesia would suggest that the line between thoughts and perception can be surprisingly blurred. What synaesthesia reveals is that the brain's sensory restrictions are not as fixed as we once thought. Visions can bleed into thoughts and the internal can be affected by the external.

So if that clever brain of yours can mirror and blend perception with internal thought, maybe the lines of our thoughts and others isn't so clear cut. Might that be why we know what someone is about to say before they say it? Perhaps that's why empathetic people have such keen insight.

Is it too big a leap to believe that these blurring of lines could link to telepathy?

Still the Scully to my Mulder?

That sentence alone should have me switching this off, but here I am.

Let's turn to what experts call the 'Theory of Mind'. A uniquely human ability to deduce what someone is thinking through the tiny clues we give away about ourselves: desire, fear, intention. We do this all the time, in crowds, pubs, offices, romantic relationships.

This is how we as people navigate social situations.

But consider this for a moment: if mirror neurons, coupled with synaesthesia and the Theory of Mind interlink, maybe, just maybe, empathetic people aren't simply attuned to the mind and emotions, but actually feel or see or hear them? Might this be actual telepathy?

Perhaps. Maybe the real question isn't if mind reading is possible, it's: are we already doing it without knowing we are?

That's it from me today, folks, but before I go, consider this: the next time you get a shiver of knowing something about someone, or that moment when a loved one's unspoken thoughts seem to echo in your own head, don't dismiss it.

Because maybe, just maybe, your brain, in its quiet, miraculous way… is listening.

I know this is some guy who is probably hosting from his parents' house without so much as a P or an H or a D anywhere in sight, but there's a bolt of possibility. That it's not completely out of the realm of possibility to question if Maggie could be telling the truth.

I shake my head and let out a long breath. I'm so desperate to believe her, that I'm trying to convince myself that the impossible is plausible.

I turn off the engine as the jingle runs, looking over to Levin's door, the blonde woman from next door waving a hand.

Christ, how did I get here? A year ago I was about to expand my business, get married. I knew my place in this world. And now I'm a guy sitting in his car listening to podcasts about hearing thoughts, who has to use Star Wars bubble wrap to find the letter J.

I've never felt so alone.

* * *

'Lick it,' Levin says pushing a green plate towards me.

'What?' I look up at him, his eyes peering over his thick glasses.

Levin rocks on his heels and points to the red squiggle in front of me.

'Lick it.'

'Why?'

'Jack, you need to trust me if you're going to make more progress; now lick the strawberry lace thingymebob.'

I hold my breath tightly, then exhale, bending down and tentatively licking the top part of the squiggle.

I stand back up. 'Now what?'

'I mean lick the whole thing. From tip' – he points to the top of the squiggle – 'to toe.'

I shake my head, but bend back over the table, running my tongue over the shape.

'Now tell me what letter it is.'

'I don't know, C?'

'No. Try again.'

I repeat the action, concentrating on the shape. 'Z?'

'Good. Again.'

My tongue is getting sore, the sugar is all gone and my tongue feels numb. He removes the strawberry lace and passes me a pen. 'Circle all the z's that you can find.' I look down to the symbols, the words that are vibrating on the page. I sit down, clutch the pen and run my finger along the symbols. And then the weirdest thing happens. I *taste* them. The z's. I can taste the strawberry, feel the sugar on my tongue.

And if I can taste letters then is it too far a stretch that Maggie believes she can—

'Nine out of fifteen. Excellent! Fancy a stroll?'

I don't have time to answer before he shrugs on his oversized mac that makes him look like he's wearing his older brother's hand-me-downs.

Levin leads me out to the back of his building. The space is small, but the sun is shining on the patch of green lawn. On it is a long blue blanket curved into a shape, like a river.

'I want you to concentrate on the blue shape, and while you do' – he pulls out a small white paper bag and shakes it at me – 'suck on this.'

I frown but take out a boiled sweet and put it in my mouth: lemon sherbet. The smell and taste immediately bring Maggie into mind. God, I miss her.

'Are you trying to give me a tooth cavity then tell me no pain no gain?'

'No.' He frowns, sucks on his own sweet. 'I want you to walk the letter, taste the lemon and tell me what letter you think this is.'

I dig my hands in my pockets and begin walking, following the shape. I repeat the journey five times from north to south, south to north.

'And? Tell me, what letter?'

'M.'

'No. Not even close. Try again.'

I sigh but give it another go. He gives me another sweet, tells me to concentrate on the cooling temperature, the colour of the leaves, the sound of my feet hitting the ground, the feel of the fabric beneath my boot. But all I see and think about is her.

'Still M,' I say. His busy eyebrows furrow. His arms fold and I can see he's trying to work out why I can't find the right letter.

'I think... I think it's the lemon. It, well' – I look to the sky, to the white clouds sliding past – 'it reminds me of someone.' The sherbet fizzes on my tongue and suddenly I'm back in Flicks, Maggie tucking her hair behind her ear, and flashing a grin at me.

'Oh?' he says, eyes sparking with excitement. 'Who?'

'A woman,' I say in a breath. 'She smells like lemons.'

'Righto. Your girlfriend?'

'Um, no. She never was, not really.' His face softens before he asks me her name.

'Ah that explains it!' He claps his hands, rubs them together and goes about manoeuvring the blue river. 'Try again.'

I do and I know in my stomach, that it's M. That the letter M tastes like lemon, and fresh air, blue skies, and it feels like happiness.

'M,' I say with a smile.

'M.' He grins.

We make our way back upstairs, another sheet placed in front of me, and this time, when he asks me to circle every 'm'. I get most of them correct.

I crick my neck from side to side as he files the sheet away.

'That's it for the reading for now. Over the next few weeks we're going to move on to more two-letter graphemes. I've got some nice tricks up my sleeves for those!' He stops, narrowing his eyes in concentration. 'You don't have a heart condition or a pacemaker, do you?'

'What? No.'

'Excellent, excellent.'

'Dare I ask why?'

'Just a little idea I had – you know those buzzers that clowns use?'

'You want to electrocute me?'

'No!'

'Phew.'

'It's a little static shock, that's all.'

I have no idea if he's joking or is actually serious. He shuffles the file of papers away and lands a blank piece of lined paper in front of me.

'Now... I want you to write a letter.'

I frown. I'm exhausted but I take the pen and paper. 'What do you want me to write?'

'What do *you* want to write? Go with the first thing that pops into your head.'

Maggie's face as she said goodbye. He must see something cross my face because his voice softens. 'I'm not going to read it, Jack, it's just for you. Think of the exercises we've been doing and let me know if the process has changed. It's to stretch that link between reading and writing.'

The pen hits the paper, my hands forming letters and punctuation. I know when to move to a new paragraph, when to leave a space.

'Dear Ma—' I stop, look up. 'I taste lemon.'

He nods, a slow smile popping a dimple beneath his beard, then moves away to the back of the room.

Dear Maggie,

My hand stills. This feels too big. Simply writing her name is making me admit that I'm not ready to let her go. *If* and this is a big *if*, she was telling the truth... how would she be feeling about the way I left things?

I have no idea if any of this will make sense on the page, but I'm hoping that Dr Levin is right and that all of these words are somehow buried deep inside my cortex.

I look over to the window, a siren going off in the distance. My senses jolt, the scar at the back of my head pulses. The words on the page are meaningless when I look back at them. The taste of lemon has gone. I rub my forehead, another headache beginning to form.

'That'll do for today.'

'I haven't finished...' I can hear the frustration in my voice.

'You can finish it on your own. It's lunchtime.'

'Oh. OK.' I fold the paper.

'Same time?'

'Um. Yeah. I'll be here.' I pull on my coat and head towards the door.

'Jack?'

'Hmmm?' I zip up my coat.

'Whoever Maggie is? Tell her you miss her. Life is too short and you never know when it can be taken away from you.'

I hesitate, my eyes following his to the wedding photo on the wall. I hadn't noticed that since visiting here, there has been no sign of a Mrs Levin.

'Thanks. I'll' – I clear my throat – 'see you next week?'

I close the door and head back to the car.

Maybe it doesn't matter if it's not real. The way I feel about her is.

And that might be enough.

* * *

The sea air whips around me as I sit across the road from Flicks. I'm working up the courage to go inside. Levin's words feel less convincing right now. I'm like Julia Roberts: I am just a man, sitting outside a cinema, waiting to ask a girl to, well, not love me, exactly, but give me another chance. To listen. To try to understand.

I check my watch. I've waited until the film will have started. Right now she will be eating popcorn and staring at the screen. I get up, the sky now dark above me. I take a moment, run a hand through my hair and step inside.

Romy looks up from inside the booth wearing cat's-eyes glasses. She blows a pink bubble, scratches her head with the tip of a fountain pen, her pencil-thin eyebrows raised as I make my approach. Her expression is curious but not confrontational. I wonder what, if anything, Maggie has told her.

'Hi.'

'Well, if it isn't the infamous Jack Chadwick,' she says, arms folded.

'I wondered if you could give this to Maggie?'

Romy leans back, her chair swinging from left to right. She moves forwards, mouth closer to the perforated glass. 'She's inside,' she explains through peach-glossed lips.

'I'm not here to interrupt her evening; I wanted her to have this.'

I look down at the cash slot, take out the letter.

She eyeballs me, long fluorescent fingernails reach out to take the envelope. I hold it tightly for a moment. 'It's... quite private.'

'I'm not going to open it or send it to the local rag to print, Jack.' My shoulders drop a touch. 'Shall I say who it's from?' she asks, all eyebrow arches and corrugated forehead.

'She'll know.'

'I'll see she gets it.' I nod my thanks and exit the building.

I follow my feet through the town, hands dug deep into my pockets. OK, Levin... let's see if you are as good as they say you are.

28

MAGGIE

I tear open the envelope, unfold the paper and rest it on the counter. Above is a poster of Sandra Bullock and Nicole Kidman's *Practical Magic* – tonight's film.

His handwriting is full of loops and swoops and I take a moment to let the implications of this land. This took a lot for him to do.

Dear Maggie,

I have no idea if any of this will make sense on the page, but I'm hoping that Dr Levin is right and that all of these words are somehow buried deep inside my cortex.

I smile; he's been to see Dr Levin. Jack's trying to read again.

I've been thinking about how to say what I want two to say but... I guess it boils down down to, I miss you. I miss sitting next to you and watching your face light up at the screen. I miss your laugh and the way your hair falls from behind your

*ears. I miss the way you sea see me. But must most of all, I
miss us.*

*I know things have moved quickly, and I know it's wrong to
feel this way about someone I've only known for a short time.
But I'm happiest when I'm with you.*

Help me understand.

Give us another chance.

We deserve that shot at a happy ever after.

Jack

I fold the letter over.

'What happened?' Romy prompts. 'With Jack?'

'I... tried to explain who I am and... It's a lot. *I'm* a lot. I mean, you've seen him. He deserves to have a girlfriend who he can at least touch for Christ's sake. Who would make his life easier. Not harder.'

His words circle my mind: *Help me understand. We deserve a shot at a happy ever after.*

'Look. I might be the last person on earth to give advice on dating and finding romantic love, but I know a thing or two about people. I saw the way you two were together and I've only seen that amount of chemistry on the screen. I spent my married life pretending to be someone I'm not, trying to force myself into a shape small enough to accommodate him. Now, I know who I am, I know what I like, and if I ever felt like dating someone other than myself then it will be on my terms with a partner who fits next to me without either of us having to bend.' She reaches out a hand then drops it. 'Show him who you are, Mags. But don't bend. You shouldn't ever need to pretend to be somebody else. Now, go.'

'But your date...'

'My date can wait.'

If I could, I would kiss her cheek.

* * *

The air is rich with the smell of seaweed, the salt in the sea mist already clinging to my hair as I scan the streets. I pull my pink fur around me, heading through side streets and along the narrow coastal road; to my right, the buildings lean forward like a crowd lining the streets to wave to an important visitor, each building different, some short and struggling to see beyond the taller forms. My lilac heels click as I make my way through town, until I see the creamy apricot light spilling out onto the kerb. I slow down and catch my breath.

It's time I stopped running away from a chance of happiness.

29

MAGGIE

The warmth wraps around me as I step inside, the bell above the door announcing my arrival.

The book club is in full swing, the semicircle of readers all throwing their opinions around, copies of the book in their hands. Conversations trail off, like the final bars of a song. Eyes all focus on me.

'Hello?' I say. Nell turns her head, stands, the booklovers throwing smiles and awkward glances. 'I'm' – my voice cracks – 'I'm looking for Jack?'

Jack strides into the room, his arms filled with books, chin resting on top. 'So I have the red one, the first in the series, and the green, which I think is the second but I don't have the—' He looks up, his steps slowing.

'Hi,' I say with a smile.

He lowers the stack of books onto the table, his hand splayed on the cover. 'Hi.'

'I... I got your letter.' Nell's eyebrows raise in Jack's direction. His eyes flash briefly to hers, then he treads slowly towards me. I can feel the group taking in the scene, looks of curiosity and tenderness. 'Thank you.'

He digs his hands into his pockets. 'You're welcome.'

'I'm sorry—' we both begin.

'Can we talk?' I ask quietly. Despite the warmth, I'm shaking.

He nods. 'We can go outside or, or... my flat is upstairs?' My heart trips at the hopeful tilt to his voice.

'Your place would be great.' He turns, leading the way, stopping to move a few chairs, clearing a path. I trail a few steps behind him. Nell catches my eye. She's on guard, a mother bear in a Minnie Mouse dress and black eyeliner. I look down and pull my arms closer to my torso. There is enough space for me to pass the group without touching them, but I keep my distance as much as I can. Jack holds open the door for me, his arm high above my head. The door swings heavily behind me, the voices behind coming back to life in a rush.

The walls of the hallway are an expensive dusky emerald green, the type you'd find in a stately home or an Oak Furniture Land ad. I follow Jack along the black-and-white-tiled floor, my hand skirting the banister that twists upwards in old dark wood.

I climb the three flights of stairs, two behind Jack. Along the walls are framed book covers: *Sense and Sensibility*, *Dracula*, *Great Expectations*, *Brideshead Revisited*, *Rebecca*, *Wuthering Heights*. At the top: *Pride and Prejudice*.

'It's through here,' Jack says turning the doorknob and stepping inside. I recognise the warm smell from the blanket I'd had wrapped around me the night at the fountain, something comforting like vanilla and nutmeg. He flicks on the lights. The large room is almost circular, the bay window split into three tall sections, dark oak shutters drawn over them.

'Wow. I'm guessing you have a view of the sea from here?'

He steps forwards, folding back the shutters. 'You can see better if I—'

He walks back to the light switch, flicking it off. Below, I can see the rooftops of the town and beyond, the lights from the harbour shimmer around the bay, a semicircle of life etched out against the night sky. The moon is hanging low, the edge of the world rolling towards us. I step closer to the glass.

'All you can see from my window is the back of a supermarket and wheelie bins. Oh, and Harrowsby Bay's answer to Banksy. Most mornings I have a new update on whether Dec and Carly are made for each other.'

Jack bends down to the fireplace on my right, striking a match, blowing gently at the flickering flame. A large brown leather chair sits in the left corner of the room, a reading lamp casting a soft light above it. There is a jumper hanging over the back and a cardboard box sitting in it.

Jack stands, hands in his back pockets. The fire spits, flames beginning to brighten the room. 'Would you like a drink?'

'Um, sure. Yes, please.'

'Do you want to sit?' He hurries across the room, picking up the box, a reel of bubble wrap sticking out of the top. 'I'll just—' He opens another door, disappearing from the room, returning with empty arms. 'Tea? Coffee? Or I've got some wine? Or a beer?'

'Tea would be great, thanks.' He nods, opens another door and disappears through, the sound of the kettle being filled punctuates the quiet. I walk over to the bookshelves lining the recessed walls either side of the fireplace, most of the spines facing the wrong way, but there are about ten facing front. If I didn't know the reason why, I'd think the décor was kind of cool, but seeing the books that Jack loves so much with their backs turned to him, hurts.

There is a record player sitting on a low box chest, vinyl records slotted neatly into the spaces below. I look down at the turntable: Bob Dylan's *The Times They Are a-Changin'* album.

'I love this album,' I say as he returns, placing two mugs on the table. He joins me. 'Really?'

'Yeah. One of my earlier foster carers used to play it on Sunday mornings. She'd let me help make French toast with ginger and marmalade. I was only with her for autumn. Then I was back in the home. She was kind to me... while I was with her.' Above the record player are a handful of photos, all different frames. I spot a red-headed girl, a man and woman with their arms around each other, heads thrown back in laughter.

'It must have been hard, moving from place to place?' Jack says joining me.

'Sometimes, but I kind of got used to it. And I got to meet interesting people, living different lives. Is this your family?'

He lifts the needle.

'Yep.' He smiles over his shoulder. 'Times They Are a-Changin'' begins.

He stands by my side as I move from frame to frame. 'That's Mum and Dad; this is my sister' – he points to the redhead, glass of wine raised in a toast with a pool in the background – 'Charlotte and that's George.' He nods towards a thinner blond with the same grin as Jack. He's dressed as Einstein. Jack stands with his arms thrown around his shoulders wearing pyjamas.

'Who are you dressed as?'

'Arthur Dent from...' He walks over to the books, eyes alight, fingers raised. He stops still, hand opening and closing like he's got cramp. Sadness and regret expands in my stomach. For that tiny moment where he seems to have forgotten that he can no longer read, can no longer see the names of the books he loves so much. 'From *Hitchhiker's Guide to the Galaxy*,' he continues, then clears his throat.

'These are the shiners...' He moves the conversation forwards, glossing over the pain that has flickered across his face.

'The shiners?'

'My nieces... one night I was babysitting and the pair of them had heard a noise and were standing at the top of the stairs like that scene out of *The Shining*. They almost gave me a heart attack.' He taps each one with his fingers. 'Jaz and Greta.'

My eyes are wide as I take them all in. His relaxed frame is back as he talks about them each in turn, their likes and dislikes.

'You have a wonderful family,' I say.

There is a photo of all of them sitting on the kind of wrap-around porches that I've seen in American movies. He gestures to the sofa and sits opposite in the reading chair. I take my tea in my hand, lifting it to my mouth.

The fire spits. Bob Dylan's harmonica plays in the background. Jack places his mug onto the table with a soft clunk. 'I've been thinking,' he begins. 'About that night... about the things you said.'

I look up at him, my throat dry, my body braced to accept his rejection.

'I...' He scratches beneath his eye. 'I didn't know how to even begin to understand. At first I thought you were scared of getting close and that you came up with a line so bizarre that I'd have no choice but to bolt.' He scrubs the side of his jaw with his knuckles. 'I could have handled it better.'

I shake my head, putting the cup back down. 'I told you I can hear thoughts. I'm surprised you didn't leg it, to be honest.' I rummage in my satchel, pulling out the letter and placing it next to my mug. 'This was a lovely thing to do, Jack. Nobody has ever written me a letter. Well, not one that doesn't ask me to pay my bill already. They're pretty rare aren't they, these days? It was really special.'

He looks across at me. Dark eyes burning. 'You're rare. You're special. I wanted you to know that.' He indicates the space beside me. 'May I?' I nod, my heart speeding up. He sits on the other side of the sofa, eyes meeting mine. 'After you left, I didn't know how to feel. I thought I'd misunderstood, or... or that you were, I don't know...'

'Crazy?'

'No, not anything like that. I was trying to make sense of why you would say something like that.' His throat bobs. 'I guess I was trying to work out why you would think that was the truth. And then I couldn't stop thinking about it, or you. I've... been doing some research.' He scrubs his hand over his mouth as though he wants to rub the words away.

'Research?'

'Yeah, podcasts and such... There's quite a lot out there when you start digging... about empaths and brain science and...'

There is a rush of something like hope. Like the moment the curtains pull back in front of the screen at Flicks, where there is the promise of something new about to unfold. All my life I've hidden my ability, kept it a secret, like Grandma had told me to all those years ago and here he is. Trying to believe me.

'You *believe* me?'

'I... I'm hoping to. I want to understand.' He tilts his head. 'Tell me more about how it works. If I touch you, will you be able to hear everything about my life?'

I shake my head, dragging my eyes up to meet his. He has no idea what this means to me, that he's trying to find a way to see the real me.

'No, not everything, just what you're thinking in that moment. Sometimes, if you're more emotional, I can see thoughts too, but that doesn't happen often. It's hard to explain, but I... I can prove it to you.'

He frowns, a line forming between his eyebrows.

'If you'd like? I can show you.'

He chews the inside of his cheek, looks away then gives me a small nod. 'OK.'

'You're sure?'

'Yeah. I'm sure.'

'Picture a place that only you know about, focus on a specific detail and describe it, like you're writing it all down. Repeat it a few times so that is the *only* thing you're thinking about.'

His eyes cast around the room as he thinks, looking up at the ceiling then back to me, a small knot of worry knitted in the corner of his mouth.

'Ready?'

He nods. 'As I'll ever be.'

I take a moment to calm my breathing, then tentatively, I reach out and cup the side of his face. The bristles of his stubble scrape against the palm of my hand. He closes his eyes as his voice rings out, clear, slightly nervous.

It's small and dark. Coats and boots are scattered on the floor.
I can smell lilac.
In my hands is a book.
The Lion, the Witch and the Wardrobe.
Please let this be real. I don't want to lose her agai—

I drop my hand and shift back as he opens his eyes, searching my face.

'It's a small dark place. It smells like lilac and you're reading a book.' His eyes widen, his expression somewhere between impressed and scared to death.

'What book?'

'*The Lion, the Witch and the Wardrobe*,' I say gently.

The colour drains from his face. And I know he's scared. The truth is too much.

'Jesus.' He flops back on the sofa.

'Nope.' I shrug. 'Just me.'

He drags his hand through his hair, his cheeks flushed. We're quiet for a minute.

'When, I mean, how did it start?'

I tell him about my parents dying, being placed in my grandma's care, the day I first remember hearing her thoughts, how they didn't match the words coming out of her mouth. I tell him about the foster homes, about Tess and Hellie, and all the while Jack listens.

'It must have been so hard for you.'

'It was. In the beginning. I've tried to have relationships, to live a normal life, but it's hard to be around people when I can hear their most private thoughts. It's not fair on them either. So that's why I've chosen to distance myself. As best I can.'

'Hence the gloves.'

'Yep.'

'That first night, when we were trying to open the fire exit... did you hear anything from me?'

I hesitate then nod. 'It was more of an impression, a lot of things pressed together. I knew that things had been tough for you, that you felt you'd lost something important. That you didn't feel whole, somehow. I wanted to help.'

He links his hands and taps his thumbs together.

'And Luke? Did you know it was him?'

'Yes.' The word comes out quietly, like an exhalation.

'I don't know how to feel about that.'

'I wish I could have told you straight away, but I wasn't sure.

Not at first and I...' I meet his eyes, my face heating. 'I liked you so *much*, Jack. And I thought that maybe, if you got to know me first... that maybe you would give me a chance. *Me*. Not this weirdo who can know *everything* about you, anytime I want. And that's why I said we should be friends. I didn't want to—'

'You could have touched me anytime.'

I look up slowly.

'Why didn't you?' he asks, head angled to the left as I consider my reply.

'Because it's an intrusion.' His eyebrows gather. 'I didn't have your consent.'

He leans towards me. I let him come as close as he wants. For the first time, this is his choice not mine. But still I'm convinced he's going to end things, that he's going to ask me to leave and wish me well. And I can't let that happen before I help him find the answers to move on with his life.

'Jack? I...' I look into those brown eyes. 'I want to help you.'

He frowns.

'Help you remember what happened, after you came out of the pub?'

'I'm not sure I want you to—'

'Never mind,' I say briskly. 'It was just an idea.'

He rushes on. 'It's not that I don't trust you. I suppose I'm afraid of what I might find.'

'So let me find it with you,' I say, my voice quiet. 'You don't have to do it alone. And if you want me to stop touching you, just say, and I will.'

He exhales loudly.

'No pressure. It's your choice.'

He pauses, as though considering if this might be a really bad idea, but then the words fall from his mouth.

'OK. It's worth a shot.'

I lay out my hand, palm side up. Jack looks down, then tentatively takes my hand in his.

'Close your eyes,' I say gently. 'Go to the clearest images you have of that night.'

His thoughts are hazy, shrouded in mist and shadow.

I'm inside the pub.
Standing at the bar.

I see Jack knock back a shot; say goodbye to a man, *Steve*, and I walk beside him as he exits the pub.

Mist swirls in places where buildings should be, all of it filled with blank spaces and shadows, in blacks and greys.

I see the couple arguing.
You're hidden from my view.

There is an image of a phone screen, where letters should be there are symbols, and beneath, the vibration of Jack's frustration.

Luke's face comes next.

'This is a little clearer since meeting him,' Jack says, but his voice feels distant; I'm deep in his thoughts, right there with him.

I feel the contact as Jack bumps into him, hear Luke telling me to watch it and a muttered curse.

His concentration is back on the phone in his hand now, fingers about to type but not quite hitting the screen. Then there is nothing but shadows. But there is something there, in his periphery.

'Look across the road,' I say.

His focus shifts, more shadows, but something darker, something that moves and an overwhelming feeling of...

Something's not right.
There's someone there.

There is a bolt of pain. I take my hand away. Jack's eyes flash open, blinking like he's parted the curtains and it takes him a moment to adjust to the light.

'Are you OK?' I ask.

He looks off to the distance, eyes scanning as he thinks. 'It was... different.' His focus back on me. 'Like you were there somehow?' He pauses, trying to put into words what has just happened. 'And not being alone, made me less... afraid, I guess?'

'There was someone else there, someone in the shadows?' I lean forwards.

He nods. 'Something was wrong; I could feel it. A threat? But it...'

'Wasn't a threat to you,' I finish.

'Exactly. I think... maybe I was trying to stop something from happening.'

'What?'

He shakes his head. 'I have no idea.'

30

MAGGIE

Jack pours us both a glass of whisky, the smoky liquid easing some of the tension. We talk about what could have happened next. He asks me more about my life, and tells me about his break-up with Vicky. There is an ease to our conversation now. We're sitting so close. My feet tucked under me, Jack's arm across the back of the sofa.

'So where do we go from here?' he asks.

'I don't know. Maybe go back to the pub? Ask around? Or ask the police to check out CCTV again?'

He smiles slowly. 'I meant... about us.'

The air shifts as we look at each other, conversation falling away.

'We all need our secrets, Jack. I'd hear your doubts, your worries... things you don't even realise you're thinking.' My voice comes out in a whisper. 'Our private thoughts should always only belong to us. That's why this can never work.'

He moves closer still, our faces a few centimetres apart. 'What if I don't want to hide anything from you?'

I take a beat. 'I've never wanted to touch anyone more than I want to touch you, Jack. God how I've wanted to. I've never wanted to kiss anyone as much as I want to kiss you. Be held by you. But I can't. You'd never have space, privacy. If I wanted, I could know everything about you, whenever I want. You'd never be able to hide anything.'

'But still, even though you were locked inside a building overnight, even though I was a stranger, you didn't.'

'No.'

'If I give you my permission, would you let me kiss you?' His voice is quiet, deep, eyes lifting to mine.

I should say no.

But no words come out.

Jack's hand moves towards my hair, he hesitates, letting it fall away. The warmth from his skin skates along my arms.

He's even closer now; I can smell the warm earthy scent of whisky on his breath. I tighten every muscle in my body; the slightest flicker of movement could undo us. His forehead dips towards mine. This close I can see sparks of amber amongst the brown of his eyes. I swallow, unsure of opening or closing my mouth. 'You have to be sure this is what you want.' My voice is hoarse, my whole body shaking.

His eyesight follows his hand as he reaches for my hair. 'I'm sure.' He takes a lock, and curls it around his index finger. His thoughts are gentle, quiet. He hasn't touched my skin yet but my whole body is yearning for more. He tucks it behind my ear.

One, two, three.

He lets out a low laugh, the sound close enough to my ear to send goosebumps running along the right side of my body.

Always three seconds.

'What's always three seconds?' I ask, my voice scratchy, my breathing erratic. He brings his focus back to me, eyes widening.

'You heard that?'

He takes a moment. Looks deeply into my eyes.

'Your hair, it always falls back from behind your ear in three seconds.'

'It does?'

He nods. 'Is this OK?' He reaches for it again.

'Ye... yes.'

He smiles. 'And this?' He moves closer, our noses almost touching.

'Mmmhmmm.'

'Tell me to stop if you need me to.'

'Same,' I say. 'If you've got any weird foot fetishes... now's the time to tell me.'

He smiles, our mouths are millimetres away from each other, then there is the faintest touch as his lips brush across mine. It's delicate, light but heat rushes through me.

> Take it slow.
> Take it slow.
> Take it slow.

He pulls back. My hand lifts to the back of his neck, not touching but ready.

'Should I stop?' he asks.

'No.' My voice sounds like it belongs to someone else, low, sultry.

'How about now?' He runs the back of his hand along the curve of my cheek and I lean into his touch.

> So beautiful.

The depth of his true feelings for me shimmers in his voice. I've never felt more beautiful. There's a flicker of fear. I can't tell if it belongs to me or him. Because if we don't stop, there is no going back. I open my eyes, my gaze drawn back to his mouth curving upwards.

'What can you hear?'

'That you want to take it slow,' I reply my voice hitching. 'That I'm beautiful.' I should feel embarrassed saying it, but there is only honesty between us now.

His eyebrows rise a fraction as he begins to steer his way through the landscape of my condition.

He turns his hand over and I lean my face into his palm and I'm hit with desire, with heat, with tenderness.

'It's hard to differentiate your thoughts from mine.'

Can you hear this?
Can you hear how much I want to kiss you again?

'Yes.' His gaze slides down to my mouth. He runs his thumb over the swell of my bottom lip.

I haven't been able to stop thinking about you.

'I can't stop thinking about you either.' He leans in, so close that we're breathing the same breath.

'Can I—' I swallow. 'Can I touch you?'

'You don't need to ask.' He drops his thumb, moves closer still. I pull back a touch, eyes scouring his. 'I *always* need your consent, Jack.'

'Then, yes. I want you to.' I let my hand find the back of his neck, warm, the tendons strong, his pulse fast. I grab onto his hair as his mouth presses onto mine. Our thoughts clamber over each other:

Oh God

I've never felt anything—

Like—

This.

Emotions explode through my whole body, the hot need of arousal, tenderness, urgency. I can't work out whose thoughts are whose. His tongue flicks against mine, awakening my whole body. I let out a small groan; my hand pulls his hair, his body closer.

Slow. Down.

He pulls back, his eyes hooded, dark eyes almost black but searching that I'm still OK.

'I've waited for my whole life to be kissed like this,' I reassure him.

'Same.'

I wrap my arms around his neck. All thoughts of taking things slowly have left both our minds.

We're lost in each other... and it's some kind of wonderful.

31

FRIDAY 8TH NOVEMBER

Jack

'So, what did you think of the film?' Maggie asks, toggling up her coat before punching in the code and locking the doors. 'Beautiful, isn't it?'

'It wasn't what I was expecting, when you said Adam Sandler I was expecting something more, I don't know...'

'Goofy?'

I laugh. 'It's an interesting dilemma, isn't it? How, for her, each of their fifty dates are first dates and yet for him, he's falling deeper and deeper in love. It's a great hook.'

In all honesty, though, my mind hasn't been on the film, it's been on the way that Maggie has started to let her guard down around me. We haven't touched since last week but there has been a lowering of her barriers. To an outsider, Maggie sitting straight, rather than leaning away, wouldn't even be a footnote in an observer's recollection, but this is a big step for her. For us.

'I love that even though she'll never be able to remember him properly, he sacrifices a normal relationship because he loves her so much.'

I don't miss the hope in her voice and I wonder if she asked Romy to play this film this week, so I could see how our relationship could work. It's timely, that's for sure. And if I'm being honest, I have been having... not doubts exactly, but I do wonder how this could work in the long term. I could never keep anything from her. I'm jumping ahead though. All I know is that it's working. That I'm happy. And that's enough, for now.

She stops, bends down and untangles the bottom of her skirt, which has snagged on the top of her boots.

We begin walking towards the White Lion, having figured going on a Friday night might give us more of a chance of finding out if anyone was there that night. But as we approach, Maggie tenses. The pub is packed. A football match must have finished, going by the sport shirts and people holding pints spilling out onto the kerb.

'I...' Maggie looks over. 'I can't go in there, Jack. Drunk thoughts are so unfiltered...'

I turn to her. 'We'll come back another time.'

'No!' she says. Despite her reservations, there is a gleam of encouragement in her voice. 'This is good. Someone might know something. This is the perfect time.' She nods to a bench across the road. 'I'll wait here.'

I hesitate.

'I'll be fine.'

I look to the pub, the Tudor frontage, the white lion rearing up on the sign swinging in the breeze.

'Shoo!' She wafts me away with a grin.

'I'll be five minutes.'

'Ten,' she challenges. 'Ask as many people as you can.' She pulls out her phone and wiggles it. 'I've got the Kindle app; I'll carry on with *The Girl on the Train*.' She pauses, looks up at me, almost embarrassed. 'Can I kiss you good luck?'

I smile and lean in, her mouth meeting mine briefly, lips soft and smiling.

'Now go!'

The air is warm inside, filled with the smell of perfume and beer, a loud cheer as a glass smashes to the floor. Conversations noisy and theatrical. She was right not to come in.

I shoulder my way through the bar. 'What can I get you?' the bartender asks through his perfectly groomed beard, his tattooed arm pulling a pint.

I order a Heineken Zero, even though I know I won't be staying, and broach the subject of the night that changed my life.

'Sorry, mate, I barely remember last Friday let alone a year ago.'

'Are there any regulars? Smokers who might have seen something?'

'There's Frank?' He nods over to a man sitting in the corner, weathered skin, blue woolly hat pulled over his ears. 'Frank!' he bellows. 'Fella wants a word!'

'Cheers,' I say, tapping my card as Frank makes his way through the throng.

I put out my hand. 'Jack.'

'What can I do you for, Jack?'

I explain what happened and ask if he remembers that night. 'Anything at all might help,' I prompt as the creases in his forehead furrow. 'Sorry, lad, nothing springs to mind.'

'Not to worry, it was a long shot. But if you do remember anything, could you give me a call?' I ask the barman for a piece of paper and a pen and scribble down what I hope is my name and number.

'Will do. Good luck, I hope you find the answers you're looking for.'

I ask a few more people, but no dice, and exit the pub scanning the bench to where Maggie is sitting, pink fur collar pulled up against the cooling sea air.

'Hey.' She smiles looking up and pocketing her phone. 'Anything?'

'Nope,' I say with a sigh.

Her shoulders slump. 'I've been googling the newspapers again. There was a robbery that night but that was a few towns over.'

I'm hit again by how much that means to me, that she would sit outside in the cold, trying to help me find the answers I need. My stomach rumbles.

'Fancy grabbing something to eat? There's a place not far. It's usually quiet...'

A siren goes off in the distance, a fire engine or ambulance. Flashes of memory fire into my subconscious: blue lights, someone asking what my name is, then a flash of something red. Red hair. Long and flowing, caught on the air. I look across the road, a deep groove forming between my eyes.

'I think I remember something.' I'm still, eyes darting to the left and right, my face tight in concentration. I take slow steps. Forward then backwards, eyes scanning the dark road opposite.

'Jack?'

I crouch down, leaning my head to the left, narrowing my eyes, viewing the street from a different perspective. 'I think...' I stand back up, hand rubbing across my mouth. 'There was a woman. With long red hair. Up ahead of me. I might be wrong but... it's something?' My voice is hopeful but edged with doubt.

'Where?' Maggie steps towards me.

'I don't know... She had long red hair, bright, like fire engine red. It was blowing out behind her.'

'Maybe you hooked up with someone?'

I laugh, shake my head, holding up my hand and tapping my ring finger. 'I was engaged, remember?'

'Right. Yeah, sorry. Anything else?'

I shake my head. 'No. That's it.'

'Should we go to the police? They might reopen your case?'

'Maybe? Let's wait until I have something more solid. Let's go eat. I can't think on an empty stomach.'

I lead us towards the American Diner in town: red leather stools along the bar, separate booths, jukebox that only stocks fifties music. I think Maggie will appreciate the vibe.

'May I?' I hold out my hand. She hesitates, looking down.

'You may, just...' She pulls out a pair of gloves from her pocket. They're mittens, a rainbow of colours. She glances at me, pulls her bottom lip with her teeth then pockets them.

Our hands meet and I focus on keeping my thoughts as neutral as possible. She bursts out laughing and drops my hand.

'What?'

'You're trying to block me by singing about my milkshake bringing all the boys to the yaaaaard?'

'Shit. Sorry. I have no idea why I'm thinking that.'

'I do. You're taking me to the American Diner?'

'Well, bang goes my surprise.'

A look of hurt flashes across her face before she replaces it with a smile. But I'm reminded of how tricky it will be, for us to have a future, for me to keep even the smallest secret from her. 'It's still a surprise to me. Let's pretend you've told me instead of thinking about it?'

'I can do that. So, Maggie' – I swing her hand in mine – 'I

thought I'd take you to the American Diner in town? They do incredible banana milkshakes.'

'That sounds like a great idea, Jack!' We laugh but she drops my hand and tucks it back into her jacket pocket. 'How did your session with Dr Levin go?'

'Good. I mean, I now hate the letter K with a passion but...'

'How come?'

'He made me eat liquorice while shaping it out of playdough. There is method in his madness though, but even though I'm making progress, it's...' I let out a breath. 'It's hard, you know?'

'And the shop?'

'I...' I think of the subletting offer I've received and the pain I felt once I'd used the read-aloud function. The hour it took to write a response that's still not finished.

'I'm not sure if I can, even with the progress I'm making. I'm afraid of making a twat of myself on a daily basis if I go ahead. Watch out!' My arm instinctively reaches out to help her avoid the huge pothole filled with last night's rain, and instead of gallantly helping her across the puddle, her instinct to avoid my hand has sent her falling into it.

'Well, crap!' She looks up at me, her body sitting on the road, hands slapping down into the water. We both begin laughing. I want to help her up, but she shakes her head.

'Shit, I'm sorry.' I try to say the words but we're both laughing so hard that my words barely make a dent in the atmosphere. She waves away my apology instead flexing the tips of her purple boots back and forth like she's sunk into a bubble bath rather than a metre-long crack in the tarmac. Our laughter dies away as she folds her legs and begins to stand, redundantly brushing down her clothes.

'See? You're worried about looking like a fool trying to recover from a stroke and look at the mess I'm in!'

'Here.' I take off my coat, but she shakes her head.

'There's no point in both of us being soaked.' She looks over to the other side of the street at a bus trundling towards the stop. 'I can't go for dinner like this. Fancy coming back to mine? I need to change.' She gestures to her clothes, nodding towards the bus.

'Yeah. I'd like that.' We run across the road and I raise my hand, hailing the bus. Maggie hesitates, eyes scanning the windows. It's empty save for a couple of teenagers locked face to face on the back seat. I step back to allow her to take a seat and go to sit next to her. She shakes her head in warning. The space is too small. I take a seat on the opposite side of the aisle. The humour and laughter is falling off Maggie, eyes trained on the window and the street passing us by. She turns back to me, a brave smile in place, but there is a sadness there. We don't talk for a while, the reality of our relationship standing between us like an extra passenger. Could this ever work? Eventually she smiles, reaches for the bell. 'This is my stop, but it's late, Jack, so if you want to go home, I—'

'I'm not tired. Unless... you want me to go?'

She inhales deeply, pulls at the cuffs of her sodden coat, chews on her nail then gives her head the briefest of shakes.

We discuss the film. The ease of before feels more constricted as we walk down her narrow street. There is a change in the air. Maggie is becoming quieter, her laughter more controlled. She gestures towards a green door. It's unassuming, but there is a charm to it, potted plants hanging overhead: glimmers of colour on a dark road.

'This is me,' she says, but the words sound overly bright. She wiggles the key, her movements taut, her shoulders tense as she takes off her coat and clicks on the lights.

'It's not as impressive as your place but' – she has her arms wrapped around her as she looks around – 'it's home.'

'I love it. It's very—'

'Cluttered?'

'You.'

'Is that a good thing?' she asks, self-conscious.

'Of course.'

'And this must be Bruce?' I bend down and peer into the fish tank. Bruce lets out a bubble as though saying hello.

'He likes you.' Maggie smiles. 'I'll be back in a sec. I need to...' She pulls at her tights. 'The kitchen is through there... Can you stick the kettle on?' She turns and rushes towards the bedroom.

The kitchen is small. Baby-blue cupboards, more plants, scented candles, spotlessly clean. I fill the kettle and look for the teabags. I open the cupboards. They're empty but for a few essentials: a bag of oats, pasta, tinned cans without pictures but stripes and words. I look for teabags, finding different sized and shaped canisters, one pink, one white, the other a dark green with gold writing on. I reach out, fingering the first symbol, hearing an echo of Bob Dylan.

C   □ ↗ ↗ ♎ ♎

Maggie moves around at the back of the flat, the floorboards creaking quickly. I prise open the container; there are a few grains of instant coffee. I think to my own, and to my parents' house, where the cupboards are packed with oils and herbs, with condiments of every variety. Behind the pasta is a plastic tub, filled with packets of instant noodles.

'Sorry!' She rushes in. 'I haven't had chance to go shopping,' she says briskly, opening the fridge and grabbing a handful of mini milk cartons like the ones at my shop and places them on the counter. She opens a cupboard door, takes out a ziplock bag with sachets of coffee inside and holds them in her teeth while grabbing two mismatched mugs and landing them beside the kettle. I step aside. 'Are you hungry?' she asks, brow furrowing. 'I can heat up a tin of soup?'

'How about a takeaway?' I ask. 'My treat?' Her shoulders drop and she leans her back against the fridge.

'I...'

'I was going to take you out for dinner and despite my mother's suggestion that I should always allow a woman to go Dutch, I'm afraid I have too much of my father in me.'

'You don't have to do that.' Her voice is quiet.

'I know. But seriously, I could kill for a pizza right now.' I tilt my head, examining her response.

'Deal, but I'm not letting you pay.'

I open my mouth to protest but she turns her back and opens a drawer, passing me a coupon.

'Sorry... I can't...' I squint at the paper in front of me.

'Sorry.' She points to the words with lilac-varnished nails. 'Two for one. You buy your pizza and I'll have the free one?'

'Deal.'

I go to put out my hands to shake hers but she looks down and we both begin to laugh.

'Jesus, what a couple!' I say. Her laughter falls away as she looks at me.

I'm about to step closer. The word 'couple' is hanging in the air.

But the power cuts out, the room suddenly in darkness.

'Oh shit. Just... wait there. Don't. Move.' There is an edge of panic to her voice. I stand still, wanting to help, but I think this is one of the times I need to give Maggie space.

I hear the sound of drawers being opened, the scratch of a match. Maggie's face lights up above the glow of a candle, her expression tight. She places it down on the kitchen side, doesn't meet my eyes, but the soft light casting shadows around the room makes everything feel that much more precarious. Maggie retreats to the lounge. After a few minutes, she shouts that I can come through.

The room is now lit up, candles casting a soft light from a motley collection in various places around the room. 'Take a seat.' She gestures to the sofa. 'I'll make the drinks before the water goes cold.'

The room is small, only the sofa to sit on. I perch on one end, my body sinking into the fabric. 'Oh!' She stops still. 'Be careful – there's a rogue spring that might bite you in the bum. That's a better spot.' She indicates to the right. I shift as she places the cup on the floor and folds herself onto the rug, legs crossed, blowing over the rim. 'It's decaf, sorry.'

'It seems we're destined to spend our time together during power cuts.' She doesn't say anything, just takes a sip, eyes on mine. 'It's a good job you have so many candles.'

'Yeah. It's... it's a regular occurrence here.'

'Really?'

She nods, shifts her body and stretches out her legs. 'I don't mind. Sometimes it's good to have quiet, you know?'

'I do. That's what I miss the most about reading. The quiet. The way you can shut off your own world, your own thoughts, how you can travel the world, take yourself to somewhere new, with people who are interesting with their own stories to tell. Far, far away from your own life, your own troubles.'

'Would you—' She hesitates. 'Would you like me to read to you?'

My heart quickens. I've not even had the guts to listen to an audiobook in months but as I look at her, I can feel a yearning that I haven't felt for a long time, like a knot unwinding.

'I'd really like that.'

She smiles and gets up. 'Right then, you order the pizza, and I'll go and see what I can find.'

I take out my phone, speak into the search engine and order. I throw in some cookies and mozzarella sticks too then warm my hands around the cup. The temperature is dropping quickly. I get up, pull back the curtains and look along the street. Lights glowing opposite, no sign of a power cut except here. I frown, notice the radiators, the thermostat dial on the wall. I can't read the numbers but can see it's set to low. I look at the many DVDs lined up around the TV, leaning in to pull a few out. A red light behind the TV flickers on and off. An electric meter, similar to one in my student house. There's a sinking feeling in the pit of my stomach. This isn't a power cut.

I look to a jam jar filled with coins on one of the shelves amongst the DVDs and knick-knacks; a label I can't read explaining the contents. I think of the cupboards, the sachets of coffee and individual milk cartons. The way Maggie devours her popcorn. There are blankets on the sofa, and next to a bag of knitting is a pair of fingerless gloves.

The weight of the reality of this 'power cut' hits me hard, my stomach tightening as I look around.

I want to help. I want to pay for her electric, her heating, take her shopping, help her in some way, any way that would make her life easier. But I know her. She wouldn't accept help, even if it's from someone who already cares deeply about her.

Could I insist? I push the thought immediately away. This

isn't about the empty meter and stark cupboards, this is about her self-respect. I won't cross any line that could jeopardise that.

'I don't have many, but I did buy *The Great Gatsby* in the charity shop down the road? I love Baz Luhrmann. Shit it's freezing, just a sec—' She disappears again and pushes in an old portable gas heater like the one my grampa had in his potting shed. 'I keep this for emergencies,' she says. 'There's not much in the tank but it'll take the edge off.' She goes about lighting it. There is a knock on the door. I take the pizzas, arranging the boxes on the floor, next to where Maggie was sitting, and fold myself opposite.

The awkwardness has dissipated now, as if we can understand each other without words.

Vicky was always a fan of grand gestures and perfectly curated 'Insta-perfect moments', but in this small room, with the soft glow of candles, it's like we've created a safe place, just for us, protected from the pressures of the world outside.

And it's perfect.

32

MAGGIE

'So, who are your pen pals?' Jack asks, covering his mouth as he speaks, eyes on the postcards above the sofa. I turn my head, looking at them.

'No pen pals.' I smile. 'Just a hobby. I sometimes clean houses before estate sales. I found a stack of them in the bin, and it felt wrong to get rid of them.' I reach out and unstick one from above the sofa. 'This is my favourite: New York in winter.' I turn the card over: '*Wish you were here, L.*'

'Have you ever been?'

'To New York?' I laugh and shake my head. 'No.' I change the subject because the truth is, I will never be able to go. 'Too many people, too many thoughts. You?'

'Once or twice. But not for a while.'

He tells me about Central Park, about Macy's at Christmas, about the Empire State Building, which leads me on to *Sleepless in Seattle* and *An Affair to Remember*. 'I shouldn't have had that third slice,' I say rubbing my full stomach. 'And the cookie.'

Jack folds the lid over the leftovers. 'I'll put the rest in the fridge. Breakfast of champions,' he adds over his shoulder as he heads into the kitchen.

I reach over, flapping the book when he sits down on the sofa. 'Ready?'

'When you are.'

'I'm not the best reader...' I begin and wince at my lack of tact.

'Makes two of us.'

'Sorry.'

'You don't have to do that, you know.' He pulls at his earlobe, shifts the cushion behind him. 'It's one of the things I like; you say what's on your mind.'

'Well, I like to even the playing field.' Christ it feels good to be able to say things like that to him. I smile over, then look down at the page. 'In my younger and more vulnerable years...' I begin. Jack leans back, his head tilted and a slow smile easing across his face as I read. As I near the end of the first chapter my back is starting to ache and I crick my neck.

Jack stretches his arm along the sofa. 'Would you like to...' He rubs his hand across his mouth. 'Shit, I can't think of a better way to say this, and I hate this word, but cuddle?' I snort, he's practically squirming as he says the word.

'I'd... yes. I think I would quite like to "cuddle". Promise me, you'll say if you need space though?'

'You mean if I start thinking inappropriate thoughts about what I would like to do to you?'

Heat rushes over my skin.

'You're blushing,' he says, looking at me with a mixture of desire and amusement. 'I promise to try and keep my mind on Gatsby.'

'You might not be able to.'

'Given the way I feel about you, Maggie, I doubt that too.' He shifts and I ease myself beside him. We're still not touching. His arm is stretched along the back of the couch.

'Ready?' I ask, positioning myself next to him, waiting to lean back against his arm. I can feel Jack trying to keep his thoughts as neutral as possible. I burst out laughing as I lean against him.

'What?' I shift away so we're not touching again.

'Your milkshakes bringing all the boys to the yard, *again*?'

'I literally have no idea why that's still in my head.'

'Just... relax, OK? I'll move away if I'm uncomfortable.' I raise an eyebrow. 'Ready?'

'My milkshake brings...' he starts singing quietly, but there is a grin as he does it. 'I'm ready.'

I lean back into the crook of his arm.

> **Thank you.**
> **For trusting me.**

I don't reply. If he could hear my thoughts, they'd be nothing but a jumble: how nice it is to touch his skin, to feel safe in his arms, to feel wanted, despite the person I am. His hand drops gently over my shoulder and I turn the page. Jack's voice reverberates through me.

> **Focus.**
> **Try to read the words on the page.**
> **Come on, you can do this.**

I hear his need and concentration as he tries to decipher the words. A line of lyrics from Bob Dylan and another song I'm unfamiliar with.

'Could you... guide my finger?' Jack says aloud. 'Beneath the words? It'll help me keep my focus on the words and the book, rather than the way...'

I want to kiss the top of your shoulder.

I try to hide the flush of heat that is no doubt visibly creeping across my neck. I take his hand.

'Like this?'

His hand is warm beneath mine.

'Yes.'

I follow his finger along the top of the next page. 'Their interest rather touched me...'

Their, i...
Where is the dot above the i?

I stop. Go back to the 'I'. 'Here.' I drag his finger over the stem of the letter, dotting it with a pop.

I continue following the letters with my fingers, a smile on my lips.

You smell like lemon.

'Concentrate, Jack,' but I'm smiling.

I take his finger over the 't'. There is a spark, a burst of excitement from Jack's voice in my head.

Wait was that a 't'?

'Yes!' I retrace the letter again, taking my time and lifting his finger off the page before crossing the letter.

Lost it.

'You'll find it again.' I twist my head, looking up at him. His emotion switches, from joy to desire.

Can I... milkshake. Boys. Yard. Sorry.

'You're going to have to come up with a better song. Back to the book, Jack.'

I burst out laughing. 'Katy Perry's "I Kissed a Girl"?'

'Sorry. I'm trying but—'

'Words, Jack. Focus on the page.'

'Right.'

'Close your eyes. It helped before.'

'"It. Seemed. To. Me..."'

S-ee

'S?' he asks.

'Yep!'

'Holy shit.'

He closes his eyes and I can hear him trying to find the letter again. As he concentrates on the letters, I occasionally hear a burst of classical music, or an image of something you would buy from an old-fashioned candy shop. But then there is a tear in his thoughts, like the letter has fallen into a void.

'How about, we stop for now, and I just read to you?'

'I can keep trying. It's working.'

'You're getting frustrated. You were relaxed when you saw the letters.'

'You're right.' I release his hand. He lifts it and it drops to my bare skin. There is a jolt, a pulsing of energy through me. He begins making slow circles on my skin. I can feel the outline of the letter: 's'. I don't say anything; I'm battling with my own desire and the little sparks his finger-tracing is leaving on my skin. Jack's thoughts have quietened. I read until the end of the paragraph then close the book, turning back to him.

'Why did you stop?' he asks, with a hint of a frown.

'Because right now, *I'm* the one who is finding it hard to focus.' My eyes drop to his mouth. 'I want...' I meet his eyes. There is a flicker of curiosity. 'Can I kiss you?'

The words in his mind and the ones he speaks are almost simultaneous.

'I thought you'd never ask.' In one movement, I'm on his knee, my arms around his neck. Like before our thoughts collide: heat simmers, need aches, want and desire pools in my stomach, as my tongue tentatively licks the tip of his.

Oh Christ.

We lose ourselves in the kiss, Jack's thoughts and my own bouncing off each other as his mouth presses against mine. His arms wrap around me, tighter. I can feel the strength of his biceps, feel the softness of my skin beneath his fingers.

You.

Taste like home.
More.

Stop.

No. Please.

Oh God.

His thoughts take form, no longer just words, but a whirlwind of images: a sense of apprehension battling against an image of my bare skin, the bones of my clavicle.

He pulls back. 'Do you want me to stop?'

I can feel him trying to control his thoughts.

'No. I don't want you to stop.'

Excruciatingly slowly, he pulls back my hair, his warm lips skimming my collarbone.

'You smell like lemons, like...'

Sunshine. Christ don't say that... Shit.

'Sunshine?' I raise my eyebrow at him.

'Sorry. For someone who spent their life surrounded by words, you'd think I could come up with something better.'

'Stop talking, Jack.' He lifts me, hands skirting along my spine. I can feel him swollen beneath his jeans. I've never felt lust like this. My hands reach up into his thick hair. I tug gently. His face lifts, mouth back on mine. My legs tighten around him. I pull back, cross my arms over my body and lift my jumper over my head. A string of words clash in Jack's mind, a sense of awe, attraction, need.

'You're beautiful,' he says. His voice is husky. He didn't need to say it; I can hear the way he feels. He lifts my hair, makes a pathway of kisses along my neck. He brings his mouth away.

'What's wrong?' I ask.

He holds my face in his hands, eyes searching mine. I can feel him trying to reorganise his thoughts, trying to form a sentence but the words are tripping over themselves.

Too fast.

'It's not. Too fast. I want this. I want you.'

I want you too.

'I don't want to rush things. We're just getting to know each other.'

'You're not rushing me. This is my choice.'

Our mouths meet, and we're lost again, in the taste of us. I pull back.

'I want you to take me to bed, Jack.' His eyes widen a touch, a flash of desire sparking behind them.

'I... believe me, there is nothing that I want more, but—'

'We've wasted enough time already.'

'You're certain?'

I take a beat. Not because I'm doubting my decision, but because I want to feel and experience this moment, let it anchor me in this new place full of security and hope. Because with him, it's so different.

Because I know what he thinks; I know what is in his heart.

So when he repeats the question, I know without any doubt that it's what he wants too. I don't need to take my time replying. Every part of me is yearning for his touch. 'Yes.'

I've never wanted anything, *anyone* more.

33

MAGGIE

I walk ahead, leading him into my room. A soft orange glow from the street lights warms the walls. He steps towards me, his silhouette outlined against the dark. Jack brushes my hair away from my cheek with his finger, his mouth nearing mine.

'If you want me to stop, say.' His voice is rough, dark eyes staring into my own.

I nod. I can't form any words. Our mouths inch closer. The pressure of his lips is feather-light, his tongue seeking out mine, gently at first. Then deeper. With more purpose. I'm on fire.

His hand clutches the back of my skirt, bringing my body closer. He turns us around, and I'm stepping backwards. His thoughts and my own are a cacophony of wants and needs. A burn of something primal between us. Our mouths mould into each other, his tongue over mine, my teeth pulling at his bottom lip, co-ordination that has nothing to do with me being able to read his mind. He lets out a small moan. My mouth opens against his, tasting the sounds of him as he lands on my bed.

I pull up my skirt, sinking over him. His hand runs up my leg, from my knees, to the outside of my thighs, my skirt riding up to my waist. I lean back, eyes not leaving his as I begin unbuttoning my blouse. His head dips, lips trailing along my collarbone, my back arching as I throw my clothes behind. It's so different than with Luke. With him, I was always trying so hard not to hear him that I was never fully present. We kiss again, each movement against each other intuitive. This isn't like when I've kissed men before. No lurid thoughts and expectations, no constant narration of how this move was going to 'drive me wild', just pure echoing of yearning, desire and awe. I unhook my bra, letting it fall to the floor. Jack stops kissing me for a moment. I lean back. He wants to look at me.

It's like a dance, the way he pulls back then moves closer, his hand gripping mine above my head, his other tracing the curve of my ribcage, his thumb running upwards. With each touch and scrape and moan, our thoughts meet. My voice, his skin, his voice, our need. If I could tell him how good this feels, it would echo his own thoughts exactly. It's like we are one person.

I grip the bottom of his jumper, yank it free, my fingers run up his spine, clutch his shoulders, his skin against mine.

I've never felt this whole.

This certain.

This complete.

'Is this OK?' he asks, breath hitching.

'God yes.' A small smile quirks in the corner of his mouth, hand gliding to the zip of my skirt. 'And this?' I nod as he trails along my ribcage with his tongue, the brush of his stubble scratching against my skin as he sinks lower. He looks up at me, undoes the button and, excruciatingly slowly, lowers the zip. I lift myself so he can pull off my skirt. He sits back, hands away from my skin now, and I'm left with my own thoughts.

It's like I've lost half of me.

He smiles and lifts my foot, and his thoughts are back. I know he's going to take his time now, that he wants me to wait, to need him as much as he needs me. He rolls down the material from one leg, feather-light fingers running up the back of my calf, my knee. He repeats the action, until the tights are discarded. He comes back up, our mouths sinking into each other.

'I've never felt this way about anyone,' he says, voice scratchy, deep.

'Me neither.' His mouth is on me again and then to my chest, his tongue sending sparks through my nervous system, then his mouth drags back down my body. He lowers my underwear, eyes on me as he does. I shiver, goosebumps on my skin despite the fire inside. His stubble grates the inside of my thigh, his mouth taking me. I close my eyes. His thoughts are clouded by desire, by my taste, by the way I feel against his tongue. I can feel my climax approaching but he pulls back.

           Not yet.

I'm gasping as he looks up at me. His thoughts back in my head, loud and clear.

     I want you to hear how I feel about you.
      Do you know how beautiful you are?
            Right now.
         Right in this moment.

And then his mouth is back on me and my hips are rising against him. This time he doesn't pull away. My whole body arches against him.

He gives me a moment to recover, kisses roaming over my skin as he traces his way back up with his mouth. Jack leans over me, the back of his hand tracing my jawline.

'I've never wanted anyone as much as I want you right now.'

'So take me.'

He stands, and I drink him in as he undoes his flies, pulls down his jeans, and for a moment I can't move, can't speak. I look at him, all of him: broad shoulders, dark hair running down from his belly button, long eyelashes, lips swollen. I sit up onto my knees, pull him back to the bed. He's hard against me and our mouths crash against each other, teeth and tongue and rough and soft. I reach out a hand, yank open my bedside drawer, pulling out a condom and pushing it into his hand. He stops, draws back. 'You're sure?' he asks again.

'Yes.' He tears the packet with his teeth, and a few moments later, he's above me. His thoughts loud and pulsing.

He glides his thumb over my bottom lip, kisses me again, and then I feel the length of him, hips against mine. My arms circle his neck pulling him deeper and closer than I ever dreamed I could.

And all I see, feel, and hear, is us.

34

MAGGIE

It's late, but I'm resisting sleep. I run my fingers through the dark hairs on his chest, his thoughts a gentle beat of joy, tenderness and wonder.

'What are you thinking?' he asks me, twirling a lock of hair around his finger.

'That I don't think I've ever felt this happy. That I never thought I'd ever be able to have this.'

He pulls me against his chest, wraps an arm around me.

'I can hear your heart beating.'

The weight of our feelings for each other flexes into the silence.

'Do you need some space?' he says gently. His hand stops drawing circles on my arm.

'No.'

'It must be loud in there.' He taps my forehead gently.

'It's not actually. You're calm; your thoughts are quieter than normal.'

'And while we were...'

'We were both loud, Jack. I couldn't tell who was who most of the time.'

His phone buzzes from somewhere on the floor.

'Do you need to get that?'

'Nope.'

He shifts, facing me. I hook a leg over his hip as he kisses me. 'No it's not too fast and yes I want you again,' I say. He deepens the kiss but the phone rings again.

I grab the back of his hair and pull him closer.

Shit. Ignore it, ignore it.

The phone rings again, demanding to be answered. He draws back and shakes his head.

'Sorry, I'd better take it.' He kisses me again. 'Don't move, OK? Stay right there.' And then he's pulling on his jeans.

I wave away his apology.

He leaves the room, phone clamped to his ear. 'Hey...' The rest of the conversation stolen by the closed door.

I lie back and starfish across my bed. Relishing all the aches in my muscles. I let out a little laugh, pulling up the covers over my mouth.

The door handle creaks as Jack walks back into the room. 'My brother.' He wiggles the phone in explanation. 'He has some news and wants us all to go for lunch at Chadders next Friday.' He chews the inside of his cheek, looks distracted.

'Oh. Flicks is showing *Sense and Sensibility*, but I'm guessing you already know the plot to that one. It's not one of my top ten...'

'Hmmm? Oh. Yeah. I've seen it actually.'

The air cools around us quickly.

'It's late,' I say. Giving him an escape route.

He nods, eyes still on the phone in his hand.

'I'll call you a—'

His eyes flash back up and he sits on the edge of the bed.

'I don't suppose Romy would let you have next week off?'

'Oh, when I mean it's not in my top ten, I'll still go and watch it...'

'No. I meant...' He shuffles his phone between his hands, the groove between his eyes deepening like he's thinking of what to say. 'Do you want to come? To lunch?'

'But I thought you were going to your parents'?'

'I am.'

'Oh! I... I don't know, I mean...' I gesture to my body with a grimace.

'I can tell them about, you know, the germ thing. And I can be by your side, ready to bounce them.'

'Bounce?'

'I can be your personal bouncer.' He pushes down on the bed, making it spring up and down. I let out a snort and he laughs. 'You know what I mean' – he lies back beside me, head propped up in his hand – 'bodyguard. I can be your bodyguard.'

'I mean, sure? If... is it not a bit too soon?'

'I think it's about the right time to meet the parents. And, well, the rest of them.'

'The *whole* family is going to be there?' I pull the covers further up beneath my chin.

'Yeah. George asked for a full house.'

He brushes my hair away from my forehead. 'So what do you think? Will you be my date?'

My heart is knocking so hard against my ribcage I'm sure he can hear it too.

'But...' What if they see the real me? Someone weird and not good enough for the man lying beside me. 'What if I'm not...'

'Maggie?' His hands are near my face. 'Close your eyes.'

I do as he says.

'I'm going to touch you, OK?'

I nod.

His hands settle around my jaw, his thumb stroking my cheek.

This is what I see.

A feeling of calm, happiness and belonging floods through my system. He describes our time together, like a rolling tape of highlights, directed with the love and adoration of someone who cares deeply about the scenes. The first glimpse of me in the cinema as the lights came on; my head thrown back laughing; my side profile as I watched the film by the fountain; the rush of need as he kissed me the first time, and the feeling of calm and belonging as I read to him.

He takes his hands away and I open my eyes.

'They're going to love you.'

35

FRIDAY 15TH NOVEMBER

Jack

For the past week, apart from my trips to Levin, I've been here in Maggie's bed, more than I've been at work. We've finished *The Great Gatsby*, and have made our way through half of *The Water on Horseback*, both of us convinced that Clarissa is indeed our Riz. I've also been forced to watch not one but *three* of the Twilight franchise; the less said about that the better.

'That's it for now,' she says.

'What? You can't finish mid-chapter!' I snatch the book from her, my eyes scanning the page. I wince as I focus on a word:

$$\text{Th} - \text{♑}$$

'Ugh. Levin and his methods,' I say trying to shake the noise from my ears. 'I had to ring a hand bell each time the flashcard read "th",' I explain.

'Ooh fun.'

'Hardly, I'm dreading that sound becoming a permanent part of my reading experience. Just read until the end. Look...' I flick the pages. 'It's only a few more pages.'

'Sorry, but no deal. You'll have to wait. I need to have a shower before we go...' She takes in my expression, her own slightly amused. 'It's really bothering you, isn't it? Why can't we finish mid-chapter?'

'Because!'

She takes the book back. Her finger automatically moves to fold the corner of the page, but I steal the book from her hands, sliding in the Chadwick's bookmark I'd bought over between the pages.

She shakes her head. 'You're such a book nerd.' She laughs, pulling my shirt over her head as I lay the book back down on the bedside table.

'You know, I could tell them I'm sick?' I start fake coughing as she throws her pillow at me.

'No way, and have them already think I'm stealing away their little prince. Not on your nelly, Jack Chadwick.' But she settles back down lying on her side, facing me.

'I wouldn't worry. I lived like a hermit for the past year. I doubt anyone has noticed *you've* been holding me captive.'

'Excuse me, *I've* been going to work and on far less sleep than usual,' she challenges.

She leans over, lips a fraction away before I nod. We've found a rhythm to our consent, tiny pauses, one leaning in after the other makes the first move. It's becoming second nature. Her lips brush mine and she pulls back, lying down and tucking her hands under her cheek.

'So what's next? Painting your body blue and climbing a giant letter Y?'

'Who knows?' I brush her hair back. 'He agrees that if I could remember more, it might open up something. I still get that headache occasionally.'

'Shall we try again?'

I take a breath. We've tried this a few times over the last week. There are little details coming more and more into focus. It's not my favourite thing to do in Maggie's bed, but still, I nod.

She shifts, moving down the bed and I laugh, peering down. 'I won't be able to concentrate if you move any lower.'

'Behave. I'm going to lie on your chest. Ready?'

'As I'll ever be.'

She rests her head against me. 'Start with leaving the pub again.'

Just like last time, I focus on everything I can remember until I'm hit by a sense of something being off. The shadow across the road moves. I hear – not my own thoughts exactly – but a feeling of something definitely not being right.

But this part is new.

Footsteps. Slow, steady, the sounds of boots against tarmac. Mine? The shadow? Buildings move, roads sweep forwards and retract, curve then rise and fall. Then I see a flash of long red hair against the blacks and greys of the shadows. My voice rings out, 'Excuse me?'

The strike comes from behind me. The pain of impact so real that I gasp. Maggie instantly pulls away, her worried face leaning over as her room comes back into view.

'Are you OK?' she asks, concerned. 'Jack?'

I'm hot, the blood rushing around my body.

'I... I think so.'

'Let me get you a glass of water.' She hurries from the room, returning with a glass, which I drain. The images start to push and shove against each other. Maggie sits next to me, face etched with worry.

'I think something was going to happen to her.'

'To the redhead?'

'I think so.'

'We should go to the police.'

I'm hesitant, but I remember so much more now. 'Agreed.'

Who is she?

I need to find out who she is.

And if anything happened to her.

36

JACK

I slip into fourth gear and glance at Maggie, watching the darkening patchwork of countryside that was the backdrop to my childhood rushing past. The mosaic of rolling fields to the left; to the right, glimpses of the coastline dipping under the setting sun keep up with our progress. Despite it being November, winter is yet to hit us in full force.

'When shall we go to the police?' Maggie asks. 'I'm sure they'll reopen your case now.' She's searching on her phone again for any mention of an attack, or a clue as to who the woman, or the person in the shadows was, but so far nothing has come up.

'Yeah. Maybe.'

We're quiet for a while, Maggie's hand furiously typing into the search bar. 'I'll check the missing people pages, again.'

The sun catches the bronzes and golds of Maggie's hair, her pupils small against the jade of her irises, and the memories of that time take on a fresh design. For so long, I had felt like I'd lost all purpose in this life, but now I'm starting to realise that the night I thought I'd lost everything was actually the beginning of something new. And now, with Maggie's help, I'm finally finding answers to the questions that have plagued me since that night.

I think back to my previous session with Dr Levin. It'd been amazing to me, the pride I felt in being able to read The-lion-sat-on-the... I didn't quite get plains, but after a few weeks of intensive reading and writing, for the first time I think that maybe, I might be able to find a way back. He's made it clear I will never be the person I was – reading will always be taxing; the alexia will never go – but the reading age of a six-year-old is better than no reading at all.

I turn onto the steep driveway leading up to the house. 'We're here.'

'Here?' Her eyes widen as she looks up from her phone. 'Your family lives on a cliff?'

I cast an apologetic glance in her direction as we pass the sign that I know reads: *Chadwick Crest.*

'And they have a *crest* named after them. Of *course* they do.' Her eyes sweep the surroundings, her head turning towards the sign as we pass.

'Kind of, my great-great-grandfather named the place after himself. A kind of two fingers up to the previous owners. He worked on the estate when he was younger, then made his fortune.'

She's alternating between pulling her cuffs down and pushing them back up her arms.

'Before we get there, it's important you know that' – I drop a gear again as I follow the gravel higher up, the outer edges of the garden wall coming into view – 'it can kind of look imposing but...'

'Holy hell.' She leans forward as the house comes into view. 'It's like Manderley had a baby!'

I round the car into the car park to the right of the house, the crest of the cliff dripping off the edge of the garden. 'I promise, it's half falling down, everywhere creaks and the majority of the furniture is second-hand and most things have a knack to them.'

'A knack?'

'Yeah, like the downstairs loo needs three pumps of the flush; the kitchen door needs a quick shoulder barge below the hinge and...'

She shakes her head and pulls at her cuffs again, hands smoothing down her trousers as though she can change the whole outfit the more she fiddles with it.

I grin over at her but she's pale. 'Hey,' I add softly. She turns her head to me, hands clutched around the tops of her arms. 'I promise you, my family are as much of a mess as me. Don't be fooled by the whole...' I wave my hand at the house. 'Chadwick *thing*.'

'So they're not perfectly groomed, articulate and charming? That makes me feel a whole lot better, thanks.'

'I know this is a lot. But I promise, I wouldn't have brought you here if I didn't think you would be comfortable.'

She breathes in deeply through her nose, holds her breath then exhales slowly. 'OK. Let's go meet the parents.' She frowns as though never expecting to ever say the words. 'God I hope I don't go all *Ben Stiller* and offer to milk your dad's nipples.'

I laugh, but she's nervous. Maybe this *is* too much too soon?

We climb out of the car. I double click the lock, as Maggie pulls her navy-blue leather coat around her, arms folded.

The cast-iron rusting garden furniture is still out, as is the pergola. Lights swing in the sea air, and flames are dancing in the paella tin/firepit that Dad insisted we brought back from a week in Madrid. The waves are loud, but I can hear laughter, the whack of a cricket bat and cheers coming from below.

'And you've definitely told them about... the germ thing?' she says as I walk around the car to her side and we head towards the house.

'Yes. They know not to touch you.'

'What else have you told them?' The wind is whipping her hair around her head, thick brown and blonde curls flashing across her face. I step towards her.

'Enough. Just be yourself.'

'I don't know how to be anyone else.'

'And thank God for that. You are the perfect you.'

'How do you do that?' She stills, hand over her eyes blocking out the sun. 'Land the perfect one-liner?'

'I rehearse them into my mirror every morning.'

'You do not.' She laughs, but she's nervously looking back up at the house.

'Ready?' I ask.

'I guess?'

I stretch out my hand and she lets her own fall into my palm.

37

MAGGIE

I can feel Jack trying to dampen his thoughts; I extract my hand from his and straighten my coat. He needs space to think. His mind is back on the redhead and the feeling that something was about to happen to her. He's remembering so much more. I'm determined to help him find out what happened to her, to *him* that night. Who was she?

'Brace yourself. They can be a lot,' he says, opening the door, head lifted. 'Hello?' Jack shouts into the large space.

The house is huge, but like Jack warned, it's not the glossy film set I imagined. Patches of darker colour blot the pale blue walls with areas that need repair, but the foyer alone is bigger than my whole lounge.

Opposite us, a staircase climbs in a curve and splits across three different landings. I half expect them to start shifting like they belong in Hogwarts.

'In the kitchen!' a woman's voice replies.

There is a sense of vertigo as I tread across the floor, as though everything in the house is leaning towards the cliff, to the sea. But as soon as I'm certain this house is going to fall into the ocean, I can feel the centre of gravity switch, pulling it back inland. It feels alive. Like it's got its own thoughts and desires, its own instinct to protect.

I step into the kitchen, olive green cupboards, large wooden counters that look like they've been lifted straight from the beach below, all sporadic curves around the edges. In the centre, a large island, a hunk of wood that looks as though it's still sunk deep into the cliff, as if the house has been built around it. The room smells of coffee, pastry and stewed apples.

At the far end there are huge double doors looking out to the darkening sky, and a table that could easily sit twelve, and where his family are all seated, looking over with expectant faces.

I misstep, Jack checks I'm OK, but it's not the volume of his thoughts or the uneven flooring that has knocked me off balance. It's like I've stepped on a paving slab that's not fixed in place. Jack takes my hand without hesitation. Time doesn't slow, it slackens. The anxiety deep in my chest unravels. His thoughts and love for his family ground me, yet unbalance me. Like I'm tapping into some deep sense of belonging that doesn't belong to me.

I look to Jack. He's smiling over at them, as they sit around the table.

> **Christ I hope they go easy on her.**
> **You.**
> **Sorry.**

There is a tiny hint of nervousness from him, a judder in his words that climbs up my spine, but it's not for himself, I realise, it's for me.

He rests his hand gently over mine. His thoughts are becoming more distant, like he's trying to calm himself, but his love for them is searing through my veins, blooming in my chest.

'Maggie!' Jack's mum, the woman I recognise from the pictures on his wall, stands with a welcoming smile. She's tall, blonde, elegant. 'Goodness, you're just as pretty as he described you! Hello, Jackson.'

'Jackson?' I question under my breath.

'After Pollock. I was quite the finger painter apparently.'

He releases my hand.

There is a feeling of emptiness without his hand in mine. Like I've been walking around with a hole inside me that I didn't know was there. Something hidden, or out of reach, like a memory in the corner of my mind.

'Maggie!' his father booms, rising from his seat. I swallow, step back. He looks like Jack, but more weathered: he could be cast as a sailor, all creases and broad shoulders, like he's used to hurling lobster pots on board. His hair is grey, longer than Jack's, wilder.

'Mr Chadwick.' I manage a smile. 'Thanks for inviting me.'

He lets out a roaring laugh. 'Mr Chadwick? Good Lord, that makes me feel like my great-uncle Rupert and Great-Uncle Rupert was a right tosser. Studied fruit flies.' He shakes his head at Great-Uncle Rupert's choice of job. 'Tom, please. Good to meet you. *You* don't study fruit flies, do you?'

'I... no.'

'Ignore him,' Jack says rolling his eyes. 'Dad thinks he's hilarious.'

'I am hilarious.' He throws an arm around Jack's head and knuckle-rubs his hair. 'At least seventy per cent of the time!' He releases Jack who straightens his hair. Tom settles himself back into the chair.

Jack begins introducing the others semi-circling the table. 'This is my sister, Charl.'

'Hi! You're not at all what I was expecting!' The redhead

wearing bright-purple dungarees with a yellow 'land girl' tie in her hair grins at me.

'Charl...' Jack shakes his head.

'What? She's not! No sign of a wooden pole stuck right up her backside like your usual type.'

Charl is bursting with energy, eyes wide and brown, strong chin, kind.

'Cool jacket. Lunch is almost ready.' She gets up. 'Shit. You can eat things made by other people, can't you? I promise I'll wash my hands.'

'Yes, it's...' I begin.

'That's right. You just can't touch people. Jackson sent us all a voice note with strict instructions not to hug you. Shame. You look huggable.'

'I do?'

'Yeah. I want to give you a squeeze.' I cast a glance in Jack's direction, eyebrows raised, his expression reading: *I warned you they can be a lot.* 'Jackson, do you think you can stop looking at her like a puppy in need of a belly rub for five seconds and give me a hand? George will be here soon, with the *news*.'

'Anyone know what the news is?' Jack asks, making his way to the kitchen island. Charl passes him a bag of limes.

'Oh, darling,' Jack's mum, Gillian, begins. 'It could be anything. Last time he had news, it was that he was thinking of getting a puppy.'

Tom leans forward but not close enough to touch me. 'Gilly has *baked*.' He grimaces. 'Best stay away from the shortbread.'

'I heard that!' She bats his arm away.

'Uncle Jaaaaack!!' There is a stampede of feet as two waist-high girls in a variety of feather boas and hats run into the room wrapping arms around his waist. He discards the bag of limes. The youngest is wearing just a feather boa and a luminous lace tutu, wild candy-floss-thin blonde hair, which is standing up like she's electrically charged. Jack immediately swings them beneath his arms.

'Take a seat, Maggie.' Gilly gestures to a seat at the end of the table.

'It's—' God I have no idea how to navigate this conversation. Words are forming in my head, like a script for an actress but without a director to steer her in the right direction. 'Lovely to meet you all.' I smile over at her, trying not to cringe at the plummy accent I seem to have adopted.

'We've heard a *lot* about you over the past few weeks.' She smiles but it's guarded. Not unfriendly but more... appraising.

'All good I hope,' I ask not quite meeting her eyes.

'I hear you've been helping Jackson sort out the shop?'

'I... yes.'

My attention goes back to Jack who is dragging the children around pretending to look for them, one hanging onto his leg, the other with her arm around his neck.

'I'm on your back, Uncle Jack!'

He's a natural with them. He casts a quick glance back at me. I give him a little nod in reassurance, and he returns his attention back to the kids hanging off him.

He's good with children. Of course he is.

I don't know why this hits me so hard. I suppose it's because having kids has always been such a foreign concept to me. Luke and I had never discussed it; it was too early in our relationship. I guess deep down I'm afraid. Afraid of something happening to me and the kid being left in the care system. If Hellie hadn't come along, who knows how long I would have been bouncing around foster care and children's homes. And then there is the issue of being able to constantly hear their thoughts. I mean, there are times I'm sure that would be helpful, but what about while I'm pregnant? What would I hear then? Seeing Jack like this though, with one girl hanging off his leg, the other on his back...

Something feels like it breaks inside my chest.

Tom pulls the newspaper towards him. His glasses are perched on his nose.

'Coffee?' Gillian asks.

'Yes, please, thank you.' She reaches for the coffee pot.

Please *and* thank you?

'Sugar, Maggie?' she asks.

Tom reads out a clue from the crossword, 'Six down, four letters...'

'Um, yes... please.' My head is spinning as I try to untangle the riot of activity around me. Jack's face is lit up as he chases the girls around the large kitchen. 'Two, please.'

'Control your kids!' Jack shouts at his sister.

'Nope, you started it,' she responds, opening plastic cartons of food.

'Milk?' Gilly asks, eyes back on the task.

'That would be great,' I reply.

She passes me the cup. I hesitate before reaching for it.

'Shit sorry, I didn't think...' She places the cups down with a clink, concern around her eyes.

'It's fine. Thank you.'

'Phew. Thought I'd fucked up at the first hurdle. Jack has warned us not to make a mess of things and here I am, practically about to hold your hand.'

I'm slightly taken aback by the F-bomb but Jack had already warned me that his mum swears like a sailor.

'Greta!' Charl bellows from the other side of kitchen as the kids run away and out of the kitchen, Jack making growling noises behind them until they run up the stairs. 'Put some clothes on!'

'Oh, let her be,' Tom adds barely looking up. 'She's not going to get hypothermia.'

Charl lands her hands on her hips. 'Do I need to remind you that I *did* get hypothermia when I was her age?'

'That's completely different.' Gilly shakes her head. 'You were in the sea and not wearing a wetsuit.'

'If I recall...' Jack adds, his dark hair flopping forward into his eyes as he reaches over for a biscuit on the counter. 'You were wearing Mum's bikini, which you'd superglued shells onto.'

'I didn't superglue them, I used Blu-Tack.'

'And you made a magnificent mermaid,' adds Tom but with his eyes still on the newspaper in his hands. 'Triangulate.' He mutters, hand pressing a biro onto the page.

'So, Maggie...' Gilly takes a sip of her coffee. 'Jack tells us you have your own cleaning business?'

'I, no, I clean; I don't own a business. I have a few regular gigs—'

'And you clean the cinema too?' My head turns to Charl, who opens a bottle of vodka and pours half of the bottle into a large glass drinks dispenser.

'Yes, I—'

Gillian jumps in, 'Such a cool place. I've been a few times...'

Tom mutters another clue to himself, pen tapping his bottom lip.

'I can't believe you got Jack to go and see *Notting Hill*,' Gilly says under her breath.

'Is that the one about the sports agent?' Tom asks glancing up.

'No that's...' I begin.

I'm trying to keep up with the discussion bursting with different personalities surrounding me, but it's hard. Fireworks of conversation are exploding in every direction; my body wants to duck beneath them. I can't remember the last time I was this close to so many people, being part of the conversation rather than spectating from a distance. I look over to Jack, warmth floods through me but I know my hands are quietly shaking. Jack turns, looking back as though I've pulled on the toggle of a kite string. He says something to his sister who rolls her eyes, and then he walks towards me.

'Tell me you're going easy on her?' he asks his family, eyebrow quirked.

'Honestly, Jackson!' Gilly says, taking another sip. 'You make us sound like the Spanish Inquisition.'

'Do I need to remind you of the first time I brought a girl home?'

Charl snorts as she twists a cap, then pulls out a chopping board.

Gillian laughs. 'What? We were being welcoming!'

'Mum, you asked her what her intentions were,' Jack challenges.

'Well... I was interested.'

'We were fifteen!'

'We were charming!' Tom adds.

'Hardly,' Charl says, as she begins chopping a red pepper. 'She dumped him before the apple crumble hit the table. Mum, are you sure everything else is ready?'

'Yes, I told you, it's all under control. Come and sit back down, Charlotte.'

The conversation continues on to other moments where their parents' behaviour caused embarrassment.

'Everything all right?' Jack crouches beside me, his words quiet. His voice cuts through the cacophony of conversation around me, like we're alone and the equaliser on the background track has been turned down.

Yes. No. I don't know. This is wonderful. This is hard.
He reaches out and I take his hand.

They already like you.
I can tell.

His words are soft, gentle yet solid. His emotions hang off each word like an accent: pride, concern, protection and something else.

And I think it might be love.

38

MAGGIE

I clutch the glass in my hand, as Jack leads me through the downstairs labyrinth of 'Chadders'. I'm hoping that Jack can't see how overwhelming this is for me.

There are photos everywhere, family history smiling and laughing up from each wall, each sideboard. Each room that Jack takes me into swells with personality.

The smell of this house is intoxicating, years of breakfasts and dinners, perfume and shoe polish, firewood and cold showers all caught in the breath of the sea breeze leaking into the house.

Jack points to a photo. He explains this is the beach below the house, their own private cove, he says smiling. He laughs, telling me about a time they took the boat out and how sunburnt Charl got, but it was only on the one side he says. She'd gotten distracted mid suntan lotion application, and she looked like a domino. 'Next summer, I can take you out. You'll love it.'

I nod, but I find it hard to swallow down the anxiety that is calcifying in my throat.

Because Jack doesn't see what I see. He doesn't see how they are all so close on that boat; that I wouldn't be able to hold their thoughts at bay. He sees me as one of them, the girl he likes, who laughs at his jokes, who could be part of a world where she can't belong.

He pushes open a heavy wooden door with a creak.

'This is the den, but it's more Mum and Dad's study now.'

I turn my head to the right. A large sofa that looks like it could fold in half if you sat on it speaks of overuse and comfort. Behind it are shelves bulging with books, some laid on top of each other, more books stacked in precarious piles on the floor. The whole opposite wall is glass, the doors leading out to the garden and the darkness beyond.

To my left is a large desk, two chairs on opposite sides facing each other. There are more books towering unsteadily, pots filled with pens and several different spectacles lying around the surface. 'This is where the magic happens,' Jack adds with jazz hands but without a hint of jealousy or resentment.

'Your parents work together?' I gesture to the desk, one chair with a red-and-brown-checked scarf over the back, the other with a thick black cardigan hanging across the shoulders of the chair.

'Yes and no,' Jack says, picking up a stray pen lid and slotting it over the tip of the biro. 'Mum never edits Dad's work. Says she's all too aware of how fragile an author's ego can be, but they work in the same space when they're at home.'

I feel like I'm intruding, despite the welcoming warmth. Jack walks ahead, lifts a latch on the glass door and opens it; the sound of the sea crashing below pours into the room. I join him. 'I can see why you love it here so much.' I look up at him. 'I bet if you had a picture dictionary and you looked up the word "home" there'd be a picture of this place.'

I squint into the dark clouds outside. A small flash so fast I think I've missed it. 'Is that a lighthouse?' I ask, catching the flash again.

'Yep. You can't always see it.'

'It's like the green light in Gatsby,' I say, my voice distant: a glimmer of hope, just out of reach.

'You're like my green light.' I look up at him. I hadn't realised he was looking at me rather than the light out at sea.

'Here you are!' Charlotte bounds into the room with a dramatic hand on her heart as though we've been missing for days rather than ten minutes. 'Lunch's almost ready! Mags, can I call you Mags?' She doesn't wait for a reply. 'You can use my room to freshen up and Jack, the' – she finger-quotes – 'parental unit want a word. They're in the library.' She gives him an eye roll.

'Sorry...' He steps away. 'I'd better go speak to them.'

'Of course.' I clear my throat.

'Jackson,' Charl says. 'You've got something on your—' She waits for him to lean closer and flicks him hard on the ear.

''Sake.' He rubs it.

'I'll pay for that later.' She grins over at me.

Greta bounds in, knocking her mum into me. Charl lands a hand on my arm in apology.

Trust Jack to fall for someone he can't quite get close to.

It's a simple and natural gesture; she doesn't even realise she's done it.

**Vicky really did a number on him.
They had their whole future mapped out, marriage, kids, the
shop...**

Charl scoops up her daughter, planting kisses over her face, and heads into the hall.

She doesn't see how her words have landed like a stone in my stomach: cold and hard. I look back out at sea.

But the blink of the lighthouse is no longer there.

39

JACK

I take a deep breath and go into the room. We call it the library but it's just a small room with a desk and wall-to-wall books and their many literary awards displayed. Basically, it's the only room in the house that has decent Wi-Fi, so they use it for Zoom calls.

Mum is standing by the window, mug of tea in her hands. Dad is behind the desk holding a book.

He puts the book down and Mum turns with a smile. I slump down opposite Dad, like I'm a student about to get detention. I pick up a paperback. Before I met Maggie, or Dr Levin, I wouldn't have got that far, let alone tried to sound out the letters on the front. Th-e b-i-g but the next word slips away, tangled in shapes and spaces I can't decipher. I put the book back down.

'We like Maggie,' Mum begins with a smile that I recognise has a subtext in the brackets around her mouth.

'Good. I like her too.'

'Oh, I'd say it's more than just liking her,' Dad says over his glasses. 'You're good together. We can see that.'

'Thank you. She's been helping me...' I tread carefully, trying to think of ways to explain how having her with me, as I try to remember that night, has opened up so much. 'To remember. What happened.'

'Oh?' Dad says, my parents casting a glance at each other.

'I think... there was a reason I was going in the wrong direction. There was a woman, with red hair, and it's hard to explain, but I think she was in some kind of danger?'

'Interesting...' Dad leans back. 'Have you been to the police?'

'Not yet.' I shrug, as if it's nothing. 'I haven't got anything concrete yet. But I will.'

'And Maggie has helped you remember?'

'Yeah. She's... patient. Listens to me.'

'That's good,' Mum replies enthusiastically.

'Dr Levin thinks that the more I remember, the less pain I'll feel when I read. It's already making a difference.'

'And it's helping you progress with your reading, then? Seeing Maggie?' Mum asks gently, coming behind Dad's chair. I don't miss the way she lands a hand on Dad's arm as if to warn him to take things slowly.

'Yeah... I mean I'm not going to be reading *North and South* anytime soon, but...'

'I should hope not,' Mum interjects. 'Most depressing book I've ever read. I've never understood the need to read the classics, like you can't be taken seriously unless you've read them. Some of my most successful authors haven't even been to university, but do you know what? They can make me laugh, and give me a happy ending when all around us the world is turning to shit. That's talent. Wailing on about the mess famous people have made of the world doesn't make for a great writer or storyteller, it simply shows us they can write a story that doesn't belong to them.'

'Deep,' I say.

'So, the shop, Jack.' Dad jumps into the conversation, his fingers tapping on the edge of the desk.

And here it is.

'I've told you, I still haven't decided. We agreed I'd try and that's what I'm doing.'

'Jack,' Mum says softly. 'It's just that, after Vicky... and we know how much the stroke took from you...'

'No. No you don't, Mum. Neither of you do.'

'No... you're right. That wasn't what I meant.'

'Your mother means that now that things are progressing with your reading that, well it's time for you to start getting more involved in Chadwick's.'

'I am.'

'Nell runs the shop, Jack. Not you. I popped in last week. She said you'd not been in all week.' Dad's voice is sharp. 'You need to take back some control. It's time to stop hiding away.'

'I'm not hiding away. I'm here, aren't I? And I brought Maggie. I'm moving forwards.'

Dad leans back. 'Yes. Yes, you are. And we are thrilled for you. Truly. But you can't be serious about her?'

I stand, angry.

'Sit down, Jack,' Mum intervenes. 'Tom, that was entirely the wrong thing to say. It's not what he means, Jack. She's lovely. And we can see how much you care for each other, and it's clear she's good for you' – she clears her throat – 'right now, but in the long term...'

'It's more than that. This isn't...'

'A rebound?'

'Fuck's sake. Of course it isn't. Me and Vic were done as soon as I had the stroke.'

'Yet you've not dated anyone since.'

'No, well I've kind of been busy recuperating from a stroke so Tinder has been pretty low on my agenda.'

Mum softens. 'It was not so long ago that you barely got out of bed. And while we like Maggie, you've only just met her, and we worry that...'

'What? That I'm happy?'

'No. But perhaps you *think* she's the perfect woman for you because... well, she's a woman who has to keep people at arm's length, isn't she? You said it yourself: she finds being around people difficult, what with things the way they are with her phobia and...'

'I don't need to listen to this.'

'Calm down.' Dad peers over his glasses. 'No need to go blowing a gasket.'

Mum takes a breath. 'Darling, you're stepping back into the world and we couldn't be more pleased about that, and you're making progress, but you've a long way to go. Opening the shop, getting back into the life that you love, that's what will sustain your future. That's what you need... whereas with Maggie, well it's easier for you to hide away from it, isn't it?'

I hesitate.

Mum walks around the desk, leans against it, her hand is cold on my cheek. 'Maggie is lovely. Really, she is, and I know you like her... But, darling, and I say this with nothing but love for you, might you be rushing into a relationship that takes you away rather than immerses you?'

'HHHHHHIIIIIYYYYAAAAAAA!!' George's voice interrupts the conversation as does the loud bang of the closing door.

Mum wipes down her trousers. 'We'll talk about it more once you've finished your time with Dr Levin, hmmm?'

I try to speak, to defend my relationship with Maggie, but no words come out.

40

MAGGIE

I climb the stairs, follow the hallway until I find the room with the pink door and push it open. I wonder if downstairs, they're all imagining me dousing myself in antibac.

There is a small step down into the room. It's chaotic, paints and canvases, an easel by the window, bright clothes scattered over the bed and floor. It smells of Charlotte's perfume, something floral with an undertone of patchouli. I close the door behind me and lean against it, heart jackhammering in my chest.

I tread towards her vanity unit and sit down. I'm pale; my hair is a disaster. I try and fail to untangle it.

Behind me, there are yet more family photos on the walls. I get up and lean into them, smiling at a younger Jack, at the three siblings with arms around each other. There are a few photos of the shiners, of a younger Charl, surrounded by friends, tongues sticking out, raising shots.

I move along to a recent photo of her blowing out birthday candles. I lean closer. Jack is in the background, arm around a shoulder.

I know who she is from the few details Jack has shared with me.

She's tall. Almost as tall as him, long gleaming blonde hair, the glint of an engagement ring on her finger. She has a slim frame like she might have been a ballet dancer or a Gwyneth Paltrow lookalike: Vicky. I take another deep breath thinking of her being welcomed into the family the same way as I have. Did Charl want to hug her because she looked huggable?

There are a few more family photos of this time, Vicky in three of them, her lying on Jack's lap on the beach, peering over her sunglasses. The next one is here, outside on the patio. Charl is the focus of the photo again, red hair blowing in the wind, but behind her, Jack and Vicky. He has his arms around her, and they look like they're about to kiss. My finger reaches out and outlines his profile. I've seen the way Jack is looking at her, because it's the same way he looks at me.

My phone vibrates in my pocket.

TESS

So how's it going? What are they like?

What are they like? Wonderful, welcoming, too good to be true.

MAGGIE

Lovely. But a LOT.

TESS

Nipped off for a quickie in the downstairs loo yet?

I shake my head. Not only is Tess *thrilled* that I've finally slept with Jack but she seems insistent on suggesting places to shag before the excitement flags.

I can't ever imagine not being excited to touch him.

MAGGIE

Get your mind out of the gutter.

TESS

Never... You OK?

MAGGIE

Yeah. It's just overwhelming. And...

I think Jack might be in love with me. I think I might be—

A loud 'Hiya!' rips through the house. I delete the 'and', hit send, give the photos one last glance and take a deep breath. Closing the door on Jack and Vicky.

My hand trails along the banister. Loud chatter and eager clacking of plates and crockery are coming from the kitchen.

I step forwards. The table is laden with food on brightly coloured dishes: chicken wings, corn on the cob, baked potatoes, little bowls piled with colourful rice, pasta... There is more choice here than I've experienced before. The buffet-style vibe mimics the room: chaotic, warm. Slightly terrifying.

At the far end of the table, Jack is hugging a man, back-clapping him affectionately. He has blond hair, and an air of Oxbridge boat race about him.

'Maggie, this is George.'

Jack turns, his arm still looped around his brother's neck.

'Hi! Good to meet you.' George charges over, arms wide. Jack is shaking hands with another man – tall, scruffy brown hair, glasses – who I've gathered is Kieran, his boyfriend.

I jolt backwards, my spine bumping into a chair, sending it clattering to the floor. I scramble to correct it. Despite the sound that stops conversation, and the way they are all looking over at me, George slows, smiles and picks up the chair.

'Sorry—' I say, flustered.

'Not to worry, you're not part of the family unless you've broken something.'

My cheeks heat, and I apologise again, which he dismisses with a wave of his hand. There is a spark in his eyes, a natural flirtatious way about him.

'So you're the one,' he says.

'Sorry?'

'The one who brought my miserable git of a brother back into the land of the living.'

The rest of lunch goes by without further incident, the air swollen with interruptions, stories and jokes.

I sit quietly next to Jack. He's moved his chair slightly further away from me. I try not to read too much into this, but part of me wonders what was said in the library.

I hold my elbows in as I reach for something that looks like rice but is dotted with pomegranate seeds. Across the table, I catch Greta giggling and picking up a straw, her eyes on Jack. She copies his movements as he sucks his straw, a crouton being held at the edge. She giggles and does the same.

He's so completely natural with her. I don't know how to imitate this ease, or crack this secret code that they all seem to know.

Jack nods, while giving Charl surreptitious glances, but she's talking loudly and pointing a bread roll at her father, while telling him he's wrong about a line in a popular novel.

Jack mouths one... two... sucks the crouton back up and then blows it across the table at his sister.

'Jack!'

Greta folds herself double, her laughter bubbling up out of her as she tries to replicate his actions again, her eyebrows pinched in concentration.

'Great.' Charl throws down her napkin. 'I can't wait to get my own revenge when you have kids.'

Jack grimaces at Greta, but they share a look of mischief before he replies, 'My kids will behave impeccably, not like these two little monsters!' He growls at Greta, who giggles.

My kids.

I take a sip of elderflower cordial, the taste dry but too sweet on my tongue. Seeing him around his family, the way that he's such a part of them is so different to the man he is when he's with me, different but somehow supercharged. He will make a wonderful father, but—

My thoughts are interrupted by George standing, clinking the side of his glass. The room hushes.

'So... I've invited us all here because as you all know, somehow I've managed to land myself with one of the kindest, most gorgeous men on the planet.' He looks down at Kieran with love in his eyes. 'And for reasons that I cannot fathom, he seems to feel the same way about me.' He holds up his left hand where a platinum ring sits on his engagement finger. 'We're getting married!'

The whole room erupts, claps and cheers, seats pushed back as they all hug and shake hands.

I don't know what to do with myself other than to smile and say congratulations from my seat and tentatively take a glass of champagne once the corks start popping.

'I have an idea!' Charl leans forward, dipping a breadstick into a pot of something that I think might be hummus. 'We should have a party! Tonight!'

My stomach jolts, my hand drawing the glass close to my chest. I want to look at Jack, to tell him this is too much, but I can't do that. They should have a party if they want to, and he should be here, celebrating with his family, not being forced to run away from it. I'm the one who should be leaving.

'Actually, we're going to get going—' Jack interrupts, taking his seat, but I don't miss the way he leans away from me slightly.

The room feels like its closing in.

'Oh, don't be a spoilsport, Jack. You don't mind, do you Mags?' Charl looks over at me. 'You can borrow one of my outfits. I have the perfect thing for you...' and she begins rattling off about a white lace dress that will fit me.

Jack jumps in, 'Charl—'

But I find myself forcing an expression full of excitement. Not forcing exactly, because no matter how terrifying this all is, isn't this *everything* that I've wanted?

'How about it, Mags? I promise to clean everything twice and I'll keep your food separate. The weather's clearing so we can have some of it outdoors. Dad?' she interrupts his animated conversation with the soon-to-be newly-weds. 'The patio heaters are all working, aren't they? There'll be plenty of space outside if you need to escape...'

'I... well, I suppose—'

I look to Jack and around the room, expectant faces poised in my direction.

'Sounds great!' I take a large gulp of champagne. When I look at Jack, even though he's smiling, there is tension in his expression as Charl leans in, talking more and more about preparations for the party, and asking for my opinions.

'And wait until you meet everyone; they are going to adore you. Just a few friends. Promise.'

41

JACK

I don't get angry with my sister often. Charl was, and is, usually my ally, but right now I'm furious. The house is *teeming* with people.

It's not unusual; our house has always been full, especially growing up. We were allowed to bring friends over whenever we wanted and because we're out of town, more often than not, it meant they stayed over. But this isn't a few friends.

My plan was to take Maggie home. Tell her my parents' worries, that they think I'm rushing into our relationship, that I'm using her to hide away from my life. Then I was going to kiss her and let her see that none of it is true. But before I had the chance, Charl was in full force. Maggie, gripping her glass, eyes like a deer – not just caught in the headlights – but like they were coming towards her at eighty miles an hour.

What else was she supposed to say other than yes? Luckily, she didn't see the reserved and judgemental look I received from my parents at her hesitation. And when I looked back to Maggie, I saw something else, a hint of happiness as Charl brought her fully into the conversation about preparations.

I should have known the minute she said promise. *Promise* meant, *I'll pick you up on time*, when she would arrive twenty minutes late, or *I won't tell her* when I had a crush on her best friend when I was thirteen, then she promptly announced it the minute said friend arrived on our doorstep.

The noise level is high. Conversations and boisterous laughter fill the hall. I step past two men sloshing prosecco over the rims of their glasses, one dressed in a sharp suit, the other with a wedding cake hat balancing precariously on his head. I pull Charl to the side. 'You said a few people.'

'I know, and I'm sorry but it kinda got added to our other WhatsApp group and, then someone mentioned a wedding theme; anyway, look, she's having a lovely time.' I look over to Maggie outside the doors, smiling at something Mum has said. Maggie is wearing a white lace dress, a white fur bolero around her shoulders.

She's breath-taking.

It hits me.

Hard.

I stare at her, my family folded around, her cheeks pink from the cold. She belongs with us. She belongs with me.

I'm in love with Maggie Wright.

And I know that a life with a woman who can hear my thoughts will be hard. I know that I won't be able to keep secrets or feelings hidden, but this past week has shown me that it *is* possible. She's never hurt if I move away and need space. She doesn't touch me without checking it's OK; this *can* work. I know it can.

I want nothing more than to take her in my arms and tell her.

I dodge two more grooms, one with a cravat and fake moustache, and make my way towards her but I'm interrupted. Charl's best friend Emily introduces me to two of her work colleagues.

I'm polite. Mum is getting too close to Maggie, leaning her head forward, her expression serious. I reckon, taking in the glow on her cheeks, and the way she is gesticulating, Mum is already a bottle down.

'Jack, this is Jenni and' – she pushes a woman forward, short, glasses like Elton John – 'she was saying she's got a publishing deal for her debut. Isn't that great?'

I make the necessary congratulatory noises and try to inch my way forward.

Emily clamps a hand on my arm. 'Jack owns a bookshop. I'm sure he'll be happy to have you in, once you're published?'

'Yes, yes of course. We'd love to have you in... Fire over your publication details and I'll get it in the diary. Sorry... if you'll excuse me, I—'

The noise around the room amplifies. A shuddering fear bolts through me. It's a cliché but the whole scene is like it's unfolding in slow motion. Mum's hand begins to reach out. I try to move towards them but I know I'm too late. Mum's hand is on Maggie's arm. Behind me, someone shouts my name, a cheer goes up, but all I can see is Maggie. She's rigid. Mum is talking slowly, not noticing the way the colour is draining from Maggie's face. The laughter and joy that I've seen over the last few hours is leaking out of her.

She looks up, eyes meeting mine.

She knows.

She knows what they think about our relationship.

42

MAGGIE

Today I've lived a life I never thought I would have. I've been welcomed into this gloriously flawed family and been made to feel, just for a day, like I could belong here. Between the banter, the food, the party preparations, there's been a pull in the pit of my stomach. Because the more they bring me into the light, the longer the shadow grows over me at the thought of losing it all.

I'd always thought that getting-ready montages only existed in movies. But there Jack was, looking up at me from the bottom of the stairs, like I was the only woman in the world. And in that moment, I believed it too. That I could be the girl they would all want to keep. Even if he didn't take my hand or hasn't touched me since his talk in the library, and even if, for most of the party, I've been here, on the veranda. Once again, the outsider looking in. Jack has tried to stay with me, but I've encouraged him to go and mingle. It's not fair for him to be the outsider too. And I haven't missed the glances from his family when he's been outside with me rather than inside with them.

Gilly joins me.

'Phew! It's getting warm in there. Mind if I join you?'

She places a glass of prosecco on the small patio table.

'Not at all. Jack's just nipped to the loo,' I say as though I need to remind her why I'm here, that I'm not a random person who has pushed herself into their lives.

'I want to thank you, Maggie,' Gilly begins.

'Thank me?' I ask, catching Jack's eye from across the room. Something shifts inside, as I meet his eyes.

There is no point trying to deny how I feel about him any more, but being here, with him and his family, just reminds me how difficult it will be for us.

But this is how love should be, right?

I can't keep ignoring the fact that I'm in love with Jack. I think I fell in love with him right from the moment he walked into Flicks.

And love... It's not supposed to be easy. That's what Riz said: *that's what love is, pain and joy and everything in between.* But still...

'Thank you for helping him find his way. Before he met you, he was closed off, barely came out of his flat. And now' – she looks over at Jack – 'I feel like I've got my son back. He tells us you're helping him find out more about what happened?' she encourages. I pause, wondering if he's told them the real truth, but there hasn't been any sign that they think I'm nuts.

'Yes. I mean, I just listen... It seems to help him feel calm?'

'Right, right. Well hopefully, with your help, we'll finally find out why he was on Fleetwood Road in the first place, instead of heading towards home.'

Fleetwood Road? Something stirs in the back of my mind. The room tilts, like the moment we'd taken off from the runway. *Fleetwood Road. Red hair.*

She pastes a smile on her face as someone calls her name,

distracted. My mind reeling as I repeat *Fleetwood Road, red hair* over and over. Gilly placing a hand on my arm jolts me back.

> **If only she was normal.**
> **She'd be perfect for him.**
> **But he can't have the life he needs.**
> **Not if they stay together.**

Each thought lands with razor-sharp edges.

'Anyway. I wanted you to know that we do appreciate everything you're doing for him. It's funny isn't it, how life turns on its own axis. One stranger ruins his life, another saves it.'

I pull my arm back as discreetly as I can, my throat dry. 'Oh fuck. Maggie, I'm sorry, I—'

'It's fine. I just... I need to...'

I begin walking into the house. She is calling my name but it's swallowed by the noise of the party, my own doubts amplified by Gilly's words screaming inside my head louder than any of the partygoers that I try to unsuccessfully avoid.

I hurry up to Charl's room and sit down on the bed. I look to the photos on the wall, of Jack and Vicky, the engagement ring, the easy way she fits with the family. I can't be with Jack, not in the way he needs.

We don't fit in the real world.

We only fit outside of it.

And Jack is too wonderful, too kind, too *alive*, to be living a life hiding away in the shadows with me.

I reach for my phone scrolling through my camera roll, until I find the photo I'm looking for. Me and Luke, pre-breakup, but the same night.

I examine the photo.

At least now I can give Jack the answers he needs to move on with his life when I walk away.

Because around my neck, being tugged in the sea breeze, is my red scarf.

And that night, I was on Fleetwood Road.

43

JACK

I take a beat before knocking on Charl's door and stepping in. I need to tell Maggie how I feel.

'Hey,' I say. She's sitting on the edge of the bed, her phone in her hands, curls falling forwards.

'Hi. Sorry, I... it was a bit much. I needed some space.'

I sit down beside her, and try to think of the best way to tell her how I feel without scaring her away. 'We should have left before it got this hectic. You've nothing to be sorry for. Charl shouldn't have...'

'What, Jack?' She meets my eyes, the green paler, more emerald than jade. 'Shouldn't have thrown a party to celebrate her brother's engagement? Of course she should.' There is a burst of laughter from the bottom of the stairs.

Her eyes go towards the door, where the laughter is dying away, more conversations filtering through.

'Maggie, I—'

'I don't fit in here, Jack... in this house, with your family.' She looks up at me. 'With you.'

Panic swells inside my chest. I'm trying to find the right words. But then I realise I don't have to. I can show her.

'May I?' She looks down at my open hand, hesitates then folds her hand in mine.

I love you.

We both register my thoughts at the same time. I can see it flash across her face.

My voice is trembling when the words come. 'I'm in love with you, Maggie. And I don't know what that means for us and our future together but I do know that you're everything I need.'

'I love you too...'

I should be filled with joy at those words, but her words are in opposition to the way she is shaking her head, the tears in her eyes. 'But I'm taking you *away* from what you need.'

Without warning, without me having the chance to move my hand away, Mum's words ring in my ears: *might you be rushing into a relationship that takes you away rather than immerses you?* I try to rein my thoughts in, try to push away all the doubt, the worries I've had about how we can have a relationship, but they come crashing through my mind, uncontrolled. Unfiltered.

I start to count, to regain control. One, two...

Three seconds.

And I'm there again, the man back in the hospital bed, clutching onto the rails for life support as she pulls herself and her hand away.

And I know I've already lost her.

Something like panic pulls at the pit of my stomach.

It takes me a moment to centre.

'We belong together, Maggie.'

'Not if it means giving up on the life you want.'

'Look.' I scrape my hand through my hair, trying to regulate my thoughts. 'I know that this is hard for you and I'm scared too...

It's natural for us both to have doubts about how this will work—'

'I know.'

'Then you know that I want to work through all of this. We can take things slower; I'll make sure' – I gesture to our surroundings – 'this never happens again.'

'You can't do that. I won't take you away from a family that loves you, that you love and belong to... You're scared, Jack.'

'Isn't everyone a little scared when they start to fall in love?'

'No, Jack. I mean...'

She lifts her chin, a sad smile in place. 'You're scared that they're right.'

I'm speechless. She's wrong. I try to replay everything I was feeling as I told her I loved her.

'That's... No. Let me...' I hold out my hand. 'I'll show you.'

She wraps her arms around herself. 'You already did.'

While her voice is soft, her words are final. Like the closing lines of a novel.

'Let's take a minute. Let me explain?'

But she shakes her head, straightens, and I can feel her pulling away from me. From us.

'I need to tell you something, Jack. But before I do, I want you to know that my time with you has been the happiest of my life. I...' Her voice is shaking. It's the same expression, the same tone, as the night she walked away. I'm not going to make the same mistake as I did last time. This time, I'm not going to let her go.

'I know this has been hard for you, so tell me; tell me how I can make it easier? We can be together; we just need to work out how.'

'You never said Fleetwood Road,' she begins. I'm disorientated, confused at the change of direction this conversation is taking. 'That's the way I go home. It avoids all the main streets.'

'Fleetwood Road? I...'

There is an echo of a memory, but whenever I tried to recall that night, all I remembered was being outside the pub. I was so certain that's where it all happened.

'Why does that matter?'

She looks at me then down to the phone in her hands.

'It was me, Jack.'

'What do you mean?'

'The woman? The night you had the stroke?'

'What?' I shake my head. 'She had red hair; it was long... It wasn't you; it was—'

'It wasn't red hair... it was a red scarf.' She turns the phone over. I reach for it, and scan the screen.

Images of that night career into my thoughts as I look at the photo. The woman, the red hair all change form.

She holds out her hand, palm up. 'Let me give you the answers you need.'

I shake my head, trying to reorganise the images of that night. She opens her palm, tears in her eyes. I take a breath, and place my free hand in hers and close my eyes.

I see Maggie, red scarf caught on the breeze crossing the road. A man, no longer a shadow, but tall, broad, watching her go. He pulls up his hood. I know in my gut that something is off. That the woman, *Maggie*, is in danger. I quicken my steps. She's up ahead; he's gaining on her. 'Excuse me?' I call out. He turns briefly then continues as Maggie talks on her phone and disappears from the main street down an alleyway. He continues to follow. I approach him; my hand clamps on his shoulder. He turns, and pushes me hard against the wall. There is a crack. My brain feels like it's splitting in two. Then nothing.

Maggie pulls her hand away, her face creased in pain as though she's been hit too.

'It's my fault, Jack.'

She wipes away a tear. 'My fault you can't read. If I hadn't heard Luke's thoughts, if I'd been more aware, if I'd walked home a different way, if I hadn't called Tess... It was stupid of me to—'

'Did he catch up to you?' I lean forwards. 'The man,' I say more urgently, eyes scanning her face. 'Did he hurt you?'

'I...'

'Maggie? Did he hurt you?' I ask, my voice louder.

She shakes her head, cat's eyes widening at my reaction. 'No.'

The feeling of relief floods through me. But it's not just relief. Ever since the stroke I have been angry. Angry with the world, with the doctors, with myself, because I never knew *why* I lost everything, but now, it means it meant something. 'You're sure, he didn't—'

'No.' She stiffens. 'I didn't even look behind me. I didn't know any of that had happened.'

My shoulders drop as I exhale. 'Thank God.' I have the mad urge to laugh. It wasn't all for nothing. I saved her. I saved Maggie. It all meant *something*. My life didn't fall apart for no reason, because she is safe. And it feels like fate. If ever there was a sign that we belong together then this is it.

'Are you listening to what I'm saying, Jack? It was my fault. I ruined your life and that was *before* you even knew me.'

'I knew in my gut that something was off,' I rush on, almost euphoric, high on knowledge. 'He pulled his hood up and crossed the street. It's not your fault. It's his fault.' I frown. 'All of this time, I worried that it was all for nothing. That it meant nothing.'

'He never touched me.' She shifts towards me tentatively, eyes glistening. 'You saved me, Jack. It means everything.' I realise I'm shaking. My eyes are still scanning her face, making sure she is unharmed. I think back to the first time we met, that feeling of familiarity.

I shake my head again, trying to banish all the dark thoughts since the accident, the feeling of worthlessness that had hounded me for so long. Then I think back to the first time I saw her, when the power came back on. 'I thought that I knew you. When we first met. Maybe I did know it was you?'

'Maybe.'

'Do you see what this means? We were always meant to be together. It's more than a coincidence I was there that night, that we got locked in the cinema together. If ever there was a sign that we belong together then this is it.'

She looks up, her voice soft, her eyes searching. 'Hellie used to say that sometimes you meet the right person at the right time.'

'Exactly!'

'And I believe that, Jack, really I do. And I think I met you at the time when you needed me most, and I'm so glad that I was that person, that I was the side character who helped you find your way. But loving me will cost you too much. And I won't let you give up the life you deserve.'

I feel like I'm free falling. 'Maggie, I...'

'Take me home, Jack.'

44

MAGGIE

Jack turns off the engine.

The rain is falling now. I picture the guests at Chadders, jackets and paper plates held over their heads as they rush inside to the warmth of the home.

He doesn't speak at first.

Mist is beginning to cling to the windows.

He had tried so hard to keep his feelings and thoughts away from me, but the truth shouting inside his mind was too loud to ignore.

I felt his desperation as he tried to block it out, but I could hear and feel his doubts, his fears, his love and his determination to make it work. He tried to push down that voice that was telling him what he could lose. All of it. Because he loves me.

Because the thing is, Jack would give it all up. The way he feels about me is *real* but he's scared of that. He's scared of what a life with me will look like, and he's scared of the future, but he's also determined. Determined to live a life with me. To throw away all his dreams. But I can't, and I *won't*, let him give up everything that he loves and needs, for a life hiding away with me.

'Can I come in?' he asks.

I turn to him. 'I don't think that's a good idea.'

'Maggie' – he looks back, hand clutching at the front of his hair – 'we need to talk about this. It doesn't matter that it was you that night. God, I'm *glad* it was you because you're safe.'

'Even so, this... this *curse*, already messed up your life. And I know you don't blame me, but it doesn't change the truth. And whether you want to acknowledge it or not, you know how difficult a life with me will be.'

'We'll find a way. I shouldn't have tried to hide that I was worried about how difficult it might be. From now on, I *promise*, I will always be honest with you. I'll tell you everything that is on my mind. I should have realised— Truth. That's the only way we can do this. I'll tell you the truth, as soon as I think it.'

I don't answer straight away, just wipe away a tear. 'Thank you, but you *can't* promise me that. There will always be things you don't want to tell me. And that's how it should be.'

'I'll figure out a way to make it work.'

'I know how much you want to carry on seeing me, but I already know too much. You still want the life you had planned. All of it. The wedding... a family, the chain of bookshops with your name above it. But this, us... me... I can't be a part of that life in the way you would need me to be.'

'None if that matters if I don't have you.'

'You want *children*, Jack.'

His expression falters.

'And I can't... that will never be on the cards for me.'

'We're rushing ahead. I don't even know if I want kids, yet.'

'But you did... with Vicky?'

'I guess we'd talked about it but—'

'I will always be in the way of everything that matters to you.

And I've taken so much from you already. Loving me? It will only cause you pain.'

'There is always a solution.'

'No.' The word is barely a whisper.

'Just, let's slow things down, take it one step at a time.'

'I can't.'

'Please don't do this. Don't give up on us. Relationships are hard and we might have more things to overcome than most couples but—'

'I can't, Jack. Not because I don't want to... because every part of me *wants* you. Wants to be *with you*. But the longer I'm with you, the harder it's going to be to lose you. And I *will* lose you, Jack.'

'You don't know that.'

'Yes... yes I do. These past two months have been the happiest of my life. You've given me a glimpse of what real love feels like, and you will never know what that means to me.'

'I feel the same way; I've never felt for anyone the way I feel about you.'

'But you will.' I soften my voice. 'Listen to me, Jack. I have to end it. Because... I don't think I will be able to recover from losing you if I fall even more in love with you than I already am.'

He's still. Processing everything I'm saying. His knuckles are white as he grips the steering wheel.

'Do you know what is so good about romance films?' I ask, my voice lighter as I desperately try to explain to him. I lick my bottom lip, finding my footing with the words I need to say. 'They give you the happy ever after without actually *showing* the after.' He frowns, head pitching to the left, eyes scanning my face as I try to explain. 'They give you the moment where the future looks happy, but they don't show the time that passes, the arguments, the divorces. They leave you with the good bits.' I smile at him, tears falling freely. 'And that's what this is... you've given me the good bits and I'm so, so happy with that.'

'Don't. Please don't end it this way. We can do this; we can find a way.'

'I don't want you to have to *find a way*... Don't you see?'

He exhales, eyes full of pain. I reach for my bag, bring it onto my lap.

'I want you to know, that for the rest of my life, I'm going to be happy. Because I got my happy ever after – truly, I did. And if we part now, then I get to imagine how our life could have turned out, just like I do at the end of a good movie.'

I put my hand on the door handle. If I don't go now, I might not have the strength. 'Goodbye, Jack.'

His voice stops me pulling the handle. 'How does it turn out?' He has tears in his eyes, his face softening. 'The end of the movie?'

I smile through the tears, through the heartbreak. 'We have a wonderful life together. We go on holidays, sit in busy restaurants, go to concerts, festivals, carnivals, surrounded by people. We go to your parents' every Friday. I hug them hello; I play with your nieces, carry Jaz on my shoulders. You propose and I go on a hen night to Vegas with *all* of my friends. We get married and have a huge wedding, so many guests that the dance floor is full.'

'Do we have a special wedding dance?' he asks, voice raw.

'Of course. We go to rehearsals and everyone claps and is amazed at our skills. We have children, a boy and a girl. You sometimes take them to work with you. They love to hear you tell them stories, and you let them choose their favourite books to go in the windows. At Christmas, we stay up late wrapping presents. I burn the turkey, but it doesn't matter because our house is filled with friends and family.'

'We can have all of that.' He smiles, his face eager. 'We just need to...'

I shake my head but I'm still smiling, even though I swear I can hear my heart ripping open. 'Please, Jack. *Please* do this for me. Give me my happy ending.'

He takes a deep breath in, looks back out of the window, the rain coming down heavier, the outside images like wax melting against the glass.

'I don't want this to be the end.'

'But it's not...' I take in his side profile, commit it all to memory. 'It's the beginning.' He meets my eyes. 'Live your life, Jack, don't hide from it. Open your shop, get married, have children and... remember me. Remember that girl you got locked in a cinema with, and wish her well. Maybe send her the odd postcard? And know that she will always, *always*, carry a piece of you in her heart.'

45

FRIDAY 20TH DECEMBER

Jack

I exit the police station and drive towards the new shop, having identified the 'hoody' man from the line-up. After I had gone in and explained that I'd made progress recuperating from the stroke, I had given a full statement. My phone vibrates and just as I have for the past five weeks, I check to see if it's Maggie, to see if she's changed her mind, but it's a voice note from Dad wishing me luck and telling me to call him if I need help.

Last week the police asked me to come in. There had been a bout of attacks of women walking home late at night in Brighton and they'd made an arrest, and they thought it might be connected to my case. I'm once again grateful that I was there that night, that Maggie is safe. I can't be one hundred per cent sure, but I'm confident it was the same guy. I hope he gets what is coming to him. My statement will add 'assault occasioning actual bodily harm' to his rap sheet so hopefully he will be going away for a very, very long time. Not as long as it will take for me to read a whole novel, but there we go.

Bayside is busy. Buses pass; workmen are putting barriers up, partitioning roadworks. The shop looms over me as I slide the key into the lock and flick on the lights, the empty shelves blinking against the harsh light. The room seems to expand as I walk in, a tension released as though it's ready to be filled with stories and life. I scan the room.

There's a few unopened letters and flyers on the floor and I pick them up. My eyes skim the symbols on one of the envelopes, my finger – automatically, now – tracing the outline of my name, to the distant sound of Darth Vader's theme tune. My mind skips back to the curve of Maggie's shoulder, my finger drawing an 's' the night she first read *Great Gatsby* to me and the loss of her hits me again.

I've replayed that final night over and over again. Tried to turn back time so I take her home instead of letting Charl convince us to stay. Said things differently when she told me it was over. I can't turn back the past, but maybe I can still change the future. Make her see that if I can do this, then maybe there will still be a chance for us. And maybe I can help *her*, just as she has helped me.

I pile the envelopes up on the wooden counter that stretches along the wall facing the window and head into the back room. It's small, a nook really. I had wanted this to be a reading room.

The polythene covering easily rips off two reading chairs, which I'd picked out last week, and I bend down. I know the tub of paint is 'Whisky-White'. I wipe my finger across the small rectangle on the front of the tin, slow my breathing and look for the 'W'. It takes me a few minutes, but I can start to see the letter form, smell clementine and cloves.

I take off my jacket and head into the storeroom. There are at least twenty boxes towering inside; each one I know is filled with classics. It was my first order, the books that most people wish they'd read. I lift one down, tear away the tape, and open it after several goes with a knife. I will never understand why book deliveries are always so hard to open. I shake my head, reach in and pull out the first book. I know it's *Dracula* by the picture on the front, but the symbols are dancing again. I hold it in my hands, tracing the letters but I still can't work out the title. Levin encouraged me to use an app. I open it and scan the front of the book. The title and author fills the room, a robotic voice echoing from the walls. I turn the hardback over and repeat the action, the full blurb and reviews rebounding around the small room. It's a laborious process, but by lunchtime, I have small piles of books ordered into alphabetised piles.

I write down the names of the stock, a page for each letter. But the notes soon become jumbled.

Google tells me where the nearest hardware shop is, and I listen to the directions; I've tried to read the usual map and I'm making progress, but I'm often distracted by the symbols still dancing on the screen.

Town is busy, the packed streets buzzing with the relief of a brief lunch break and Christmas shoppers. I dip into a café, use the app again to read the menu, the words read out loud through my ear pods. Nobody looks at me, or notices what I'm doing. I'm just a guy listening to music while picking out his lunch.

I pay and then eat my sandwich while I follow the direction from Google Maps until I locate the hardware shop and find the sandpaper.

The streets are still busy, despite the threat of rain in the dark, heavy clouds. There is a souvenir shop, postcards slotted into a white plastic frame that tilts to the right. I slow down, my hand reaching out. The card is split into quarters, little snapshots of this small bay. I trace the letter B and the opening bars of 'Bohemian Rhapsody' pound in my chest. I've got to give it to

Levin; it might be madness, but some of his methods are definitely working.

Once back in my shop, I pull out the sandpaper and plastic alphabet stencils that I'd brought with me. They're the same as the ones I bought Jaz for her birthday. I turn the sandpaper over, draw inside the stencils then cut them out. Twenty-six symbols at my feet, which I carefully trace and place around the room. In the store cupboard, I take the stack of thrillers and begin placing them in piles next to the sandpaper letters.

It's dark when I finish. My eyes are stinging, my fingers blistered, and my back is already starting to seize, but most of the stock is sorted into genre and alphabetised. I dig my hands into my coat pocket, checking for my keys, my finger catching on the edge of the rectangle of cardboard. Beside the new till is a pen and I reach for it, not letting myself think too much. I write Maggie's name and address on the right side of the card.

I miss you.

Jack

x

I attach a stamp from the stationery drawer and pocket the card, and as I drop it into a postbox, and picture Maggie standing on her sofa, attaching it to the wall, the hole inside my chest begins to fill a little.

46

FRIDAY 10TH JANUARY

Maggie

'He's gorgeous, isn't he?' I ask Derek. We're sitting side by side, his leg nudged against mine as we watch *Chariots of Fire*. He frowns, and that resistance that his dementia has forced in place is lowering. Today is a good day. Sometimes, he's so scared of letting his true feelings out that it's like a steel wall is locking his true identity away, but today, it's softer, more like lace than metal. 'You'd make a good couple. He'd give you a run for your money though.' I nudge him. He lets out a small scoff and I pass him the box of Turkish delight that he enjoys.

Christmas has been and gone in a flurry of chocolate orange, Baileys and some of my favourite movies watched with Tess: *The Holiday*, *The Man Who Invented Christmas*, *It's a Wonderful Life* and Bill Murray's *Scrooged*.

Flicks doesn't quite feel the same as it once did. I still work one shift... although I've switched days with Claire and helped her find a new babysitter, a kind girl, Ambika, who I bumped into at the corner shop and was looking for work. Friday night felt too raw. To be there without him. And the first time I tried to watch *Dirty Dancing*, my eyes kept flitting behind me, checking the door, and let's face it, that film deserves more of my respect.

I toasted the New Year with Riz, while we watched *When Harry Met Sally* with a bottle of cheap fizz and I tried not to think of how Jack and his family were seeing the New Year in.

I've finally set up my own website, and have a few clients on my books. Some of them through my flyers dotted around Flicks and local shops; others who have found me through word of mouth. It's a small fledgling business but it's mine and it's starting to build a steady income. I've even started to save a bit each month so I can get a new car. Or maybe even a van if things keep going well.

Derek flashes a grin at me. 'Oh I don't know... I've always been quite athletic.' He pops the sweet in his mouth, a dusting of white powder falling onto his jumper.

'You old devil, I bet you are.'

Ravina pops her head around the corner. 'What are you two sniggering about?'

'Never you mind!' Derek taps his nose, but I can see the fog is rolling in. He's trying to work out why he's watching a sports programme.

'Shall I pop on *Gardener's World*?' I move away from him, and select the prerecording that he seems to like. I stand and wipe my hands on my trousers.

'Mags? Could I have a quick word?' Ravina smiles and beckons me towards two chairs in the corridor.

'Sure. Everything OK?'

'Yes, it's been a good day today, although Mrs Davenport in room thirty-nine threw her bedpan at me.' I grimace as she points to the small mark on her forehead. 'Thank you for visiting Derek. I know how much joy you coming here brings him.'

'It's a pleasure – anything I can do to help make his days a bit brighter. It's like he can feel the loss of William, but he can't understand why he's in pain. I try to distract him as best as I can.'

She nods. 'And you do and, well, I've spoken to the powers that be, and we wondered if you'd be interested in a more permanent position?'

'A job?'

'Mmhmmmm.' She nods, brown ponytail swinging. 'Not as a carer, but as a companion? Just a few hours a week... We'd love you to be part of the team.'

'I...'

I don't know how to react. I want to say yes. Of course I want to say yes. I would have to leave the department store job, and then I could fit it in with the rest of my cleaning, but being a proper member of staff would be difficult.

'Thank you. But... can I think about it? I have a condition and...'

She nods. 'I know.' She looks at me with understanding, I wonder if Riz is somehow behind this job offer. 'But you seem to be adapting?' I press my lips together and look along the corridor where a young couple are looking at each other with worried eyes as they take in their surroundings, then I pull myself back to Ravina's hopeful expression. 'Just think about it and let me know? If not, well... keep on doing what you're doing. The place is brighter for having you here.'

* * *

Riz's room is two flights up, at the end of the corridor with windows that look out towards the southernmost tip of the bay. There is laughter from inside her room and I give the door a quick knock before I go in.

'Maggie, darling!' Riz's face cracks into a red-lipsticked smile. 'Meet Phillip!' She leans forward on her chair, the table between them scattered with playing cards and what suspiciously looks like brandy in the bottom of their cups. 'This is the girl I was telling you about.' He is still tall despite his age, skin marked with years of a happy life threaded around the skin of his eyes and mouth.

'Ah.'

My brows furrow at the look of sadness that flashes across his face. The type that stems from understanding someone, before they've said anything.

'Nice to meet you,' I reply, regardless of the expression on his face. I walk to the window, pulling open the curtains a little more. From Riz's room, I can occasionally see Jack's lighthouse. I hadn't noticed it at first, but sometimes, if the sky is clear I get a glimpse. It's like I can feel the turn of its cogs, the rhythm of it. The pull of safety it brings. I picture Chadders filled with family and laughter, the lighthouse keeping a watchful eye. Warmth settles in my stomach, my thoughts linking to each imaginary turn of the lamp: I was right; I was right; I was right. I turn my back and lean against the sill.

'Phillip used to be a psychologist.' She looks at me pointedly.

'Really? How interesting.' I give her an equally pointed stare.

He dips his head in response.

'Well.' He lands his hands on his knees and pulls himself out of the chair, wincing as he does. 'Damn these old bones.'

'Oh shush, you have a lot to be grateful for. Can't bloody stand all the moans and groans around this place. Many folk don't get to this age; we should all be walking around with permanent smiles as far as I'm concerned. Hitting your eighties is a damned lottery win if you ask me.'

'You're right, you're right.' He grins at Riz, all white dentures and sparkling eyes. Still a handsome man, I bet he had his pick... and looking at the way Riz's hair is clipped up and the shade of her lipstick, I reckon he still can. 'Good to meet you, Maggie.' He shuffles towards the door, leaving his hand on the frame before meeting my eyes. He hesitates, like he's about to give me some sage advice, but then throws Riz another smile and leaves.

'Soooo Phillip huh?' I wiggle my eyebrows up and down suggestively, steering well away from his profession.

'Oh, behave yourself. One whiff of sexual tension would likely send his blood pressure skyrocketing.' She shifts in her seat, winces, sucking in air sharply. I head towards her, hands twitching at my sides as she struggles to shift the cushions behind her. 'Are you all right? Do you need me to get a nurse?'

'To shift a few cushions? Absolutely not. I'm fine, just a bit stiff is all.'

I take the recently vacated chair and shift it back, but I don't miss the way Riz is clenching her fist as though she's holding her pain in her palm.

I know better than to ask Riz again but I will speak to Gloria, the nurse on duty. She's hiding something from me. I'm tempted to touch her, but Riz is as proud as they come, and it's not for me to go pickpocketing her thoughts, no matter how much I want to.

'Now, I've been telling Phillip all about you and your... problems and he thinks it's all down to deep abandonment issues.'

My eyebrows rise sceptically. 'That's not what this is.'

'So, you're not afraid of being cast aside, left alone?'

'Everyone is afraid of that.' I reach over and grab a biscuit.

'True, but it doesn't stop folk from at least giving it a go. Tell me, have you finally come to your senses and been in touch with Jack?'

I shake my head, chewing with frustration. We've been over

this conversation more times than I can count. 'You know I haven't. I'm not good for him, Riz.'

'See! This proves Phillip's theory! You're scared of being abandoned and thus are protecting yourself from letting anyone get close to you.'

'Rubbish! I'm not seeing Jack because I will hold him back from the life I know he wants. As I've said. Repeatedly.'

'Humph. Just because you keep saying it doesn't mean it's true. You're not being fair to him or to yourself.'

Tears spring in my eyes and I look away to the window, feeling the pulse of the lighthouse, the pulse of that life I was part of for a brief moment.

Her voice softens. 'Forgive me, love, but my time on this glorious earth will soon be at an end and I hate to go before I see you living your life, not hiding away from it because you're afraid of being cast aside. Answer me this, Maggie, do you want to see him?'

I let out a long breath. 'You know I do.'

'Then go!'

'I can't.'

'Poppycock. You mean you won't.'

'Yes. That's exactly what I mean. I won't stand in the way of him living the life he wants, Riz.' No matter how much it feels like my insides are on fire.

She shakes her head sadly. I straighten and reach for another biscuit, swiftly changing track. 'So what's the goss around here, apart from you and Phillip getting it on after lights out?'

'Mrs Khan from room sixteen has kicked the bucket.'

Mrs Khan had become one of Riz's partners in crime, as she liked to call her.

'Oh no! I'm so sorry.'

'It's a shit. She slipped off in the middle of *Midsomer Murders* and she will be furious that she didn't find out who put the poison in the loganberry jam... but there are worse ways to go. She'd had her supper first and she had her family around her so that's something. I'd hate to leave this mortal plane on my own.'

She glances up and Gloria the nurse walks in. Gloria, as the name suggests, is bright and cheerful, pink hair backcombed like a ball of candyfloss. 'Time for your meds. Oh hello, Maggie. Didn't see you sneak through.'

'She's like a spy this one – stays close to the shadows. That's why she only comes to see me at night.'

'Shush, nobody but you is supposed to know about my secret identity,' I joke, at the same time pushing away thoughts of seeing Jack. I glance at the pills Riz tips into her palm, spotting a pink one that I haven't seen before.

'Gloria, tell me' – Riz throws the pills to the back of her throat and gulps a glug of water from her glass – 'if you met a tall, dark and handsome man, who is clearly head over heels for you, who is successful and funny and kind, would you let him go?' I shake my head and roll my eyes at Gloria, my attempt to dismiss Riz's tone.

Gloria lets out a deep throaty laugh but wags her finger at Riz. 'I'm still not going to answer that. Leave the poor girl alone; she has her reasons.'

'Thank you, Gloria. I do,' I challenge, folding my arms in front of me.

Riz lets out a long sigh. 'Youth is wasted on the young.'

Gloria sits beside Riz, checks her pulse. 'Will you stop doing that. I'm old and still alive, no amount of checking is going to stop me marching towards the pearly gates.' Gloria shakes her head with a smile but there is concern pulling at the edges. 'Right. Bedtime for you,' she adds standing.

'Absolutely not. Not until Maggie tells me that she's going to go to Jack and lets him know what a magnificent fool she's being.'

Gloria tuts and shakes her head. 'I'll be back at nine to make sure you're behaving yourself.'

'Well?' Riz challenges as Gloria leaves. 'You're not going to decline a dying woman's wish, are you?'

'Riz, I love you, but in this case yes. Yes I am. I know what I'm doing. It's for the best.'

She lets out a pffft.

'I know you think we should be together but it's not as simple as that.'

'Poppycock. You think that life is always easy?'

'No. I know first-hand that it's not.' There is a snap to my words and she softens.

'Did I tell you that the first time Art asked for my hand I said no? He was too good for me, you see. Came from money, was distinguished and always behaved impeccably... all the things I wasn't. But do you know what I discovered? That I was *everything* he needed. He'd grown up with the weight of expectation on his shoulders, and I was able to fill in all the little gaps that made him into the person he was always meant to be. His parents thought I wasn't good enough for him, but I was, and he was a better person for meeting me. You see, my lovely girl, what makes a person the best version of themselves is when they find all the gaps in themselves and fill them with the things that matter. I said no to my Art, but then I realised the reasons I was saying no were nothing to do with him or his family; they were to do with me. I needed to fill those gaps, those little parts of me that I thought weren't good enough. It took me a year, but I filled those parts of me with life and experiences that I needed to become the best version of myself. I needed to fall in love with *me* before I could fall in love with *him*. Do you see?'

'I...'

'Fall in love with the person you want to be, Maggie. Take all of those holes and cracks that are holding you back and find a way to mend them. It's not being with Jack that you're afraid of, it's being left alone.'

I don't tell her that's exactly what I'm afraid of. I can't give him what he truly wants, and in the end, being together will only end up hurting us both.

'Now enough chat, it's time for the new series of that bonk-buster and it's time you stopped spending your evenings with an old bird like me.'

'I like spending my nights with you.'

She shakes her head and shifts. There is a flash of pain and she clamps her mouth tightly. 'As I say... youth is wasted on the young.'

FRIDAY 14TH FEBRUARY

Jack

'Happy Valentine's Day!' Nell shouts.

'Nice jumper,' I say, looking at the skull and crossbones sitting on top of what looks like a dissected heart.

'Thank you. Festive isn't it? Seeing as we're both loners for the most romantic day of the year, I thought it was fitting.' She leans over me, peering at the screen. 'What you up to?'

'Just organising the release dates into genres... I thought we could do genre-themed displays depending on the most releases of that month? April is looking pretty cosy crime heavy so... maybe one of those murder mystery nights?'

'Oooh, nice idea. You going to do it here or...'

'I thought here first? See how it lands?'

'I'll check it out and get the costing up.'

'Do you mind?'

'Of course not. I do everything around here anyway,' she quips even though it's not technically true. At least not any more.

'About that... I wanted to talk to you about something.'

Her face falls a touch as she takes in my more serious tone. 'You're not going to fire me, are you?' She laughs but the laughter catches in her throat. 'You're not, are you...?'

'Take a seat.' She perches on the end of a stool and I drag the other over to face her.

'Nell, I want you to know that how much I appreciate everything that you've done for the shop and for me since, well, since I lost my shit. And as you know things are changing—'

'Fuck. You are going to fire me, aren't you?'

'What? No! I'm offering you the permanent managerial position.'

'Really?' Her short black fringe shoots up to her hairline.

'And... I haven't worked out all the details yet so it won't come into play until next year, but I want to introduce a profit-share system... depending on if you want the job or not.'

She taps her bottom lip thoughtfully. 'Do I get to have multi-coloured Post-its?'

I shrug. 'It's up to you, you'll be in charge.'

'Can I do my speed date with a book night?'

'Again. It's up to you.'

She lifts her chin and puts out her hand. 'Then I accept.' She shakes my hand then laughs. 'Oh come here you great baboon!'

'Baboo—?' But my question is lost as she's pulled me into a hug and I've currently got a mouthful of her hair.

'Right. What time is it?'

'Almost five.'

I grab my coat. 'I'll be off then, things to do, places to go, people to see...'

'Um, Jack? On the subject of people to see...'

'Hmmm?'

'I saw Maggie. Last week. At Flicks.'

The mention of her name is like a gut punch. My fingers stumble over the buttons of my jacket.

Nell scratches the top of her head. 'She looks good. Although her date was a bit weird.'

My stomach hits the floor.

'Date?'

'Yeah, short bloke, red in the face... manic smile?' She shakes her head. 'The vacuum, you dummy, but you should see your face.'

'Very funny. How did she...'

'She's fine.'

'Good. That's good.'

'Good?'

'What do you want me to say, Nell? She ended it, and...'

'Look, all I'm saying is she, well... she's still single and so are you and... It's just that you're doing so much better and maybe it was simply about timing, you know?'

'You mean if I didn't have my head up my arse when I was with her?'

'I wouldn't put it quite like that but—'

'Yes, you would.'

'You're right. Yes, I would.'

'I can't, Nell. She made it clear that she doesn't want to see me.'

'I know. And usually I would be one hundred per cent in the girl's corner and not encourage you in any way to, you know, go against a woman's clear wishes, but I am also a woman who dates women...'

'So what are you saying? I should rock up to the cinema with a bunch of roses and beg her to go out with me?'

'Have you lost your mind? Of course bloody not. But maybe

you could... offer an opportunity? Like, I don't know, mention of a *new bookshop opening*?'

I shake my head. 'She wouldn't be able to. It'll be too busy and...'

'Look. I am usually always on team girls, but for some unknown reason, I am always in your corner. And do you know what? Maybe she needs to get her head out of her arse too?'

I take a second, a hesitation. Outside, a loud car horn grabs my attention until I land it back on Nell. 'If...' a grin flashes across her face as if she knows what I'm going to say '...and it's a big if... what if she doesn't come?'

I swallow down a flicker of hope or maybe it's fear? Part of me wishes she'd never said anything, but in my heart, I know this might be another chance. My only chance.

'Then at least you know you tried. And come on. What have you got to lose?'

A lorry screams to a halt as I step onto the kerb. The noise jolts me from my thoughts of Maggie. I wait for it to move on, fiddling with the silver book on my keychain. I could send her another postcard. I mean, that's not too intrusive. I look to the right, cross the road behind the lorry, opening and shutting the keyring like the start and end to a new chapter.

48

MAGGIE

This will be the first Friday shift at Flicks that I've done in a while. Nell asked if I could swap shifts with Claire tonight. I hesitated at first, but *The Notebook* is on tonight, one of my all-time favourites, so I agreed.

I unfold my legs, the lines from the cord carpet imprinted on the outsides of my thighs. I've been learning mindfulness. Phillip agreed (with what I'm sure was more than a little persuasion from Riz) to be my unofficial therapist. Riz says it helps him feel useful.

I mean, it's not like I've told him the real reason why I'm seeing him, but I have explained that sometimes it feels like my head is filled with so many people's thoughts (I bluffed and said I was always conscious of what people thought of me) that I can't hear my own. He says I need to turn up the volume on my own thoughts, the thoughts that matter, so that my own voice overrides the outside noise. I've tried my best to stay present in the moment... to imagine reaching out and turning up the volume on my own thoughts. I imagine a dial, like the one on the DVP at Flicks, I start at one, then when I'm calm, I turn the dial to two. I focus on my breathing, on the fabric of my clothes, the smell of the flowers in his room. And it's helping, kind of. It's hard to concentrate on my own breathing and the sound of the birds outside when a carer on the verge of quitting puts a gentle hand on my arm. But still, I'm trying. Trying to fix those broken parts of me, just as Riz had suggested. I need to learn new ways to navigate my life, just as Jack has.

Over the past week, every day, for at least half an hour, I've been trying to take myself deeper into my past. Phillip thinks that the fact I can't access my earlier memories is the key to turning the volume up so I can't hear the 'extra' thoughts. And that sometimes, when we're filled with anxiety, when life is too hard to tackle, our 'wonderful' brains find ways to distract us, to bury the pain behind other thoughts, other things to protect us from discovering what may hurt us, *like white noise that we get used to*, he said. I didn't say that in that case my mind has practically been a rave for my entire life. But still. I've tried to picture the house that I have flashcard-like images of. There's the cherry tree outside. But the house is always too far away. The pathway never gets to the door. Yet every day I attempt to go further, and every day, I'm getting a little closer. I'm trying. But I'm not there yet.

As I climb into my car, the sun is beginning to set behind the haphazard buildings. The Jack-shaped hole is still pulsing inside my chest cavity, but I don't want that to go. It's good to still feel his loss because it reminds me of what I had, a true romance, just like the film, but without the drug dealers and, you know, Christian Slater.

And life is mostly good. I still haven't accepted the job officially, but I'm spending time with more of the residents at the home. I have a few new cleaning gigs, so yeah, life is good. I turn the key again but there is nothing but a groan, a shudder, and a loud bang from my exhaust pipe. No, no, no, no. I turn the key again, foot furiously pumping against the gas pedal.

Nada.

I climb out, picking up Henry and lifting him out from the back seat, where he's strapped in like a toddler.

'Here we are again, Henry.' I think about the night of the storm, the night I met Jack. Maybe something good will come out of this? That thought is squashed as I stand in front of Fleetwood Road. Roadworks, no pedestrian way through, a yellow diversion sign glowering at me. Crap. I let out a long breath. If only this road had been closed the night of Jack's stroke, things would have been so different. Right now though, I need to think. I can do this. It's – I check the time on my wrist – half four. By the time I get to the main high street, it will be almost five and the shops will be closing. I dig my hands into my pockets and pull on my thick sheepskin gloves and start walking.

The minute I turn the corner to the main high street, my stomach bottoms out. The path is buzzing with people. Heart-shaped banners and cuddly toys line the shop windows, and couples galore are strolling hand in hand. Valentine's Day. I expand my lungs, give myself a quick pep talk and give Henry a tug. I look left and right, cross the road and begin making my way.

I manage to avoid people on the whole, and it's actually quite nice, being around the buzz and loved-up atmosphere. The breeze bites at my nose; the sea to my right is churning, but it's not aggressive. It's as though it too is caught up in the feeling of festivities. The unmistakable hint of seaweed and sand is refreshing, despite the deep rumble of trepidation inside.

There are a few close calls: a woman with a toddler who escapes his reins and runs straight for me, luckily, the mother abandons her bags and grabs him just in time. There's a gaggle of teenaged girls with tiaras on their heads; and another jogger brushes my arm, but his thoughts were on his wife and the look of joy on her face as she'd opened a gift in a small square box. The sun has started to set as I catch the glow of lights from Jack's store up ahead. I cut a glance up to the windows above, no lights on. He's probably safely away in the new shop anyway.

I'd seen Nell a few weeks ago. She'd told me he was doing well, that he had practically moved to the new shop and she'd suggested in a not-so-subtle way that maybe I should get in touch. A horn from a car parps loudly, making me jump, the driver two-fingering at a cyclist who is powering down on the pedals, thick headphones on his ears.

My phone begins to buzz in my pocket. I turn my back, facing the sea opposite, wheeling Henry with me as Heritage Retirement Home flashes on the screen.

'Hello?'

'Maggie, love, it's Gloria. I... it's Riz.' The sea churns a little more, larger waves crashing against the rocks as my pulse begins to race. 'I'm afraid—' A lorry pulls up next to me, letting a car on the other side of the road come through, stealing the rest of the sentence. Nausea swirls inside my stomach.

'Hello? Hello?! Can you hear me? Gloria?' I jam the phone closer to my ear and begin walking back the way I came, the lorry still so loud I can't hear. Finally the lorry begins to move away.

'Gloria?' I ask again.

'It's her time, love. It's her time.'

Every part of me feels like its falling. Like the cracks in the pavement are widening and I'm dropping down into them. I look around the street desperately. A bus is coming along the street and I step out into the road, my hand up. The doors hiss open. I scan the inside; it's busy but I clutch Henry towards my chest. Words fall from my mouth at the driver, words about Riz, about

Heritage, the address. He nods and tells me he can get me there, and that it's on his route.

I sway as I drop Henry to the floor. The seats are full – rush hour on Valentine's Day – of course they are.

I have two options, to stand swaying and bumping against the other passengers, or to take the only seat next to a woman reading a book. I brace myself:

> **Why is she carrying a vacuum?**
> **Should have got the earlier bus. I'm going to be late for**
> ***EastEnders*.**
> **When I get home, I'll make a to-do list.**

Images of lives and homes bounce around my head, a collage of daily lives, love, regret, stress, tiredness, family, romance; the cacophony of emotions tap and snip and stroke at every part of my body. I'm holding my breath but take my seat. I nudge away from the woman. She's young, dark hair pulled back, thick green coat wrapped around her. I sit. There is little space as her bags are sandwiched beneath the window, and my leg presses against hers. I close my eyes. Her voice is calm and rhythmic as she reads, her thoughts entirely focused on the plotline of her novel. I let her words conjure up the image of a woman riding on a dragon, high up above a fantastical landscape. But the images are blotted by my own thoughts, images of Riz, the pink pills, the pictures on her wall, the laughter and sparkle in her eyes as she told me about her life, her loves.

Gloria's words that told me Riz is a private woman and it wasn't for her to tell me anything Riz wasn't happy to share herself. I should have touched her. I shake the thought away.

Nothing worse than dying on my own. Riz's words crack open the images of the girl flying on a dragon and instead I'm filled with desperation.

She will not die on her own.

I will not let that happen.

The journey seems to take forever and I'm biting my nails; the driver glances at me in the rear-view mirror.

'Quick detour!' he shouts. I hear a collective groan and mumbles run through the bus. 'Sorry, folks.' I can feel eyes on me, but the girl on the dragon has landed and there is a battle ahead of her. The image snaps shut and the woman instead turns to me, a hand on my arm. I meet her eyes, wide, blue, and feel a wave of compassion, of kindness. 'Is there anything I can do?' she asks. I realise I'm crying. My cheeks and my throat wet.

'I... my friend is dying and I don't want her to be alone.'

I hear the kindness in her thoughts, a flicker of some of her own grief, an aunt, a call taken in the middle of the night.

'I'm sorry too, for your aunt.'

Her brows pucker. 'How did you—'

The bus screeches to a stop. Doors whoosh open.

'Here you are, love, as close as I can get you!'

'Thank you,' I say. The woman nods, still with a look of confusion.

I lift Henry, brushing past people, each with thoughts of kindness and concern as they watch me make my way out of the bus.

I don't stop to think, I just run.

She will not die alone.

49

JACK

I get up from the reading chair, placing the children's book about a magical eagle on the table. The author, Patrick Shaw, is coming to the opening in two weeks' time. My progress is slow, but I've got to page five of twenty and only had to use the app six or seven times. Reading is a different experience now, filled with tastes of strawberry laces, music, the smell of rosemary or mint when I read the grapheme 'sh' and lemons, always lemons. Since getting all of my memories back, the pain has gone. Do I wish I could read like I used to? Of course I do, but there is also something... more in the experience now. I read books like nobody else and that is something to be grateful for.

The bookshelves around the shop are full, the paint on the walls fresh and clean. There is a separate bar to the side of the store, book-spined wallpaper behind dark wooden tables. I'm going to introduce open mic nights, and Nell's idea of speed dating with a book is starting to feel more like a possibility, too. I hope it's enough to make it a success. I make my way to the door, postcards as similar to Maggie's as I could find, are tacked to the wall to the right, some the same places, and others are stills from films. Levin is standing outside. His dark hair is wild and his cheeks are flushed. I swing the door open. The street is lit up, and after the council grant came into action, there is rarely a night that's not busy, even at this hour, but tonight it's teeming with activity.

'Thought you were going to leave me freezing my naughticles off.' I bump an eyebrow as he steps through.

'Naughticles?'

'Had the snip years ago. My late wife named the boys naughticles.'

'That's too much information.' I shake my head, closing the sounds of traffic and Valentine's Day behind him. He unbuttons his coat, looking around.

'No such thing. Well, what a place, eh? Looks great, Jack.'

'Cheers.' I gesture to the bar. 'Coffee? Tea? We have beer on tap...'

'Ah no thanks. I won't beat about the bush. I wanted to give you this.'

He unpacks a pile of paper, bound together at the top with a bulldog clip. I glance down. 'Um, you do know this will take me about a decade to read?'

'I know, I know, and call me sentimental but still. I'm pretty hopeful my career is going to take an upward swing when I publish this, and, well, it felt right that you should have it first. It's my first draft. It needs a lot of work yet...'

My finger follows the first letter. Ffff. Then the next. Iiiii. Nnnn. My brain pulls away but I force it back with a snap. Din? I let out a breath. Ggg. Fiiiinnnndddd-ing. Finding. The familiar Darth Vader death march leaves me with no qualms about the last word.

'Finding Jack?'

'I know it's a bit on the nose, and well, I can change it if needs be, but it felt right somehow.' He crunches his gloves in his hands. 'I can change the title if you want?'

'No. No.' The lump in my throat bumps up and down. 'That's a great title.'

He gives a little nod. 'Oxford University Press are interested in the pitch and, well, it might help. Others. You know. Like you. You're my best case study.'

I laugh. 'Thank you, Dr Levin. For this and for everything. I know I wasn't always the easiest of patients.'

He taps his palm with his gloves and smiles. 'It was an honour, Jack, really. And if I might be so bold... but I'm very proud of you.' He looks around, eyes lighting up as he takes in the shop. He gives me a slightly awkward pat on the shoulder, clears his throat and pulls his gloves back on and heads to the door.

'If you don't mind, I'd like to pop in. Once in a while?' He pulls up his collar and tries to pat down his wild hair.

'I'd like that. I...' He turns back at my words, bushy eyebrows puckering up. 'I... I never thought that I'd ever find pleasure in books again and, well, thanks. Again.'

'Truth be told, I was on the verge of giving up. You came to me and validated my research. I'm just as grateful to you as you are to me.'

He puts out a hand and I shake it. It turns into this weird man hug, hand-shaking, shoulder-clapping affair. I close the door behind him, pull down the shutters and stand looking at the inside of Chadwick's the Second with my hands in my back pockets, and a swell of pride in my chest. I check the clock on the wall, the hands hitting ten past ten: happy time Maggie used to say, when the clock is smiling. I wonder what she's doing, if she's noticed the time too.

I'm about to turn off the light when a postcard falls from the wall. I bend, pick it up, see Ferris Bueller looking up at me with his rebellious grin. We never did get to watch it together, but having it in my hand makes me feel closer to her, reminds me of the first night we met. I clutch it in my hand, make my way to the counter, pulling open a drawer. I don't let myself think too much about what I'm doing, just peel a save the date sticker off a sheet with the opening day and time and stick it on the back. I write Maggie's address, stick a stamp on and put it in the pile of envelopes ready to post in the morning.

50

MAGGIE

Gloria meets me at the door.

She goes to hug me. I'm too caught up in my thoughts about getting to Riz that I don't pull back in time.

**Poor love. Multiple myeloma.
Blood cancer.**

There's a rush of compassion, and fleeting thoughts of Riz over the past months, becoming more tired and not eating. A brief conversation where Gloria suggested calling me and Riz being adamant that she didn't need a fuss over her feeling a bit under the weather. I pull back.

'Am I too late?' Relief rushes through me as Gloria shakes her head. 'No. No, love. Let's get you to her, shall we?' She takes Henry from me, pushes him behind the desk.

The corridor feels longer than ever, like it goes on for miles, each door slanted, the walls closing in as I walk. The sounds of my boots clicking with each step.

Gloria pushes the door back and lets me through. I pass the

small living area, her photos smiling up at me, her life so full and vibrant despite the darkness flooding my thoughts.

Riz is lying back, her hair clipped with a green-emerald butterfly. Her lips are pale, her breathing shallow. I sink into the seat beside the bed, shifting in closer.

'Talk to her, let her know you're here,' Gloria says gently. 'Just press the buzzer if you need me.'

'Is there anything that can be done?' I ask, my voice breaking.

'No, love. When it's time, it's time. And she was adamant, right from the first day she walked in here and asked for a room with a view of the sea.' She gives me a smile. 'I did try to get her to tell you, love. But she'd made her choice and you know how head-strong she is.'

'Thank you. I appreciate that.'

After Gloria leaves, I pull the chair closer, leaning in. 'Hi, Riz, it's me. Maggie.'

She doesn't respond. Tears fall freely down my cheeks as I look around the room. It feels as if something is missing and I realise it's her scent. The perfume she always wears: flowery with a spicy under-tone. Her nails aren't painted either. I stand, look around for her vanity box. I take out her perfume, bringing it to my nose. So many memories flicker, like old photos developing. The day she hired me, Jack laughing with her, Riz slamming down a winning hand of cards. I go back to the bed, lean over and spray some on her neck.

'Can't have you meeting St Peter without looking and smelling your best, eh?'

I click the lid back on and then reach for her lipstick. I twist the gold casing, red velvet: soft and rounded by her mouth. I lean over her, dabbing the stick against her lips. 'There. Much better.' I put the lipstick away and reach for her nail polish. Her hands are lying beside her, flat on the soft blue blanket. I twist open the bottle, gliding the brush against the edges, and begin painting her nails. My throat is tight with the distant pulse of her. It's calming, no thoughts, no sounds, just... calm. I move to the other side of the bed, repeating the process.

'Keep still or you'll smudge.'

I move back, hearing her voice as if she were speaking. *No chance of that is there.* A small laugh turns into a choked sob. I return to her bedside. Time passes; the room darkens. I open the curtains as far as they will go. The sky is full of stars tonight and the moon swollen, low in the sky.

I continue to talk. I tell her about my life, the truth about why I couldn't touch her, about why I can't be with Jack.

'Thank you,' I say quietly. 'For being such a good friend. I'm going to miss...' I swallow. 'I'm going to miss you.'

A strange sound comes from her throat and I push the call button.

Gloria steps into the room. Soft feet in Crocs. 'OK, love?' I shake my head, throat closed.

'She made a weird noise. A—'

'It's all normal.' She sits beside Riz, takes her pulse, strokes her hair back and straightens the bedclothes. 'It won't be long now. You might want to hold her hand?'

'I...' I shake my head.

'I know it's difficult, but it'll help. I promise.' She gets up and leaves the room.

'The first time I met you,' I begin. 'I thought you were the most incredible woman. All those pictures on your wall, all of those adventures, but it's not the places you've been to or how many of the Fab Four you met, it was this confidence, this love of life. That's what made you incredible.' I pause, wipe my cheek with my sleeve. 'You looked past my problems and instead made me feel normal, you know? No, normal isn't the right word, you made me feel special. But in a good way.'

Riz lets out a long breath and panic slices through me. I get up, sit next to her. And with grief and pain in my heart, I take hold of her hand.

And then.

There is a pull. A tug inside.

I don't only hear her thoughts. I see them. As if I'm in the front row at Flicks, looking up at the screen.

You want to buy me a drink? Why?

The picture in her mind is so clear that I can smell the polish of the wood on the bar, hear the music in the background, the conversations around us, feel the warm heat of the room and then I see the man in front of me, *her.*

Because when you walked into the room, I didn't realise there was part of me missing.

The weight of her hair is heavy at the base of her spine. She looks to the mirror behind the bar, blows out a plume of cigarette smoke through scarlet lips that I can taste.

Poppycock.

The image shifts, another time, her hair feels shorter, the same man, dark messy hair roguish smile, glasses, thick jumper. I can smell his cologne, mint and burning wood. He drops to his knees, a bolt of fear shooting through her, I can hear the sting from the words falling from her mouth.

No. I'm not the marrying type.

I feel pain as her back turns and she walks away.

Images flicker past, seasons changing: Riz working hard, camera in hand, loneliness, the ache of something missing, then love.

All-consuming, unwavering love.

There is another rush, feet running along a pavement, her hand banging on a door, Art's face as he opens it, beard, clothing crumpled, glasses askew, a breathless feeling tight in her chest.

I love you.
Took you long enough.

The memories speed up, image after image after image: laughter; friends filling her house; the sounds of a saxophone playing; dancing with Art in her arms; snaps of scenes behind a camera; the sounds of gunshots; panic and adrenaline; mountains from outside a tent; the cool morning mist on her shoulders; more laughter, time slipping by in photo-snapped shots.

Art gets older, and life takes on a slower pace. But there is still laughter, still an all-consuming love. Art is hunched over papers, with a cigarette in his mouth, then I hear doors slamming, arguments, tangled sheets, thinning hair, aches and pains, laughter, contentment.

The images are starting to lose their colour, and the sounds and smells are more diluted. I see a door opening, a policeman, a coffin, a walk home alone, the fear of life without him.

The images are getting smaller, more distant: fading.

'Riz?'

There is a blinding flash of light, and an overwhelming feeling of freedom. I see two solid doors opening; there is a swish of fabric. I look down and there is a clutch of flowers in my – *her* – hand. 'Moon River' is playing and I realise we're in a church. Rows and rows of guests stand and turn. But they're like smudges in the periphery because all we can see is the man at the end of the aisle: glasses, a smart suit and obliterating love as we begin walking towards him.

The images around us fade, and the final image, as the lights burn brighter, is Art, his hand outstretched taking her hand in his.

Silence.

The room I'm in comes back into focus, Riz's hand limp in my own. A sob escapes my mouth as I lean in and kiss her forehead. Still warm, still her.

I glance to her photos by her bedside with a smile, taking in the time: ten past ten – happy time. I reach over and press the buzzer and wait. I cast a glance around the room, a flash of light in the distance. I get up, open the windows to let her spirit soar. The white light winks in the far distance.

'Say hi to Art for me.'

51

FRIDAY 21ST FEBRUARY

Maggie

I don't sleep. I don't eat. I don't work.

I don't know how a week has passed since I said goodbye to Riz. I pull the duvet tightly around me, as I shift into the corner of the sofa where I had leant against Jack. I try to capture his smell, the feeling of his arms around me, to gather some comfort from my time with him, but I can't stop Riz's life passing behind my eyes. It's like I've lived her life right alongside her. It was a privilege, but the aftershocks have left me with a life that feels empty, a scrappy home video with dodgy sound and pixilated images.

The letterbox snaps open and closed, post sinking on top of the rest of my bills for the last week that are piling up on the floor along with flyers for takeaway pizza that I have no appetite for. I bury myself deeper into the warmth of the duvet.

I close my eyes, but the terror Riz felt when Art proposed, the fear of not being good enough churns my stomach. I knew she had turned down Art when he first proposed, but it was like a sidenote to her story, always told with a laugh and a shake of her head, but that's not what it was. Not anywhere close. The roll of loss and regret keeps sucking me under, and I know it's not just Riz's emotions I'm feeling.

For the last few months, I have forced my own emotions beneath the conviction that I made the right choice, for me, for Jack. But then the image of Art at the door and her reasons for turning him down fell away, and instead, she stood before him, exposing her heart, giving him the most vulnerable part of herself.

The happiness of her life that followed that decision keeps playing on repeat.

I try to shake the gnawing feeling of regret. I have managed to create a life where I'm happy and safe. Being alone has never been something to be afraid of; it's my sanctuary, a place where I can't be harmed and can't harm others.

My phone vibrates again. I send another message to Tess to tell her I'm fine. She's in Amsterdam where an agent is going to see her gig. I hope this is the turning point of her career. An unknown number flashes up on the screen. It's been trying to contact me all morning. I suck in the stale air simmering around me and accept the call.

* * *

Outside Riz's house, life is carrying on without her. Her door is still bright red like her lips and the windows glint in the sun. I take slow steps and rap on the door. It swings open, a man – suited and booted – greets me. 'Margaret Wright?' he asks. Kind brown eyes behind thick-rimmed glasses, a gentle lapping Jamaican accent. I nod but don't step inside. 'Kingston Green,' he puts out his hand.

'Maggie.' I gesture to his hand with a nod. 'I have a...'

What? What do I have? The ability to hear thoughts, to hurt the people closest to me? To push people away?

'Condition. I can't touch people. No offence,' I add at the quizzical look.

'Of course, let me...' He turns and takes some confident strides back. My purple boots click against the tiled floor and I pull my coat further around me. The house feels so cold, so devoid of life, so... empty.

Kingston Green smiles at me and sits down at the oak table. I pull out a dining chair and sink into the fabric.

'I would imagine you're eager to find out what this is all about?'

I nod.

'I have been instructed by Messrs Bassett and Wick as executor of the last will and testament of Clarissa Hancock. I'll cut straight to the chase, if that's OK with you?' I nod again. Words lost beneath the fog of her loss. 'Clarissa has—'

'Riz.'

'Sorry?'

'Her name is Riz.'

'My apologies. Riz... named you as her sole heir.'

'Sorry?'

'As sole heir, you are now the owner of this beautiful home.'

'I can't be.'

'I know this may be quite a shock and of course you will need time to process.'

'She left me the house?'

For a second I can hear her laughter. See the sparkle behind her eyes at one last hurrah.

'She did, and a rather generous inheritance.'

He passes me an envelope with Riz's handwriting looped across the front.

'Perhaps this will explain in more detail?' He throws me a kind smile.

My hand is shaking as I run my finger along the seam of the envelope, ripping it open.

Dearest Maggie,

So it seems I've had my last waltz.

Please don't be too sad. I've had the most wonderful life, filled with colour and texture, love and loss and everything in between.

Forgive me, my dear girl, but – if you can't say the things that need to be said when the end is near, then when can you? – don't waste your life on what-ifs and the fear of the unknown.

You are a spectacular woman, Maggie, full of spark and kindness, brimming with energy and love that is bursting to get out.

I wipe away the tears that are falling, going back to the paper in my hands.

Life is there to be lived, my darling girl, and you're not living it. Life is a gift. Don't squander it worrying about what could happen, protecting yourself from the pain you may not feel. Or protecting others from you. We all have to take a risk if we're going to live.

It doesn't matter what might happen; all that matters is you open that great big beating heart and let life in.

This house is yours. Call it payback. It's not a gift, it's to repay my debt of gratitude for all the kindness you've shown

*me. Fill it with laughter, with love, and a full life. Travel the
world, my beautiful girl. Take that fear that is holding you back
and kick it in the teeth. Use it.*

*Fear is power. The things we are most afraid of are usually
the things that are the most precious.*

*Phillip says that psychiatrists don't fix people, they just
help them find the key to unlock the answers to their own
story. Find the key to yours. Open the door, Maggie love.*

Riz

I close the letter, reeling.

Kingston talks through the next steps and I follow him out,
closing the door behind him, and stand still outside this empty
house waiting to be filled.

I walk back to my flat, my mind full of all the things I've seen,
that I have been told, her words and the vast empty rooms that I
had seen through her eyes brimming with laughter and music
and friends and love. How can I own a house like that and do it
justice? Do Riz justice? I slide the key in the door and look
around at my small space crammed with souvenirs and pictures
of places I've never been to; to the bookshelf filled with DVDs of
fake lives that I've fake-lived from in front of a screen.

None of this is real.

Not one part of this house reveals my life. My memories. My
experiences. My home is a set, a carefully choreographed collection of things to make it look like a home when in reality none of
it belongs to me.

I bend down and pick up the pile of bills and flyers. My hand
stops shuffling and I stare at the postcard in my hand. It's Ferris
Bueller, lying back in a white T-shirt with the slogan talking
about life moving by quickly, advising you to look around before
you miss it.

I turn the card over – today's date and time for the opening of Jack's shop. How long has this been sitting on the hall floor?

Every part of me wants to go, to walk into his shop and hold him in my arms. But I can't. Too many people. Too many thoughts, memories and emotions that don't belong to me. Even with the progress I've been making with Phillip, I know I can't do it. And it'll hurt too much to say goodbye to Jack again.

I drop the card.

And fall to my knees.

Find the key. Open the door, Maggie love.

I look down at my open palms, to the hands that have read and stolen people's most private thoughts and emotions.

Take all of those holes and cracks that are holding you back... and find a way to mend them.

I look down to the creases and lines branching across my palms, my own life etched out in front of me... waiting.

I take a deep breath. Focus on my ability. Just as I did when I tried to help Jack find the answers he needed. It's time for me to stop listening to the thoughts around me. I need to turn up the volume, to feel, to see, and to listen to myself.

I wrap my hands around my body. My movements intentional. My focus sharp.

My mind centres. I listen to the sound of my breath, the low steady beat of my heart inside my chest, the way my skin feels beneath my fingers: soft, cool, taut.

I close my eyes.

I picture my hand reaching for the dial. And slowly, while I concentrate on my breathing, I turn up the volume higher, past two, three, four, taking my time until the dial reaches ten in the hope that's enough to hear the echoes of memories that have been buried for so long.

I lived in a small house.
There was a path.
A cherry blossom tree.

An image comes... blurry at first, but becoming sharper the more I listen, the more I take myself inside my own mind. I walk along the path that leads to a small cottage with the cherry blossom tree outside. The key is heavy in my pocket; my fingers lock around it. I hear the clunk as I slide it in the keyhole, the click of the mechanism as the door swings open.

Flashes of a little girl, of *me*, of something I've pushed down inside for so long, bursts free from somewhere deep within me.

I'm sitting on a knee, a story about an enchanted wood is being read. I look at the woman.

Mummy.

Her face rips through my emotions, long curly hair, green eyes gleaming up at me. She passes me a cuddly toy in the shape of a fish.

What shall we call him?

Her voice. The cadence of her words, a soft accent, a Cornish burr.

Bruce.

The tinkle of my own laughter runs up and over my arms.

Another memory now, there is the smell of popcorn. I look down to my feet skipping then swooping over the grey carpet. We stop, hand in a ticket. We're at a cinema. I'm high up. My hands being held by warm ones; shiny purple shoes bouncing against a chest. I can hear laughter and I turn, looking down from my place on someone's shoulders.

A deep voice now.

Daddy.
Time to get down, Pumpkin.

Strong hands are under my armpits, there's a rush of lightness as I'm lifted and placed on the floor.

They take hold of my small hands, nothing but love in their eyes, as they swing me forwards and backwards.

People I haven't been able to picture my entire life are suddenly clear, like they're on screen, in the same way as Riz's memories were. Mum's green eyes the same colour as mine, Daddy's wild curly hair.

The lights dim, my hands clutching my cuddly fish, the seat throne-like to my small body, little hand dipping into Mum's popcorn.

A car then.

It's dark outside, fireworks off in the distance. I can feel the heat of the blowers, the swipe of the windscreen wipers. Dad's voice:

Look.

A finger pointing towards the sky, Mum looking at me over her shoulder. I can taste something sweet on my tongue: cherry cola.

I watch Daddy's hand move the gearstick. My feet in small polished purple shoes dancing from side to side. There is another boom of firework to my left. I throw Bruce forward:

Look, Mummy! A flying fish—

Sounds then.

Metal. Heat.

The world upside down. A tightening of a belt across my chest.

I gasp, a scream coming from my mouth long and low and high and short.

There is an emptiness in my chest.

I'm now in a room with white walls. A woman in a grey jumper and baggy black trousers leaning forwards:

> *Take all of those memories.*
> *Hide them away until you're ready to deal with them.*

I don't know who she is. I don't like her. But I like the idea of not thinking about them. It hurts too much. I miss Mummy and Daddy.

On the wall are posters and pictures, one of them is an iceberg the shape of a volcano and a calm sea. I like that. I want to be there, on that iceberg. The woman's voice drones in the background, but I'm picturing myself climbing on top of that iceberg, looking down into the cavity below. I should be cold but I'm warm in my big fur coat and patent lilac shoes.

> *It can help to hold your worries and fears in your hand.*
> *Imagine filling a bubble and blowing them away.*

I'm cross at the woman. I don't want to blow Mummy and Daddy away. I want them to wait for me. And the ice is pretty and cool. It will put out the fire; it will keep them safe.

Next to the photo of the iceberg is a cartoon picture of a boy.

He's sitting cross-legged, a big smile on his face, the words: '*Good Listening*' are written in jaunty handwriting. I'm thinking about how happy the boy is. Around him are words: **Think. Know. Listen.** I like the boy and want to be like him.

The woman is still talking, but my eyes have dropped to the sign above the sink. A hand inside a red circle and big red strikethrough and the words: **Don't Touch. Stay Safe.**

Here, inside my flat, my hands want to release their grip on my arms, but I don't let them. I take myself deeper into my past.

I'm a little older now.

I don't remember a woman with curly hair and green eyes, or a man with me on his shoulders and a kind laugh. Now I see other people's homes. Images of my childhood flash by, things I've never looked at before: a warm hug from a foster mother, a robust laugh from a foster father playing Snap! with me. A deep sadness pulls me away when I return to the children's home. Christmases, Easter egg hunts, and the feeling of being ripped away from the warmth and safety of a ready-made family on repeat. Of not understanding why they say one thing and do another.

The tapestry of my childhood is made up of hundreds of stitches of hope, hope that this family would be the one to keep me; that maybe this time, I wouldn't go back to the children's home. Always living half a life, being half a person, half a daughter, half a sister.

I see kind families extending a helping hand towards me only to pass me back when the damage in me was exposed. That quiet girl with big wide eyes and dimples who they let into their home soon became a child who would scream when kindness touched her, would push and kick when she couldn't process what and who it was she could hear inside her infantile mind.

And so that little girl had learnt that the only way to protect herself from the cruelty of hope was to carve a space around her where hope couldn't get in, where she wouldn't get hurt, where she was the only person in control. Where she could hear the truth, not the lies they said about being welcome. Wanted.

But I'm not that little girl any more.

A sharp pain rips through me. My body feels like it's splitting in two but I wrap my hands tighter and tighter around myself, feeling and seeing everything that I've kept hidden from myself for so long.

I release my hands. Nausea rushes through my body, hands gripping the carpet. My body is aching, shaking, thick snot beneath my nose, my face wet.

That empty cold space inside me is flooding with warmth.

I was loved.

I was wanted.

I had a family.

There is a boom, a flash of white and then—

52

JACK

I pull at the collar of my shirt. It feels too tight but I know it's just nerves. Nell pops another cork and half fills glasses while Mum arranges canapés on a silver platter. Dad is in the corner nursing a glass of red, while he reads the blurb of one of the new arrivals. I sidestep Charl who, glass and book in hand, is already heading for one of the beanbags at the back. 'Call me if you need me!' she says taking a huge bite out of a sausage roll.

'Any good?' I ask nodding to the book in Dad's hand. 'It's been done before but...' He taps the hardback. I love that sound. That bracken echo that links it back to the tree that broke it's back to be here. 'The reviews are stellar.'

'May I?' I take the book from his hand, turning it over. My eyes run around the outline of the letters, I smell rosemary, hear the melody of *Swan Lake*, taste lemon.

The N-igh-t
And the Immm■□▢♎♓♌●
D-ay lll-igh-t

The bell above the door rings and I glance up, my heart crashing back into my boots with every new customer that isn't Maggie. I know it's a long shot, I know this would be too much for her, but my hopeful heart keeps being drawn to the bell.

'The Night and the Im-something Daylight?'

'Impeccable.'

'Good title.'

'Hmmmm,' Dad reluctantly agrees.

Nell walks towards me; an anxious pull around her mouth. I check the time; it's almost half seven already. I scan the room. Patrick Shaw is nowhere to be seen. In the children's corner, eager kids are clutching their books while watching the magician I'd hired to keep them entertained. Parents are sipping wine and watching on, waiting for the author. Who is late. Fifteen minutes late. Probably a cancelled train but I can feel the swell of concern. The big pull of tonight is his appearance. This could cripple the reputation of the shop before it's even had a chance.

'Patrick can't make it,' Nell says.

'What?' I look to the eager children.

'Been sick on the tube, and let me tell you, that is not something anyone should be privy to hearing.' She shudders.

Fuck.

The shop is even more full than before. Patrick's recent stint on *Between the Covers* has made his coming here more prominent than I had originally planned. I was pleased, but the minute I make this announcement, the atmosphere will deflate like a popped balloon.

'Don't worry, I can fix this.' Mum squeezes a hand on my arm. 'I'll ring his agent—'

'No, I... I can sort it. But thanks.'

'Darling, I know we pushed you to do this on your own but that doesn't mean we're not here for you if you need help.'

'I know. And thanks. But I have an idea.'

If I can keep them entertained long enough to get their attention, I might be able to pull this off.

The magician has finished and the children are starting to fidget. My eyes land on the book folded next to the chair, ready and waiting for Patrick to talk about his book and the story behind it.

'So... what are you going to do about...?' Mum gestures to the children who are fidgeting like they're sitting on a pile of nettles.

I swallow, eyes on the book. The magician gets up and makes her way across the room. I speak quickly, she passes me her pen, and I make my way over to the desk, pull out the ticket list, and hide my activities with my back, before sitting down in the creaking reading chair in front of the children.

I can't mess this up. The kids are already getting bored, and I've seen more than one glance at smartwatches from the parents. I can't ruin this. Not now. Not after how far I've come.

'Hi!' I clear my throat. 'I'm Jack and this is my new shop. What do you think? Pretty neat, eh?'

Neat? How old am I, seventy?

The children look up at me unsure how to answer.

Greta sniggers and mouths 'neat' to her sister.

'Mr Shaw couldn't wait to meet you all, but he's got a poorly tummy and can't come.' The faces that look at me are already becoming bored, bottoms are shuffling and the parents seem to have with tight lines where moments ago full smiles were clamped over glasses of wine and chocolate-covered pretzels. I get it. I've seen my nieces' tantrums and they are not pretty. I'm losing them fast so I revert to the best way I know around grabbing kids' attention. 'He's been...' I act out violently farting, wafting my hands. The kids giggle and the unease in my stomach settles a touch. OK, so I may have got a bit carried away with the vomiting actions and louder farting noises, by the expressions and furrowed brows of the Waitrose brigade, but the children are in hysterics. Right. Time to calm them down.

'But... I've been told that this book is magical but we can't see the magic until the final pages.' I raise my eyebrows knowingly. Eager and curious glances from the children, sceptical and challenging looks from parents, who are probably wondering if the next part of my act might actually include real farts and vomit. I turn to the back of the book and show the page to the eager faces.

'I can't see anything!' A boy with glasses and scruffy hair scowls at the book, rising up on his knees.

'Ah well that's because it will only appear once I've read the story.' I grin and there is a buzz of excitement. 'But first I have to tell you a bit about me.' I hold up the book with the invisible writing on the back page.

'You know how you can't see any words? Well, that's a little bit like me. I can't always read what is on the pages of a book.'

'That's stupid. Why do you have a bookshop if you can't read?'

'Conner!' A short sharp voice from a mother who is reddening quickly looks to me and mouths 'sorry' but I shake my head and smile to her.

'You have a very good point. But you see, sometimes, you have to learn new things. Even when you're a grown-up.'

'I thought that's why we have to go to school? I don't want to learn when I'm grown up.'

There is a murmur of laughter from the parents standing at the back.

'Ah well. You keep learning even when you get really, really, old... like me.'

I turn the cover over, glancing at the chocolate-smeared faces. Jesus. I've run marathons in forty-degree heat. This might be harder. I point to the title and slowly trace the words.

'I'm going to be brave now and try to read this to you, but I may need a bit of help, is that OK?'

'I'm red group in English. I can help you,' a girl of about five pipes up, dark brown ponytail swinging.

'You are? Brilliant.'

I take a deep breath, ignore the way my hands are shaking, and turn the page.

'It... was... on a c-o-'

Lllll-dddd

'Cold n-igh-t...'

There is hushed chatter in the background but I don't take my eyes off the page.

Wh-e■

I turn the book around and put my finger under the word. The words are hard to find, my senses on overload. But the kids don't get bored, they pay attention. 'Can you help me out with this one?'

Bodies are propped onto knees, as they crane their necks to see. There's a chorus of 'when!'

'Amazing. Thank you.' I turn the book towards myself and continue reading. It takes me longer than I would like, but I guess there is something exciting about helping an adult to read. A realisation seems to sink in with parents, that this isn't some kind of ruse to keep the children entertained. I glance up to the looks of compassion and something like understanding passing their faces. I get to the last page where the Eagle finally flies and finds his family. I know the final line because it's the tag line on the front of the book and the press release and the posters in the window display.

'Sometimes, you have to fall... to let the ones you love fly.'

Prompted by the parents, the kids begin to clap. My family are standing at the back of the shop, clapping and cheering like I've won an Oscar.

53

MAGGIE

I open my eyes. The front door is tilted to the right, my cheek against the carpet. Outside, the light is starting to dim. I wince as I sit up. I don't know how long I have been passed out for. My body should be ice cold, but there is a warmth radiating from deep inside.

Christ, maybe I've had a heart attack? I stand, hand against the wall, my balance still off. Something feels different. I rub my arms, beneath my fingers. My skin feels warm.

My eyes are drawn to the floor, to the postcard from Jack. I bend, hold it tightly in my hands. I'm raw. My skin feels sunburnt and tender to the touch.

Something has changed.

I feel different.

I glance down to the card and scan through the details.

Jack's shop opening is tonight. My eyes take in the fleeting light outside.

My instinct is so finely tuned to protect me, that a barricade of worst-case scenarios flits through my mind, but if I'm ever to break the cycle, if I'm ever to stop living my life in fear of being cast aside, then I need to change that. I need to.

I hope I'm not too late to repair the damage I've caused.

Don't waste your life on what-ifs and the fear of the unknown.

I can do this. I can go.

I grab my keys and open the door.

'Come on!' I turn the key again but my car won't start no matter how many times I try. I reach for my phone, swiping my finger across the screen. The last train leaves in twenty minutes.

I can make it.

If I run.

My legs are already burning as I run along the street. I side-step and dodge the shoppers, and hold my hand up in apology as I cross in front of a car about to pull out, but most people seem to see my desperation and are happy to move out of my way. 'Sorry!' I shout as I almost career into a group of women strolling in a haze of expensive perfume. 'Coming through!' I yell as I push through the doors into the tiled floor and high-ceilinged train station, scanning the screen for my train.

'Now arriving at platform four, the seventeen forty-nine train to...'

Shit!

I dig deep, take the steps to the overpass two at a time. The train is already thrumming against the platform. There is a loud beep reverberating through the air as the doors begin to close.

'Wait!' I shout. 'Wait!' I push my hand through the closing doors. A man holding a bike, head to toe in blue Lycra, and a furiously trimmed beard takes me in, eyes widening as his hand slams on the open button.

My throat is dry, and I'm so out of breath, I can barely speak as I climb on.

'Thank you,' I gasp.

'No bother,' he replies. The train is packed, but I'm too busy trying to catch my breath, my hands on my knees, blood rushing to my face.

'Would you like a drink?' I'm confused for a minute, then he passes me an unopened bottle of water. I sag with relief.

'Thanks.' I reach out, tentatively reaching for the bottle.

The train jerks, my balance lost.

I slam into him.

I brace myself, waiting for his thoughts to shoehorn their way into my subconscious.

Oops. I... the... nev... min...

I look down to where his hand is under my elbow steadying me.

'You OK?' he asks. 'You're as white as a sheet.'

I can hear him. But it's fainter than usual. Not whole words, but fractured pieces.

A flush of gentle heat spreads through me.

Damn it. I forg... ot... br... d

What is happening? I jolt slightly. My own thoughts so much louder than his.

'Sorry, would you mind if I...' He frowns as I place my hand on his arm. 'I feel a little dizzy,' I say in explanation. I close my eyes and concentrate. His words are faint. Still there, but the more I concentrate on my own thoughts spinning through my mind, the louder my voice becomes, and the more distant his. I'm in control of the volume, the dial still set at ten. It's just as Phillip told me. I'm in control.

The sound of my own heart beating, and my own jumbled

thoughts is first and foremost in my mind... His is like an echo, so quiet that I'm having to concentrate on them. My eyes flash open.

'I can't hear you properly...'

'Sorry?'

'I...' A bubble of laughter explodes from my mouth. I cover it up, but laugh again. I grip his arm. 'I can't hear you properly!' The guy looks at me as if I have lost my marbles, and who knows, maybe I have?

I let him go and look towards the carriage, people are standing, swaying as the train makes its way towards Jack.

For my entire life, I have been different. I've unknowingly adhered to that sign above the sink in that small room with the poster: *Don't touch. Stay safe.* Lived my life trying to be the happy boy sitting with his legs crossed: *Think. Know. Listen.*

Losing Riz, loving Jack, finding the key and opening the door to myself means that I can open up to all the joys and fears that come hand in hand with a life filled with possibility. A life I want to grab with both hands.

'Thank you. For the drink. I'm going to see if I can find a seat!' He raises his eyebrows in an 'ohhhhkaaay...' movement.

I try not to get too excited. It might come back. The thoughts might get worse and be louder next time. But still, I move away and begin stepping into the main part of the carriage, my arms bumping against elbows, legs brushing past man-spreaders. And still. The thoughts are only whispers.

The train is pulling into another stop and I step aside. A woman with a thick black topknot and bulky blue jacket sets a small child on her hip as she gets up and tries to reach down for her suitcase above. I hesitate. What if this new *thing* wears off? But the words come from my mouth, regardless of my concerns.

'Would you like me to hold her?' Words I never thought I

would say are tripping out of my mouth like I'm used to saying them every day.

Her shoulders sag with relief. 'That would be great.'

She passes the warm bundle into my open arms. I prepare myself, but as the little girl wrapped in a bright pink sleep suit lands in my arms, and as the sway of the train means I bump hips with the teenaged boy reading his phone, no coherent thoughts push their way into mine. Just a gentle roll of vowels and the odd snap of *mumma*, but I'm having to concentrate hard to hear them. I let the tension inside relax. Instead, I focus on the powdery-sweet smell of her, feel her tiny pudgy fingers reaching for the silver stud in my ear. 'Hello,' I say. She doesn't look at me, instead her wide blue eyes are transfixed by my earring. 'I'm Maggie.'

'Thanks, you're a lifesaver,' the woman says and I pass the little girl back, the soft hum of her thoughts easing away like a dandelion seed floating away on the wind.

'You're welcome,' I say. 'Anytime.' The woman nods and shifts her way through the aisle.

Anytime.

I sink into the recently vacated space. I can't control the grin that is stretching across my face. I must look unhinged but I don't care.

I'm coming, Jack.

MAGGIE

I run from the station, my breath hot and dry, until I'm standing outside the shop. New paintwork, book displays and gifts arranged behind the clean window. I take a moment to calm my breathing and tame my hair. And mustering every ounce of my newly discovered control, I reach for the door and open it.

He doesn't notice me come in. All eyes are on him as he reads, that voice I love so much, steady, deep, soft. I stand to the side, obscured mostly by a bookcase.

'Turn the page! Turn the page! Turn the page!'

'There's still nothing there!' A red-headed boy scowls and folds his arms.

'Ah, but that's because you haven't activated the magic yet.' Jack reaches to the table and picks up a torch, flicking it on and passing it to the boy.

Jack's eyes tear away from the children as I step out from behind the bookshelves.

The room stills.

His eyes meet mine, dark, intense.

'That's my name!' Jack's gaze is pulled away from me, back on the children letting out squeals, heads turning, eyes almost popping out of their sockets as names emerge on the back page of the book under the torch's beam.

'And mine!'

He passes the book to a little girl with brown pigtails and asks her to pass it around with the torch, then gets up.

We walk towards each other. The room quietens. Like the tension, and love, and hope is expanding into the room. We stop short of touching. In my periphery, Jack's family, customers, Nell... all eyes are on us. It's only been a few months, but I'd forgotten how tall, how *Jack*, Jack is.

'You came.'

'I did.' I smile, my whole body shaking. 'You did brilliantly just then. Amazing.'

'I can't take all of the credit. I had help.'

I look to the right. Nell watching on with a soppy smile.

'I...'

How to begin to tell him everything that I want to say? How to tell him, in Riz's words, how much of *a magnificent fool* I've been. All that comes is:

'I've missed you.'

I step closer.

Jack looks pleased that I came, but I don't know how he feels about me, don't know if he even wants me in his life any more. 'I know that I hurt you, and that I'm not the easiest person to be with...' His expression is hard to read: understanding maybe? Is he going to agree that walking away from us was the right thing? I power on, 'And I really *really* don't expect you to forgive me for walking away without fighting for you, for us, and I totally get it if you don't want to—' The words fall from my mouth in a rush, bursting to get free.

'What are you saying, Maggie?' He tilts his head, eyes scanning my face.

'The thing—' I let out a breath, my throat tight. 'The thing is. I couldn't remember. What it is to be loved. To be part of a whole instead of watching from the outside. And, and... I've come here with no expectations because I know loving me will be hard and I know I'm not perfect and—'

'Love isn't supposed to be perfect, Maggie.' His eyes darken, that seriousness, that sincerity, which I love about him rising to the surface. 'Love is made up of all the broken pieces that make us *us*.'

Us. He said us. My heart is pounding so hard I fear I might crack a rib. 'I said goodbye because I thought I couldn't give you a full and happy life—'

'But what if the only way I can have that... is by being with you?' he asks, stepping closer, eyes fixed on me. 'Even if we drive each other nuts on occasion. Even if it's *not* perfect. God knows I'm not.'

'But I think you are, Jack. I think you are perfect.'

'I snore.' He moves a little closer.

'I sneeze when I'm full.' I step closer.

'I'm moody.' Another step.

'I'm a morning person.' We're almost touching now.

'I can't stand it when people crack the spines of books.'

'I like cracking the spines of books.'

He scrunches one eye, flinching.

'That was a deal-breaker huh?' I ask, chewing my lip.

He moves closer still, a fraction of space between us.

'No one is perfect.' He's so close now that I can feel the warmth from his skin, smell that familiar hint of clove and vanilla. 'But maybe we are perfect together?'

Yep. Definitely going to crack a rib. 'Do you think so?'

'I do. And if we don't at least try to live a perfectly imperfect life together, I think we will regret it for the rest of our lives.'

'I think...' My voice cracks. 'I think my whole life, I have been making my way to you.'

'So *stay*. I mean, of all the bookshops in all the world, you did walk into this one...'

He leans forward, a hand hesitating by my cheek, ready to wipe away the tears falling down my face.

'For fuck's sake, Jack—' Nell says despite the children at the back of the room. 'Just kiss her already.'

He smiles, slowly, and looks into my eyes.

'May I?'

I wrap my hands around his neck.

I love you.

His lips brush gently across mine, and there's that tug, that invisible thread that latches me to him. We lean into the kiss, warm, desperate, relieved, passionate, his strong arms holding me tightly. He pulls me flush against him, lifting me from the ground, turning me around slowly. There are whoops and cheers and claps behind us, but all I can hear is my own heart beating, my own words:

I am loved. I am loved. I'm loved.

EPILOGUE
MAGGIE

Charl has her arm linked through mine as we push through the crowds lining Fifth Avenue. The September sun is high in the sky skimming above the skyline. Across the road, leaves flicker and glint in the warm autumn sun. Behind me, tall buildings scrape the skyline, Greta's hand clamped in mine.

'He's going to miss it!' I cast a hurried glance around me, popping up on tiptoes to find him but there is no sign. The parade started fifteen minutes ago. Bagpipers have piped past; a marching band drummed their way along the avenue, snare drums and the sound of feet marching echoing around the crowds. Jack had to take an urgent call, something about the new extension of Chadwick's the Third. His first shop stateside. Flags wave as lederhosen-clad men and women dressed in Oktoberfest outfits are throwing sweets from the raised float being pulled along by a station wagon.

The atmosphere is buzzing. Families, from all walks of life, are leaning over the barriers as the floats pass by: some with disco music playing and dancers on the small platforms; others with cartoon characters: a giant Sonic the Hedgehog and the cast of *Frozen*; all waving flags, giving out pretzels and sweets to the crowd as they move further along the avenue.

'Let's wait here,' Charl says. 'I'll text him and tell him where we are.'

Sometimes, when I wake in his arms on a Saturday morning at Chadders, with the sounds of his – *our* – family downstairs, I panic that I'm living a dream. That when I wake up, I will be alone in my flat with only Bruce for company. But I never wake because this is my life now. I'm living my happy ever after. And life isn't perfect, just as Jack said that day in his shop. He still has days where reading exhausts him. Sometimes I have days where everything I try to do in my new house goes wrong, and I have to call an emergency plumber. Jack curses when he trips over my shoes that I never put away, and I wake up in the night and have to give him a gentle nudge to turn over so he stops snoring. But since I gained control over my gift, life has opened up in a way I never thought possible.

My house, 53 Pickford Avenue, is slowly filling with things from our travels. Photos of us, me and Tess on our nights out, and the Chadwicks in all their colourful and loud glory. My shelves are filling with snow globes and souvenirs from every city and seaside town we have visited, including the day where Jack taught me how to kitesurf. And the night we went to see Tess as she sold out at her first Hammersmith Apollo set. She's touring now, and is finally beginning to see herself the way I have always seen her.

Hunting for the perfect place for his next shop has taken us to Paris, to Rome, and now, New York. The place that I've seen on the screen so many times, and here I am, part of it.

People bump into me, and while I still have the urge to pull myself away from the crowds, to hide in doorsteps and quiet corners, with each day that passes where I can listen to my own thoughts above anyone else's, it gets easier to live in this beautiful, messy world. Occasionally, thoughts will find their way through, if they are upset or angry, or when I'm lying next to Jack and he's overwhelmed with love for me.

I still visit Heritage, and Derek. His thoughts are getting harder and harder to hear, but occasionally they will be a memory of William. I try my best to keep those memories alive for him, to give him – and some of the other residents – comfort. But for the most part, my thoughts are just my own.

Now, back to the task in hand... where *is* he?

Another float is approaching. Oktoberfest-themed women are swinging beer steins. The outside of the float is decorated in red, white and blue balloons, flowers, and flashing fairy lights.

'Where's Uncle Jack?' Greta tugs on my hand. I crouch down.

'He had to take an important phone call, but he'll be—'

Through the speakers, a twang of feedback, then a voice:

'This goes out to a very special woman—'

It *can't be*.

'—who wanted to see something spectacular today.'

Greta shakes her red pigtails, hand pointing towards the float. 'I said *there's* Uncle Jack!'

I stand quickly, eyes frantically searching until they land on Jack. He's standing on the float, wearing Ferris Bueller's leopard-print waistcoat over a white T-shirt, microphone in hand.

'Gotcha,' Charl says loudly by my ear, turning her camera first to me then to the float. The first bars of 'Twist and Shout' begin. I clamp my hand over my mouth, laughter climbing up my throat. Tess is behind him, wearing the full on lederhosen and a grin that she used to hide. She's swaying and dancing the way we used to in a locked room with headphones on, and now here she is with the crowds of Manhattan dancing with her. She used to protect herself with jokes so people wouldn't tease her about her looks, her weight, but now – my heart is so full just watching her – here she bloody is. And she is magnificent.

Jack continues miming to 'Twist and Shout', John Lennon's voice powering out as he encourages the crowds to twist and shout with him. And while he looks one hundred per cent embarrassed, he's captured all the moves, his dark hair blowing in the breeze. His eyes search the crowds, looking for me as the float moves slowly towards us. Our eyes meet and he gives a little shrug and grins, beckoning me over.

'Oh no...' I say but Charl pushes me forward and parts the barrier. 'I can't!'

'Oh yes you can!'

Jack continues miming, reaching out his hand as he sings the part about me looking so good. He steps down to the edge of the float, hand outstretched.

Oh Christ. I take in the look in his eyes and shake my head with a laugh.

He's replaying the whole scene. I have no idea how he pulled this off. My heart is jackhammering against my ribs... He planned this. The trip, getting us here for the famous Von Steuben Day parade, arranging everything so I could be part of the movie that I have loved and watched for so many years, always the spectator never the star. I reach out a hand, warm in his cold ones, and climb onto the float. The crowd are cheering, flags waving as he puts his arms around me.

'You're nuts!'

But Jack just grins and carry's on singing as he twirls me around. Surrounding us, the cheers from the crowd are getting louder, Tess flinging sweets and flowers like she belongs on Fifth Avenue. As the song comes to its feet-stomping crescendo, he brings me into his arms, and dips me like I'm on *Strictly*. 'Jack Chadwick...' I run my hand along his cheek. 'You are my hero.' He kisses me, and there's that familiar zing, that yank inside like there is a chord latched between us, pulling us closer. I'm laughing as he pulls me back, his dark eyes scanning my face.

'Happy anniversary.'

'I can't believe you did this.'

'I wanted to give you your dream,' he replies. Both of us are out of breath. He tucks a lock of hair behind my ear as I stroke the side of his face. 'You already did.'

He wraps one arm around me and continues waving to the crowd. I follow suit, looking out at the throng of spectators cheering with phone screens pointing our way.

My eyes snag on a little girl on her father's shoulders. She's wearing an astronaut outfit: thick white fabric, puffy white glove, face inside a plastic dome, hands waving an American flag. My hand stills for a second as I think back to myself as a child, to the little girl who learnt to stay safe by keeping love away.

I wish I could hold my younger self, let her know that it'll all be OK. I would tell her that it's good to be scared. Love hurts. But it also heals. I'd hold her close and let her see that she doesn't need to be alone to be safe. Safety comes from letting love in, not hiding away from it. I would pull her closer and tell her that love isn't like it is in the movies, or books.

It's, so, so much better.

Jack kisses the top of my head and I look to all the phone cameras pointing our way: I'm finally the leading lady in my own romance story.

But then again...

I always was.

I just didn't know it yet.

* * *

MORE FROM EMMA COOPER

Another book from Emma Cooper, is available to order now here: https://mybook.to/EmmaCooperBackAd

ACKNOWLEDGEMENTS

Every Saturday afternoon, I go to the cinema with my best friend to whom this book is dedicated. We go and watch anything and everything, but my romantic heart is always pining for a good old romance. As I'm sure you will have guessed, I'm a total sucker for eighties teen movies so I hope you'll forgive the indulgence for the films mentioned... If I'm ever lucky enough to be locked in the cinema overnight (with as many snacks as I want!), these are the films I would love as company.

So often, I had thought about writing a book set in a cinema and I'm so glad I've finally found a way to write it! There is a kind of reverence to watching a film with strangers... alone but together. My busy life is put on hold for a few glorious hours as I sit in front of the big screen, rant and laugh with my best mate (during the trailers and before the film starts... I'm not an animal!) and I always feel so refreshed when I come back out, blinking into the daylight.

I'm sure it comes as no surprise that I also find the same kind of relief when I walk into a bookshop. I adore the smell of books, the lowered voices of the customers, and the whisper of a turned page. And so *The Truth About You and Me* is my love letter to books and film. I hope you find as much comfort in reading this as I did in writing it.

Behind every book I write, there is always a team in the background helping me, and never more so than with this book. I don't mind sharing with you just how tricky this one has been to write. Creating a romance when the two main characters can't touch has been a challenge to say the least! But I have loved following their love for each other and helping Maggie and Jack on the road to recovery – I hope you have fallen in love with them as much as I have.

So onto the thank you part! I'd like to mention first how grateful I am to my readers, and to all who pass on dog-eared copies of my books into eager hands, who take out my books from libraries, buy them from charity shops, download it onto their e-readers, or listen to my characters come alive by the wonderful actors through the audio versions. No matter how you read my books, I am forever grateful. You have all given me my dream, and I want you all to know how fundamentally important you all are to me. You're the reason I get my arse in the seat day after day, when frankly, I'm often just desperate to click on the TV and watch old *Buffy* and *Supernatural* episodes. So, from the bottom of my heart, thank you.

Massive thanks, as always, to my agent Amanda Preston, who has been with me from the start of my publishing career, and who is always, *always* there to champion me on, to give sage words of advice and to laugh with. I will be forever grateful that you continued to read my submission, even when the arm of your glasses was broken, and you were about to go on holiday! You are an absolute goddess and your support will never be something I take for granted.

To my editor, Rachel, who is incredibly astute and supportive. Thank you for taking my *very* shitty first draft and knocking it into shape! You've been incredibly patient and understanding throughout the many rounds of edits... you're an absolute power-house of a woman. I'm so thrilled that I get to continue working with you.

Huge thanks to the whole Boldwood team for all of your hard work, and for thinking of fresh and innovative ways to get my books out there. I feel very blessed to be published by you.

Further thanks go to Candida Bradford and Helena Newton for their guidance, enthusiasm and eagle editorial eyes – you're both rock stars.

Thank you isn't quite big enough to say to my wonderful colleagues at Jericho Writers. I adore working with you all. Special mention goes to Kat Ashton, Verity Hicks, and Imogen Love who are always there to answer my questions, and who keep the utterly fab UNWC course running. Total superstars, the lot of you.

To my very talented colleagues and fellow tutors, Holly Seddon, Megan Collins and Anna Vaught... thank you for the laughs, the support, and being the absolute best folk to work with, I'd be lost without you!

Further thanks go to my UNWC mentees both past and present. Thank you for sharing your work with me, and for joining me in the mornings for our writing sessions, you make my 'work' days so much brighter. I feel incredibly honoured to be part of your writing journey... being your mentor brings me more pleasure than I can say.

And where would I be without my writing tribe?! Massive thanks to Josie Silver, Kim Nash, Caroline Hulse, Natali Simmonds, Clare Swatman and S J King for all the support, chats, and yummy breakfasts. You are all blooming ace.

To the bloggers and whole bookish community who are the often unsung backbone of the publishing industry: Linda Hill, Anne Cater, Rachel @rararesources, The Fiction Café, The Savvy Writers' snug, Em @EmDigsBooks, Claire @Secretworldofabook, Jenna @book_club_momma and Telford Book Club – with another special mention to Kay and Carrieann who work tirelessly encouraging new readers and supporting local authors including those further afield. You are all absolute wonders and I can't thank you enough.

Special thanks goes to Kathryn @tealeavesandreads for taking the time to have a Zoom call and for sharing details of her day to day at her gorgeous bookshop. I didn't get a dog in, but I did make the boxes hard to open!

Raising a large glass/bottle of wine to Emma Jackson, Claire Ashley, Amanda Hedison and Teresa Merry. Thank you for being you, and for all our lunches and nights out... less thanks for the hangovers that inevitably follow!

On the subject of hangovers, moving swiftly to my incredible mum. I'm running out of ways to say how much I love you. Thank you for everything you do and for being the person you are... you selflessly give us all so much and we're all incredibly grateful to you and Chris. Oh, and we're definitely hunkering down at yours when the apocalypse hits!

To my mad loud and always loving Evans family – I love you all. I'm grateful every day to be part of this loyal, wild and incredible family.

Jac, you are the best mother-in-law I could ever have hoped for and more. Thank you for the love, the giggles, and the Sunday salad bars. You are more loved than you could ever know.

To my dad for his love, his support and most importantly his legendary BBQ's! And to the glamourous and beautiful Terry for putting up with my father and for being so kind, funny, and for hand-selling my books to all her friends.

On to my favourites! To my talented, clever and gorgeous kids who make us so incredibly proud and thankful every day: Ethan, Ally, Max and Delilah, keep being you because you're all perfect.

Last, but never, ever least... my Russ. Thirty-one years with you still feels like not nearly enough. Thank you for filling my days with laughter, for challenging me, and for loving me into the best version of myself. You are my home, my heart, my world. Thank you for being the leading man in the greatest love story I'd ever hoped I could live.

ABOUT THE AUTHOR

Emma Cooper is the author of highly acclaimed book club fiction novels and is known for mixing humour with darker emotional themes. Her debut, *The Songs of Us*, was short-listed for the RNA contemporary novel of the year award. Her work has since been translated into seven different languages.

Download your exclusive bonus content from Emma Cooper here:

Visit Emma's website: https://emmacooperauthor.wordpress.com/

Follow Emma on social media:

facebook.com/EmmaCooperAuthor

x.com/ItsEmmacooper

instagram.com/itsemmacooper

tiktok.com/@emmacooperauthor

ALSO BY EMMA COOPER

The One Before the One

The Truth About You and Me

BECOME A MEMBER OF

THE
SHELF
CARE
CLUB

The home of Boldwood's
book club reads.

Find uplifting reads,
sunny escapes, cosy romances,
family dramas and more!

Sign up to the newsletter
https://bit.ly/theshelfcareclub

Boldwood

Boldwood Books is an award-winning fiction publishing company seeking out the best stories from around the world.

Find out more at www.boldwoodbooks.com

Join our reader community for brilliant books, competitions and offers!

Follow us
@BoldwoodBooks
@TheBoldBookClub

Sign up to our weekly deals newsletter

https://bit.ly/BoldwoodBNewsletter